THE MAGICIAN'S LIE

 This Large Print Book carries the
Seal of Approval of N.A.V.H.

THE MAGICIAN'S LIE

GREER MACALLISTER

THORNDIKE PRESS
A part of Gale, Cengage Learning

GALE
CENGAGE Learning·

Farmington Hills, Mich • San Francisco • New York • Waterville, Maine
Meriden, Conn • Mason, Ohio • Chicago

LIBRARY OF CONGRESS CATALOGING-IN-PUBLICATION DATA

Macallister, Greer.
   The magician's lie / by Greer Macallister. -- Large print edition.
     s cm. -- (Thorndike Press large print historical fiction)
   ISBN 978-1-4104-7756-9 (hardcover) -- ISBN 1-4104-7756-8 (hardcover)
   1. Magicians--Fiction. 2. Large type books. I. Title.
PS3613.A235M34 2015
813'.6--dc23   2014046466

Published in 2015 by arrangement with Sourcebooks, Inc.

Printed in Mexico
1 2 3 4 5 6 7 19 18 17 16 15

"The unnatural, that too is natural."

— Johann Wolfgang von Goethe

"Those who tell their own story, you know, must be listened to with caution."

— Jane Austen, *Sanditon*

"There is no trick . . . you simply lie down in a coffin and breathe quietly."

— Harry Houdini

Chapter One

Waterloo, Iowa
July 23, 1905
Six o'clock in the evening

Tonight, I will do the impossible.

The impossible is nothing new to me. As I do every night, I will make people believe things that aren't true. I will show them worlds that never existed, events that never happened. I will weave a web of beautiful illusion to snare them, a glittering trap that drags them willingly with me into the magical, false, spellbinding world.

Before that, I will gather my strength. I will remain motionless, barely even breathing, here in this chair, while preparations happen around me, to me. I feel the feathery touch of brushes on my cheeks, on my chin, as my face is made up for the stage. I feel a heavy thumb press down on my eyelid. Another hand lightly, lightly edges it with kohl. Fingers twist and pin my hair into place, snap a heavy gilded bracelet onto my wrist. It's not possible to ignore the hands, but I focus on not reacting to them, on not reacting to anything.

I go through the act inside my head, rehearsing my patter and my gestures, seeing the whole night unfold. I welcome the crowd and take charge of the theater. I produce hats from nothingness. I transport coins through the air with a snap of my fingers, turning gold into nothing into gold again. The details of each scene bloom and dive and swarm through my head as I picture the evening from first curtain to final bow, here in the chair, silent and still. Without giving any outward sign, I dance on the inside, hearing every trilling and tender note of the music, practicing every elegant step.

When it's time, I rise on command and step into the dress held out for me, bowing my head. The dress is always last. This is how we proceed every night, and at least in this way, tonight is the same as every other. The hands close up the back of the dress, waist to neck, and then turn me around to pass three tiny buttons through three tiny loops, covering my throat, and my costume is complete.

Onstage I will act as I always act. I will do

many impossible things. I will make mysteries of scarves and coins, enchant the audience sweetly, misdirect their attention to take them by surprise. I will entertain and flatter. Then I will close the show, as I always do, with the Halved Man. I will cut a man in two, severing him through his trunk, and he will scream for mercy as the blood pours forth. The audience will be unable to believe what they see, but neither will they be able to reject it. It will look entirely real.

Then I will heal him. He will spring up whole again, wiping away the blood from an expanse of flawless skin, as if there had never been a wound. My healing powers are legendary, though no one really knows their true extent. They don't know how I wish away my own injuries, the cuts and bruises, the burns, the broken bones. It isn't part of my legend, but it's part of my life.

I'm escorted to the stage, as I always am, another set of footfalls moving exactly in concert with mine.

This is the routine now, every night.

This is the life of the most famed female illusionist in the world, very nearly the only one in existence, the life I have made for myself through luck and talent and sheer will. This is the life I have decided to leave

9

behind. This is the life I will end.

Tonight, I will escape my torturer, once and for all time.

Tonight, I will kill him.

Seven o'clock in the evening
The magician raises the ax high over her head, lets it hang there a moment, then brings it down in one broad stroke.

The sound of splintering wood rings through the theater. At the same time, there's a scream. It sounds like an animal, but Holt knows it's a man. It's the man in the box, a box the woman onstage just drove an ax straight into. Blood gushes out over the sides of the box, pooling wetly on the floor. He almost vomits.

The blood's got to be fake. This is an act, he reminds himself, all an act.

His friend Mose whispers, "Like I told you, right? Never seen anything like it!"

"Never," agrees Officer Holt.

As latecomers, they're standing all the way at the back, behind the seated crowd, and he looks over the heads of several hundred silent Iowans, holding their collective breath. Even from here, he has a clear view of the stage. Earlier in the magician's act, there were elaborate sets, like a life-size replica of ancient Rome, with a dozen danc-

10

ing slave girls and lute players galore. Now there is only the magician, and her ax, and a man's head and feet protruding from the ends of a long box like a coffin on tall wheels, now half-split through the middle and seemingly soaked with blood.

She raises the ax and swings it down again, workmanlike, as if it were only wood she's splitting. The man bellows once, twice more, and then falls silent.

The audience waits.

When the magician tosses away the ax, it clatters to the floor with a sharp report, but she doesn't seem to hear it. She lays her bare hands on the splintered wood and slowly, slowly pushes the two halves of the broken, bloody box apart. She shoves half of the box offstage to the right, returns to the center, and shoves the other half offstage to the left.

Holt finds himself leaning forward, rapt.

At the edges of the stage, ribbons of black smoke rise in slow currents. The smoke swirls and grows, spreading in inky clouds toward stage center, until the magician — standing with her long, pale arms thrust into the air, waiting — is swallowed whole.

There is a noise like a thunderclap, and the black smoke turns white.

Another noise, and the smoke is gone al-

11

together, along with the magician.

Then there are murmurs from the front of the theater. A disturbance in the audience, shifting motions, turning heads. Something's happening in the front row. Holt can't see what it is, trapped in the back with his roiling gut. He wants to surge forward. He burns to know how this all ends.

All at once, everywhere around him, applause breaks out, so loud it hurts his head. People gasp, whisper, cheer. The magician is on the stage again — how, when did she get there? — with her arms outstretched once more. The sight of her takes what's left of his breath away. Her face floats like a moon above the high neckline of her sparkling black dress. One porcelain cheek is splashed with blood.

Then he sees what has amazed the audience. She welcomes to the stage the man from the box, whole again. The man grins and waves. Once broken, now healed, as if the horror and the blood of minutes before had never been.

It's too much for Holt, and he turns tail, pushes open the back doors, stands panting in the lobby. He hears Mose follow him, not too close behind. He stares at the nearest unmoving thing to try to steady his head.

It's a poster for the magician, the Amazing Arden. She stares out proudly with one blue eye and one that's half blue, half brown. Her body hovers above a halved coffin. Strange stuff. There are other words too blurred for him to read. The fault is probably not in the words.

Mose says, "Steady there, Virgil," and claps him on the back.

"Not sure why you thought this would help," Holt tells him dryly.

"Take your mind off your troubles."

"Kind of you to try."

"If magic won't distract you, I know what will," Mose says and leads him down the street to a tavern, half-empty, friendly, dark.

They drink and talk of innocuous things: whether the lack of rain is stunting this year's corn, how little Janesville has changed in twenty years, how the taste of lousy gin seems to get better the more of it you drink. They don't talk about Mose's promotion, or their rivalry, or Iris, or Holt's bad news. Holt asks politely about Prudie and the baby but is relieved when Mose only says that they're well. Talking about their wives could open doors Holt doesn't want opened tonight.

They are still there three hours later when the door of the tavern bangs open and

13

someone calls, "Sheriff Huber!" While Mose leaps up to answer, Holt remains on his stool. He sits by himself and drinks yet more gin he should leave alone. Unlikely he'll ever be sheriff. His hand creeps toward the small of his back from habit. He forces it back down.

When Mose calls to him, it takes a few long moments for him to hear and stir himself from his reverie.

"Holt! Up and out," says Mose.

"What?"

"It's a police matter." He points at Holt. "And you're police."

"Twenty miles down the road. Not here."

"Doesn't matter. You won't be there in an official capacity. But you're going to want to see this."

Holt rises as best he can and follows.

A few hours' time has transformed the theater and not for the better. The house lights have been turned all the way up, making visible the wear on the empty seat cushions, the stained and faded carpet. The voices of a small crowd near the stage carry all the way back as the two of them head up the center aisle.

Holt catches the metallic tang of blood on the air right away. The bile rises in his throat

14

again, and he fights to keep it down. Pouring cheap gin on top of today's news and tonight's gore has hollowed him out like a rotten stump.

He keeps moving, forcing himself forward, even when he hears Mose frame the question, "All right, who found the body?"

"Stagehand," says one of the men in uniform. There are several, standing in a tight circle in front of the stage, heads down, staring through an open trap door. Holt joins the circle and follows their gazes down. Underneath the stage, there are another half dozen officers, clustered around the remains of the Halved Man trick. Where there are more officers, there are more lamps, and the space under the stage is almost as bright as day. He can see clearly despite the distance and the drink.

The long, coffin-like box is split in half, nearly pulped in the center by the magician's ax. The stains near the center are cherry-red, clearly fake stage blood, but the spreading pool of liquid around the base of the box is a darker red, somewhere between wine and rust. One half of the box is empty. A man's dead body has been jammed into the other half. As he watches, two of the officers free the body from the box. When he sees what sorry shape the dead man is

15

in, he stops watching.

Mose calls gruffly to one of the officers onstage. "And they're sure who it is?"

"Confirmation from these two," says the officer, indicating a pair of trembling girls off to the side. They clutch each other's sleeves and wipe their eyes over and over again. "Tell them what you told me." But the girls are unable to string a sentence together, and at last the officer says, "It's her husband."

"Whose husband?" asks Holt, thinking he means one of the girls.

"The magician's."

Mose says, "So where's the magician?"

"Nobody knows."

"Obviously, we'd like to talk to her."

"Obviously."

Her trick, her husband, almost certainly her doing. Of course she's wanted for questioning. Holt pictures that ax falling again, the matter-of-fact way she brought it down, without hesitation. The image is so clear in his head that he thinks he feels the blade.

He should go home. He didn't sleep last night, just lay in his bed in a panic, and it's starting to catch up with him.

He taps his friend on the shoulder and says, "Listen, I'm going to get on the road."

"Just let me —"

"No, you need to stay. Good luck, Sheriff Huber. I think you may need it."

"Why don't you stay the night?" Mose asks. "We've plenty of room."

"No, thank you. Really need to get home. Iris'll worry," he says, all of which is true.

Outside in the warm night, the summer air does little to clear his head. He swings his leg over his horse and lowers himself into the saddle inch by inch, angry that he has to be careful about it. The alcohol has dulled the pain enough that he can almost forget it, but not quite. It still gnaws. He's sore from the doctor's poking and prodding, as if the wound itself weren't bad enough. At least he can put this place and this day behind him now. He turns the horse's head toward Janesville.

Fifteen miles down the road, still five miles from home, he slows at the crossroads. The night is silent and warm. For a moment, he pictures himself turning right. Continuing east toward Chicago and Ohio and New York City and the Atlantic Ocean, none of which he's ever seen. Throwing caution to the wind and spurring the horse as fast as he can go, galloping across the open flat land till they're both gasping. Hunger is what makes up his mind in the moment.

17

The lighted window of a restaurant just before the bend, perched here for travelers at all hours, draws him. The road will be there afterward either way.

He ties his horse out front, goes inside, takes a seat. Late as it is, just past midnight, the only other customer is a gentleman in the corner with his head down on the table like he's asleep. Reading the menu, Holt wipes his face with a handkerchief and feels the alcohol sweating out of his pores. He asks for coffee, but this time of night, they don't have a pot ready, and the waitress disappears to put one on fresh. Every single thing on the bill of fare sounds delicious. Fried ham and creamed hominy, roly-poly pudding, and blueberry pie. He could hardly go wrong, whatever he chooses. As Iris says, hunger is the best sauce. He loses himself for a moment, thinking of her. She doesn't yet know the news he heard today. He isn't sure what to tell her. Or what to tell anyone. No doubt they'll force him to resign, give up his position as the town's only police officer. Who will he be then? Would Iris still love a nobody, if that's who he becomes?

The bell atop the door frame jingles. He glances up from the menu for just a moment, and when he does, the whole world shifts.

In the doorway is a young woman in a long cloak, gripping a valise. Since he last saw her, she has wiped the fake blood from her cheek.

He wastes no time, standing from his chair and meeting her in the doorway, before she can step farther inside. He reaches for her elbow and says, "Ma'am?"

She seems much smaller now than she did onstage. She stares up at him with those odd, mismatched eyes. One blue eye, like a regular eye, the left one. The right one, half brown, half blue. Divided right down the middle, straight as a plumb line. Even if her sparkling black gown weren't peeking out from under her cloak, which it is, the eyes would have given her away.

He says in a clear, firm voice, "I'm Officer Virgil Holt of the Janesville Police Department. I'm placing you under arrest, ma'am. On suspicion of murder."

"Murder!" she exclaims, blinking, her hand flying to cover her lips. "Sir?"

"Don't be alarmed, ma'am. Just come with me and we'll discuss it," he says, reaching for her elbow, which he almost manages to hold for a moment before she bolts.

They struggle in the doorway, and the bell

jingles madly as he maneuvers her outside. As they jostle and his shoulder slams into the door frame, the thought strikes him — he shouldn't be doing this, it's dangerous — and he relaxes his grip just a little.

She breaks free and runs as he stumbles, righting himself quickly, but not quickly enough to hold her. When he looks up, he sees her untying his horse and neatly balancing on the rail to hop up onto its back. He lets her. Because when he whistles for his horse, it brings her over to him, and he smoothly mounts up into the saddle behind her while she's still figuring out whether to jump. The horse knows him well enough that he doesn't even need the reins. He locks both arms around the magician.

"Don't fight," he says. "We both fall off and get trampled, that helps no one."

She still struggles for a moment but seems too afraid of falling off the horse to put her whole self into it. She seems even smaller to him now. The top of her head is just under his chin, and her hair is twisted into ropes and knotted together. A clove hitch, like a hunter would use.

"I didn't murder anyone," she says, her voice hoarse and uncertain. "Who's murdered?"

He doesn't answer. Back in the restaurant

doorway, he can see a shadow. Either the waitress coming out to see what's happened, or that other patron, if the noise woke him. Best to go before anyone sees. He can't stay here and conduct an interrogation on the back of a horse. He needs to find out what she knows, what she did.

North then . . . or south? If she's guilty, he should take her back to the theater in Waterloo immediately and hand her over. Mose is probably still there. But the horse, eager for his hay bed, starts moving in the direction of Janesville, and Holt lets himself — lets both of them — be carried. He'll sober up on the way. He can always bring her back. He's an officer of the law and bound to do the right thing, except he's not sure what the right thing is just now.

If she's guilty, she'll be the most famous criminal in the state in years. And he'll be the one who brought her in. They won't be able to force him out then, wounded or not. He needs all this to go his way. She could change everything.

Holt's head is buzzing and clouded, but the horse knows the way home.

Janesville, Iowa
Half past eleven o'clock in the evening
The station is a single room, not much more

21

than a wooden box with a door on it. There's a chair and a desk and a window. Only the gas lamp on the street outside gives any light to see by. He drops her into the plain wood chair like a heavy bag of feed, a solid dead weight. She sags forward. Her reddish hair, now escaped from its intricate knot, is a nest. He pulls away her cloak and valise and throws them near the door, which he locks, then grabs his uniform belt from the nearby hook and buckles it on in haste. Wearing his gun helps clear his head a little. He turns back toward her and sees she isn't moving. As he steps closer to examine her in the dim light, his foot slips on loose sequins. He loses his footing a moment, unsteady.

She is up out of the chair on her feet, a blur of motion. Instinct kicks in. He throws himself at her, arms around her knees, and brings them both crashing to the floor. Again he tells himself these exertions are dangerous. It's exactly what the doctor said not to do. But the doctor couldn't have foreseen this circumstance, and anyway, now he's in it.

He hears the air go out of her lungs. He's breathless too but recovers faster. A second chance. This time, he'll do better. He hauls her body up onto the chair again, shoves her against its back, and secures her wrists to the chair with the pair of handcuffs from his belt.

Will it be enough?

Officer Holt goes to his desk, feeling his way in the dark and shoving his own chair out of the way, and retrieves four more pairs of handcuffs. He'd use more if he had them. He affixes all four pairs to her slim wrists, one after another after another, to total five. He loops the chains through the chair back's straight wooden slats as he goes.

She's breathing. He can see her shoulders rising and falling. Mose told him all about her on the way to the theater. That half-brown eye is believed to be the source of her power. She uses it to hypnotize the audience into swallowing her illusions. He should avoid looking into it, just to be safe.

Just as the last cuff clicks into place, her voice ragged, she says, "I am not an escape artist. Perhaps you've mistaken me."

"I know what you are," he tells the magician.

"You have the advantage of me then," she replies.

"I told you, I'm a police officer."

"And yet you wear no uniform and you smell like a wet dog drowned in gin."

It stings that she's right. Now that his

hands are free, he lights the lamp. "I'm a police officer, and you're a suspect in my custody. Those are the facts."

"Are they? And what am I suspected of?"

"As I told you when I arrested you, ma'am, you are suspected of murder."

"Whose?"

"Your husband's."

"Husband? Me? That's a laugh." And she does laugh, a short dry bark. But she shifts in her seat.

"Not a laugh. A fact. Your husband was murdered in Waterloo."

"Clearly, we're not in Waterloo anymore, are we? They have buildings. And electric lights. And a police force that isn't made up of twelve-year-olds. Is that a mustache on your face or a pigeon feather?"

He opens his mouth to strike back and then shuts it again. He shouldn't be in this situation, but he is, and he needs to make the most of it. Whether he finds her company unpleasant doesn't matter. Whether she is a murderess is the only question. Once he has his answer, the right course will be clear.

"I'll thank you not to insult me, ma'am," he says and moves his hand a few inches, resting it on the butt of his gun.

Her eyes flick down and then up again,

and he knows she gets his meaning.

"Please," she says, in a softer voice. "No more 'ma'am.' Call me Arden."

"Due respect again, m—" He swallows the end of the word. "Due respect, I'm certain that's not your real name."

"It's the only name that matters, isn't it? The one on the posters. The Amazing Arden, the Alluring Arden, the All-Powerful Arden. Depending on the poster, depending on the town. And what town is this?"

"It's called Janesville," he says.

"Not very big, is it?"

"Big enough."

She says nothing for a few moments, and then her bravado seems to crumble all at once. "This is ludicrous," she says, sounding half strangled. "I don't — I don't even know — if it's — I didn't kill anyone, officer."

He expects to find her looking up at his face, watching him, reading him. But she is only staring down at her boots.

"Ma'am?" says Officer Holt.

When she meets his eyes, he sees the wetness on her cheeks. She's crying. Now that she's still and silent and facing him, she doesn't look like a powerful enchantress. She looks like an exhausted young woman in the grip of enormous sadness, helpless beyond words. It almost melts his heart. Almost.

He pulls the handkerchief from his pocket but immediately sees his mistake. He can't offer it to her. With five pairs of handcuffs holding her wrists fast to the chair, she doesn't have a hand free to take it.

"Just dab at my eyes, please," she says and raises her face toward him. "The salt stings."

He can't help but notice, while wiping the tears from her cheeks, that her skin is smooth and lovely. There's something childlike about her, though she's certainly not a child. If he had to guess, he'd put her about halfway between twenty and thirty. A little older than he is, but not by much.

"Thank you. Now, due respect, Officer Holt," she says, sounding resigned. "Let me say this again. I am not an escape artist. I am an illusionist. I could conjure a dove from nothingness if you like. Or I could pour a glass of milk into a hat, which will later prove to be empty. That's my business."

"You know your business. I know mine."

Her soft voice turning more insistent, she says, "Look, you're a lawman. I understand. You think you need to do this. But you don't. We can end this now. Let me go."

"And why would I?"

"If you don't, you're killing me. Is that what you want? To be my executioner?" She stares up at him fiercely, and he wants to feel superior, looking down on her, but he doesn't. It's the eyes. The half-brown eye, to be specific. As if she can see him on the outside and the inside at the same time. He doesn't want to be seen.

"It's not up to me. You'll get a trial."

"The supposed witches of Salem got trials," she says with obvious bitterness, "for all the good it did them."

He unfolds and refolds his damp, streaked handkerchief. "I can promise you a fair shake."

"Can you? Some think a trial with a judge and jury is justice, sure. Other people have a different idea of it. People who'd lock me up with vagrants and violators and let things take their natural course."

He can hear the edge of desperation in her voice now but can't tell whether she's put it there on purpose. He answers firmly. "Ma'am, I'm sorry; I have no choice."

"We always have a choice. Sometimes it's just the will we lack. And again with 'ma'am'? You won't call me Arden?"

"No." He folds his arms and avoids her gaze. He stares out the room's only window, as if she's not even interesting enough to

27

look at, which of course she is. All else aside, she's a beautiful woman. But there is too much else to put aside.

Beyond the window, it is pitch-black. Darker than it should be. The gas lamp must have gone out, and now nothing is visible. No grass, no streets, no trees, no town. Just black. They call this the dead of night for a reason.

"Officer," she says at last, "could you at least do one small thing for me? Could you unbutton my collar? I — it's a little difficult to breathe."

It could be a trick, of course, but he wants her to trust him. So he reaches out for the buttons at her throat, taking care not to look her in the eye and keeping the hip with the gun on it on her far side, well out of reach.

There are three tiny buttons on the high lace collar of her gown, and once all three are open, he can see the vulnerable hollow at the base of her throat. He can also see a deep bruise across the front of her neck, a spreading purple mess roughly an inch high and several inches across. He spreads the lace of the collar open with his fingers to get a closer look. The bruise is a single thick line running side to side, as if someone had tried to behead her with something blunt. It is more pink than blue, with no yellow or green at the edges.

"Is this fresh?" he says. "It looks fresh."

"It doesn't matter."

He takes out the handkerchief to dab lightly at her tears, which have started again.

"It's entirely your choice, officer," she says. "To turn me in or let me go."

She's right, of course. He has to make the decision. Capturing a notorious murderess would change everything for him, but at the same time, what if she's innocent? The truth of what she's saying can't be denied. The law is perfect. The men in charge of executing it are not.

"Tell me then," he says. "Tell me what happened."

She does something he has not yet seen her do. Not in the posters. Not onstage. And certainly not since he recognized and apprehended her in that restaurant.

She smiles.

The Amazing Arden looks at him out of her half-brown eye, tilts her head, and asks, "Where does a person's story begin?"

Chapter Two

1892

A Night's Alteration

Where *does* a person's story begin? Mine starts with a hole in the middle, a hole where a father should have been. I must have had one, but the truth was that no one wanted to say out loud who he had been, if they even knew. I was raised in my grandparents' house in Philadelphia. My name was Ada Bates. There was plenty of room and plenty of money, and I grew up straight and strong.

In my earliest memories, I remember my mother as a cello. She and her instrument fused: a deep voice, a wasp waist. She wielded her bow fiercely, the notes soaring high and plunging low until the very windows trembled in their sills. I heard her at a distance, practicing at all hours, from down long hallways and behind closed doors. As she and my father were never married, she must have been in disgrace, but she never seemed to feel it. She was always cheerful as a songbird in those days.

She taught me music herself, though I was at best a middling student. From her, I had inherited milk-white skin, large eyes, and a cleft in my chin, but the other side of the family delivered a tin ear. My singing was perpetually flat and my piano clumsy. I still looked forward to the lessons, because I rarely heard or saw her otherwise. Once a month, we both had our hair dyed from its natural red-gold to a more sedate brown, a tradition my grandmother had started when my mother herself was a child. I looked forward to those days, when we sat side by side for more than an hour, but they were all too rare. The rest of the time, a freckled governess named Colleen woke me, managed my days, and bid me good night, and I took my daily meals with her instead of in the dining room with my mother and grandparents. Except for music, my education was conducted by a series of tutors: French, history, grammar, drawing. All my tutors were so alike in demeanor — pale, cool, severe — that I believed when I was very young that they were all brothers and sisters from the same family. When not engaged in lessons, I was nearly always reading, my bookcases filled with Shakespeare and Seneca, Emerson and Donne. Reading was learning, and learning was a matter best conducted in privacy. My grandmother never trusted the schools.

As it turned out, my grandmother would have done well to be even more distrustful.

In 1892, when I was twelve years old, my grandparents arranged what was to be the greatest opportunity of my mother's life. At considerable expense and trouble, they secured passage for her to travel to Europe for an audience with Franco Faccio of Teatro alla Scala in Milan, for whom she was to perform. If she impressed him, she might have a place with the orchestra as a first chair and soloist, appearing before large audiences to great acclaim.

And she might have amazed Signore Faccio with her skill at the cello, and she might have been a great star, except that she sold the tickets and traded away her best jewelry and gave the money instead to a man named Victor Turner, who had been her music teacher for several years and would later be a frustrated farmhand, my stepfather, and the love of my mother's life. The day that she would have left for Europe became, instead, the day they ran away.

And that day, they took me with them.

Heaven knows why. Someone else could have stood witness at their wedding, which was the only service I seemed to perform on the journey. I stayed silent and didn't ask questions. I didn't want them to think better of the choice.

Our destination was Jeansville, Tennessee, where Victor's brother Silas owned a small farm outside the town, growing hay and breeding horses. Victor was a versatile teacher, a master of everything from singing to piano to woodwinds and brass, and his plan had been to teach music to the families of the town. It took only two weeks for this plan to fail. The people of Jeansville were suspicious of newcomers. No one owned instruments, of course, and even if they'd had the money to pay a singing master, it would have been seen as too frivolous. He may as well have been selling champagne coupes or china shepherdesses. With unwise optimism, they had paid ahead a full year's rent on the house, and the rest of the money wouldn't stretch far enough to make a stand in a different town. Therefore there were only two possibilities: crawl back to Philadelphia in supplication, or stay. Had this been my mother's first misadventure, supplication might have been more tempting. She'd been forgiven the first time and given another chance. But she knew she was no longer welcome in her parents' house. With the second chance squandered, there would be no third.

A new plan was hatched. Victor's brother Silas was a fat man with a thin wife, and she had been complaining about the isolation of their farmhouse, which was too far from her friends' houses in the town. She was as dedicated to the art of complaint as my mother was to the cello, and her virtuoso work had finally reached Silas's ears. So they and their son Ray moved into the rented house, and my mother and Victor and I took occupancy of the farmhouse. It seemed like a fair trade. With no job prospects that matched his skills, Victor began working for his brother as a farmhand, and in this way, our cobbled-together household found its new equilibrium.

I began attending school for the first time, which I did not enjoy. I was an indifferent student at best and insolent at worst. My manners, so carefully inculcated by my high-society grandmother and the etiquette experts she had paid to reinforce her, were unraveling rapidly. Never having set foot in a classroom with other students, I didn't see the point of sitting still or waiting to be called on. Even when these things were explained to me, I resisted. They seemed silly. If I knew the answer, why shouldn't I say so? If the lessons bored me, as they often did, why shouldn't I find something better to do? My teacher wore her hair in two braids over her shoulders like a girl, and she seemed to know only answers that had been written down for her by someone else. Besides, the classroom was always too warm. It stank of chalk, spit, and cheap slate. I missed my shelves of books, all of which we'd left behind. I missed the idea that behind those cloth covers lurked endless surprises — spare slashing lines of poetry, or the rhythmic cadence of a play, or characters who, despite being only invented, sprang warmly and fully to life. There was none of that in our simple schoolroom primers, none at all. Their singsong phrases were, only and always, exactly as expected.

With all of its drawbacks, however, this new life had one commanding advantage over the old. I was in my mother's company for hours at a time. She was the only one of us with the luxury of rising late, so I didn't always see her in the morning before I started down the road to school, but she was always there when I came home in the afternoon. She would hand me the cloth to wipe the dust of the road from my shoes, then we took a small glass of milk each, seated at the kitchen table in silent companionship. At dinner every night, I drank in the novel sight of her lovely, animated face and the reassuring hum of her smoky voice. After so long without her, I found her slightest attention intoxicating. I could subsist for a week on one of her smiles.

After dinner, she would often sit down with her cello between her knees and coax the most beautiful music from its strings. If he wasn't in the fields, Victor would sing to accompany her. I wanted to do more than listen but had nothing musical to contribute, so I began to dance. Mother had taken me to New York a handful of times to see the ballet, and I emulated what I remembered of the ballerinas' movements — long graceful arcs of the arms, fluttering pointed toes, the basic arabesque. My dancing made my mother smile, so I did it at every opportunity.

I took to it so well that my mother decided I should have more formal training, but of course there was no dance school in Jeansville, nor possibly in the entire state of Tennessee. I was in no rush to leave, of course, so I asked if it might be possible for her to handle my instruction? She agreed that it was. She wrote away to a woman in Russia for lessons, and we regularly received letters of detailed instruction. Eagerly we put these into practice. The Cecchetti method involved repetition of motion after motion. But not carelessly, not just with a mindless echo. Every motion was important, and it needed to be performed consciously, with purpose. One day, I would make a certain set of motions with my leg, the next day, a set of motions with my arm. One week was the right side, one week the left. It took discipline, and while I may have been undisciplined in other areas of my life, in dancing I was absolutely obedient.

And all was well. We were happy.

Until a boy named Ray changed everything.

CHAPTER THREE

Janesville, 1905
Midnight

"What kind of fool do you take me for?" asks Officer Holt.

"I beg your pardon?"

"No, you don't. I suspect you don't beg anything."

She looks up at him, all wounded and meek. That face of hers, it's too nimble. He reminds himself what she does for a living. Day in, day out, she fools people. He can't let her do it to him.

He says, "This story of yours. It isn't real. It isn't true."

"It is."

"*Jeansville?* You expect me to believe that?"

She stammers, "Officer, sir, truly, I don't understand what you mean."

"What's the name of the town we're in now, ma'am?"

She looks down at her lap. "I'm sorry, I don't remember. The last few weeks have been . . . trying. So I'm not entirely clear in my mind."

Of course she understands. She's just pretending not to. It infuriates him. "I'll help you. It's Janesville."

"Yes, sir."

"Janesville," he says, "and you expect me to believe you were raised in a town called Jeansville, that the two just happen to have similar names, and that you didn't just make up the name of a town like you're making up this story?"

"Believe it or don't," she says with a little fire. "It's the truth."

"I don't want to hear this anyway. I want to hear about the murder. Tell me that part."

"I will. When I get there."

"Talk about the murder or don't talk at all," he says, disgusted. He wanted to hear her out, to let her explain her innocence, but he thought it would be the matter of a few minutes. That doesn't seem to be what she has in mind. He needs to rethink everything.

He eyes her ankles, still free. Maybe he should cuff them too. They look small enough. Onstage, her dress was long enough to reach the floor. Now that she's sitting down, he can see everything below the knees. Her fancy little silk boots are smudged and caked with dirt. Those boots probably cost more than he earns in half a year, but that's not why he's staring. He's trying to see if any of the smudges are dark enough to be blood.

He turns up the lamp, but the circle of light doesn't reach far. As small as the room is, more than half remains in shadow.

"Officer!"

He looks her in the face. "Didn't I tell you to be quiet?"

"As I live and breathe," she says, gazing up at him, examining. "You really are rather handsome. Wasted on a town like this, I suspect. Are you married, officer?"

She keeps looking up at him as if she genuinely expects an answer. He should blindfold her. He shouldn't look her in the face. Heaven only knows what powers that eye has. If she bewitches him, all those handcuffs might as well be hair ribbons.

He crosses the room in four long strides and grabs for the telephone.

"Wait," she says. "What are you doing?"

"Calling the sheriff in Waterloo. Turning you in."

She bucks against her restraints, eyes wild. "No!"

He lifts the receiver and places his finger on the lower grip slowly and deliberately, making a show of it, making sure she sees. Ready to signal for the operator. Ready to change the game.

"I lift my finger, and she'll come on the line. All I have to say is your name. It'll be too late to turn back then. Now are you going to tell me about the murder, or . . ."

"Please don't," she says. Fear is written on her face, in great large letters. "I'll tell you everything. I will. I promise."

Satisfied, he hangs the receiver on the hook switch and sets the telephone back on the desk. Relief floods him at the successful bluff. He'll be damned if he hands her over to Mose without knowing what she's done. The glory should be his. Everything depends on it.

"So tell me," he says, folding his arms. "Why did you kill him? Your own husband?"

"I swear, I didn't know there was a murder until you told me I was arrested for it. Honestly."

"Honestly?" he scoffs.

"Yes. I still don't even know . . ." She trails off.

"Know what?"

"Anything! Where was he found? Who found him? What happened?"

41

Her desperation — wide eyes, rapid breath — seems genuine. How is he supposed to tell the fake from the real with her?

He wants to let her stew, so he opens the top drawer of the desk and rummages around, extending the silence. The only thing in the drawer is an apple. The acid in his stomach rises in anticipation, but he doesn't let himself eat it. He has a better idea. If there's an advantage to be gained from feeding her, he'll gladly stay hungry.

He stands up, polishing the apple on his sleeve, his mind zooming forward, figuring out a plan. "You're hungry, aren't you?"

"Yes, very."

He holds the apple toward her, from a distance. "Would you like this?"

"Of course," she says, with an edge of anger. He needs to tread carefully.

"If you'll answer my questions, it's yours," he says.

Gently he brings the apple close to her mouth, and she leans as far forward as the cuffs will allow. She takes a great large bite, and he feels the sensation travel all the way up his arm, an invisible vibration.

"You're toying with me," he says in a neutral voice.

She chews and swallows. He can see the knot of it in her pale throat.

He offers her another bite, and she takes it, sinking her teeth in, tearing off a sizable chunk.

"You can take smaller bites," he says. "I'm going to let you eat the whole thing."

She makes a noncommittal grunt and keeps chewing with gusto.

Holt brings the chair from the desk and turns it to face away from her. He slings his leg over the seat and sits down in it backward, folding one arm across the top, extending the other toward her, with the apple in his hand.

Trying to sound gentle but confident, he says to her, "You're not telling me what you did."

She mumbles around a mouthful of fruit. "I'm telling you who I am."

"Let's try something different. Tell me who *he* was. Your husband, I mean. The one they found under the stage, after the show, in Waterloo. Dead and bloody, stuffed into the Halved Man apparatus, right where you left him."

She stops midchew.

"Your dead husband," he continues. It's time to put on more pressure. "Blood everywhere. Bruises, cuts, broken bones. Someone hit him and hit him hard. You, I suspect. It's amazing what damage a woman

43

can do when she wants to."

She turns her face away, looks down. He offers her the apple again, its hollow white side, but she makes no move toward it.

Quietly she says, "He was beaten?"

"Badly."

"Did you see the body?"

"Yes."

She asks, "Did you see his face?"

Something in him makes him reach out for her chin and pull it forward again. He wants to look her full in the face. With his other hand, he puts the white, bitten side of the apple in front of her mouth. He says, "Eat."

She takes a smaller bite this time. Her eyes don't leave his as she chews and swallows it, her nimble face a storm of emotion. She looks angry and pleading and hungry and confused. A faint sheen of sweat is starting to form on her brow, under the tendrils of reddish hair. She takes a second small bite and chews it, his fingers on her jaw feeling every movement of muscle and bone, and he sees again the knot in her throat as she swallows.

Then she says, "Please. Did you?"

"No," he lies.

She drops her chin toward her shoulder, and he lets her. He thinks she looks queasy, but he might be flattering himself, thinking he has some effect on her.

In silence, he feeds her the rest of the apple. She eats it all, down to the core and the seeds. At last, he is holding only half an inch of stem between his thumb and forefinger. He reaches out with his handkerchief and wipes a spot of apple from the corner of her mouth, and she says softly, "Thank you."

The air in the room is already stale and hot. He wishes the one barred window, eight feet up the wall, would give him fresh air to breathe.

He makes a decision and rises from his chair, moving it away to give himself room. Then he drops to his knees at her feet, putting one hand on each ankle.

"What are you doing?" She edges back, rocks herself against the chair. The legs move a little. She inches back but he holds on. Then she wrenches hard and pulls one leg free, trying to kick him.

"Easy!" he shouts.

Her dirty boot catches him in the shoulder, causing a sharp hot pain, which he hides. He shoves the kicking foot down hard and shifts his body sideways so he's sitting on it, pinning the wild leg between his body and the chair. He prays the exertion won't damage him, but if it does, so be it. He's gambling anyway. He's betting that she's a prize rich enough to win him security, the security that began slipping away three months ago when he interrupted a man robbing a bank and slipped away even further this afternoon in a doctor's office in Waterloo.

She tries to kick again, wrenching her body around, straining against all five pairs of handcuffs. When none of that works, she lets out a howling, piercing scream.

"Easy, I said! I'm not going to hurt you! Be quiet!"

"Get away!" she shouts.

He uses one hand to hold her foot in place while the other unlaces the boot. She keeps moving and shifting and twitching. He could explain to her why he needs to remove her boots, but it wouldn't soothe her, so he isn't going to waste the words.

"I'm not going to hurt you," he says one more time instead.

"You don't understand," she says. She says it over and over again, quieter and quieter, "You don't understand, you don't understand, you don't understand."

At first, he's afraid it's a spell. Some kind of incantation. But it goes on and on, as if she's compelled. It doesn't seem like she's trying to bewitch him; she doesn't even seem to know he's there.

When she finally pauses, breathless, he says, "That's right. I don't understand. Why don't you explain it to me?"

In a low clear voice, she says, "Okay."

CHAPTER FOUR

1893–1894
Invisible Knots

The following June, I turned thirteen, an unlucky number. I was becoming a young woman. Mother showed me how to fashion my hair into a neat, low chignon instead of a braid down my back. My hips and breasts grew, and although I would never be a violin, I was no longer a flute. These changes didn't bother me. But other changes did.

When the harvest began, not long after, a slight adjustment was made to the bargain we had made with Silas. He and his wife continued to rent the house in town, but because their son Ray spent long days working on the farm, someone decided — it was never clear who — that he should come live in the farmhouse with us.

Ray was sixteen that summer. Before he moved into the farmhouse with us, I could count on a single hand the number of times

I had seen him. All I knew of him was that in childhood he'd narrowly escaped dying of a fever that had carried away his three younger sisters. Whether the fever had made him more precious or he had always been so, his parents fawned over him like a little prince. Like Victor, he worked for Silas as a general farmhand; unlike Victor, he seemed perfectly suited to it. He was built for physical labor, his arms and legs as thick as tree trunks. You could see his mother in the pale hair and aquiline nose, his father in the broad frame and cleft chin. His head was topped with an unruly crop of blond curls. As the summer went on, they got blonder in the sun. In the evenings, he ruined the triangular pleasure of our after-dinner entertainment by sitting in a chair and staring silently.

I admit that I disliked him from the beginning, before I had much reason to do so. I'd caught my mother's attention but feared I could lose it again at any moment, so I didn't want his competition. In the beginning, he spoke so rarely that I thought perhaps the fever had left him touched in the head. Therefore I was equally annoyed whether he stared at a spot on the floor, or at my mother's hands on the cello, or — as he most often did — at me.

As the weeks went on, it seemed that he was always nearby, always lurking. The character of his attention changed. Every interaction with him was fraught. I would pass through the hall toward my room, flushed and exhausted from a solid hour of rigorous pirouettes. He would appear soundlessly to block my path, the sour tang of a day's sweat on him, forcing me to stop short. He wouldn't touch me. He reached out as if to lay his palm against the side of my cheek but then would pause just an inch or two away. He stared into my left eye, the flawed one, as if he could unlock a secret from it by staring. I blinked as little as I could. He didn't say a word, and when I stepped away, he let me go.

I thought I might mention it to my mother, but what could I say? It sounded silly to complain that he sometimes looked at me and, on occasion, almost touched me.

It sounds silly even now. Even now that I know what was coming.

For my birthday, my mother had bought me a rather extravagant gift. It cost enough that I later heard her and Victor arguing about it, him cursing that it was too much money, which it no doubt was. The gift was the tallest mirror I'd ever seen, a breathtakingly flat and large piece of silvered glass in which I could see the reflection of nearly my entire body. My room was otherwise unadorned, only a faded hand-me-down quilt on the bed and a thin gray rug covering perhaps a third of the floor, so the mirror seemed all the more remarkable. The oval frame was dark wood, simple and lovely, with a subtle pattern of carved leaves. Mother insisted that it would help me correct my posture and perfect my positions. It did both of these things, but I also just liked to look in it and see myself, examining the tiniest details of my own appearance. I stared at the shape of my earlobes, one of which seemed ever so slightly higher than the other, and at the faint short hairs along my hairline, which stirred with my breath. I could finally see how odd my eye looked, how clear the dividing line was between the brown and the blue. I could see the speckles of shifting color in the iris and watch the pupil grow larger when the sunlight from the window faded at dusk. I brought my face so close to the mirror my breath fogged its surface, then made a game of holding my breath to see how long I could keep it clear.

My pleasure in the mirror outlasted its novelty. Even three months later, when I was back in the daily routine of attending school, I often wished I was at home with the mirror instead. My behavior in the classroom grew worse, and my reputation with it. Mother was informed of my unwillingness to comply with the rules. I couldn't puzzle out how she felt about it. In front of the young teacher, she told me this misbehavior couldn't continue and promised I would be disciplined. In private, she said nothing. At the dinner table, she only told Victor that the classroom seemed to be run by a recent winner of the Harlan County Jump Rope Championship, and it was too bad the schools here weren't better. When Silas's wife remarked one evening that she had heard I was a discipline problem at the school, my mother replied archly that the brightest children were known for being the most unruly, then changed the subject to the weather.

So I continued to comply with my teacher's directions when it suited me and do otherwise when it didn't. More than once, this led to a punishment where I was placed in the corner of the classroom and made to raise my arms while holding a book in each hand. This had no deterrent effect whatsoever, since it was an exercise that strengthened my arms for dancing, and my mother complimented the improved elegance of my arm positions in fourth and fifth.

One afternoon, when I had become so annoyed with the remedial nature of the reading lesson that I simply got up and walked out of the school, I snuck back into the house and headed upstairs. I was so focused on keeping my footsteps silent to avoid detection that I didn't see that Ray was in my room, standing in front of the mirror, until I was a few feet from his elbow.

Ray had a straight razor in his hand and was drawing it along his abdomen, making a long shallow cut, and little beads of blood were beginning to well up from the flesh.

I breathed in.

His eyes opened wide and met mine in the mirror. I lowered my gaze. His cotton shirt was unbuttoned and open down the front, and in his reflection, I saw them all. Scars. Scars that followed the lines of his ribs, outlining them in ghostly white, so you could see the shape of the skeleton underneath his skin. He had cut himself again and again, neatly and deliberately, over and over. How long would something like that take, I wondered. Months? Years?

"Get out," he said, almost growling.

"It's my room," I said hotly. "You get out."

He spun and grabbed my arm with his

free hand, the other hand clutching the open, gleaming razor. The blood began to run down his skin but did not drip.

"You keep this to yourself," he said. "You understand?"

I forced myself only to shrug.

He lay the flat of the razor against the bare skin of my forearm, then my neck, then my cheek. The metal was cold. The ripe odor of his sweat swarmed up around me in a cloud.

"You will keep this to yourself," he repeated.

"I will?"

"If you tell your mother what you saw, I'll tell her that you invited me here to your room to seduce me."

"That's ridiculous," I said, keeping my eyes locked with his so I wouldn't look down at the blade and panic. I didn't think he meant to hurt me, just scare me, but I also knew his hand could easily slip.

"Is it? You're a lonely girl. I'm a handsome boy."

"Are you?"

He laughed. "As you like. You're an insolent girl. I'm a well-behaved boy. I do what I'm told and you don't. You shouldn't even be here. Who would they believe?"

I was uncertain of the answer. He never misbehaved, not that anyone caught him at.

54

I was a known troublemaker. My mother had defended me when it suited her, but this was more serious. Certainly she knew something about young girls misbehaving, or I wouldn't exist.

And the longer Ray stared at me, the less sure I was that he didn't mean me harm. There was something in his eyes. The intensity of his gaze was becoming almost too much. I forced myself not to look away.

"Now that would be a lie, of course," he continued. "You seducing me."

"Yes, it would."

He tilted his head and gave me an appraising look. "I wouldn't mind a tumble, of course, if you're inclined."

"No, thank you."

"Lord, blades do make people polite, don't they?"

An answer didn't seem necessary. The steel on my cheek was no longer cold. It had drawn its heat out of my skin.

"Do you believe in magic?" he asked abruptly.

"No."

"I do. I think everyone has a little. I'm trying to find mine. And yours."

"I haven't got any."

"You don't know that, not for sure."

I needed an angle. I tried one. "So what

do you think yours is? Your magic?"

"Not sure yet. Something to do with healing. I survived a sickness I shouldn't have survived. It killed my sisters, but it spared me. Don't you think that's a clue to something?"

I let my eyes flicker down toward the razor, still against my cheek. "Seems you're more likely to hurt than to heal."

He smiled at that and let the razor drop. I didn't let the relief show.

"Hurting and healing are two sides of the same coin," he said.

"A funny coin."

"You'll understand someday. For all your faults, you're a quick learner. We'll talk more about this, someday soon."

He folded his razor, wiped the blood from his torso with a cloth from his pocket, and buttoned his shirt back up to the neck. And then he left me there. I listened to his footsteps grow fainter and fainter, the thump of work boots going down the stairs and across the floor, and when the sound of the front door closing finally came, I let out the sigh I'd been holding so close.

I looked in the mirror. No one would be able to tell I had just been terrorized. Everything about me was exactly as it should have been, except for three faint marks. In the three places he had touched me with the razor's blade — the arm, the neck, the cheek — there was a thin line of blood, not my own.

The marks were a simple matter to wipe away.

He was right, of course. I was too scared to say a word. I didn't think I'd be believed. And besides, what had really happened? He'd done more damage to himself than to me.

That time.

Later that year, Mother took it into her head that I could be sent to a dance school. We had settled long ago that there were no schools nearby, but she opened up the possibility that I could attend one far away and board there.

She had often told me of seeing Marie Bonfanti, the prima ballerina assoluta, dance at Niblo's Garden in New York City. Madama Bonfanti had retired from the stage some time before. But Mother had read the news that Madama had opened a ballet school in New York, where she taught the Cecchetti method. Mother thought the youngest and most tenderhearted of her New York cousins might be willing to use a little influence on her behalf, if properly approached with flattery and eloquence. There was no question of help from my grandparents. A letter from the lawyer had made that clear some time before.

In addition to New York, letters went out to Boston and Richmond and Charleston. Even to San Francisco, and once to Chicago. Abroad, they went to Moscow, Paris, Venice, Bonn. In a fit of optimism, my mother even bought me a valise, so I'd be ready to go.

It sounded like a fantasy, but I encouraged it all the same. The school in Jeansville was tedious at its very best, and I had several years left to go if I stayed. And I worried about Ray more and more. The idea of ballet school sounded like my only reasonable chance at escape. So I practiced and practiced and held out hope.

It was 1894, and I was fourteen years old when my mother received the letter from Madama Bonfanti. She presented it to me at breakfast, her cheeks pink with excitement.

"What do you think of *that*?" she said with delight, flipping the cream-colored envelope down onto the wood of the table.

She had already slit the envelope across the top, so I tugged the letter out. The faint smell of lavender wafted upward as I unfolded it to read:

We will be at the Biltmore Estate on Wednesday 13 September taking our leisure with the family. If your daughter is as talented as you say, you may bring her to dance for us on that afternoon, and we shall see her.

Mother said, "To dance for Bonfanti. This could be magic, Ada. It could change everything. If she likes you, she could take you to New York. You could enter her Academy. We're so lucky she'll be so close by. Oh, it must be fate!"

"She lives at this Biltmore?"

"Oh no, oh no. Biltmore is the home of the Vanderbilts. A palace, nearly. I've read about it in the magazines. They're still building it, but it's already famous across the country. The biggest family house in all of America."

"And it's in Tennessee? Why?"

"Over the mountains, dear. In North Carolina. But it's close by enough, less than a day's ride. Oh, I can barely imagine. Madama will be in a relaxed mood, receptive. They're still building the home, but Mr. Vanderbilt might be there — maybe they'll even invite us to stay! Oh, I don't know

59

what you'll wear . . . your practice gowns are worn to shreds . . ."

I heard her words but not her meaning. Estates and mountains and coach rides. Too much at once.

She grinned at me, a blinding smile. "This is your chance, Ada, your chance. You could go to her school! You could be a ballerina!"

I finally started to grasp what she was saying. "Madama Bonfanti . . . of the Academy . . . wants to see me dance."

"Yes!" she exclaimed.

"On the thirteenth."

"Oh. Oh!" she said, rising to pace the floor. Her bare feet made no sound. "The thirteenth! That's tomorrow! The mail must have been delayed . . . We'll have to leave in the dark. The note says afternoon, but no particular time? That's good. But Victor's gone with Silas to the horse fair in Montclair. They won't be back. I'll have to ask Raymond to drive us."

"Don't do that!"

"Why not? We can't go just the two of us. Even if it were proper."

I couldn't explain, so I stayed silent.

She mistook my look for another kind of nervousness, and she reached out and touched my arm. She usually only did that to correct my positions. It was a magical

60

day indeed.

"Go practice," she said. "You needn't worry about the details. Just make sure you're ready. Not too much, just your usual exercises. Make sure you're graceful. She'll want to see you graceful."

Nearly tripping over my own feet in my excitement, I dashed up the stairs. I was already wearing my practice garments, a loose dress over my camisole, enough to cover me down to my calves but give my legs freedom to extend fully. In my room, I donned my pointe shoes and practiced in front of the mirror until the sun went down. As I danced, my confidence grew. This would be the moment. I was strong. I was talented. I would show Madama all my skill in a handful of bravura moves, a sequence of *pas de chat* and *pliés, pirouettes en dehors* and *fouettés en tournant*.

In the evening darkness, I dressed in traveling clothes and squared my shoulders, telling myself I was capable of changing my future. When Mother called me outdoors, I strode downstairs and outside with my head held high.

When I saw Ray standing next to the coach, I faltered a bit on the inside but left the smile on my face. I told myself I couldn't let him rule me, not through fear, not in

61

any way. I told myself that someday soon, I would need to stand up to him. But this wasn't the time for it. If this excursion went well, if I impressed Madama Bonfanti with my grace and talent, I would be gone from this place and never have to worry about him again.

"Your mother told me of your good news!" he said. "Such an opportunity."

The forced, jolly note in his voice jangled my nerves. There was something foreboding about it, something dangerously false. I remembered how he'd touched the razor to my cheek and smiled, murmuring his threats.

Mother waved, only her white glove visible from the interior of the coach. "Isn't it lovely?" she said. "We're so lucky to travel in such style!" She looked happier than I'd seen her in months. This trip was as important to her as it was to me, if not more so.

Ray extended his hand to help me up into the coach. I didn't see how I could refuse, with Mother watching. I paused for a moment to straighten my skirts first, collecting myself as I did so.

"I suppose I'm just your lowly cousin," he said merrily, loud enough for my mother to hear. "No doubt you'll forget all about me when you're famous."

Finally I took his hand and put my foot up on the step. He smelled of sweat and old hay. As he boosted me up into the carriage, he bent close to my ear, whispering softly enough that only I could hear him.

"I hope you know I'll never let you leave," he said.

I twisted to face him and nearly fell. He put his other hand up to catch me at the waist and kept me in place, staring up at me, with a cold and steady smile. He twined his fingers into mine, clinging in a way that was not at all brotherly, and I strained as hard as I could to free myself from that grasp. Once, twice, three times. At the end, with a look that reminded me it was his choice and not mine to make, he let go.

Released, I sat down hard in the back of the coach. Mother chattered away, speaking about me but not to me, praying everything would be all right when we arrived, since everything in the world depended on everything being all right.

I heard Ray climb up to the driver's seat and call out to the horses, snapping the reins against their backs. The coach lurched forward.

We rolled on, heading toward a hopeful future, through the dark.

CHAPTER FIVE

Janesville, 1905
One o'clock in the morning
She pauses, taking in a deep breath and
sighing it out. He finds himself waiting, with
a quickened pulse, for her to start speaking
again, to tell him what happened next. But
he shouldn't get drawn in, he tells himself.
He shouldn't care. It's just a story. Most
likely not true in any case. Most likely
calculated to tease out the exact feelings
he's having right now: equal parts sympathy
and dread.

He tells himself that he has a good reason
to let her talk, though. She's exhausted.
She's anxious. If she is lying, the longer she
talks, the more likely it is she'll slip up. Give
her enough rope, as the saying goes, and
she'll hang herself. An apt phrase. They
hanged that woman two years ago in the
Oklahoma territory for what she'd done to
a child in her care. Iris had cried for a full

week about it, the story was so appalling. He wonders what she'd think of this story. Will it be a tragedy? Or something else, by the end?

"So let's say," he says, "that this whole story is true, and I can trust everything you say, and you're innocent. You didn't kill your husband. Who did?"

"If someone killed the husband of a famous magician," she says, tilting her head as if the problem were theoretical, "there are some obvious suspects."

"Like the magician."

"Besides the magician. Maybe someone who hated the magician and wanted to punish her. One of her enemies."

"You have enemies?"

With a grim smile, she says, "Some days I think I have nothing but."

"You think it was someone out for revenge?"

"Or the victim could have enemies of his own. It could have nothing to do with her — with me — at all."

"True. What kind of man was he?"

"I can't even begin to tell you," she says, her voice oddly unsteady for a moment. "Honestly."

"Stop using that word. The more you say it, the less I believe it."

She doesn't respond.

He circles behind her, his footsteps heavy and echoing against the bare wood floor. He begins to undo a set of cuffs, examining her as he does so. One wrist has been recently cut deeply. There's a perfectly straight three-inch-long slash, dark with old blood, against the pale skin. Unfortunately it's already healing and too old to be evidence of a struggle tonight, when the murder was committed. Still, it interests him.

"How did you injure yourself? This cut on your wrist?" he asks casually.

"Things happen on the road," she says. "Heavy equipment shifts at the wrong moment. The illusions have so many moving parts. I don't know half the time what happens."

"And the bruise on your throat?"

She makes a noncommittal noise, a verbal shrug, but he sees her shoulders tighten. There is enormous tension in the back of her neck. Of course she can't relax in the situation he's placed her in, but he saw the change come over her when he asked about the bruise, not before. He'll ask again later. For now, he has another plan. He has two pairs of the new adjustable Lovell cuffs, which should be just enough.

He hangs the first pair of Lovell cuffs from

his belt and begins work on the second. Once the second pair of cuffs is likewise free, he circles around in front of her. He toys with the dangling cuff, opening and closing it. The metal clicks each time he pushes the teeth down against the pivot bar and then thumbs the release button to pop it open again. Like his footfalls, the clicks are loud and sharp in the enclosed space. There are still three pairs of cuffs on her wrists. They both know where things stand.

"Now," he tells her, "I'm going to finish taking your boots off. I'm asking you to let me. Will you?"

"What if I say no?" she asks.

"I'm asking as a courtesy, ma'am."

She sits up straight with a bright false smile and thrusts her right foot out at him, the mostly unlaced boot hanging.

"Here you are then," she says.

He lowers himself slowly to his knees in front of her, then takes the foot in both hands. Then he adjusts his knee to pin the free foot back against the chair. If he's kneeling on her foot, she can't kick him with it. A mere moment of cooperation on her part doesn't mean he'll let his guard down completely. He's tired, not stupid.

The lamplight flickers, and he works on the unlacing in silence. It's so quiet in the room that he can hear the leather and string rasp against each other. When the boot is unlaced, he pulls it off and tosses it away. He does the same with the other boot. She's quiet but not still. When he's done, he can feel the warmth of her foot. It squirms in his hand like an animal. The dead silence of the night outside hangs heavy. He can hear his own breath but not hers.

In the quiet, he remembers how tired he is, and that isn't good. Cuffs or no, she needs to be watched and guarded. Sound will help keep his eyes open and his mind clear. He should get her talking again. Her story will be something to hold onto when the exhaustion threatens to drag him into unconsciousness.

"You aren't telling me what I want to hear," he says. "I asked about the murder. You're telling me this other story instead."

"They're all the same story."

"Which couldn't start a little closer to the end?" He takes one free pair of handcuffs and latches it first around the leg of the chair. He opens the other half of the cuff and draws it forward, circling it around her ankle, pushing the clasp until it clicks shut.

She says, "Where does yours start, officer? Did you play cops and robbers as a boy and find yourself always on the angels' side? Or is this just a job to you, a way to line your pockets? Is it the first thing you ever wanted to do or the last?"

He was right; the Lovell fits, on the largest setting. In a pinch, it seems, a woman's slim ankles can stand in for a man's thick wrists. He repeats the motion with the other pair of cuffs, linking her other ankle to the leg of the chair, so both ankles are trapped. "What difference does that make?"

"It makes your story different," she says. "How you came to be who you are. And if I wanted to know your story, I'd want to know it from the beginning."

"You don't want to know my story."

"I do, actually. Very much. But I'm not the one in charge here, am I?"

"No." He's glad to hear her acknowledge it. "Well, it isn't a long story. I was born here, grew up here, plan to live here my whole life."

"I bet you were one of those charmed boys. You have the air. Always the best at everything."

"Second best," he says before he can stop himself.

"Who was the best then?"

"No point in telling you, is there? If you don't know him?" Despite her visit to Waterloo, Mose Huber's name wouldn't mean anything to her, even if he were inclined to share it.

"I'm interested," she says.

Her eyes are shadowed from this angle, and he can't even tell the half-brown eye from the blue one. He wishes he had a real jail to put her in. She is too close this way. He thinks again of what she did onstage, how rapt he was, and he realizes he has to ask.

"What I'm interested in," he says, "is the Halved Man. How does it work?"

"It's fake," she says flatly. "Fake blade, fake blood, trap door. That's all."

"No, explain it to me. What's the secret of the trick?"

"What kind of magician gives away her secrets?"

"One who'll be hanged if she doesn't."

Quietly, leaning in, she says, "Is that what you think they'll do? You think they'll hang me?"

"Without a moment's hesitation," he says.

She stares at him with her lips shut tight.

They sit together in silence, two figures in two chairs, on the fringes of the circle of lamplight.

After a time, the magician says quietly, "Here in this room, while I tell you what there is to tell, it's just us two. And these are all just words. Once I step outside that door, there's a whole real world again, and that frightens me more than I can say."

"I understand that," he replies, offering his own honest response. "There are things in the real world that scare me too."

"Such as? I'd like to hear."

He opens his mouth to answer her, but another noise drowns him out.

The telephone is ringing.

It is a long, rattle-clanging, uneven sound, and it takes them both by surprise.

Holt freezes.

The telephone rings again. It makes a brittle echo against the close wooden walls, sounding louder and louder in the tight, small space. He feels like he's sitting inside a drum. It wakes the pain in his head, which he had almost managed to forget. No forgetting it now.

He tries to be logical, fighting for clarity against the noise and the drink and the lack of sleep. No one from Waterloo knows he's found her. It can't be Mose. Or could it? There are only a handful of telephones in this part of the state, and no reason for anyone to call from farther away at this time of night.

Iris, then, it must be Iris. The telephone in his house, installed so he can be reached at any hour, is one of the handful. He's not ready to answer the question he knows she has. She wants to know what the doctor said, whether anything can be done. He can't tell her, not yet. Especially not with this one watching. But he wants to answer just to make the ringing stop. The sound makes it almost impossible to think.

Maybe now is the time to strike. He raises his voice to be heard over the telephone's ring. "Did it surprise you? How much blood there was? When it was for real?"

She shakes her head. "I wasn't there. I told you, I wasn't there. I was already running."

"If not the murder, what were you running from?"

The long, shrilling metal clang sounds, falls silent, and then starts up again. His head is beyond buzzing now. Aching. Howling.

She says, "I didn't even know anyone was dead. You have to believe me."

A ring and a silence, a ring and a silence, while their gazes lock.

Putting his face close to hers, he says, "Why did you kill him? Your own husband? How could you try to cut him apart?"

She blanches, visibly, and says, "Did you say cut?"

He turns his back on her then, turning as if to answer the telephone, but only to hide his face.

"Tell me!" she shouts. "How did he die?"

The telephone rings and rings. It takes all he has not to fling the door open and run outside, away from the sound and from her, gulping in fresh air. Instead he breathes his own breath again, growing unpleasantly warmer, struggling to stay put.

His mind soars and races. What does she mean? Is it possible that she's telling the truth, that she had nothing to do with the murder? She is waiting on his answer. All the more reason to stay silent. If he waits for her to speak, there might be some clue in what she says next.

The ringing sound stops, blessedly, and the magician speaks into a longer silence. "What happened to you, anyway? The way you hold yourself. Stiff. Like you're afraid of breaking something."

He tries to hide his shock. "Don't know what you mean."

"Look, I want to tell you everything," she says, sounding sincere. "I do. I will. But it won't make sense to you yet."

He doubts murder could ever make sense to him, but maybe it's time to humor her a little. For now. She seems to relax when she tells her story. If vinegar doesn't work, he's capable of honey.

"Then what would you like to tell me?"

"What happened next. When we arrived at Biltmore, where I was to dance for Madama Bonfanti."

"Go on, then," he says.

The phone blurts a strange, smothered half ring, and they both hesitate, waiting for the rest of the ring to come.

When it doesn't, she starts her story again.

CHAPTER SIX

1894

The Flying Cage

After many hours, the light in the coach changed from dappled to bright, and I raised myself to look out. We had come out of the wooded area onto a lawn that seemed to stretch for a mile. Beautiful, flat grass, as green as an emerald, the likes of which I'd never seen. I couldn't imagine the work it had taken to make it so lush, so even, so perfect. And I could smell flowers too, a distant hint of roses in the still, warm air.

The jouncing stopped as we turned onto a steadier, smoother path, and in a moment, I got a look at the bulk of the house itself.

I gasped.

It was a castle. It was too enormous, too grand, to be called a house. Great jutting spires soared toward the sky. I had no words for it, other than the words Mother had used to describe the capitals of Europe:

majestic, substantial, sublime.

The gray stone walls soared up, impossibly high, into sharp turrets. The roof itself was steeply gabled, and the lowest floor was marked out with a series of arches, a single one of which could have embraced our entire house back home. Columns of windows held huge panes of glass the size of the coach we rode in. I counted two dozen windows without even trying, and that was only on the side facing the coach. Behind the house, the mountains rose gracefully in the distance. My gaze kept skipping from window to arch to turret to gargoyle and back again. There was far too much to take in at once.

The wide iron gate stood open for us, and a neat gravel drive extended between two perfectly flat and green spaces of lawn. And again, the smells, of flowers and grass and sweet pure nothing, crashed over me. It felt almost unfair that there should be a place so beautiful in the world when there was such ugliness elsewhere. My grandparents' home had been large and well-appointed, but it had no more similarity to this home than a hut to a palace, or a single lit match to a forest fire.

The drive took us under a broad stone arch, off to the side of the main entrance, and brought us into an enclosed courtyard. A groom took the horses' reins, and in the face of the house, two great tall front doors swung open with a whisper. I realized afterward there must have been two or more hidden servants pulling them aside, but in the moment, it seemed like magic.

Just inside these broad doors, I could make out the dim shape of another inner door, and on both sides of it, clusters of figures who stood waiting. Black-coated men and white-aproned women. Mother had warned me to expect only the servants at the gate, and though I was still a little disappointed to see no one of note awaiting us, it was best that I not be presented yet. Now I only looked like an ordinary, every-day girl, nothing worth their time or attention. It would take dance to transform me. For today and possibly forever.

I clambered down awkwardly, by myself, yanking my hand back with a jolt when Ray offered me his arm. I hadn't forgotten what he'd said just before we left home, and it preyed on me. The trip had done me no favors. My hair tumbled out of its poor restraints.

"Good heavens, you're in disarray," said my mother, as if seeing me anew now that we had arrived. "Get yourself cleaned up."

"Yes, ma'am."

We were separated and taken to different rooms. I was unsure whether my mother's presence would have been reassuring or unsettling. So much depended on the next few hours. In any case, I wasn't given the choice.

Soon enough, I found myself alone in an enormous bedroom, lushly furnished and streaming with light. At the center of it all was a four-poster bed so broad it could have fit eight girls my size lying shoulder to shoulder. The luxury of the place left me shaken and uncomfortable. It seemed so foreign, so unnecessary. Why was I even here? What did I expect? At the back of my brain, Ray's threat was echoing. I needed a way to calm down, to feel myself again. What could I do?

I slung my pointe shoes, the ribbons of which were tied together, over my shoulder and lit out down the long, foreign hall. If discovered somewhere I shouldn't be, I could always say I was lost. It would probably be the truth anyway. I quickly lost track of where I had started, and since I had no idea where I was going, one hallway was as good as another.

Once I found my way outside and I could see across the broad back lawn to a series of outbuildings still under construction, I knew my destination. No one stopped me as I slipped out the door and walked barefoot across the lustrous grass toward the cluster of wooden buildings, half shells. The most complete building was the one I wanted. I opened the door a crack and edged my way inside.

A barn. Like everything else here, grander than ours at home. Clean and unfinished and smelling of freshly cut boards. I breathed in the smell deeply — it helped settle me a little — and I explored with interest. I looked up to see a completed hayloft at one end and a long narrow beam reaching to the far end to brace the sloped roof. The idea came to me instantly. This was what I needed, for confidence. I'd walk the crossbeam en pointe.

Before I could think better of the impulse, I hastily climbed the ladder and donned my shoes, tying the ribbons around my ankles, and then I started across.

I concentrated every bit of my attention on the small circles where my toes hit the beam. At the start, it was easy. My toes in the pointe shoes took up less than a third of the beam's width, so it wasn't hard to land each foot firmly. With each step, the hollow toe box echoed against the wood, through the empty barn. I heard a scurrying else-where in the barn, maybe a mouse or a rac-coon, but I didn't want to look away from the beam. I focused and made it to the far wall. I dropped down onto the arch of my foot to make the turn, carefully, one hand against the wall, and started back toward the loft.

Thud went my toe box against the wood of the beam. Right toe box, thud. Left toe box, thud. One after another after another. I felt myself speeding up as I took the last few steps, nearing the end of the beam, and expelled a sharp breath as I reached the safety of the loft again. I hadn't realized I was holding my breath at all. I set my feet flat on the long wood planks of the loft and stretched my arms up elegantly, striking the established pose of first position.

I heard Ray before I saw him, his voice all too near, saying, "Nicely done."

He stood in the loft, only a few feet away from me. His slow, sarcastic applause ech-oed off the bare walls of the barn. I nearly stepped backward to distance myself from him, but behind me, there was only empti-ness on both sides of the beam.

"What a wonderful performance," he said. "Very graceful. You really are a lovely young woman. And a secretly powerful one, as well."

"Not today with your nonsense," I said. "Leave me alone."

"I only want to pay you a compliment. Show you my appreciation."

He was standing at the top of the ladder, the only way out. In trying to escape him and find a quiet moment to gather my strength, I'd put myself in the worst position possible: utterly alone with him, no one knowing where we were.

I said, "Thank you. Now get out."

"No, I don't think so," he said.

I crossed my arms over my chest. My practice garments had always seemed modest enough before, but now, I felt exposed.

"Come over here," he said. "I want to appreciate you."

Instead of answering, I calmly sat down on the floor of the loft and began a stretching exercise, pointing my right toe and bending my body down over it. I moved as if he weren't there. Maybe if he thought he wasn't bothering me, he'd give up. I pointed my other toe and stretched my body out in the other direction. If he took the trembling as exhaustion and not fear, I had a chance.

"Very well, I'll come to you," he said and quickly crossed the space. He dropped his body behind mine, pressing his chest against my back, and before I could move, he already had a firm arm around the front of my shoulders, holding me in.

"How dare you!" I shouted. "Let me go!"

He had been wheedling and flattering, but now his voice was hard. "Shout all you want, little thing. The house is far away. No one's listening."

He took his free hand and slid it up my knee, toward my thigh, and higher. When I grabbed his paw to haul it off me, he slid his other hand up to grasp my breast. I tore it away, but he moved and it was back again. I began to panic in earnest.

"Stop it."

He hissed, "Let's try it once. You'll never know otherwise whether you like it."

I tried to scream. He put his hand over my mouth. I tried to bite it, but he was too strong. He let go a moment and then used both hands under my legs to flip me over onto my face, and I could taste blood where my teeth cut the inside of my mouth. The raw pine boards scraped my cheek. When I could feel cool air behind me and the extra weight of my skirts lying heavy on my back, I knew it was my last chance. While he fumbled with the flap on his breeches, I got my knees under me, and with a great fierce burst of all my strength, I drove my heel straight back, right where his legs met, hard.

Oh, how he howled.

I scrambled up to get free, but he was still between me and the ladder. One hand clutched between his legs, where the pain was, but his other hand was free and ready. I looked at him and said, "Let me go!" but I could see plainly the rage in his eyes, and I knew he wouldn't just step aside.

I lunged for the ladder anyway, hoping.

He caught me up in his arms, and in another world, with another girl and another boy, it would have been romantic. But I was me and he was him, and my heart flailed madly in my chest like a bird in a too-small cage. He held me in the air, one arm behind my neck, the other under my knees, my feet swinging free, and when he started to walk, I feared he might intend to knock me unconscious so as to do what he pleased unimpeded, but what he did instead was take three steps to the edge of the hayloft and, with one single sweeping motion, throw me free of the earth, into the empty air.

I fell fast and landed like a stone.

The heavy thump of my limp body landing echoed hollowly off the walls of the empty barn.

The first breath into my screaming lungs was heaven. Then came the pain. All over at first. Eventually it focused into a sharp, vicious ache in one leg, all the way from ankle to waist. I knew then how I'd landed, and what I'd broken.

I bit the inside of my mouth so I wouldn't scream. Not that I thought silence would save me, but it felt important. I needed to control something. I couldn't control how far I had just fallen. Not just fallen, but been thrown. And the person who had thrown me was still above me, still here, and we were as alone as we could be.

I could hear him coming down the ladder.

He walked across the bare wood floor toward me. I tuned him out. I focused on the pain instead and felt the worst of it radiating from the ankle, howling.

Past the pain, I could hear his footsteps until they slowed and stopped right next to me.

I forced my eyes open and looked up. His eyes met mine.

"If you tell them, I'll kill you," he said and stepped over me on his way to the door.

I lay on my back on the bare wood and thanked God for my life, even through the pain. Because it would only hurt for now.

Because he could have done more, and I stopped him. Because a bone is just a bone, even broken.

I lay there on my back a long time. It felt like hours, though it couldn't have been. I got up when I realized my options: I could lie down in pain with a broken leg or I could stand up in pain with a broken leg. So I stood. The pain washed over me again, draining my will, and I made fists of my hands and forced myself to remain upright. Under my breath, I chanted to myself, *I will heal, I will heal, I will heal.* I wished it to be true. I needed it to be true.

Slowly, I began to work my way back toward the house. What had been a few minutes' dash before was now a torturous, slow progress. The pain still roared at me, not allowing me to forget it for even a moment. I was taking a small joy in having made it so far across the green lawn when I looked up, and what I saw brought me to a complete halt. Off in the distance, a handful of figures reclined in chairs under a broad white tent. I wanted to collapse into the earth and disappear.

I saw myself with their eyes. Had everything gone as planned, I would have strode across the lawn toward them in a spotless shirtwaist, my arms and legs elegant, the picture of confidence and grace. Instead I was limping, half hopping, doing my best to keep the weight of my body from resting on the injured side at all. My pale satin shoes were smeared with green streaks. I was soiled and poor and deeply flawed. Had I been able to run away, I would have. Instead I continued, doomed, until I was close enough to see their faces and for them to see mine.

A man's figure detached itself from the group and hurtled toward me, and my heart seized up until I realized it wasn't Ray. The man picked me up and carried me back to the group without a word. Whoever he was, I was grateful to him.

Then I saw Mother, looking horrified, and Ray, who had no doubt found a way to insinuate himself in the group and make it seem like he'd been there the whole time. But my eyes locked on a hook-nosed woman with a gold-tipped cane. Her black hair was shot through with steel gray. She could be no one but Madama Bonfanti. Her dress was high-necked and dark, and she looked as solid and graceful as a grand piano.

There was one awful moment of silence while they took me in, looking, seeing, despairing. Unbelievingly they stared, and there was nothing to say, until there was.

"No!" Madama Bonfanti cried. "What is this? You have brought me a broken girl!"

"The pain is less already," I said, but no one was listening to me. I was an object to be handled, not heeded. The man lowered me into a chair. Another voice explained that there was no doctor on the estate, and the village physician was of little use, but the cook would bring laudanum, which would take some of the pain away. Another chair was settled next to mine, and Mother sat down in it. She exclaimed over me, her voice pinched and shrill.

"Dear God in heaven! What happened?"

"I fell."

"From where? What did you do?"

I planned to answer her, but then the hands exploring my ankle twisted it to the side, and I yelped in pain, trying to pull it away.

Under her breath, Mother hissed, "Stay still, you little fool."

I was stunned dumb by her anger, which had never before been directed at me. I wanted to look at her face, but I was afraid. I despaired that I'd failed her so completely.

"I can't — this — this is awful," she said. "Where's Ray? Ray, come here!"

"What?"

He appeared. I couldn't shrink any smaller than I already had, but I looked away from him. It was all I could do.

I was invisible to my mother anyway, who was peppering Ray with questions. "Didn't you set that horse's broken leg last month? Don't you know about these things?"

"I am not a horse, Mother," I whispered, and my heart was hammering again. Because Victor had noted how good Ray was at identifying which horses were healthy and which were prone to accidents, and I had never thought much about it before, but maybe he was doing more than observing. If this boy could intentionally injure a person — a girl — he was certainly capable of doing the same to a horse. Not to mention the damage he'd done himself. Suddenly I couldn't get the image of his scars out of my head. That ghostly rib cage hovering over the real one, present with him everywhere.

Lost in my private hell, I paid no attention while he barked instructions to the servants and bound my leg up in a makeshift splint. If I thought about what was happening, I might shatter like a china cup flung against stone. Instead I retreated into my mind, leaving the broken body for others to deal with in my absence.

The promised laudanum arrived, mixed into a cup of sweetened milk, and I was pressed to drink the whole thing. It helped me retreat even further into myself, wrapping me in a soft cushion of a haze.

When I looked up, Madama and the others were gone. The visit was over even though we were still here. After that, the estate's hospitality was generous but curt. No one can provide bounty while withholding approval in the same way as the rich. I had forgotten it from my childhood, but I never would again.

After some time — the hours became liquid, flowing, impossible to grasp — we were informed that it was unsafe to go on the roads in the dark, and we would be staying overnight. We were led by silent servants down long, silent hallways to our rooms. There was a pale, beribboned nightdress laid out on my enormous bed. The freckled face of my servant guide reminded me of my old nursemaid Colleen, but I couldn't muster a thing to say to her, and she remained stern. She spoke one sentence, to ask if I'd like assistance undressing. I could only shake my head from side to side. She backed through the door and pulled it shut.

As soon as she was gone, I exploded in inappropriate laughter. I was light-headed from the pain and its remedy, nearly out of my mind at the absurdity of the entire situation. A room this sumptuous, a bed so large laid with such rich linens, a wardrobe larger than the pie safe at home, and all just for me. And I didn't deserve any of it. My laughter became hysterical. I plastered both hands over my mouth to try to contain it, frightened of being heard and labeled ungrateful, and finally knelt on the floor next to the bed to smother my laughter in the thick cotton coverlet. I kept my face down until the hysteria subsided. When I had mastered myself again, I left my own dress laid out on the floor in the shape of my body, pulled the soft nightdress over my head, and climbed up into the bed like a mountaineer making the summit.

My head heavy with shame and my leg aching in its brace, I wouldn't have slept a wink, except that the feather bed was more comfortable than I would have ever thought possible. Even as my head hit the pillow and I was cursing myself out for a foolish girl, listing off ways I could have avoided letting matters come to this, my thoughts were cut short by a deep blessed unconsciousness as dark and soft as a panther's fur.

In the morning, Madama Bonfanti was not there to bid us farewell. White-aproned women brought us our breakfast, thick slices of warmed ham on featherlight biscuits so delicious I struggled not to wolf them down like a savage. Black-coated men hefted our bags and showed us out. Ray climbed up into the driver's seat of the borrowed coach. Because of my leg, Mother put me across the long seat in the back, so I didn't even have to look at him. It was a small mercy, considering.

The road was long and rough, and every bump on it shot through my leg like fire. I'd asked for another dose of laudanum but was given barely a drop, with the lecture that sometimes people who took too much of it simply stopped breathing, not that I had any way of knowing such a thing. Despite the burning pain, I kept my mouth firmly shut the whole ride home. I wouldn't scare Mother by moaning, and I wouldn't give Ray the satisfaction of knowing how badly I was hurt. If not for him, I would have danced. If not for him, I might have found a way out, been taken to the school in New York, had a new life to live. I couldn't let the fury take me over, so I couldn't open the door to it, not even an inch. I only let my mind go blank, for myself. That was all I wanted. To forget.

After the first night's dinner back at home, eaten in near silence, Mother suggested Ray inspect my leg to see how it was healing. I didn't dare speak against her, knowing how angry she must be with me for my failure. So I sat in our best chair and endured the humiliation of Ray's wordless inspection, his hands roaming over me with full license while my parents looked on. Ray's obvious joy was more painful to me than the injury itself. I knew he was indulging his secret fantasy of being a healer, imagining somehow that he was knitting my bones back together with the power of his mind. When he suggested it again the next evening, I said, "No, thank you, I feel entirely healed." That night, it was a lie, but it was the truth soon enough. After only a few weeks, I'd regained the use of my leg. Mother exclaimed over how quickly it had healed and credited Cecchetti with keeping me in such good health.

My body made a complete recovery, but there was a permanent change to my mind. There were so many what-ifs. If my mother hadn't fallen in love with Victor. If we hadn't come to Jeansville. If I hadn't started dancing in the evenings. If we'd never been invited to Biltmore. Without all these, I never would have practiced my balance on the beam, and I never would have let myself be broken in pieces. Things would be so different. There were so many other lives I wasn't leading, all because of a handful of choices, mostly made by others. I swore to myself that in the future, I'd make my own choices, right or wrong. Then at least when things went haywire, I'd know exactly who was to blame.

CHAPTER SEVEN

1894–1895

Flight of the Favorite

Nearly six months later, two things happened in rapid succession. I happened upon something I shouldn't have, and I made a crucial mistake.

The rainy winter came upon us and gave way to a cool, dry spring. The men were plowing and planting, preparing for the summer ahead. My mother needed assistance with an especially heavy load of groceries she'd brought home from town, and she directed me to fetch one of the men from the barn. I feared I would likely find Ray there, as he was most often caring for the horses, but I had no choice. Mother had softened in her attitude toward me now that so much time had passed since the disaster at Biltmore, and I felt that we were once more on solid ground. I didn't want to jeopardize that.

94

I stood in the doorway of the barn and shouted, "Raymond, my mother needs your help. Come now."

No answer. I took one more step inside. "Raymond?"

The air inside the barn was heavy with hay dust and thick with an animal smell. Suddenly, a horse cried out with a strangled whinny. I had never heard such a cry. I rushed in the direction of the sound and arrived at a stall to see Ray seated at a dappled mare's front right foot, which was in a sling to keep her from striking out with it.

The hammer dropped from his hand when she kicked, and his grip on her leg was lost. She cried out again and shook her head fiercely, mane flying, against the air. I could see a metal spike protruding from her foot. Not from the edges of the hoof where she was shoed, but in the tender center. She had to be in terrible pain. I reeled.

"Leave that horse alone!" I shouted.

"I'm trying to get the spike out of her hoof, you fool," said Ray.

I knew next to nothing about horses, but I could still see through his lie. "You'd want a claw hammer for that. Not a mallet."

He reached down, gingerly dodging the horse's swinging leg, and grabbed the fallen mallet.

"What do you want?" he asked.

"Right now, I want you to step back," I said. Shockingly, he complied.

I stepped past him into the stall, laid my palm against the side of the horse's neck, and spoke to her in a quiet voice. When her eyes were no longer rolling back in her head, I lowered both hands as quickly and smoothly as I could to the spike in her hoof, so as not to startle her, and yanked hard.

Luckily, it came clean out straightaway. Thank God I'd caught him on the first stroke. I flung the spike away, and it landed almost silently in the deep hay at the far end of the stall. The horse whinnied and twitched, but she didn't strike out at me. I stroked her neck gently and stared at Ray, still standing just inside the open door of the stall, the mallet in his hand.

"You ruin everything," he said petulantly.

"What? You were trying to destroy this poor horse, and I ruined it?"

"I would have healed her."

"That's ridiculous. You can't heal any-thing."

"I healed you, didn't I?"

"No," I shouted, my pent-up anger all let loose. "You broke me."

"Stupid girl. Do you have any idea how long it takes a broken leg to heal? Weeks, even months. I sent healing powers into your leg, and you healed in days."

"You broke my goddamn leg in the first place," I said, nearly hissing in my fury.

"Damaged things interest me. Especially if I damage them."

He hefted the mallet, testing its weight. It made me nervous. Without moving too quickly, I backed out of the stall to put some distance between us.

"Anyway," he said, "the story is the important thing."

"And what's the story?"

"I found the poor horse with a nail in her hoof. I risked my safety to free her. And I suffered for it."

Uncomprehending, I asked, "Suffered for it?"

I saw him lift the hammer, and in a flash, I realized I was well within range if he chose to throw it, but that wasn't what he had in mind.

He brought the hammer back toward his own face, and the flat metal of the mallet connected with his nose, and all of a sudden there was blood everywhere.

I couldn't stay a moment longer. I fled.

When my mother asked, I told her there'd been no one in the barn, and anyway, I was strong enough to help her unload the groceries myself. We started to the work, and spoke no more about it.

But I couldn't get that image out of my head. Swinging the hammer back toward himself, a look of unearthly calm on his face. Indifferent to the coming pain. I knew then that he was capable of anything.

Saturday nights, our two families always came together for dinner, one Saturday at the house in town and the next at the farmhouse. I had found Ray in the barn on a Thursday, and two days later, all six of us gathered at the farmhouse dinner table. My mother had prepared roasted chicken and turnips, not one of her better meals, sadly dry and bitter. Starting late, she had never become much of a cook. I could see Silas's wife pushing the food around on her plate with evident disdain. I redoubled my efforts and ate with feigned enthusiasm so I would be able to ask for a second serving. Ray's nose was hugely swollen, an ugly red shot through with violet, which I noted with grim satisfaction. I wondered if his belief in his healing powers was shaken. Clearly he had made no inroads on healing this injury, and I hoped it was causing him great pain.

At length, Silas said, "Son, are you going

to tell the ladies what happened to your nose?"

"Got broke," Ray said.

"The boy's being modest. He was trying to remove a stuck nail from a mare's hoof and she kicked him."

"Kicked in the face by a horse?" I said loudly. "He could have died."

"He got almost out of the way," Silas said, slapping his son on the back. "Barely got grazed as a result. Quick reflexes, my son."

"Well, thank goodness he wasn't hurt worse," exclaimed my mother. "That's quite lucky."

"Unbelievably lucky," I said. No one reacted.

"I hope the horse will be all right," my stepfather said.

"She should make a full recovery," Ray said. "I caught it in time. If she'd been walking around on it long, the nail would have been pushed further in, and it would have festered."

"Can't make a business on injured horses," Silas said.

"You're certainly blessed to have the boy's aptitude," added his wife.

I couldn't believe it. They accepted his story, flat out. No one at all saw through it. They didn't even try.

My stepfather said, "On a different subject, I don't suppose anyone has seen a shepherd puppy on the farm lately?"

"No," my mother said, and I shook my head, not trusting myself to speak.

"Neighbor stopped by to ask if we'd spotted it. Belongs to his daughter, and she hasn't seen it in a week. Of course, the girl is distraught."

I immediately looked over at Ray, but nothing showed on his face. He took another bite of turnip and chewed slowly.

"That's strange," said Silas. "Two other neighbors are missing dogs too."

Ray muttered, "Maybe they've all run off together. Like the dish and the spoon." His father smiled at this, and his mother laughed.

I cringed. I couldn't stand thinking about what might have happened to those dogs. If Ray had gotten to them. If he had a mind to experiment. Scientists had been experimenting on dogs in England for hundreds of years, even taking blood from one to put into another. If I had learned that in my science lessons, Ray could have learned it too. He might want to hurt them in order to heal. What he would do with the idea made me ill.

It was a small thing compared with the

other wrongs, but it was the last straw.

After dinner, in the kitchen, I was alone with my mother. I hesitated to speak at all, but I made myself ask, "Don't you think it's strange, about the neighbors' dogs?"

She paused to consider it, handing me a plate to dry. "These things happen. There are animals in the woods. It's not the city."

"I know."

"Are you so concerned? You needn't be. None of the wild animals around here are dangerous to us."

"I'm not concerned about animals. I'm concerned about — humans."

"Humans?"

"That there might be . . . bad people doing things to the dogs."

She wiped her hands on her apron and picked up another plate to wash. "Oh, Ada. That's not likely."

"It's possible."

"Yes." She sighed. "It's possible. But why would you want to think about such things? It's not good for your mind."

"It could be Ray," I blurted.

Her hands stilled.

I went on, the words spilling out. "He might have hurt those dogs. He hurt that horse. Mother, he hurt me."

She didn't look at me. She looked down

at her hands. She said, "He hurt you? How?"

"At Biltmore. He found me and he tried . . . he wanted . . ." And I found I couldn't say it. Not to her. It was too shameful, and I was too ashamed.

"Ada?"

The accusation hung in the air, incomplete, unbelievable.

"Enough," she said, lowering her voice. "You want to accuse this boy of — of I don't even know what. You have this fantasy that three missing dogs means something nefarious. I doubt it means anything at all. Honestly, Ada, this is appalling behavior."

I whispered, "I'm sorry."

Her face softened then. I saw it change. "You don't need — oh, darling, I'm sorry too. I am. But you see, you must be mistaken."

Tentatively, I said, "I don't think I am."

"But you must be," she said again, squaring her shoulders, speaking quietly enough that we wouldn't be overheard. "Here's why. Because we all depend on that boy's father, for our lives, for everything. We're only here because he allows it. If Ray hurt you, if he's done something wrong, then I will have to tell Victor. Victor will have to tell Silas. Silas will have to respond, and I think you know Ray won't be the one he'll punish. We will all suffer instead. Our family. Is that what you want? You want us out on the street with nowhere to go?"

"Of course not," I said in a whisper, feeling the hot sting of tears under my lashes.

"So you were mistaken. Weren't you?"

"Yes, ma'am."

She said, "I'm so sorry, Ada. Once upon a time, I was stronger than this."

I was afraid to breathe, let alone to speak, so I simply continued to cry, clutching the dish in my hand as if it could give me some kind of solace. Her eyes were dry, but I could see her knuckles turn white as she clutched her own dish, her head bent and staring down into the sink in front of us.

"You're old enough to hear it. I was ready to lose my whole world for your father," she said quietly. "He wasn't ready to lose his for me. He didn't love his wife. Everyone knew that. Her parents offered him so much money to stay that he couldn't refuse. He didn't refuse. He didn't love me enough. I worshipped him, but in the end, he was weak. And it didn't matter how strong I was, if he wasn't."

"Victor was strong enough. He loved you enough. He was strong enough to run away with you."

Grimly, she said, "By then, neither of us

had all that much to lose."

I watched her wipe away a tear, and I realized I would never see her quite the same way again.

"Now we have even less," she said. "And I can't lose what little we do have. I can't."

My powerful, beautiful mother, my songbird, my cello. She was only an ordinary woman, and one who felt herself at the mercy of the world. She was right. She wasn't strong enough.

"No more of this," she said, dunking the dish in her hand under the surface of the water. She swished it from side to side and scrubbed at it even though it was already clean, then handed it to me to dry and return to the cabinet.

And that was all.

That night, I lay awake, castigating myself for my error, over and over. Maybe if I'd gone about it differently. Maybe if I'd come right out and said it, told her about what he'd done to me in the barn months before and what he'd done to the horse and himself that day, maybe then she would have to take my side. If I'd done it right, maybe I could have made it all come out differently. Come out better.

But I knew that she was right. Ray was his

father's pride and his mother's pet. There was no chance they would take a word against him seriously. I was the trouble-maker, the upstart, the bastard girl. I'd botched the confession to my mother, and if I tried to bring it up again, I knew she wouldn't listen. Now I was the girl who cried wolf, even though there really was a wolf, and I had every reason to think the wolf wasn't yet done with me.

Those poor dogs. That poor horse. That horrid, whispering voice when he'd said *I hope you know I'll never let you leave,* and later, *If you tell them, I'll kill you.* I realized then how foolish I'd been to stay this long. It could be fatal to stay longer.

My mother had told me she couldn't save me. If I wanted to escape — to live — I would have to save myself.

Rising silently, moving through the dark on practiced, careful feet, I fetched the valise my mother had bought me for ballet school. From my bureau, I took two plain dresses; from the kitchen, a half loaf of bread. I paused before I left, thinking of writing a note for her, telling her not to worry about me and that I'd left by choice, but I was too afraid. It would take time, and even if I left a note, there was no guarantee she'd see it. I heard creaks and snaps from the floorboards of the old house, and I didn't know whether it was my imagination or someone rising in the night. It wasn't worth the risk. If Ray found me trying to run, I knew he would hurt me, and I feared he would kill me. There was no coming back from that.

There was only onc thing I needed to do before leaving. I dashed across the grass toward the barn, shoving open the huge door and not, as I'd been warned a thousand times to do, sliding it shut behind me. I wanted to throw open the doors of every stall, sending our whole crew of mares, foals, and stallions sprinting out into the night, but the thought of my mother stopped me. If all the horses were gone, it would be too obvious what I'd done. Silas's wrath would come down on her. Instead, I walked directly to the stall of the mare I'd seen Ray attack. I could free one horse, at least. I could even ride to freedom on her back, if she let me.

I crouched down to open the door, but I hadn't foreseen her eagerness to break free, and I'd no sooner undone the latch than she charged the door, knocking me back. I fell to the ground, my head striking the floorboards with a thud, and then the horse was on me. I rolled, almost by instinct, hoping to shield my head. Hooves were all around, like thunder in my ears. I could only curl myself as small as I could and pray for luck. It was all over in a few moments. I had a distant awareness of retreating hoof beats, and on some level, that pleased me, but I was afraid to move and afraid to open my eyes. My body was frozen in shock, the blood so cold in my veins that I couldn't tell at first whether I'd been injured. Had I ruined my chance at escape?

As best I could, I stretched my body out to test its state, and a searing pain in my hand woke me from my trance. I held the hand out to look at it. It was clear that the outer two fingers had been caught under the horse's hoof, broken and possibly crushed, down to the first joint of each. At least it was my hand and not my foot, I told myself. I could still walk. And I didn't have time to indulge the pain. I had to get moving. So I sprinted north through the back field, skirting the edge of the neighbors' land. I rejoined the road on the other side of town, where there was no one to ask questions.

Where could I go? Not back to my grandparents' house, which was an unknown distance in an unknown direction. I doubted they would welcome me, child of an unknown lecher and a known cheat with whom they had explicitly cut all ties. I knew almost nothing else of the world, only stories, nothing real. I only knew one place to go, unsuited as it was, and so I went there. It took much longer to go on foot, but at least I had two strong legs under me this time.

I walked with my aching hand raised to keep it from filling with blood, a solitary young woman on a long road, one hand in the air as if she had the answer to a question.

CHAPTER EIGHT

Janesville, 1905
Half past one o'clock

"If I could, I'd show you what that looked like," she says and twists her hands so the cuffs rattle against the wood of the chair.

"If I wanted to, I'm sure I could picture it," he remarks dryly. She doesn't need to remind him that her hands are trapped. But the sound prompts him to circle behind her and examine her hands again. "Which hand was it?" he asks.

"The right."

He kneels behind her so he can see clearly and leans in as close as he dares. The cut on her wrist stands out, although it seems less severe than he first thought. The fingers on both hands look straight and unblemished.

"This hand doesn't look like it's ever been broken."

"It was a long time ago, officer," she says.

He retrieves his chair and sits down across from her again. He leaves plenty of room between them, but he wants to be on her level. He wants to look at her; not up, not down, just at. Into those blue-and-brown fairy eyes.

"What year did you say?"

"I didn't say, I don't think. But it was 1895. Ten years ago."

"And you were how old?"

"Fourteen. I was born in the summer. When were you born, officer?"

"Winter," he says.

"And how old are you?"

"I'm not making conversation when I ask you these things," he says, leaning forward with his elbows on his knees. "I'm trying to get the facts. What few facts there are in this story of yours."

"And what's your opinion?" She cocks her head.

"Of your story?"

"Yes."

"I think it's not true."

"Well, it is true," she says, sounding insulted.

"I think your story isn't true, and I think you're a murderer, and I think if someone put a knife in your hand, you'd stab me without a moment's pause."

Her breath catches in her throat. He hears it, clear as anything. He knows what it means: weakness. So he presses.

He says, "You've stabbed someone, but you didn't like it."

She doesn't say anything at first. When she speaks, her voice is soft and hesitant. "It's not a thing a person can like."

"Some people do," he says, trying to sound sympathetic.

"Those people are monsters," she says. "I'm not."

"I know you're not." He'll flatter her, if that's what she wants. "You're sensitive and smart and you've had terrible things done to you, so I don't blame you for striking back."

She eyes him, this time out of the all-blue eye, and says, "Oh, officer. Don't be obvious."

His optimism disappears. He stands up and turns his back so she can't see his face. It isn't fair. He has all the power and none of it. The ceiling seems lower than it did an hour before, the room smaller, though he knows that's not possible. So much is riding on this night. He can't afford to lose control.

She breaks into his reverie, saying, "Now I want to ask you a question. When you didn't answer the telephone. Is it because

111

you're not a police officer?"

"What?"

"Well, you could be an impostor. Maybe that's why you brought me here instead of taking me to the authorities in Waterloo. People do it, you know. They pretend."

He walks over to his desk and grabs the nameplate, which he turns around to face her. "Officer Virgil Holt."

"I don't doubt there is one. I just doubt you're him."

He bristles. "You're not convinced by the gun?"

"The gun is a detail. Details can be misleading."

"And the whole station?" He gestures at the room and its contents. A real desk, real walls, two real people. "Is the station a detail?"

"I never said it wouldn't take some doing."

He says nothing. Let her wonder, he tells himself.

In silence, he kneels at her feet to check the cuffs around her ankles. He wishes he had more than five pairs of cuffs. It's not logical. If she knows how to escape from one pair, she knows how to escape, period. But still, six would be better. Or eight. Or ten. At least she can't enchant him. If she could, she would have done it already. Wouldn't she?

"It's interesting," she says, raising her chin. "I still don't think you understand. Escapists use different equipment altogether. They'd have chains and not just the cuffs. Ropes too. A straitjacket. You think I'm Houdini?"

"Houdini is a genius," says Holt. "And you're only a murderer."

"Murderer? Not murderess? You deny me the badge of my sex."

He gets an idea and grabs the heavy, glittering fabric of her stage dress at the hem. He folds it back on itself, exposing her legs fully several inches above the knee.

"Heavens! So forward!" she says, as if to make light, but there is a brittle, tense note in her voice.

At that moment, he smells her, the true her, underneath the wet silk and salt. She smells like burnt orange peel, is it? Or lime? Or both? He's tempted to lean closer but braces himself, reins himself in. He is a married man and an officer of the law.

"Which leg did you say you broke?"

"Did I say?" she asks. "It was the left."

He inspects the left leg closely through the sheer stocking that veils it. An absolutely perfect leg. Pristine.

She goes on, "If a break heals cleanly, there's nothing to see."

His hands come up to her knee as if of their own accord, and he runs them both down the sides of her calf. It is warm and smooth. Oranges, she smells like oranges. He exhales and feels her body stiffen under his touch.

Her voice even more tense, she says, "You should know that, and I suspect you do."

Suddenly he realizes what's making her nervous. Him. He immediately lets the heavy beaded hem of her dress drop back into place, covering her legs, and settles back on his heels. "You don't have to be afraid of me. Not that way. I am married."

She shrugs her shoulders as much as she can, given her restraints. "That wouldn't stop a lot of men."

"It stops me."

"Your wife is lucky she has you."

"Your experience with marriage isn't as good, it seems."

"No. I've never been happily married. What's your lovely wife's name, Virgil?"

"Does it matter?"

"I'm telling you everything about me. I told you where I came from and the name I was born with. I told you everything that happened to me, even the worst things. I told you —" Her voice catches but she plunges ahead. "I told you what Ray did. Tried to do. Every detail of my life, no matter how small, is open to you. I think you can tell me your wife's name."

He swallows hard and says, "Her name is Iris."

"Thank you."

He doesn't know what to say after that. He knows he's given something up, but he doesn't see how it could do her any good to know it. His wife's name isn't a pass code. It isn't going to get her anywhere.

"Now, let's discuss the night of the crime," he says. "If you didn't commit the murder, where were you? You cut the man in the box in half with an ax, you finished out the show, and then — what?"

She gapes at him.

He explains, "What came after is what I mean. Tell me that."

In a voice of wonder, she says, "I don't believe it. You were there."

"What makes you say that?"

"I use a saw. Always. I only used an ax once, and that was last night, in Waterloo."

He's in trouble now. "Maybe I misspoke. Or misremembered. It was something sharp is all."

"No. No, I don't think so." She leans

forward in her seat as far as she can, visibly excited. Life comes back to her face, color to her cheeks. "You were in Waterloo, to see my show, and you were heading north from there the same as I was, and that's what brought you to that restaurant. It's all so clear."

Her air of triumph is irritating. It shouldn't matter that he was there, but he feels like it gives her some kind of power over him, to know that he's seen her in her element. Even now, she seems less a prisoner than before.

"I didn't go there to see your ridiculous *show*," he spits.

"So why were you there?"

"Visiting a doctor."

"Why? Because you were shot?"

Shock washes over him, through him. "How — how did you know that?"

"Lucky guess," she says with a hint of a smile. "The stiffness I asked you about. It's partly in your legs, but not entirely. You carry it in your whole body — it has something to do with your back. Lower back, I think. Like you're protecting it. And you're a police officer, so guns are your business."

She's gotten close enough to the truth on her own that he doesn't see the point of hiding the rest of it. "And so it was."

"Who shot you?"

"I interrupted a robbery at the bank. Three months back." He doesn't want to relive it. He tells the story as if it happened to someone else. "Got the man to lay down his weapon and the money. Didn't see his accomplice, who shot me from behind. Twice."

"But you survived. That's close to a miracle."

He lets himself sit, lowering his body onto the desk facing her, leaning forward. "Is it? They got the one in my leg but the one in my back is still there. Next to the spine. The doctor in Waterloo is the best for miles around. I wanted him to take it out. He said it was too risky. Too close to the nerve. If he goes after it, there's a good chance of paralyzing me, so he won't operate. Flat out refused."

"It still seems like a happy ending. Isn't it? Aren't you better off alive with a bullet in your back than dead, with or without one?"

"You'd think so, but no," he says grimly. "The human body isn't like a block of ice or wood, holding steady. Over days or weeks or years, the bullet could move. If it moves too far toward my spine, I'll lose the use of my legs. Or if it migrates — that's the word

117

he used — toward a major organ, I could bleed to death from the inside."

"Oh," she breathes.

She sounds sincere. She sounds like she pities him. It brings him up short for a moment. Her pity for him is wrong, so wrong, when he is the one with the gun and the cuffs and the power to put her on the gallows, and she is alone and weak and handcuffed, still, to a chair. He doesn't want to be pitied. He wants to be whole.

"That's my story," he says. "Now tell me yours. Tell me what comes next. How did you turn from a girl who liked to dance into a living scandal onstage every night, cutting grown men in pieces?"

"I'm getting to that," she says.

He says, "I'm listening."

It's only after she begins her story again, her voice as smooth and warm as a pillow, that his eyes come to rest on her throat. And he notices, with some surprise, that the bruise that piqued his curiosity earlier is gone, as if it had never been there at all.

CHAPTER NINE

1895

Lady to Tiger

At night I went. And along the way, for the first time in a long time, I thought of my father. Who had he been? What had he bequeathed me? Right now I didn't need my mother's elegance and grace. Both were useless. I needed determination and confidence. And in the absence of my father, I assigned him those qualities so they would be mine too. My mother had called him weak, but I chose not to believe what she'd said. She had been searching for a way to justify her own choices. It was the first time I realized that we all bend and shape our stories to fit our own ends. It was certainly not the last.

To say I climbed over mountains would give the wrong impression, but still, it was true. And those are different on foot than they are in a carriage. But you go over a mountain the same way you go over any road in the end. Step by careful step. As long and dark as that walk was, there was still a joy to it, because I was making my own way. No one would stop me, no one would hold me down, no one would be using me for their own ends. Whenever I thought I might fall down from exhaustion, I breathed in the sharp pine-scented air and reminded myself that whatever else I was or wasn't, I was free.

At last, the road sloping down under my weary feet and the sun a white ball of fire in the clear blue sky, I arrived at the land surrounding the Biltmore and saw the castle itself rising up against that selfsame sky like a fortress. I'd reached it. The building's pale stone walls rose so high and so steep that they took my breath away, what little breath I had remaining.

Even from half a mile away, I could see the differences from the last time I had visited. They had built more rooms onto the back, wedging a new great wide wall of stone against the others. The seams were invisible, but I knew the old shape from memory. The west wing too had shifted its shape and was finished with a graceful turret. There were more statues in the nearby courtyard, cherubs and horses and a marble

Diana. I could see curtains in windows that had previously been bare. Everywhere I looked, the place was different. I was different too, of course. I avoided looking to the west, where I knew the barn must be finished by now and in use. This was a place where my life had been changed forever. I hoped it would be so again, this time for the better.

I waited for nightfall. The plan I had in mind would be easier to manage in the dark. In the meantime, I retreated deeper into the forest, hunching next to a burbling stream. I let my aching, swollen fingers trail in the cool water, wishing they would heal, and either the coldness of the stream or the power of my imagination dulled the ache until it was no longer the only thing I could think of. Something tickled at my brain — a half-formed idea that maybe the wishing really did make a difference, as I had wished my broken leg healed and my recovery did seem surprisingly quick — but I wasn't thinking entirely clearly. The bread had run out long before, and I was so hungry I felt my stomach might touch my spine.

Darkness came. I edged closer to the house, lingering where the trees were thinner, and watched the sun set behind the massive stone walls. At first, I could see light glowing from windows in every part of the house, but as the evening wore on, the glow broke into scattered spheres, lesser by the hour. Once the sky turned from dark blue to utter black, only a few small pale lights flickered in the highest and lowest windows as the servants finished the last of the evening's work and carried their candles up to bed. I watched as the final light in the final window went dark.

There was barely a sliver of moon and a speckled pattern of distant stars high above. I crossed the dark lawn until I reached the lowest, smallest door. No noise, no movement. There was only silence in the great house.

I opened the door slowly and stepped inside.

The room I entered was the laundry room, hot and dark and damp like I imagined jungle air must be. The water in the vats was still warm, but the fires were out. In the dim light from the window, there was just enough light to make out shapes and edges, and along one wall, I saw what I'd come for.

The uniforms hung there, all in a line, identical. Black and white. White and black. One after another after another. Because they were all the same, it was impossible to tell one from the next.

That was what I needed and wanted. To blend in.

Thankful for the warmth of the room, I stepped out of my dark homespun dress, moving in haste. I slipped the white blouse over my head and the jumper over the blouse. I smoothed my tangled hair as best I could and tucked it up under the cap. The water of the stream had carried off the dirt from under my fingernails, but broken fingers were not so easy to wash away, so I also pulled on a pair of clean white gloves, gritting my teeth against the pain. My own clothes I tucked into a bundle, and after exploring a warren of bins and cabinets, I found what I hoped was the safest corner, and there I squirreled the bundle away.

Once I had the uniform on, I took a candle from a shelf near the doorway and lit it with a long match. I could hide better in the dark, but because a real servant would have a candle, I needed to have one too. I could hide best in plain sight. So I put on my most correct posture and walked down the hall to find a task to keep busy at.

As hungry as I was, I avoided the kitchen, fearing that once I started eating, I might never stop. I couldn't be discovered there, where I clearly wouldn't belong. I knew from my grandparents' house how closely cooks kept an eye on things. Anywhere else in the house would be better.

Almost as soon as I began exploring, I was lost. Even with the candle, I could only see a few feet in any direction, and the place was an utter maze of doors and halls and stairs. I had remembered the impression from my last visit that the place was simply too large to be comprehended, but this time it was truer and more frightening. Every step was fraught. There was no way to know if I was moving away from danger or into it.

The first hallway I followed dead-ended in the vegetable pantry, a room that smelled overwhelmingly of earth, and I had no choice but to double back the way I'd come. I thought I was headed back toward the laundry, but the next door I opened took me into the unfinished swimming pool, an absolutely cavernous room lined with gleaming white tile where my every footstep echoed like a gunshot. I hustled up the nearest staircase and down a carpeted hall to escape, trying to move quickly but not too quickly, my heart hammering underneath the stolen uniform. After this, I carried my shoes in my hand, trying my best to move soundlessly. I wanted to pause and savor the beauty of the carpets, plush and lovely under my feet, but instead I only gave thanks that they muffled my footfalls and kept moving.

On the third floor, I tiptoed down long hallways full of identical doors, like something from a storybook, and had to choose at random which to open. My breath caught in my throat each time. The way the moonlight streaked across the bed in one of the guest rooms tickled the back of my brain, but I wasn't sure whether it was the room I had slept in after my accident or just another indistinguishable in its luxury. My leg gave a twinge, and I quickly backed out of the door and shut it tight.

When I finally found the front of the house, I knew I was in the right place at last. These were the most formal rooms; it made sense to fuss over them. Here there were stone fireplaces half a head taller than my own head, carved with intricate stone acorns and branches and a thousand other dust-collecting places. There were chimney-pieces and side tables and cabinetry. Here, there was work to do. I applied myself with great relief. When it felt like there was no more to do in one room, I moved slowly to the next.

What with straightening furniture and shaking out curtains and squaring carpets, I spent several hours at labor, and before I was found, the sun had come up. After the uncertainty of scrambling around this huge house in the night's nerve-racking darkness, there was something reassuring about the light.

The one who found me was a round-faced woman with her hair pulled back in a perfectly formed bun. Her dress was plain but didn't match the uniforms from the laundry. Clearly she was in charge. I tried not to meet her gaze, but she pinned me like a butterfly in a box. I hovered on a high ladder, my good hand on a thick braided cord holding back a sunshade from a huge, spotless window.

"You. Come here. I don't know you," she said.

"Of course you do."

"No, miss. I do not know you because I did not hire you, and no one I did not hire works here. Do you understand?"

"I understand."

"So how did you get here, Miss . . . ?"

Hastily I said, "I can be of use. Please don't send me away."

She sized me up again.

"Get down from there," she said, and so I did. Standing face-to-face with her, I found her a full two inches shorter than I was, a fact which did not make her even a mote less intimidating.

"You should know better than to lie," she said. "That eye of yours gives you away. Makes you memorable. Never pretend you're someone I wouldn't remember."

"Yes, ma'am." And yet if she had seen me last time I was here, she didn't seem to recognize me. It gave me a thrill of confidence, which I certainly needed.

"Tell me your name."

"Ada Bates." No need to carry a lie if the truth would do.

"Miss Bates," she said, "this is your lucky day."

She didn't tell me why and I didn't ask. I found out later one of the servant girls had caught her arm in the mangler not ten hours before, while doing the evening's wash, and could no longer do her assigned work. More help was needed. The angels were smiling on me, in their way.

The woman in charge said, "Report to the laundry room and tell Miss Fischer, the one with the long black braid, that Mrs. Severson sent you."

"Yes ma'am!"

"If you do a bad job, I will dismiss you."

"Yes ma'am. If that happens, I'll dismiss myself first."

I almost caught her starting to smile before I turned to go. It took me half an hour to find the laundry room again.

I wondered if perhaps I should have lied about my name, but it quickly seemed it wouldn't matter. First names, in this household, went unspoken. I was always Miss Bates. Same went for the others. It was always Miss Godwin and Mr. Madison, Mrs. Severson and Mr. Shelby.

The servants in my grandparents' house had shared rooms, but here we each had our own, and I couldn't believe my luck. Each morning, I rose in silence, alone, and had a few moments to myself to work through my exercises, keeping my arms and legs in their accustomed condition, reaching gracefully up to a ceiling higher than I'd ever had at home, though it was less than half the height of some of the rooms on the first floor. On occasion, I was able to steal a few morning moments to dance elsewhere in the house, and they were a great blessing. Executing a blazing fast string of thirty turns across the long open floor of a ballroom let me imagine for the first time that I was on a real stage, and the feeling was intoxicating.

My dancer's body came in handy. I was

stronger than the typical girl of my age, and after my hand healed, I was the most able of all the girls at Biltmore. In the laundry, we repeated many movements over and over — dunking the sheets into the hot vat, stirring them around and around and around in the soap, lifting them out, heaving them into a different vat of cleaner water, stirring again and again and again. Even when we used the mechanical drum washer, it took strength to lift and spread the linens over the racks in the drying room and to fold and carry the dried sheets to closets on every floor. Repetition was nothing new for me. It was almost as if this was what I had spent my life practicing for. I knew it wasn't, not really. But I also knew that for now, it was good enough.

I found that my strength was not the only thing that set me apart, although I held the secret close. One day, another girl and I reached out for an iron at the same time, believing it cold, but it had already been left on the stove to heat, hot enough to burn. We both seared our fingertips, and they rose up in bright red blisters. Almost out of habit, I wished my fingers would heal quickly. The next day, I was surprised to see the blisters on her fingertips just as red and angry as the day before, while my blisters were already starting to fade. The next day, hers were slightly less red; mine were gone completely. I knew it made no sense that a wish had made the difference, yet I couldn't see any other explanation. I certainly couldn't tell anyone. If it sounded impossible to me, to others it would sound like insanity.

It was weeks before I thought to wonder how my deserted family felt back in Tennessee, how worried they probably were about me, and after that brief fleeting thought, I went right back to not thinking about them again. I was convinced I'd been right to go. The bones I'd broken had healed, but that didn't mean that I'd never been injured in the first place. I didn't forget that. I never would.

At Biltmore, I discovered I was a quick learner when it counted. Not only did I learn how to use lemon juice to bleach wine stains from a tablecloth and to iron velvet with the nap, never against it, I learned all about people.

All of them kept secrets, and nearly all of them had bad habits. It fascinated me how many people thought they'd managed to keep their vices secret when to the rest of us they were as plain as day. I didn't mean to eavesdrop, but people were careless. I learned who had been sent here after dismissal from a convent and who had a brother in prison back in Ireland who she sent all her wages to. I also learned things by observing — happening to notice when certain people tended to absent themselves from company and where they went when they did. Miss Godwin had a weakness for nicking canned peaches from the pantry. Mr. Carlisle snuck cigarettes behind the garden shed.

A few months into my life at the Biltmore, it was because of Mr. Carlisle that I made another important discovery. Mrs. Severson was shouting her cap off for him, swearing he'd promised to make a delivery that very afternoon. I knew of his cigarette habit, and so I snuck off to fetch him. He was, of course, behind the shed, and as soon as I told him the situation, he took off like a shot. I stayed outside and didn't run after him. Partly because I wasn't the one in trouble, and partly because I wanted to stand in the sun for a moment and drink in the smell of green spring plants growing.

That was when I saw the young man.

He emerged from the other side of the shed and strode toward the rose garden, which was at that time about three-quarters complete. When it was finished, it would be spectacular, long formal rows in the English style, but the rows had not yet been fully planted. As best as I could tell, he was my height and not far from my age. He had dark hair that looked like it was wet. There was something magnetic about him. He set my arms tingling. I wanted to know more.

The dark-haired young man passed behind the high trellis into the garden. I hustled forward and arranged myself behind a thick cluster of climbing roses, the vines and leaves and buds and blooms obscuring my outline, and made myself be still.

I watched him for half an hour, not even noticing the time pass. I only felt the tingling of my arms, a hotness in my throat, strange shifts in temperature that had nothing to do with the sun. From time to time, I caught glimpses of his face — a sharp cheekbone, an arched eyebrow. He dug down into the dark ground with a spade until he was satisfied with the size of the hole and then carefully, gracefully, he lifted a rosebush from its resting place on the ground and settled its roots inside. He was what I imagined Adam in the garden to be — somehow part of the earth while master over it.

After the new bush was in the ground, he crouched down next to it. He sprinkled water slowly and lightly over the new roots, lowering his hand into a bucket of water and lifting a scooped handful at a time, careful not to displace too much soil. And when he stood back up and drew his forearm over his sweating forehead, the underside of his muscled arm framed against the blue sky, a swarm of buzzing surged up into my temples and I felt faint.

I was afraid to step out from behind my trellis and greet him because I wasn't supposed to be there, and if he asked me any questions, I was just the kind of girl who would have to answer them.

And I didn't want to speak to him, I realized, because that might break the spell. He might be stupid or mean or angry. He might not like me, and I wanted him to like me, because I liked him. I felt sure that someone so tender with a plant would be just as careful with a person, but then again, finding out more might mean disappointment. He would have to have some kind of flaw. We all did. And as long as I never spoke to him or saw him again, he'd remain perfect.

And so he did, for a time.

CHAPTER TEN

1895

Metamorphosis

The seasons passed. Without the vegetable
dye my mother used to apply to it, the red-
gold color of my hair started to show
through, especially at the crown of my head.
I piled my hair under my cap anyway, so no
one much saw it, but I became fond of taking my hair down and looking at how red it
was, how quickly I was growing into my new
self.

As for what had happened in the garden,
it frightened me. Scared of ruining my
fantasy, I didn't go out to the garden again
for weeks, though I considered it nearly
every day. I ventured no further from the
house than the statue of Diana. She helped
define my limit. I pictured the boy, his
hands gentle, his body tense and strong,
and I treasured that picture. But I stayed
inside with it and kept it to myself.

In a way, even though there were many of us, the huge estate felt lonely. You could tell that the mansion's best days were yet to come. You could look at the rooms and imagine them filled with rich people. Rich people reclining on the couches, or standing in the dressing rooms waiting for people like us to dress them, or taking their leisure on the lawn under lovely linen parasols on a summer afternoon. It was clear that this was the house's destiny. But so far, it was only in our imaginations. We did have occasional guests, but they would generally tease Mr. Vanderbilt that they'd traipsed to the wilderness for his sake, and they thought perhaps once Biltmore was truly finished that it might really be something. Even the servants' dining room, built to seat thirty of us, in those days was never more than half full. The swimming pool that had so frightened me that first night was finally completed but had yet to be filled with water. The bowling alley had a gleaming, polished floor and an impressive aspect but was still not stocked with balls or pins and remained as quiet as a church.

In 1895, we welcomed our first large party, a full score of guests, for Christmas. With great fanfare, the master of the estate declared Biltmore officially open to invited visitors. The preparations kept us hopping for weeks. Every night, I slept the sleep of the dead.

We decorated nearly every surface with spruce, from the fireplaces to the light fixtures, and covered the walls until they looked like living things. Men were sent out to denude whole sections of the forest and brought in heaps and armfuls of branches, and the heavenly smell filled every room of the house.

We bedecked the house in ways large and small, finishing off the spruce garlands with red ribbon bows, changing out the table runners, tying glass ornaments on thin, nearly invisible threads to dangle merrily in each first-floor window. Every guest room needed to be in full and festive readiness, and linens upon linens flooded the laundry room on top of our usual work. It seemed a deliveryman was knocking at the back door every hour. The kitchen and pantry over-flowed with the makings for not just the Christmas feast but a Christmas Eve seated supper as well and three days' worth of enormous breakfasts and lunches. With little time to dance in the mornings, I found myself humming and stretching my limbs out secretly as I went about my other tasks, as if the instinct was threatening to burst out of me whether or not I let it.

The eve of Christmas, we added festive touches to our uniforms — holly in the hair of the women, mint leaves on the men's lapels — and served as we were meant to serve. We treated all the guests with outwardly identical deference, but some were more famous than others, and we all secretly jostled to have the honor of attending the stunning soprano Madame Nordica and grave but cordial Governor McKinley. Drinks were served in the grand parlor, with dozens of fragile glasses borne on silver trays up and down the back stairs and laden platters of hors d'oeuvres brought up by dumbwaiter.

When the time came, the entire party was ushered down the grand staircase — that sight alone made them gasp in delight — and seated at table for seven courses, using every fish fork and ice cream spoon in the estate's collection. We brought foods to table that most of us had never even seen before, bearing caviar and truffles as if they were grits and succotash. It was a mad scramble downstairs to achieve a tranquil appearance in the dining room, like a duck seeming to glide upon the water but paddling madly all the while. But all was charm and grace at the dinner itself, soup to nuts. At the end, we cleared away the last of the delicate china and steered the company to yet another parlor where coffee and brandy lay at the ready. Our collective sigh of relief afterward was so deep that it might well have been audible.

After a quarter hour of lovely piping after-dinner music from a trio of French horns, we bundled the whole visiting party into elegant carriages for a late-night turn about the grounds. Even the carriage horses, matched white stallions, were decorated for the occasion, with jingle bells on their reins and red velvet ribbons braided into their manes and tails.

Once the jingle bells faded into the distance, the mischievous Mr. Bullard stepped forward and said, "And until they return, let's play!"

The more cautious among us, myself included, made some noises of concern, but we were quickly shushed by the more adventurous. The grooms agreed to stand watch at the door so we'd have fair warning of the party's return. The rented musicians with their French horns were quickly urged into the side room and a bowl of punch produced, and impromptu festivities began.

Some of the group grasped hands and

began a partnered dance. I stood aside, thinking I would only watch. But once the first deep trill of the French horns sounded, the dancing itself was like a spell that came over me.

Only the first few motions were mechanical. I raised my arms over my head and began with a pirouette, then swept my whole body forward and extended my fingertips as if to embrace the great far ceiling, and from there, I let the music carry me off. I stretched and bent, leapt and flourished, every movement quick and lovely and joyous, until an unknown time later when the music began to fade.

The sound of applause brought me back to the room almost reluctantly, with a warm haze of delight still lingering in my limbs. Many of the servants were watching me, and their applause was directed toward me, so I bobbed my head in a quick acknowledgment. It gave me a warm feeling, their admiration. Cheeks flushed, I stepped back toward the wall.

Mr. Bullard handed me half a cup of punch. Thirsty, I drank it in a few fast gulps. The horns continued to play, and I must have been swaying along. I felt the music swelling inside my body deep down, nudging me into motion again.

"Let's see you dance some more!" cried Mr. Bullard, who had never previously shown signs of getting carried away, but I obliged.

To impress him, I brought my arms up in second position, struck a haughty, high-chinned pose, and set myself up to spin clear across twenty feet of open floor in a sharp series of piqué turns. Before the Christmas preparations had started, I'd done it a hundred times. But after the punch, I wasn't spotting correctly. When you do piqué turns, chaîné turns, or other sharp spins, it's essential to spot. You focus on a place on the wall and turn your head quickly at the end of each spin, fixing your eyes on that spot again, and it keeps you level. You don't get dizzy. But I spun out of control, and instead of ending in the corner I aimed for, I ended by thudding into something soft.

I looked into the eyes of the something soft. A man, just about my size, almost too close to make sense of. High cheekbones, a straight thin nose, and small lips. Thick, dark brows with a pointed arch at the far end of each. Blue eyes, clear and infinitely deep. I recognized him then. His was a face in perfect harmony, strong and sharp, and not so different close up than it had been glimpsed from afar.

His eyes were turned upward, so I followed his gaze to the door frame above our heads and saw the mistletoe hanging there, a sprig of green sharp leaves with a cluster of perfect white berries, and then his face was very close by my face, and his eyes closed, and he lowered his lips to mine.

It was a sweet, soft kiss, and it was over in a moment.

We stepped away from each other at once. The music resumed. The world started to move again. My lips felt both numb and aching, as if I'd nibbled horseradish. I felt a hundred eyes on me, but when I peeked back at the rest of the servants, it was as if nothing had happened. The swarm of chattering and murmuring voices continued without break. The music piped on. No one was turned our way.

"It's very nice to meet you," he said.

"Roses," I blurted.

"Beg pardon?"

"You tend the roses," I said.

He smiled then, and it was like sunshine. "The roses, yes, and the pond lilies, and the tall grass, and the forests around us. Whatever the master wants to grow, or not grow, on the land. How did you know?"

"I saw you once."

"When?" he asked. "Hasn't been much growing lately."

"In the summer."

"That long ago? And you remember me still? How flattering."

I blushed from the roots of my hair down to the collar of my uniform and well down underneath the cloth.

"But where are my manners?" He thrust out his hand. "Clyde Garber."

We shook hands. "Miss Bates."

"No," he said. "What's your first name?"

"Ada."

"You have beautiful eyes, Ada."

"Thank you." I dropped a fast curtsy.

"No, I'm not being polite." He extended his hand again but with the palm turned up. "Will you dance, this time with me?"

I wanted to reach for that hand, wanted it badly, but I felt myself teetering already. "I'm afraid not. The punch has left me dizzy."

"You should sit. Come this way." He beckoned for me to follow him into the next room, the library, and I did.

There, it was cooler and less crowded — empty, in fact — and I settled my body onto a soft couch next to a tall bookcase. I expected to feel his weight drop onto the cushion next to mine, and the thought sent a pleasant shiver up my legs, but there was nothing. I looked up. He was facing the bookcase instead.

"Have you read any of these?" he asked, gesturing toward the books.

"I don't think I'm allowed."

"You're that obedient? I didn't take you for a child."

"I'm not a child."

"How old are you?" he asked.

"A lady never tells."

He stared me down. There was an intensity to him that I found unsettling and comforting at the same time.

"Fifteen," I said. I knew I looked older, because the other girls said so, but the truth would do well enough.

Chuckling, he said, "That's what I thought."

"How old are you?"

"Seventeen," he said. "But I feel like I was born much older."

"Tell me what you mean."

"Another time. You should take a book or two whenever you want. They never check. I take them all the time."

"You steal Mr. Vanderbilt's books?"

"Borrow. I borrow. And mostly when Mr. Vanderbilt is traveling."

"What do you read?" I asked him.

"Come here, I'll show you," he said, and I did. As I stood next to him, he ran his fingers along the spine of each book as he talked about it. I was close enough to feel the warmth of his body and smell the mint in his lapel, and the music drifted in from the other room while he talked to me about the beauty of Shakespeare and Donne and Zola. When I told him I'd read all that and more, he grinned and nodded and said what a pleasure it was to talk to a well-read woman for a change. He went on to tell me about a particular book called *The Picture of Dorian Gray,* which he had just finished reading but had not had the chance to place back on the shelf. While he talked about that book, he stroked the spines of the books on either side of the empty space. I began to imagine his fingers stroking my body instead of the books, those careful long fingers against my bare skin.

I couldn't help it. I reached out for his hand. He turned his body toward mine. The intensity of his gaze unsettled me and I froze, fearing I'd been too bold. But then, as if it were the most natural thing in the world, he entwined his fingers with my fingers, and his lips came down on mine.

The second kiss was different from the first. Hotter and sweeter. Instead of the brief firm touch of the kiss under the mistletoe, I felt his tender, playful mouth against mine, shifting and asking and answering all at once.

My body, with a will of its own, drew closer to his. I felt his fingers on my neck, the calluses rough against the tender skin but his touch nimble and teasing, setting my nerves atremble. I'd imagined the touch of his fingers, months ago, and they were exactly as gentle and graceful as I'd imagined.

Then I heard shouts from the other room and realized belatedly that the music had stopped. The riding party had returned. They'd come flooding into the entryway at any moment. Mr. Garber might not be obligated to receive the guests and assist them, but I was. My absence would be noted if I stayed.

I broke away from him, my cheeks flushed. "I'm sorry," I whispered. "I have to go."

His hand was still on the warm flesh of my neck. He let it linger there a moment longer as he said, "Ada, it was a true pleasure." Then it fell away, and he left by another door.

Late that night, after the guests had been carefully tucked under their fine duvets, with that day's elegant gowns packed away and different elegant gowns laid out for morning, I went to bed with a strange, hollow feeling in my stomach. Some of the less discreet girls gossiped in the laundry room in great detail, and I knew what men were capable of on a good day, or during a good night. There was a storm in my blood, however calm I looked on the outside.

I had cherished a private fantasy of this young man, but now I had something new. The warmth of him, the rumbling sound of his voice, the sweet yielding pressure of his lips on mine, the feeling of those hands. It was almost too much all at once. The dizzying possibilities. I imagined him next to me as I lay down to sleep, picturing his head sharing my pillow, those sky blue eyes closing slowly, his face so close to mine that I could feel the stirring of his breath. I fought sleep even as I welcomed it, stretching out those moments, thinking, wondering.

How do we know what love feels like? Especially the first time we feel it? I was unprepared. For the first few days, I couldn't stop stroking my lips with my fingers, grazing them against my chin, touching the places he had touched. He was more than on my mind. He was everywhere I looked, even when he wasn't. Had he thought me a silly girl, too simple and too forward, or would those tender moments ripen into something more lasting? I wouldn't know until I could talk to him again.

CHAPTER ELEVEN

Janesville, 1905
Two o'clock in the morning

When she falls silent, he speaks into the silence, softly. "And did you grow up to marry this young man?"

She cocks her head and says, "Was your wife your first love, officer? We love more people than we marry, most of us."

"You didn't answer my question."

"No, I didn't."

Her even, logical tone makes him angry. It's a tone for discussing a tedious sermon, not danger or love or murder.

"I'm going to ask another question. And this time, I want you to answer. Do you understand?"

"Officer." She sighs. "I don't want to talk about the murder."

"I know. That's not what I'm going to ask about. I want to ask about your magic."

"My magic?" She says it with a slight laugh.

"Yes," he says, "your magic," and reaches out to touch her throat, holding aside the edges of her lace collar to see it clearly. He was right; the bruise there is completely gone. The whole of her neck is pale and unblemished.

His fingers still on her throat, he looks into her face and says boldly, "The magic that helps you heal. You mentioned it. You realized, at Biltmore, that you were making it happen, that you were healing yourself. With a wish."

She eyes him out of the half-brown eye with something resembling respect. Perhaps she thought he'd forget, given the length of the night and her story. Then again, she must know the claim is extraordinary. "I suppose we could dance around it, but what's the point?" she says.

A different air altogether has come over her. There's a new tilt to her chin, a different angle in her carriage. She's proud of what she can do. *As well she should be,* he thinks.

"So," he says, thinking of her neck, her wrist. "Bruises. Cuts. What else?"

"Bruises disappear. Cuts seal themselves up. Broken bones become whole again. As simple as that."

"How long does it take?"

"Small things, just a matter of hours. Longer for something more serious. As I'm sure you've figured out from what I told you."

He remembers the story of the leg broken in her fall, the fingers crushed by a horse's hoof. How quickly she healed afterward in both cases. The story she's telling him may or may not turn out to be the story of the murder, but it has very useful information in it all the same. Information that could, he's now realizing, change everything. He doesn't just have to decide what to do. He has to decide what to believe.

"So Ray was right."

She flinches, hard. He immediately regrets saying it.

"He was wrong about himself," she says, her mouth tight. "He couldn't heal. But me, yes. I can."

"It's served you well."

"It's helped me survive," she says.

"Where do you think it comes from?"

"How could anyone know that?"

"You must have ideas. Ray thought he —"

"For God's sake," she says sharply, "don't talk about him. I'll tell you what you want, all right?"

"All right."

"It might have something to do with my father, whoever he was. That was one possibility, that he had some kind of power and so I inherited it from him. Or it could have something to do with the fairy eye." She points to her half-brown, half-blue eye, the dim light glinting in its depths. "But I'm telling you, I don't know. I only know what I can do. And now you know it too."

"I know what you claim," he says, suddenly skeptical. This whole story, he has only her word to believe. He knows what he thought he saw. A bruise that was there and then wasn't. But he doesn't truly know what her powers are, if that's where her magic starts and ends. He needs another way to investigate.

Then a dark shape on the floor catches his attention. He can't believe he's forgotten it until now. He'd been in such a hurry to get her into the chair that he'd thrown these things aside. He reaches down, shakes the cloak away, and puts his hands on what the cloak has been hiding. A little charge of excitement runs through him, toes to fingers. People can resist questions and bend the truth until it breaks. Objects can't.

"Where did you get that?" she shouts when he lifts the valise up onto his desk to open it. The wooden chair legs clatter against the ground, almost like a horse's hooves.

"When I brought you here. I brought this too."

"Don't open it. You hear me?" She rattles her cuffs. "I said don't open it. Those things are private."

"If you want privacy, you should probably not kill people," he says, opening the bag up and shaking its contents out across the wooden desk top.

He doesn't know what he expected to find. Several changes of clothes, perhaps, and money. Things a fleeing murderer would need. Yet the only objects that tumble onto the desk are a brown fur muff, a folded men's razor, and a small leather-bound book. Holt opens the book to its first page, and finds that he's holding a copy of Shakespeare's *As You Like It*.

"Can you explain these?" he asks.

"I suppose I could. You don't give me much of a reason."

He tries to soften his voice. "It would be a nice gesture. I'm not your enemy."

"What a funny way you have of showing it."

The razor has a polished bone handle, worn to a gloss with long use. He opens it up and looks at the square-tipped blade. No blood. It doesn't mean anything, unfortunately. She's not a fool. She'd be smart enough to wipe a blade clean.

He sets down the razor and picks up the book, idly flipping its pages, pretending to be casual. In truth, he wants to rattle her. If these things are hers, if she treasures them, he will put his fingers on them all. He wants her to get upset. She's an emotional creature. Other than the handcuffs, it may be the only advantage he has on her.

"Officer," she says softly.

"Yes?"

"I'm not a monster." But there is no force in her voice. It is barely a declaration. There are more questions than answers underneath it.

"Yes, all right."

"Don't you see it matters to me? That you know that?"

"I don't see why," he says.

"Because I know what monsters are," she says. "And I can't be in that company."

"So tell me what you are, then. If not a monster."

"A fool," she says.

Chapter Twelve

After Christmas when we took the spruce branches down, we found that they had oozed a sticky sap over every nearby surface, and the sap had hardened while we celebrated. After seven full days of work in the laundry room, we finally had to give one set of curtains up for rags. The lesson was clear. Next year we would not use those branches for decking the halls again.

And I began to wonder where next Christmas would find me.

Would I still be here? I was a servant now, and not a bad one. But the feeling I'd had when I danced for the other servants and they applauded me, I wondered what it meant. My mother had wanted me to dance on the stage. Could I do that, if I tried? How would I go about it? I enjoyed the applause more than I'd ever enjoyed the dancing.

There had to be something to it.

I made excuses to find my way into the library again over the next few weeks, and when *The Picture of Dorian Gray* was returned, I took it for my own use and read it avidly. It was not a nice book, but I could see how he'd been compelled by it. And tucked into the very last page was a simple note: *Garden, when you can. C.*

The first time I went to meet him among the roses, there was only conversation. The second, I knelt next to him in the dirt while he plucked out weeds, and he drew his fingers slowly up the length of my arm as we talked, setting every inch of my skin on fire. The third, we made plans to meet in a different place — a quieter, more private one — and that was where we met thereafter.

We met in the billiard room, which saw very little activity when there were no guests. It smelled of new felt and spilled whiskey. We talked little during these meetings, fearful of having our voices heard. But when he talked, he talked of leaving. He asked if I was content washing bedsheets and sweeping floors or if I wondered what else I might do out there in the world. He said I was such a smart girl, so clever and beautiful, that I must know I was meant for larger things. An agile mind like mine was wasted in the body — such a lovely body, he hastened to add — of a young drudge so far from a city of any import. He asked if he were to leave, would I go with him? I would not, I said. And the subject was dropped, until the next time he raised it, testing to see if my answer had changed. It hadn't. If he found this frustrating, he didn't say so. He would ask, and I would refuse politely, and he would fall to kissing me again, and such talk was easy to set aside in favor of more pleasant and pleasurable things.

Almost every night, there was time for a few stolen kisses, a handful of whispered words. His words were always flattering and tender. In addition to my eyes, he complimented the fragile bones of my pinkie finger, the shell-like curve of my ear, and other parts of me that weren't strictly visible. His words were lovely, but his kisses were what truly held my attention, along with the unbearably exciting thought of where the kisses might lead.

One evening as we pressed together against a heavy oak billiard table, his lips traveling slowly and tenderly up my neck, we heard voices. Quickly we separated. He cocked his head toward one door, listening to confirm the direction of the sound, and grabbed my hand to lead me out through the other exit. We scurried along in near silence. Down the hallway, there was a staircase, and I followed him down without hesitation. At the foot of the staircase, instead of continuing down the hallway to another room, he doubled us back into a kind of storage space under the stairs, a dead end, out of the way. There we paused and waited, listening, until we'd heard nothing for several minutes but our own breathing, shallow and quick.

We resumed kissing, but something had changed. In the alcove under the staircase, we were more hidden than before, more alone, more protected. The air felt close, intimate. My lips parted wider for his. I stepped closer, pressing more tightly against him, and in answer, he pushed me back against the wall, my bottom lip between his teeth, his knee between my knees.

Then his hand was inside my dress, his fingertips rough against the delicate skin of my breast, and I lost my breath for a moment. The world narrowed to a small, small space. The pleasure was almost too much to take. I wanted more. I wanted everything.

If the blood hadn't been rushing in my ears, all my attention on his skin against mine, I would have heard the footsteps. As it was, I only heard the voice.

"Separate at once," the booming voice ordered, and I obeyed by instinct. We drew away from each other with a jump, although Clyde imposed himself between me and the intruder, which I took as chivalrous. Cheeks burning, wanting to disappear, I made myself look at the man who had interrupted our tryst.

It was the master of the house.

We rarely saw Mr. Vanderbilt, and even when we did, we never spoke to him nor he to us. I'd heard his voice before at a distance but never so close up. He had a lamp in his hand, casting a puddle of light around our dark hiding place. He wore a black smoking jacket over his shirt and trousers. There was no doubt who he was speaking to or what he'd seen. My mouth felt sore and swollen.

"You, Garber."

"Yes?"

"Go to your room now. I do not want to hear of this behavior again. If I do, no matter how valuable I find your skills, I will have you dismissed. You understand."

"I do." He nodded briskly, turned the corner to scuttle quickly up the stairs, and was gone. I heard the sound of his footfalls fading.

I moved to follow, and Mr. Vanderbilt caught my arm. "Young lady, just a moment."

"Sir?"

Then, oddly, he grinned at me. His teeth were white and gleaming under his thick mustache. "Oh, my dear, you look terrified."

"Is that amusing?"

"No," he said and let his smirk slip into a gentler smile as he released me. "I have to remember I was once as young as you. You and your young man. I was foolish too at your age."

I couldn't help raising my chin. "I'm not foolish."

"Oh, I know you don't think so now. When you look back," he said, "that's when you'll see."

I opened my mouth to protest and he held up a hand.

"Shush. I only want to give you some words of advice."

I waited.

"When it's like this. When these things happen. You'll need to control yourself," he said. He gestured up the dark stairs after my departed companion. "He won't be able to. Nor will any other young man."

I stared at him dumbly.

"It's up to you. Do you understand?"

"Yes, sir."

"It appalls me when people think they don't have agency. We all do. We all have will. So use yours where and when it counts."

"Yes, sir."

He waved me off and I went. I had been chastised but neither punished nor dismissed. It seemed almost a miracle. That night, I played the scene over and over in my head. The hot, sweet urgency of skin on skin. The master appearing, as if from nowhere, to deliver a message, raising his lantern like a priest with a censer. The more I considered it, the more it felt like a blessing. I'd been prevented from doing something foolish. Where it went from here was up to me.

I made myself confront the facts. I was a servant in a grand house, and I could either work hard and earn my keep and make concrete plans, or I could moon about, tumbling into sin with a boy who whispered honeyed words against my ear and made my nerves sing but who had never promised me anything in particular. Besides, I had no time to waste on something uncertain. Any spare moments I could snatch went to dancing — regular exercises in my room every morning and whenever I could slip away, taking advantage of empty ballrooms and hallways — and that was real. Could I spare the time for anything that might not be?

And if what I felt for him was real, all the worse. I'd seen what happened when people fell in love. Love was responsible for all my mother's poor choices. Without the mistake of conceiving me, without running away with Victor and sacrificing her comfortable life, who knows what she would have been? I couldn't be so foolish. I reminded myself that I had to make the right choices so as not to be subject to what others would have me do for their own ends. I would have to be levelheaded. Mr. Vanderbilt was right about that. No other heads were to be trusted.

The spring was a rainy one, full of murky, shadowed days. The garden was easy to avoid. Whenever I went through the library, I forced myself not to peek inside the books. If there were notes, I didn't collect them. The clandestine meetings halted. On occasion, I would spot Clyde from far away, and when he tried to draw nearer to me, I dodged him. I knew he wondered what had changed, and I burned to go back to the seductive simplicity of our late-night meetings. My body missed his.

Over the weeks and months, I altered my

routine to avoid walking through the still, silent library altogether. I couldn't help but see and feel his absence every time the sound of my footsteps echoed off the walls. It was easier just to close the doors and take the long way around.

Half a year after Biltmore's first Christmas was my sixteenth birthday. We generally didn't fuss over birthdays, but Mrs. Severson thought that it would be good practice for the servants to prepare a birthday cake and plan a birthday party, knowing that soon the house would begin receiving more and more guests. It was good that she had us practice. There had been some turnover in the staff since the Christmas feasts, and Mrs. Hartwell in the kitchen had to bake three cakes before one turned out right.

I played the guest's part and was led blindfolded out of the house across the lawn. When the blindfold was removed from my eyes, I gasped aloud.

The garden was utterly transformed. It was like a fairy story, the kind where little elves set out a banquet during the mortals' sleep. The roses were in bloom, a riot of color, almost too perfect. A long table was laid among them, with a white tablecloth and all sorts of lovely silver, and candles for when the sun went down. My chair was decorated with yellow-hearted peach roses. When I took my seat, a wreath of miniature white blossoms was set upon my head. I felt like the Queen of the May.

I cut the cake, listened to the whole host singing, and acted appreciative, as I was asked to. There were games and music. Hours went quickly.

It was a lovely party. I told Mrs. Severson so and added, "Isn't it a fine day?"

"I have something for you to make it even finer," she said.

She handed me an envelope, and I slide the single sheet of paper from it.

"From your mother," she said, and I froze. Because I could see the writing on the fine paper, and although someone had signed my mother's name to the bottom of the page, I knew it was not her handwriting.

"How?" I asked, but I wasn't listening to the answer. I was reading:

I could not be happier to hear that my darling daughter is safe with you. It will be a week before I can make the proper arrangements, but I shall arrive the day after her birthday for a visit. I long to see her again and treasure the chance for reunion.

You do not know how happy you have made me.

My mother had certainly not written it. I didn't know for sure what Ray's writing looked like, but it wasn't Mother's and it wasn't Victor's, and I knew who had the best reason to be deceitful. The cold shiver this knowledge sent up my spine erased the warm summer day around me, turning it winter.

The housekeeper was saying, ". . . and I couldn't help but share it. Though perhaps you would have been happier with a surprise."

I must have mentioned Jeansville to her or to another servant; all she would need was that and my name, which she had. The town was small, and anyone would know where such a letter should be delivered. Mrs. Severson couldn't possibly know what she'd done. She thought I'd be happy, but this was the end of everything. So suddenly. My new life, over. My safe place, gone.

"Miss Bates?" she asked.

Quickly I realized I shouldn't show my anger. "Thank you. There are no words."

"Tomorrow will be a free day for you. So you can spend it with her."

"Again, thank you."

She smiled brightly, an uncommon sight, and I returned the smile as best I could. Tears came to my eyes. I hoped she would think they were happy ones.

Then I couldn't stand it anymore. I had to escape. I turned my back on her, on the whole party, in the gathering dusk. Someone called to her and she didn't follow me. Instead of striding across the grass back to the house, I ducked into the garden shed.

The shed was musty, and only a bit of light crept in through the slats. The smell of raw earth was overwhelming. I sat down on an overturned bucket, careless of the dirt, and put my head in my hands. The wreath of flowers slipped from my head and fell to the ground. Ray was coming for me. I hadn't escaped him. He was on his way, and tomorrow he would be here. I was too stunned to cry, but my head was buzzing so loudly with thoughts and fears and panic that I almost didn't hear the door to the shed creak open and then closed again.

"I wish you a very happy birthday, Miss Bates," came a familiar voice.

I stood, watching his shape in the half darkness, waiting for my eyes to adjust. I knew that shape.

"Ada?" he said, softer this time, less sure.

"Mr. Garber," I said. "Thank you for your

kind wishes."

He drew close. "Are you quite all right?"

"I will be," I said, not believing it.

Then he was nearer, and nearer still, and he lowered his face to mine for a kiss. I had nothing in me to resist. There was something in the familiar smell of his skin and the warmth of his breath that took away the present pain, and I clung to him, lost.

After a few moments, he pulled away and said, "I'm sorry. I didn't mean — I wanted to tell you some news."

I nodded silently, granting permission.

He said, "I'm leaving."

On another day, he might have shocked me. In the current case, it wasn't the worst news I had heard that day, or even that hour. "You really are?"

"Yes. I'm going to New York," he said.

"But you do good work here."

He said, "I can do more and better in New York. You of all people should know."

"Me?"

"I've seen you dance."

"Just the once," I scoffed. "And months ago."

"No," he said. I realized what he meant. He'd watched me, some stolen moment, when I didn't know he was there. It was both terrifying and exciting to know.

Looking down at me, something changed in his face. "My God, those eyes of yours," he said. "I've never seen eyes as beautiful."

"You haven't seen enough eyes."

"Trust me. I've seen plenty of eyes."

I suddenly realized how alone we were, how close we were, how dark the shed was. If we wanted to seek comfort in each other's bodies, we could. Having him this close brought back all those buried feelings in force. I forced out a question. "Do you have enough money for the train?"

"No," he said, "but the train isn't the only way."

"It's not?"

"There are ways. There are always ways, if you know them. The cook needs fresh crabs from Washington for Mr. Vanderbilt, and I've done enough favors for her that she'll send me along in the cart, no questions."

"Washington isn't New York."

"Let me finish. From Washington to Baltimore, that's almost no distance at all. I could even go on foot. I have cousins, my mother's cousins, who can house me in Baltimore while I work to build up more money. If I have enough money, there are trains and steamships to New York, and if I don't have enough money, I can stow away."

"You've thought about this."

"I don't do anything without a plan."

My muddled brain clearing at last, I was beginning to develop a plan of my own. Quietly I asked, "When are you leaving?"

"Tonight," he said.

"I'm coming with you."

He looked at me in a way I didn't think anyone had looked at me before. Certainly not in the way Ray had, not like an animal to be subdued or an object he had a right to possess. Almost the way Mrs. Severson did after I managed to repair a crack in a teapot that she had said she didn't think could be repaired.

He said earnestly, "Do you mean it? You'll come?"

I drew back. His earnestness made me uncomfortable, and it was too much all at once. He hadn't forgotten me, as I hadn't forgotten him, and now we were thinking of the very same thing — escape — each for our own reasons.

"Yes," I said.

Whatever his plans, the choice was a simple one for me. Stay and be caught by Ray, or leave and be one step ahead. And on my own, I had little chance of making my way much of anywhere, not before the next day's sunrise. I knew too little of the world. Clyde knew more. That would be

168

valuable.

We nodded at each other like dumb puppets, and he told me where to meet him and when, and I walked back to the house a changed girl once more. Twice during the evening as I was packing my bag, I heard a soft knock on my door, but I knew it must be Mrs. Severson, and I ignored it. I wouldn't tell her that I was leaving. I would simply go. All unknowing, she had done enough harm with my secrets already.

That night, we climbed up into the cart behind the cook, and when the horses lurched forward, I felt my heart rise up. I was headed into the unknown once more, but at least I wouldn't be there when Ray arrived. No one would know where I'd gone; no one could give up my secret. I took the feeling as a sign that I was making the right choice after all. That what I was leaving behind would be a fair trade for what was to come. Time would tell, in any case.

CHAPTER THIRTEEN

1896

The Phantom Bride

The journey took more than a month, and it was both comfortable and uncomfortable, right and wrong, tense and lovely.

In Washington, we posed as brother and sister, assigned to separate rooms in a travelers' house, seated together only at dinner. Quietly, when no one else could hear, we told each other our stories. He'd cared for his three younger brothers after his mother had died in childbirth with the youngest one, and his father didn't care if anyone was happy or sad or in pain or hungry as long as they kept themselves quiet. He'd lived in North Carolina all his life and taken many jobs to make money, but when he found his talent for tending growing things, Mr. Vanderbilt had actually found him by reputation and asked him to come to Biltmore. He'd been at Biltmore for a year when the great landscape architect Mr. Olmsted, who had designed the grounds, had come to survey his handiwork and was so impressed he praised him and shook his hand.

That was the day Clyde had decided to leave Biltmore and go to New York. Mr. Olmsted was working on a project there, a great park, and could certainly use one more pair of talented hands. Clyde would have followed him immediately, but he feared running out of money more than anything else on earth. Growing up so poor had taught him what it meant to decide which brother would go hungry on a given day, and he could never live that close to the bone again. He couldn't let it happen. Not to his family, should he ever chance to have one, and in the meantime, not to him. He stayed at Biltmore another year to set aside some savings, and the rest I knew.

When he asked for my story in return, I told him almost everything. My invisible father, my early childhood in my grand-parents' house, my mother's marriage, life on the farm in Tennessee. Why I danced. How I'd come to the Biltmore for work. I left out any mention of Ray. It thrilled me to realize I could pretend Ray never existed and no one would be the wiser. So from that day forward, I never spoke of him out

171

loud to anyone.

When Clyde and I left Washington, we agreed to walk to Baltimore to stay with his mother's family, hoarding our meager funds. Our sole topic while walking was pure mathematics: how could we stretch our pennies to feed ourselves each day for the absolute minimum? If we slept on the ground every night, would we have enough money for steamship passage up the coast? We haggled over nickels, cents, even half cents. The weather remained muggy and hot even as the sun began to set, and our bags, sparse as they were, grew heavy. When we came across a grand old pine as big around as the Biltmore's greenhouse, we agreed to spend the night under its low, sheltering branches. During this pause, we finally broached the subject that had been simmering under all our conversations, so far unspoken.

He knelt carefully and unrolled a blanket on the ground under the side of the tree that was farthest from the road. I joined him on the blanket, but at the far edge. As the sun set the rest of the way and darkness descended around us, I felt smothered in layers of dust and grime, which I could do nothing to scrub off. Instead I reached up to unbraid and rebraid my hair slowly and with great care.

We didn't speak, but even in the blackness, I could hear his breath and sense his nearness. When I was almost done with my braid, I could tell he had made his way halfway across the blanket, then closer and closer yet. I set one hand on the blanket to steady myself, and he found it with his own hand. I knew what he would do next, and I neither scooted away to make it harder nor leaned in to make it easier. I felt his other hand reach out for me. He lightly stroked the line of my jaw and brought my face to his for a kiss. The kiss was sweet and soft, a tender reminder, and it was hard for me to break contact. But I did.

"I'm not certain we should start that again," I said.

"Why did we ever stop?"

"I didn't know if I could trust you," I said and realized I meant it. "I didn't know your intentions."

"My intentions were that we enjoy each other's company."

"And?"

"I like how kissing you and touching you feels," he said, his voice a soft deep rumble in the darkness. "I can tell you like it too. Isn't that enough?"

In the darkness, unable to see each other's

faces or bodies, we had only our words to do all the work for us. I let my silence speak for me.

He said then, "Maybe it's not enough, I suppose, for a girl like you. But I can't make any pledges."

"I never asked for that."

"I'm eighteen years old," he said. "I need to make my name, build my career, before I'm fit to make any promises for a future together."

"I didn't ask for a future."

"But don't you want to take some pleasure in the present?" he asked.

I answered honestly. Maybe I shouldn't have. "I don't know."

"Look, Ada," he said, reaching for my hand again, entwining his fingers with mine. I let him. "You're a charming and wonderful girl."

"Flatterer."

"I mean it. I enjoy your company. Very much. Why did you agree to come with me, if you don't enjoy mine?"

I was glad I could tell part of the truth. "I do enjoy you. I do. But I agreed to come with you because it's the fastest way to get where I need to be. Not to snatch some thrills along the roadside."

He chuckled quietly. "At least you agree

that I'm thrilling."

I laughed at his confidence.

He went on, "I hold you in very high esteem and I would never hurt you. You can count on that."

"Can I?" But his answer had charmed me, and the question was gentle, not pointed.

"I can at least say this," he said. "I'll never keep my sentiments a secret."

Those words sprung immediately to my mind three nights later in Baltimore, where he sank to his knee in front of his mother's cousins and asked me for my hand in marriage.

We had all gathered in the parlor after the evening meal, under the pretext that we'd be listening to one of the young ladies practice a new song on the piano. I walked toward the sofa but was ushered toward the room's finest and most well-padded chair instead, a place of honor usually reserved for the hostess, and I should have known then that there was a reason. Instead I took my seat, as did the others, and I was still watching the empty piano bench and waiting for our songstress to begin when Clyde Garber placed a small decorative pillow on the ground in front of me with great deliberation.

Once he had settled his knee on the pillow and taken my hand in both of his, he swallowed twice and squared his shoulders. Then he said, in a voice that trembled just a little, "Miss Bates, it would make me the happiest man in the world if you would do me the honor of becoming my wife."

It was almost like falling from the hayloft again, with my breath crushed out of my body, only instead of exploding with pain, I exploded with joy. He wanted me. He was offering me his whole self, for the rest of our lives. All he wanted in return was my whole self. I gave it.

Looking up at me with those blue eyes, his hands clutching my hand, sincerity plain on his face, he was utterly irresistible. I didn't even hesitate.

"Yes! I'll marry you," I said.

The cousins broke out into applause, and he got to his feet and chastely kissed my cheek.

"I'm sorry there's no ring," he said.

"I don't need a ring."

"Nonsense," piped up the eldest cousin. "You'll borrow mine." She slid a worn gold ring off her own finger and handed it to my new fiancé, and he slid it onto the fourth finger of my left hand, and tears sprang to my eyes.

They applauded again, and he beamed at

me, and it was like sunshine.

The next morning, we decided to look at the garden, and when the cousin whose garden it was realized she needed to post a letter instead, it transpired that the two of us were alone together. He held my hand lightly as we walked until we were out of sight of the house. Once we were safely alone with no one in earshot, I turned to him and flashed my newly ringed finger and said, grinning, "I can't believe you did this."

"I can't either. I'm sorry I didn't warn you beforehand, but I didn't really plan it — the idea just came to me, and I knew it would be perfect. I'm so glad you went along. That money will be all we need to get the rest of the way."

It dawned on me, slowly and powerfully like a poison in my blood, what he was saying.

"Ada?" he probed.

I didn't want to ask. I didn't want to know the answer. But I had to. "Went along? So you don't —"

"Oh," was all he said.

I watched the realization dawn on his face, and I was ashamed. He thought I'd know it wasn't real. He started to stammer an explanation, an apology, something. I didn't need to hear it. The look on his face, the single word *Oh,* told the whole story. He reached for my shoulder, and I stepped aside. I didn't want to be comforted. Not by the person who'd hurt me, not that way.

"I understand," I said. "For the money."

"For the money."

We didn't talk any more about it. Not one word.

I hated myself those two weeks in Baltimore. We were both trying on a life that wasn't ours, but he seemed at peace with it, and I couldn't stop thinking how I'd been duped. How wholeheartedly amazed I'd been when he spoke those words, and how quickly I'd agreed to yoke myself for life to someone who was such a mystery to me that I hadn't realized how deep his layers of untruth went.

But what I hated myself for wasn't just the initial foolishness. It was the ongoing lie, and that even as I knew it was all unreal, how I delighted deep down in the untrue things we said. He addressed me as "dear" and gazed upon me with a fond expression. Every time, my heart nearly exploded in my chest. He committed himself so wholly to the lie that it was too easy to believe he meant every word. And when I responded with "thank you, love," or "see you tomorrow, my darling," on some level, I wasn't pretending. He didn't love me. He wasn't my darling. And yet I lay in bed every night a wakeful and aching creature, seeing what I wanted so close by, pretending I had it, but knowing it wasn't really mine.

When at last it was time to keep moving north, I saw the slim envelope pass from the cousin's hand to my false fiancé's, and I pasted on an empty smile. I gave her back her ring. I felt bad that we had deceived them — they all seemed so kind — but things were working out exactly as we needed them to. With the dollars in that envelope, we wouldn't starve. It was enough to get us to New York within the week, and it would house, clothe, and feed us once we were there. We didn't discuss the fact that we'd lied in order to get it. In a way, things that weren't said out loud didn't happen. If we didn't acknowledge things we didn't want to be true, we could keep them hidden in the dark. I'd learned that at my mother's knee, after all.

New York City, our destination, had only been a distant, hazy image in my mind. As we rode down Houston Street on a horse cart, it became utterly, astoundingly real.

The city was immense. The buildings were so tall and the streets so wide that I couldn't take them in. And the people. So many people, everywhere, beyond counting. Like grains of salt in a shaker or the blades of grass on the Biltmore lawn.

"How do you like it?" Clyde asked me, sitting stiffly only inches away. Since we'd left Baltimore, each day had been like a summer storm — one minute warm, the next cold. He would crack jokes and then fall silent for hours. He smiled too much for no reason. I would hold my body apart from his deliberately but then, when we were close together like this, find myself staring at his lower lip, fighting with all I had not to lean over and press my lips there. If his skin brushed mine by accident, I jumped like a flea. There was no peace with him.

But now, the city demanded my full attention. There were too many sights and sounds flooding my senses. So many people, such tall buildings, the smoke and the rails and the hats and skirts and horses. So much black silk. So much marble and stone. So much of everything.

"It's too much," I blurted. "It's too big."

"It's not. You haven't even seen a fraction."

"There's more?"

"There's always more," he said. "It's New York."

"How much do you know of New York? I thought you lived in North Carolina all your life."

He shrugged. "I may have been here once or twice."

"When?"

"A while ago," he said. "That's not important."

It was then that I started to wonder if any of the stories he'd told me were real. I'd been in his sight every single day for a month and he in mine. I'd met his family. I'd pretended to be his betrothed. When he lied, I shared his lies, and we had made up our own untrue story together. But he'd betrayed me, shocking me with the fake betrothal, and the fact that I'd shared his lies didn't make them more forgivable. He couldn't be trusted. I would need to act accordingly.

We edged down a noisy, tight street. Carriages whizzed past us, all too near, and I shrank away from them at first. I made myself get used to it. I tried to focus on specific, small things. The man with the fruit cart and his pile of oranges. The storefront with the striped awning advertising NOTIONS. When we turned the corner onto a

181

narrower street, the pattern of the cobble-stones changed, and the sound of the horses' hooves changed into a different rhythm, each clop-clop ringing out more clearly, which I could hear above all the voices and noise if I concentrated my attention.

The hooves slowed and stopped. I looked at the house ahead of us. Red brick, three stories, with five steps up to a solid front door. The whole block of houses was identical except for the color of the brick. They were neither grand nor miserable, but they were town houses, linked one to the next like paper dolls with no space between. The only sky was up; the only green was a single, sad tree on the other side of the street, halfway down. So many doors and so many windows, but the feeling was still one of being closed in.

"My boardinghouse," he said, pointing to it, and then, "and yours," pointing two doors down.

That settled it. He'd be too near. I couldn't trust myself. I wanted to feel unmitigated hate for him, but it wasn't that simple. There was only one way to make sure he wouldn't charm me again, against all my judgment. I made my plan and acted. "I'm going to need some of the money."

"What?"

Holding out my hand, forcing myself to smile lightly, I said, "I should really get half, you know. Of the betrothal money. I'll take less though. I just want to secure my rent."

"Your first month is already paid. You don't need any money."

"You'd leave me in the city without a nickel?"

"I'll take care of you. We'll meet up tomorrow, and I'll give you some then."

"Now," I said. "What if I want some supper?"

"I can't just hand you money out in the street."

I kept my hand stubbornly extended. "You can so. I have faith in you."

Grumbling, he reached into his pocket and struggled to peel off a couple of bills without exposing the money to the air. I saw his point — the street teemed with strangers, and it was unwise to wave money around in front of others who might want it — but I knew the danger if I didn't secure my part now. Perhaps he intended to meet me the next day and share the money as he said he did, but he couldn't be trusted. He had said he wouldn't keep his sentiments a secret, but that was exactly what he'd done with his false proposal, and he was guilty of it even now. I had no idea what he was thinking or feeling. And because of that, I was hiding my true feelings and plans from him as well. Either way, I had to take advantage of the moment, since we might never share another one.

He leaned close to me and said, "Put your arms around me then."

"Why?"

"Do you want it or not?" I belatedly realized he meant the money, not the embrace. I edged forward into his arms. His body was warm and his scent flooded my nostrils, and for a moment, I wanted desperately to sink into him and give myself up. But I felt his fingers discreetly searching for my hand and pressing the money into it, and the gesture brought me back to consciousness.

"Thank you," I said softly.

"Come meet me tomorrow. Right here. Nine in the morning. All right?"

"All right."

"We made it."

"We did."

"We'll talk tomorrow. And we'll find our way."

"All right," I repeated.

"All right." He smiled a soft smile at me. How could he think everything was okay? Everything was not okay.

I watched him mount the steps into the boardinghouse and turned right toward my own destination.

I only stopped at the boardinghouse two doors down long enough to ask after the deposit. One had been placed, and when I explained my situation, the woman was happy to give me back three weeks' rent as long as I forfeited one. She gave me the location of her cousin's boardinghouse in the next ward over and swore not to tell my dangerous husband where I'd gone. Before leaving the house, I secured both wads of money deep in my undergarments. I couldn't afford to lose my stake to pickpockets.

Then I hoisted my valise and off I went, down the teeming street into the unknown.

CHAPTER FOURTEEN

Janesville, 1905
Half past two o'clock
"Didn't I tell you? I was a fool," she says.

"That's not what it sounded like to me."

"Are you even listening?"

"I'm listening."

"So," she says, "now you know one of my weaknesses. I believe the things people tell me."

"I think we all have that weakness."

She says, "I don't know. You don't seem to believe much of what I'm telling you."

"Well, these are . . . extraordinary circumstances."

She grins at him, almost like a friend. It disarms him. On one hand, that's not what he wants, but on the other hand, why should it matter? Why not tell her everything? It won't change what needs to happen. He needs to decide whether to keep her or let her go. Her feelings on that matter, he already knows.

He goes on, "So you fell in love and trusted someone. It happens. At least you learned his stripes quickly enough."

"It felt like love," she says. "Or what people had told me love was like. Was your wife your first love, officer? I asked you before, but you didn't answer."

"She was," he says.

"And how long have you been married?"

"Two years."

"You're what? Twenty-two, twenty-three?"

"Thereabouts," he admits.

"Then you've loved her longer than she's loved you."

She's uncannily good. By now, this doesn't surprise him. "Why would you say that?"

"If you loved her in your teens, and she loved you in her teens, you'd have married in your teens. Isn't that the case?"

"She had another suitor, for years," he says. "A steady." Perhaps the story will help her think of him as a young man in love, not just a police officer. Help her open up. Tell him more of the truth, especially when and where it counts.

She cocks her head and smiles up at him. "The young man who came in first at everything, when you came in second?"

"The very same."

"But you came in first when it mattered. She married you."

He shakes his head. "Because he married someone else first."

"Who? And why?"

"A girl named Prudie. The sweetest you'd ever meet. She moved to Janesville when we were all twenty, and the whole story was written from the moment she arrived. Mose would be the leader and she would follow."

"And your wife — Iris, was it? — isn't that way? A follower?"

"Not at all," he says with a fond smile. "She's like you. She speaks her mind."

"But you love her and she loves you. Isn't that all that matters?"

"It should be."

"It isn't?"

This part is harder to be honest about. He's never said it out loud to anyone. "I was always her second choice," he says. "I can't forget that. She settled for me because she couldn't have what she really wanted, and I was the next best. Is that anything to build a life on? And now . . ."

"Now you're injured," she says, catching on.

"As soon as they find out how bad it is, they'll dismiss me. Force me out. What good is a police officer who can't physically catch a criminal?"

"You caught me."

"I was lucky," he admits. "You're smaller than most criminals anyway. And now I want to hear more about your magic."

"What else is there to say? At Biltmore, I suspected that my healing was extraordinary, but I didn't truly believe in it for years. I know how easy it is to make tricks seem like magic. But I asked Adelaide once if she'd ever heard of people with healing powers, and she had some astounding tales to tell. The mind is stronger than the body, and some minds more than others."

He's confused. "Who's Adelaide?"

"Didn't I tell you?"

"No."

"Are you sure?" Her face is stony.

After their easy confidences, her coy resistance now sets him off.

"Listen," he says, jabbing one finger at her for emphasis, "stop dancing around it. If you want any chance of leniency, any chance at all of not going to prison, you're going to need to work with me, not against me."

"You think I'm working against you," she says.

"Yes."

She kicks a little against the cuffs. They

rattle and tighten against the legs of the chair.

"Let me show you how agreeable I've been," she says.

She locks her gaze on him, stares into his blue eyes with her blue-and-brown ones. Setting her bare heels against the ground, she begins to lean back, slowly, carefully.

The front two legs of the chair scrape against the floor and rise into the air. Not by magic, just leverage. She shuffles one foot forward then the other. Then she shifts her weight forward again, setting the chair back down.

He gets a sicker feeling in his stomach.

The cuffs are no longer locked in position around the front legs of the chair. Her ankles are linked to nothing. She has lifted the chair legs right out of the cuffs. In barely half a minute, if even that.

She crosses one knee over the other, and the circle of a steel-gray cuff dangles from her slim ankle, swinging gently back and forth, hanging empty in the air.

"There's no way to lock the cuffs around the legs of the chair," she says. "When the seat is bolted straight onto the legs like this, there's nowhere to catch them. A different kind of chair would work, one with a bar between the front legs closer to the floor, but not this one."

He forces himself to keep his eyes on hers instead of glancing down at the chair legs to see what she's talking about. He doesn't want to get up from his perch on the edge of the desk. Moving would mean she's had an effect. He has to remain calm, or at least appear that way.

She goes on, "If I were going to run, I wouldn't have shown you the weakness in your plan. I would have manipulated you into adding more weaknesses until your entire plan was weakness, until I could easily break free."

She'd known from the beginning that the ankle cuffs were useless, and he hadn't seen it. He wishes he were thinking more clearly. He needs to. To hear her story, to make his decision, to turn this situation to his advantage. So he doesn't lose what little he has.

"It's not enough, of course," she says, jiggling her foot so the empty cuff bounces in the air. "I'm still cuffed to this chair. Even if I could get free of three pairs of handcuffs, which I can't, you'd just tackle me like you did before. I'd be right back where I started. And that door is still locked. Isn't it?"

He gets up, then picks up her discarded boots and carries them away, setting them next to the front door, off to the side. He

191

thinks about twisting the knob to make sure it's locked, but she's watching. It'll be all right, he tells himself. No one will interrupt them from the outside, and from the inside, he's doing everything he can.

"Isn't it?" she repeats to his back.

Enough, he thinks. Instead of answering her, he draws himself upright, all business.

"Tell me about this Adelaide," he says. "Now."

Chapter Fifteen

1896–1897
The Bullet Catch
New York City was not an easy place to live in 1896. Maybe it never has been. Life there is dark and noisy and crowded. The only smell I remembered from my grandparents' house was plum pudding at Christmas and clean sheets the rest of the year; in Tennessee, I had become acquainted mostly with the smell of dirt and horses and hay; at Biltmore, grass and soap and roses. Here every smell was on top of every other, good or otherwise. Garlic and perfume and manure. Silk and smoke and mud. Voices came at you the same way: a trilling woman's soprano shouting out the price of oysters, overlapping with a Sicilian shopkeeper's dusky accent and two German teenagers arguing at full volume, blotting out a whispering group of Irish girls on their way to work.

Positions were not hard to find. The engine of life needed to be fed. Boardinghouses needed to be run, the stately mansions of Fifth Avenue needed servants of all stripes, and restaurants needed people to cook and serve food. But running away from Biltmore gave me the opportunity to try something new, and the theaters all up and down the city needed performers on their stages every night, to feed the people in a different way. I wanted to dance on the stage for the people of New York.

I was out of practice from my journey up the coast. I'd been exercising every day, but in a stealthy and halfhearted fashion, trying to keep quiet. A *port de bras* was silent and so was a *rond de jambe,* so I'd kept those up, but I'd neglected anything noisier. I could feel the difference in my body, the weakness in my ankles where there had previously been strength. Once in New York, I quickly resumed the Cecchetti exercises as if there were someone watching me do them, as if someone were keeping track. On the rare occasions that the hallway in the boardinghouse was empty, I practiced my *chaînés tournes,* but the rest of the time I practiced in my room, tuning out the smell of boiling cabbage and the impassioned cries of my neighbors as best I could. That way I regained my full range of motion: *temps levé, fouettés en tournant,* my full vocabulary of *battements.*

I'd taken a shared room at the boardinghouse that the other house's proprietor had directed me to. I thought about moving again, in case Clyde convinced her he wasn't the abusive husband I'd made him out to be. His charm could undo my hastily made plan in a snap. Unfortunately I knew almost nothing of the city, and even staying where I was, I knew the money I had would last exactly four and a half weeks. So instead I threw myself into the search for employment, and miracle of miracles, I found it. I did what I most wanted to do and found a job dancing onstage every night.

The show was *The Belle of New York* at the Casino Theater, a musical about a modest young Salvation Army worker in love with a playboy who believes he loves someone else and then finds he loves the modest young lady after all. Toward the end of the show, she somehow becomes more noble by singing a horrendously naughty song. The entire enterprise aspired to elegance while also satisfying the audience's need for vulgarity. It was a huge hit. A dancing chorus filled the stage first as sober soldiers and later as flouncing tarts, and I was one of the chorus, though I was more impression than actual person, dancing as far back as I did. I never got to watch the entire show and be swept up in it like the audience did, but there were still moments that whisked me away. The playboy's first entrance, radiating confidence and charisma as he settled a white rosebud into the buttonhole of his fine evening jacket. The modest young lady's ballad, sung alone in a tight spotlight on a huge and deserted stage, the longing in her voice exquisitely pure and painful. Their kiss at the close of the show, brief and merry, a perfect tableau of celebration and romance and joy.

The girl sharing my room was a young Englishwoman named Clara who worked the night shift at a garment factory south of Canal. Her pay was better than mine, and she offered to get me a job at the factory, but I couldn't stand to be stuffed up like that. And I'd found what I wanted as a dancer. As much as my feet ached and my cheap costume itched, I was a performer, dancing for a theater full of people, for their joy, for their applause. There was a thrill in that I had never felt anywhere else.

Every night, the curtain came up and the curtain went down. Beforehand, I was lost in the itch of the costumes and the smell of the greasepaint and the bustle. Afterward, I was fully exhausted, as if I'd been dancing for ten hours and not just two. In between, things were a blur. But the blur in the middle was the happiest, most amazing blur, and I felt truly myself at every moment.

For nearly five months, all I could think of was survival. That was enough. The show's schedule was punishing, nine shows a week, including the weekend matinees. To condition my body to better handle the two hours of dancing, I needed to rededicate myself to practice and exercise, which also took time. There was always something to do, even if the range of things that needed doing was much narrower than it had been at the Biltmore. It was exhausting. The weather outdoors went from a hot summer stink to a cold winter chill, and as the months passed, the sun began to set before I left for the theater instead of after the last show ended, but other than that, little changed day after day after day.

By December, I was more settled. They raised my salary at the theater, which very nearly shocked me into a heart attack, since all they'd told any of us since the day we started was how worthless and weak we were. But apparently, I wasn't too worthless and weak to be promoted straight up to second line, and with second line came fifty extra cents a week, which made a world of difference to my body and my spirit.

I thought of my mother then, for the first time in a long while. She had probably assumed the worst. I should have left her a note when I fled or written her a letter sometime after. It crossed my mind a hundred times, but I didn't put pen to paper, even though it would have been such an easy thing. Had she seen the note that Mrs. Severson sent, or did she still wonder what had happened to me, with no news from any quarter? I should have done things differently. But now I felt it had been too long. I couldn't quite brush the thoughts away, but as the days passed, they occurred to me less and less often, and I made peace with myself again for a time.

The theater was dark on Christmas Day, so I spent the day at a roof garden sipping at cups of eggnog with Clara, who referred to me charmingly as her flatmate, and several of her coworkers. She and I had paid for the eggnog between us, and every time one of the coworkers downed another cup, I winced. I was calculating figures in my head the entire afternoon. Clara and her friends gossiped about people I didn't know and fell deep into discussions of methods for sewing and stretching and cutting fabric that I could barely understand. It was not as festive a holiday as it could have been. But the eggnog was warm and rich. I could see the buildings of the city arrayed like dollhouses below. And at the end of the day, we strolled home arm in arm, our cheeks pink with cold, caroling our voices hoarse.

The new year began as the previous one had ended, in a busy city with no particular friends but no particular enemies, and all told, I was happy, in my way.

Then January came.

Days that change your life don't always feel momentous. It's hard to know when or where the whole world will shift into something new. You can only stay alert and watchful and take things as they come.

The year 1897 was an eventful one in the world. It was Queen Victoria's Diamond Jubilee, a huge celebration. Mr. Stoker published a novel called *Dracula,* the artist-pervert Oscar Wilde was released from prison, and in New York, they held a ceremony to dedicate the tomb of President Grant.

And I saw a woman shot in the face, to wild applause.

January started gray and bitterly cold. By

the second week, it began to warm, and there was no snow, which gave me the opportunity to save streetcar fare by walking to and from the theater. The days were short, and it seemed always dark. One evening when I exited the stage door of the theater into the usual darkness, someone was waiting in the alley. I caught the smell first, a sweetish smoke, and then a blur of motion caught my eye.

I moved closer, carefully, and the shape resolved.

There was a man in the shadows, in light-colored clothing, smoking a large pipe. He spoke to me in a bright high voice, saying, "Good evening, young lady." I couldn't place the accent.

I said, "Good evening," and started walking past.

He said, "Wait a moment, please. I'd like to speak to you."

"I need to get home, sir."

"Ma'am," the voice corrected, and I took a closer look. Despite the breeches, the smoker was a woman. A large woman. Not fat but simply large, like an Amazon, built on a grander scale. My fear lessened somewhat without draining fully away.

"I'll get right to the point. My name is Adelaide Herrmann," she said, tapping the bowl of her pipe against the heel of her hand. "I have a show. I think you might be suited for it."

"What kind of show?"

"Magic," she said.

My first instinct was revulsion. Magic made me think of Ray, who had been convinced he and I both had magic in us and had tortured me for it. But then I realized she probably wasn't talking about real magic, if in fact it existed. She'd said *show*. That was a different animal.

She was looking at me very closely. She put her hand out and gently turned my shoulder, turning me toward the streetlight. I could feel the warmth of the light on me, against my cold skin.

"You have a very classical face, did you know that?" she said.

"I suppose not." No one had told me I had a classical face. Not even the underhanded Clyde, who had admired me, in his way.

"You could do a lot with that face."

"I'm sorry?"

"It isn't about the face really, of course," she said. "I need a dancer."

"What kind?"

"Your kind. I saw you in the show, and I think you can do what I need done."

"Which is?"

"Better that I show you. Come with me."

She turned down Broadway, and after only a moment's hesitation, I followed. The scent of pipe tobacco was more pleasant than most of the smells of the city, so I was happy to trail behind her in that cloud. I shouldn't have trusted her, but I did.

There were people on the streets, which usually made me feel safe, but these weren't the people I was used to. It was full dark. Nighttime revelry had begun. There were policemen around, but it didn't look like they were doing much policing. At least one had a girl in one arm and a drink in the other. I tried to keep myself to myself as we went and trailed Madame Herrmann like a shadow.

Ten blocks later, she turned left onto a narrower street and left again into an alleyway, and we went in at a small door.

The stairs were narrow and dark, and I followed her pale shape up through the darkness. The room behind the stage was large and mostly empty, except for several trunks lined up against one wall. Madame Herrmann rummaged in a trunk and threw a few things aside. Two kinds of cloth and something furry. I didn't look too closely. The next thing she found, she held out to me. Long blond ringlets dangled from her clutched hand.

She said, "Put this on."

"Ma'am?"

"Put it on," she said. "I may have a very important opportunity for you. But I need you to put on this wig so I can see you in it."

I tucked my hair underneath the horsehair cap and yanked the wig down over the top of my head. It smelled of old sweat. I held in the gag. I knew whatever opportunity this woman was offering me would rely on my doing what I was told, and I had a strong feeling it was an opportunity I wanted to know more about.

"Go over there," she said, pointing toward the brick wall. When I faced the wall, she said, "Turn around," so I did and faced her.

"Should I —"

"Just stay still," she said.

I left that ratty wig on my head and didn't even blow the hair out of my eye although it itched something awful, and I stared at a brick in the wall that the mason had nicked and overgrouted to make up for it. I only blinked on occasion, because when a powerful woman who smells like rosewater instead of dung tells you to stay still, you know everything depends on exactly how still you can stay, and for how long.

After a few minutes, she said, "Well done, you can move now. What's your name?"

"Ada Bates."

"Eh, no good. We'll change that," she said. "You'll start overmorrow."

"What will I start doing?" I asked her. "You haven't said."

"Young lady, you are going to have the most wonderful life with us. You have no idea."

She was dead right, on both counts, as I would later discover. I didn't think to ask her how she had picked me out of the crowd. I was no more prominent in the show than a dozen other girls. I was the one she had waited for, and I was a fool not to inquire why. But it was an unexpected, mad night, and I was caught up. And perhaps there was a part of me that was afraid it was too good to be true and asking questions might break the spell.

"Fifteen dollars a week, first week in advance," she said and pressed two bills into my hand. Real money. I only made ten fifty in the chorus. If I'd been a giddier girl, I would have run off right then, but I was levelheaded enough to know why Adelaide had given me the money up front. She wanted me to know there was plenty more where that came from.

"I still need to know what the work is," I said.

"What you'll do for this money, it's nothing you need be ashamed of," Madame Herrmann said matter-of-factly. "Tell you what. Tomorrow night, come to the Metropolitan Opera House. You'll see something amazing. And you'll understand what my magic is about."

I agreed to come, accepting the ticket she handed me. And I tucked the money into my blouse. So whatever ended up happening, I'd come out ahead, just a little.

The next night, I was delayed by some minor tragedy of Clara's and then by a slow streetcar, and in the end, I was almost half an hour late for the show. I hoped I wasn't missing the whole thing. Still I paused when I saw the majestic bulk of the Opera House. It was a tall, yellow brick box with square corners and a triangular peak on top, crowned with a rosette window. Its color stood out clearly among the darker bricks of the other buildings nearby. I scurried around the side and in at the nearest door, handing my ticket to a grim-faced usher. I entered the back of an enormous auditorium, rows and rows and rows of seats stretching out toward a stage.

Adelaide Herrmann was onstage, I could see in the first instant, and she would have commanded attention even if she hadn't been facing a sea of guns. Her robes were almost Oriental, but not adorned. Behind her, a series of great Greek columns rose, white on white, and had something less amazing been happening in front of them, they would have been enough to stare at. But there was this woman. And from the apron of the stage, a firing squad faced her, guns at their shoulders.

I stared in dumb fascination at first. I simply couldn't grasp what was happening. And then, I could.

She was a great, grand woman facing down a crowd of men with their guns pointed toward her heart, and as I watched, one man stepped forward and pulled back the trigger of his rifle, and I couldn't help myself — I shouted "No!" — but no one even turned to look at me, and when I heard the loud report of the gun crack through the silent air, I closed my eyes and prayed to God for a miracle.

I still had my eyes closed when the thunderous noise began. I grabbed immediately for the door frame, thinking perhaps it was an earthquake, since I'd never seen or heard one, and you can't understand a new thing until you've had the experience of it. But the noise was not an earthquake, nor an explosion, nor a steam engine.

It was applause.

I'd heard applause, but not from the back of a room this large, so full, so strong. I realized that not only were the seats on this level full to capacity, but I could hear a whole crowd in the balconies above me, clapping their hands together in a waterfall of dozens, hundreds, of individual acts of praise. The firing squad had laid down their guns, except the dumbfounded man who had stepped forward to fire, and the statuesque woman stood there before them. She looked unharmed. She extended her fist toward the audience, turned it so her fingers were facing up, and uncurled them like the petals of a flower.

I was too far away to see, but I knew from the presentation what she was showing them: the bullet.

The crowd around and above me leapt to their feet, applauding even more wildly. The applause surged and echoed around the high walls and ceiling of the enormous Opera House, and whatever thrill I'd felt from applause before was like a pale shadow of this new, powerful, crackling energy, and

I never wanted it to end.

She was still signing autographs by the stage door when I found her a half hour later, and I waited a half hour after that until she'd finished. I couldn't help thinking she was moving quickly for someone who'd been shot. There wasn't a spot of blood or gunpowder anywhere on her pale robes. I wondered what the secret of the act was. What if she could actually do magic? Did she have some power that allowed her to snatch a fast-moving bullet out of the air? If there was a trick to it, I certainly couldn't guess what it was. All I could do was be amazed.

Once the last stragglers were gone, I stepped up to her and said, "That was amazing, Madame Herrmann."

"Wasn't it though?" she said, and from a fold of her elegant robes, produced her pipe. "Adelaide Herrmann, Queen of Magic, first successful performer of the bullet catch in America. Though she is not American. As I'm sure the papers will say. Which is acceptable. As long as they say something, and in large type."

"I have some questions," I said to her.

"I have some answers. Let's get a drink."

We sat at the tavern for hours, and she

answered my questions, every last one. Although she had come to New York City for the bullet catch and sometimes performed here, her magic show was not based in the city. They traveled by train on the vaudeville circuits. She was the star of her show, as she should be, but she used a team of assistants in her various illusions, and they were one short at the moment. A young person with a good amount of talent and a willingness to work hard could find success with the Great Madame Herrmann's show. Her voice was wistful as she told me that she herself loved the stage and was never happier than when she stood in front of a thunderstruck crowd, performing. And in her words, I heard the echo of that amazing, all-embracing storm of applause, and I knew I was ready to sign on for the adventure. She was offering me another audience, and I was hungry for it. The promised salary of fifteen dollars a week instead of ten-and-change didn't hurt either. And with bed and board provided — even if that room was on a moving train, it was still no cost to me — I'd have far more of that salary to keep.

And still in the back of my mind, the fear of Ray was there, logical or no, and if by chance he came to look for me in New York, he would never find me. I would be on the move constantly. What better way to be invisible than to never be still?

When the light began to touch the sky outside, she said, "Settled then. We're off to the station."

"Now?"

"Now."

"My things are back at the rooming house," I said. "I need to go pack them up."

"Ah, no need," she said. "I'll send a boy to take care of it. He'll get your things. The address, write it down."

I did as she said, printing in careful letters. I wasn't used to having other people do things for me, but as it turned out, I got used to that quickly enough.

CHAPTER SIXTEEN

1897–1898
The Dancing Odalisque

My entire life changed immediately, which actually made the change easier. I simply had to let go of everything I knew and welcome whatever came my way. I learned to brace myself while sleeping on a swaying train so I wouldn't roll off the mattress, change my dress in a roomful of other women without exposing my private flesh, and wash my entire body in under five minutes in bathwater I was neither the first nor the last to use that evening. I learned to study the schedule in advance and find out which nights were one-night stands in small towns instead of longer engagements in larger ones, since the food was often better in the small towns but we were threatened with being left behind if we took too long over dinner. The train pulled out when the train pulled out, and Madame Herrmann wouldn't wait on anyone. When we left a male assistant named Billy behind in Oconomowoc one night, Madame reminded the assembled company that she was our boss, not a friend or sister or confessor or nursemaid, and above all, she was a woman of her word. I heard enough to know that her warmth upon meeting me was not characteristic. Those who crossed or disappointed her could expect anything from a shout to a slap or some of each. I resolved to do nothing to provoke her.

As for the job itself, learning the ropes on Adelaide Herrmann's traveling show was nothing much like either of my previous positions. Neither the discipline nor the routine were as strict as they had been at Biltmore. There was little in the way of training; we were expected to figure things out on our own. And while I remembered a friendly atmosphere backstage on *The Belle of New York,* here I received only a chilly reception from my fellow dancers. The girls' railcar was divided into sleeping berths, four beds lining two walls, and mine was shared with three girls named Scarlett, Marie, and Belladonna. When I had little luck with them from the first, I analyzed my behavior to try to figure out what I'd done. Had I been unkind? Too haughty? I couldn't remember having done anything to offend. Then one night when Marie was in her cups, she told me flat out: with one of the four bunks empty, a girl could enjoy some small measure of privacy when male visitors came calling, knowing no girl was trying to sleep either above or below. When I moved in to occupy the fourth bunk, I'd ruined everything. I had no urge to bed down with men in the company just for the sake of it, and even if I had, I wouldn't have confided it to these girls, so we had no common ground for conversation. What free time I had I often spent with a book, but these three were hardly readers. It turned out the dancer I was replacing had been forced to leave the tour because she was in the family way. I'd have been much more shocked by that news if I'd learned it earlier.

When I joined the Great Madame Herrmann's show, they were midway through a circuit around the Middle West. It was still possible to book a single act into a theater individually, but many theater owners had allied with each other to form circuits, so that a set roster of acts would tour together, making the booking process easier on all participants. A season might consist of many circuits or only one. Ours would be many, assuming this first circuit went well enough for us to book the next. We went as far east as Muncie and as far west as Wichita, with many stops in between — the Majestic in Dubuque, Turner Hall in Galena, the Creighton in Omaha, and many more. We crossed our fingers against the snowstorms, having heard plenty of sad tales of trains marooned by bad weather on this circuit, but our luck seemed to hold, and we performed all our shows on schedule. The foolhardy but resourceful Billy, who we'd left behind in Oconomowoc, caught up with us three days later in Davenport and went onstage that night without fanfare. It took more than such a mundane disappearance and reappearance to make an impression in our remarkable world.

The illusion Madame hired me for, and the only one I performed during my first month with the company, was the Dancing Odalisque. It was one of the simplest illusions in the act. The set gave the suggestion of a painter's studio, with easels and paint pots scattered about and a trompe l'oeil window of streaming "daylight" positioned upstage right. I was wheeled out in an enormous picture frame and appeared to be a painted girl coming to life as a real one. The secret was that it was never a painting. It was always me. What looked like canvas was a trick of the light. So all I needed to do for the first sixteen bars of the music was remain perfectly still as I was wheeled out. The seventeenth bar was my cue to extend my arm and begin the slow, gradual awakening of my dance. The steps themselves didn't matter, she had assured me, as long as the dance took up the right amount of time. At the end of my piece of music, I returned to the picture frame and settled into the same position I'd held on my entrance, and Madame Herrmann strolled out in a painter's smock, clouds of sweet incense hovering low around her feet, and gestured to "turn me back" into the painting. I remained stone still, barely daring to breathe. She rested one hand on the edge of the frame and wheeled it offstage — with some help from an invisible stagehand who had snuck onstage under cover of incense — and we left the stage empty as the music shifted to a light, lilting melody setting the tone for the next illusion.

The Great Madame Herrmann's show, and the entire rail-bound enterprise supporting it, seemed huge to me. Besides the dancers and assistants who appeared onstage, there were a dozen others who worked behind the scenes. Six men were required to manage the props, setting up and breaking down. In addition, there were specialists like Jeannie, who sewed and repaired our costumes, and Hector, who looked after the animals. There were two dozen humans and two dozen animals in our entourage, including a full-grown Bengal tiger that seemed to regard me about as favorably as Scarlett, Marie, and Belladonna did, with even less provocation.

This all seemed like the largest possible company to me, but I was quickly informed that the company had been much larger six months earlier, when Madame's husband Alexander had been in charge. He was a very well-known magician, a proven draw, performing a two-and-a-half-hour program booked into theaters as a solo act. But his health had begun to decline, and he'd decided — possibly on the advice of Adelaide, who was not only his wife but his assistant — to book into a vaudeville tour. The money was good, the demands less onerous, and the tickets practically sold themselves. In October, he booked into a six-month circuit. In December, he died. And it was that circuit we were now completing, his wife having picked up where he left off as best she could. Her employees might not love her, but she provided a good living and had a good hand at keeping the wolf from the door.

Jeannie was the one who told me Alexander's story. She was an excellent source of information and the closest thing I had to a friend. After more than a year spent in either Biltmore uniform or Broadway chorus garb, there was something I found irresistible about the variety of fabrics and embellishments at our disposal, and I couldn't resist stealing a few moments in the costume closet here and there. We fell to chatting, and she invited me back whenever I liked. Jeannie was a short woman, and her voice was low and raspy like a man's, but her body swelled as generously above and below as the native fertility figures on the shelves of Mr. Vanderbilt's smoking room, the ones we'd only given the most perfunctory dusting. She'd been sewing her own clothing since she was a child in Abilene and had taken in whatever fancy work was needed there, of which there wasn't much. But her talents were in great demand at the local theater, where Madame, on tour, discovered and claimed her. Jeannie worked her own sort of magic on torn skirts and sleeves, making things good as new or even better. Her needle absolutely danced. There wasn't a gown she couldn't improve, expertly spangling a bodice or whip-stitching rows of lace to a skirt even as she kept up a steady stream of patter. I loved to listen.

Adelaide's costumes commanded attention without being immodest. Her Oriental robes showed her shape at the waist but were otherwise wide and flowing. On a typical night, she might change her gown three times, and each was a marvel. A soft underrobe of thin cambric was overlaid with a heavily embroidered satin piece that extended all the way to the floor in front and back, meticulously worked with Kelly-green birds and beaded gold branches. For an illusion where she was to play the lady at home, Madame wore a tea gown with frills at the collar and cuffs and pronounced leg o' mutton sleeves, the height of fashion for such a character. Her most elaborate gown was for her Cleopatra. This had a bodice so laden with stones and beads that it easily weighed twenty pounds atop a gauzy skirt and train, with long swinging chains of beads that dangled from the waist and bounced merrily whenever she moved. Jeannie was responsible for keeping all of these neat and tidy, as well as sewing new costumes whenever Madame thought it necessary and extending the same attention to the dancers' and assistants' costumes. It was also Jeannie's responsibility to secure the fresh flowers Madame wore in her hair every night, a circlet of gold with a small cluster of white blossoms on each temple. We had fake flowers for contingencies, but Adelaide hated them, and on nights Jeannie couldn't find fresh flowers, we all held our breath just a little bit through the whole performance.

As for the rest of us, the dancers and assistants, our skirts only reached our knees. Our arms were bare from the elbow. The costumes were modest by the standards of the Broadway theaters, but they would have shocked the stuffing out of Mrs. Severson. I had a sudden urge to write her a picture postcard and show her where I'd gone but instantly thought better of it. Let the past be the past, I told myself. Magic was where I had a future.

But the thought stirred something else within me, and I needed to settle it finally. I wrote a plain note on plain paper and posted it from Chicago. I didn't sign it. It said simply, *I am well.* Whether my mother saw it or not I couldn't say, but it helped, knowing I had made the attempt.

Then I threw myself into the future. The time that the other seven dancing girls spent figuring out how to divide up only four eligible boys between them, I spent learning. I watched the entire show, all through, every night, choosing a different angle from one night to the next. Unlike my experience on Broadway, where I was on and off the stage constantly for the whole show's two-hour duration, I had time before and after my appearance in the Dancing Odalisque to spare. Madame Herrmann was often the headliner, but because there were plenty of other acts on the bill and an audience still in their seats, we couldn't load up our sets and equipment and be on our way until the entire evening's entertainment was finished. When our part of the show was over and the other dancers crowded into the wings to watch Miss Ella's Comedy Joy or the Singing Gardini Sisters, or made themselves scarce for other, lustier purposes, I picked our show's illusions apart one at a time.

The Dove Pan was a shallow silver dish with a lid that could be used to produce anything the size of two fists or smaller. It got its name, of course, from hiding doves. Adelaide used it to produce a sweetly singing finch. It was an easy matter for me to find the pan's false bottom and to realize that from then on, the audience never saw what they thought they saw.

Slightly more challenging was the Light

and Heavy Chest, a trunk that couldn't be raised from the stage by any number of people in the audience but that Adelaide herself could lift one-handed with no visible strain. I examined the trunk many times from all angles, inside and out, and found only one clue: the top and sides of the chest were ornately carved, expensive wood, but its bottom was made of bare, flat steel. I shadowed the prop master for two weeks, trying to ferret out the secret. It was the night we didn't perform the illusion that gave the game away — I asked why, and he muttered that there was no space under the stage. At the next theater, I snuck under the stage during that portion of the act, finding a large metal box with a switch on the side installed on the underside of the floorboards, with an assistant there to operate the switch at the right moment. When Adelaide cued the assistant with two sharp stomps of her foot, he flipped the switch and the box hummed with electricity. Moments after came the roar of the crowd. Of course. Activated, the electromagnet held the wooden chest directly above it in place, and no one short of God could have pried the metal bottom of the chest away.

And yet this knowledge did nothing to disrupt my enjoyment of the show. Even when I discovered the secret behind the illusion I loved most, it ruined nothing. From the beginning, I had been transfixed by the illusion Lady to Tiger. It was a simple, impossible thing, where Madame magicked a large empty cage into existence on the stage, strode purposefully into it, and then reached outside the bars to draw a set of curtains closed. When only moments later an assistant drew the curtains aside, Madame was gone — and a large, roaring tiger was there in her place. I never volunteered to be the assistant in this act. I was extremely concerned about losing a finger, or worse, to the tiger. But I wanted to know what the secret was, so I watched every night and scrutinized every aspect of the illusion until I figured it out.

By looking closely, I could tell that the back of the cage was solid when Madame walked into it and the base of the cage was a raised platform about half a foot off the stage floor. There had to be a reason for both. I guessed that there were two hidden compartments: one in the back to hide the tiger before its appearance, and one in the floor to hide Madame after hers. I was certain of it and confirmed it with the prop master one night outside Lancaster. He outwardly grumbled that I was too inquisitive for my own good, but he gave me that look like Mrs. Severson had given me when I'd done something impressive, so I paid little attention to his grumbling. And even after I figured out the secret of Lady to Tiger, I continued to watch it every night just as avidly. I knew that Madame was not the tiger, that the tiger existed separately as a real flesh-and-blood animal at all times, but I still believed somehow. In that moment where the switch was made, I was seeing a woman transformed.

And Madame always was a tiger in her way. She retreated to her railcar every night for a brandy, and it wasn't unusual, late after dark, to hear a glass breaking against the wall. She didn't share confidences with us, nor we with her.

As I became more intrigued by magic, it seemed Madame became more intrigued by me. In that first circuit, she added me to five more illusions, nearly half the act. She renamed me Vivi, and my name appeared in the program alongside the other girls'. Two months in, she gave me the coveted spot of handing her the first deck of cards for the first act of the evening. For this, I wore a gauzy, elegant white dress so beautiful I was terrified I'd ruin it with makeup or lamp-black or the droppings that Madame's doves sometimes left just offstage. I made a beeline to Jeannie immediately after I stepped offstage to get it safely back into her care.

After my third successful performance in this trusted role, Madame summoned me to her railcar for a nightcap. Somewhat nervously, I went.

We sat ourselves on the comfortable velvet couches. Madame drank brandy. Not having much tolerance for alcohol, I asked for a cherry liqueur. If I disregarded the soft, regular thrum of the engine propelling us through the night, it wasn't like being on a train at all. There was carpet under my feet, Impressionist artwork on the walls in gilded frames, and an arched, dark blue ceiling painted with gold-white dots to give the impression of stars. It was like sitting in the front room of a fine hotel or a wealthy woman's parlor. It didn't have the grandeur of even the smallest room at the Biltmore, but it was elegant and plainly expensive, proving that things didn't need to be large to impress.

We made pleasant small talk for a while, and I waited to see if there was something she wanted to say to me. I thought she must have invited me for a reason. I was right.

"You're a smart girl, Vivi, aren't you?" she began.

"I can't rightly say."

"False modesty will get you nowhere, girl. I expect better."

I swallowed and said, "Then yes, Madame, I am the smartest girl currently in your employ."

"That's better. And I know you're observant, and I know you watch the whole show every night. So I have a question for you. What could I be doing better?"

"You do everything well."

"Hmph. Cut to Hecuba."

"Pardon?"

"The point. Get to it, dear."

"Okay." I took the gamble that she meant what she said. "When you do the Dove Pan. You tend to turn to the right at a certain point in the patter, after you say 'sweet music.' "

She nodded.

"It obscures your face for the left side of the audience. They can't see you, and they stop listening. You lose them."

Nodding more and smiling, she said, "I suppose that's right."

"It's still a wonderful illusion, and I wouldn't change anything else about it, but just make sure you're facing forward and you'll keep them all entranced."

"All right then, Vivi. Another question. What's missing? What, in your opinion, should I add to the act?"

My answer sprang instantly to mind. "Why not the bullet catch?"

"Oh dear," she said, clearly surprised.

"I mean, it would be a great addition. Bring the house down. It was amazing. You amazed me, amazed all of us."

Madame poured half her drink down her throat, swallowed, and said, "Well, I hope you remember it well, because you won't be seeing it again."

Made bold by the fear that it might be my only chance, I leaned forward and asked, "So how does it work?"

"How do you think it works?"

"They can't be firing real bullets, can they?"

"Yes and no. We have audience members come up and inspect the guns, and there are real bullets then. You remember only one man fired. He was talented enough to palm the bullet and replace it with a flash charge after the inspection."

"But then your life was in his hands."

"His, and the others', and the audience's," she said grimly. "Because what if his flash charge was packed too solid? What if one of the other men fired? What if an audience member, suspicious and clever, slipped something solid into the barrel of that gun? People have died doing the bullet catch for all those reasons."

"Then why did you do it?"

"Before Alexander passed" — here she crossed herself — "he'd whipped some newspaperman into a frenzy, boasting that he could do the bullet catch though he never had before. The booking was made and the press set. Then he was taken from us suddenly, and what could I do? I needed to make a splash, to establish myself as a magician in my own right, and the opportunity was there in front of me. If I canceled, I'd have to claw my way up from nothing. I'd already lost what mattered most. I couldn't lose more. I kept the date."

I asked, "Weren't you afraid you'd be killed?"

"Not afraid, no," she said. "I knew it would be my answer one way or the other. If I did it successfully, I'd keep our slot on the circuit, and then I'd tour with Alexander's illusions and make my own name from there. If it killed me, it killed me. And I wouldn't have to worry about anything else, because I'd be dead."

"Thank God you survived."

"I doubt he had much of anything to do with it," she said and drained her drink. "In any case, I won't be adding that to the act. But you'll tell me if you have any other ideas, won't you?"

"I will," I said.

She raised her empty glass to me and grinned. "To good ideas, Vivi, wherever we can get them."

From the beginning, I'd been favored by Madame — who I now thought of as Adelaide — but after that conversation, things became even clearer. I'd found my place. As we began our second circuit in the summer of 1897, Adelaide began to teach me the illusions, one by one. Not just the assistant's part, which I already knew, but the main action and all the little subactions that made it up. Our new circuit took us through the northern states, beginning in Western New York with Shea's Garden Theater in Buffalo, through Pennsylvania to Ohio and Indiana, then running northward through the entirety of Michigan, with a special performance to entertain the summering crowd at the Grand Hotel on Mackinac Island.

Another girl, a newer girl, took my place as the Odalisque, and Adelaide built a new showpiece around me, called the Slave

Girl's Dream. She herself had played the Slave Girl in Alexander's act. Aerial suspension was not so unusual to see on the stage, but it was often done by lifting prone girls on tables, providing plenty of room for ropes and wires. This was a different approach. She had the proper equipment fetched from the storehouse, and I had to admit, I blanched the first time I saw it. It looked more like a torture device than a tool of magic.

I stripped down to stage undergarments — modest enough to cover me more than real undergarments would, but still clearly meant as intimate — and submitted myself to the preparations. The contraption was a large harness of steel and leather, and as I struggled to catch my breath, Adelaide strapped me in. A rigid, slightly curved bar of steel ran up the right side of my body from the armpit to the knee, with another thick bar encircling the waist. Two bands of leather strapped me to the metal, one running over my left shoulder, the other between my legs, looping back and attaching to the bar at the waist.

"This will be tight," said Adelaide, grunting as she buckled the shoulder strap, "but take my word, you do not want it to be loose."

Next she brought out a steel pole, painted black, that attached to the steel bar at a right angle. I was raised into the air by the pole, bearing the entire weight of my body on a cold three-inch piece of steel in my armpit, and it had never been clearer that the control I'd used in the Dancing Odalisque had been mere child's play.

When we performed the Slave Girl's Dream, the curtain came up on a simple pallet, where I lay as if sleeping. Adelaide, representing a goddess of sleep, danced around me, and as the music swelled, I began to hover in the air. She then whisked beautiful garments from nothingness, garbing me in several flowing costumes of glorious silk, as if I were dreaming of wearing my mistress's rich clothes.

The effect was amazing. I couldn't see it myself, but when I saw the faces of the audience beholding it, I knew what they were seeing. I appeared to float in air with no support whatsoever, the gauzy edges of my rich garments fluttering in the air currents, the onstage lighting carefully directed to highlight my outstretched body and not the black pole holding me up in front of a black backdrop.

I was amazed by the illusion and thrilled to take part, but I also felt it was badly misnamed. What I thought — but did not say to Adelaide for fear of insulting her husband's memory — was that no slave girl would dream herself draped in a series of lovely garments. She wouldn't waste her efforts on a fantasy of silk chiffon and ribbons. A slave girl, given the ability to dream without limits, would dream herself free.

Once I debuted in the Slave Girl's Dream and my billing in the program was second only to Adelaide's, my fellow dancers' attitude shifted from somewhat distant to downright hostile. Not that any of them truly envied my position. They weren't ambitious girls nor greedy ones. None of them felt the strong affinity for magic that I did, the thrill of the rare opportunity to learn from the best. They were just insulted not to be asked and annoyed that I would be somehow raised above them, in both senses of the word.

As a group, they never went too far — no pranks, no violence, no threats — but instead punished me the way they themselves would have hated to be punished: with silence. They didn't realize I didn't mind silence, and in many situations, preferred it. So they ignored me, and when new people were added to the company, they were quickly counseled not to associate with me. The new Odalisque smiled at me when she met me, for example, but then never again. And that was all right. Lonely, of course, but hardly upsetting, once I got used to it. I was a good ear for Madame and for Jeannie, in different ways and for different reasons. I was respected by the stagehands and prop crew, who recognized my appreciation for the machinery. I didn't feel the lack of other company.

Instead of socializing, I worked and I learned. In the same way I'd once followed the Cecchetti method to point the toes of my right foot over and over and over, I made a habit of practicing and repeating all the elements of the illusions I needed to know. I wasn't sure whether or not I had talent, but I knew I had discipline. Over and over, I palmed a coin; over and over, I shuffled a deck. Then I went beyond the bounds of the illusions, past those specific moments, to the moments between and around them. I perfected all the gestures. Gestures were the currency. More so than any other part of the illusion, the way you drew people's attention with a lifted hand or a swept arm would be responsible for the success or failure of the trick. Misdirection. This is where my dance training gave me an unusual advantage. I practiced long, graceful arcs that traced the sky and subtle, winking flicks of the wrist. I practiced, for hours, taking one long stride downstage. I practiced until I found the perfect way to peek over my shoulder, as if I hadn't meant to, so that the audience would be compelled to follow my eyes in that direction. In some way, it felt like Mother would be proud of me, if she'd known.

Another old ghost was on my mind, thanks to the other girls' constant obsession with men and boys. I thought of Clyde and the stolen moments we'd spent in the dark nighttime hallways of the Biltmore. How intensely delicious those kisses had been. How much I'd looked forward to his lips brushing softly against my neck, his fingers traveling up my thigh. How my whole body grew warm at the sight of his eyes closed in pleasure, seen dimly through the veil of my own lowered lashes. I thought of our journey up the coast, the betrothal and the betrayal, and how things might have been different if he'd warned me beforehand that his proposal would be false. If he hadn't told me, unprompted, that I could trust him, and then immediately demonstrated that I couldn't. Without that, and my lost faith that followed it, perhaps we would have continued to meet after our arrival in New

York, and perhaps those meetings would have escalated to their natural conclusion. I might have let him possess me, consume me. But had it been love? I thought it was. I longed for him in every way. But whatever our feelings were, they had never truly been consummated, and even from what little I knew about love, I knew it had certain requirements.

In any case, Adelaide was showing me by example how to live without love. She mourned Alexander and never sought to replace him, yet her life was full. A wealthy former rail baron in Toledo attended three shows in a row and proposed marriage to her after the third, but all she did was laugh. She never spoke of love or marriage or companionship, except in reference to what she had lost. Perhaps I was a widow like her, only without the marriage to precede it.

That wasn't to say there weren't temptations and occasions here and there. After a matinee in Akron, a rather handsome young man presented me with a cluster of daisies and invited me to meet him for a cup of tea at a nearby shop two hours hence. I asked Jeannie for advice, and she insisted I go, just to have a story to tell. Unfortunately, the story I told her afterward was of the young man's very ungentlemanly attempt to grope me without prelude during a stroll along the river. He was easy to resist, especially when he declared petulantly that everyone knew girls who took to the stage were wanton strumpets, and who did I think I was kidding? Luckily he didn't press his case, but he did make me suspicious of every townie waiting by the stage door thereafter. No doubt some of them were decent enough chaps, whether they carried daisies or tulips or Queen Anne's lace, but I gave them all the cold shoulder. Sorting the wheat from the chaff was more effort than I cared to expend.

Closer to turning my head was one of the prop boys, a ginger-haired young man named Harry. He had merry brown eyes and a neatly trimmed beard, though he looked barely old enough to grow one. Harry told me he liked my eyes, a compliment of which I had fond memories. He kissed me one night, gently, in a dark hallway in the Bijou in Union City, after a sudden snowstorm canceled that night's performance. The kiss was pleasant, but only just. I felt nothing a tenth as strong as what I'd felt before. Mild enjoyment was not the stuff of love. I told him I couldn't entangle myself with anyone in the company, that I didn't believe in romance on the road, but that I thought he was a wonderful young man that some other young woman would be lucky to have. He took it well enough. Eventually he left the company to marry his schoolyard sweetheart and go to work in her father's feed store. I always imagined I'd been a bit of an adventure for him, given that these things are all relative.

In our third season, midway through 1898, we were all forcibly reminded of the potential harm love, or its approximations, could do. The boys and girls of the company were resourceful in their way, always finding places to meet before, during, and after shows. More than once, I took a wrong turn in an unfamiliar theater and found my colleagues groping each other in a storage closet. More than once, I would see boys and girls alike wolfing down their dinner on departure nights, excusing themselves after only a few minutes, so they'd have the better part of an hour for other activities before the train pulled out.

There was a particular romance between Chloris, who had replaced me as the Odalisque, and a boy named Jonah. Jonah was an athletic boy in his late teens, but with hooded eyes that made him look older. He often played the villain in illusions where innocent young girls were threatened, which was amusing, given that he was the youngest and most innocent among us. While many of the other boys would simply go around to every girl in turn, trying their chances, Jonah only had eyes for Chloris, and you could tell which days he was in her favor by the spring in his step.

One night, he climbed out of the boys' railcar and across the top of the moving train to the girls'. He lowered himself gingerly through the trap in the roof to land almost silently among our bunks. Chloris thought it was charming that he couldn't wait until morning to see her, rewarded him with a few kisses, and sent him back before the other girls could wake and raise a fuss. On the way back across the roof of the cars, for whatever reason, he slipped. When he didn't report to the theater the next morning, the truth came out. A search party was sent back to follow the track. We never saw his body, but his parents came to claim it, and I had never seen Adelaide so grave and sorrowful as when she received them. Chloris refused to set foot on the train again, sobbing uncontrollably just from the sight of it. We were due to play the Globe in Louisville, six hours away, that evening. I stepped back into my old role for a few shows until we could hire a new Odalisque. I didn't dare refuse Adelaide when she assigned me the illusion, but it gave me a dark, nervous flutter in my belly. Every night as I waited on the stage, perfectly still, I thought of the bad ends both the Odalisque before me and the Odalisque after me had come to. I might be no luckier. We'd all shared the same costume, the same wig, the same abilities. I feared what else we might share.

CHAPTER SEVENTEEN

1898–1900
Second Sight

Over the next few seasons of the Great Madame Herrmann's show, I learned and grew and changed, building my confidence and knowledge, feeding on the energy of applause. We continued on through the rest of 1898, 1899, and the blazing festivities that welcomed the beginning of 1900. Other companies took a month or two off for summer break each year, but Adelaide didn't believe in it; she spent two weeks in August sorting through the goods in her storehouse to refresh the year's planned illusions, and then we were back on the road.

We still toured the Middle West each year, but we added new circuits and extended our reach, even playing major theaters on the East Coast — Ford's Grand Opera House in Baltimore, Low's Opera House in Providence, the Howard Athenaeum in

Boston, and a hundred other theaters. The company had grown larger, with more employees onstage and off. For music, we had previously depended on local musicians at the theaters we visited, but Adelaide decided we should travel with our own orchestra and hired capable players for brass, strings, and woodwinds. She selected both the players and the music carefully to make those five players sound like twenty-five. Belladonna and Scarlett were still dancing girls, though Marie had gone home to Utica, and there were more than a dozen girls all told, in various roles. Jeannie had an assistant, a bright girl named Cecily, and three more prop boys joined the company, there were so many sets and illusions and apparatuses. The tiger was still with us, as well as the dogs and rabbits and most of the birds, though Madame had decided to part with a handful of doves and finches. She replaced them with a half dozen snakes. Five were small and bright green and lively, and the sixth was ink-black and huge, resting in a heap of coils that seemed to stretch in every direction. We were told none of them were venomous. Hector decided he was getting too old to travel around the country in the company of beasts, especially the hissing variety, so a man named Isham was hired to manage the animals, but we saw him only rarely. He didn't seem to enjoy the company of humans, and they returned the sentiment. Isham smelled no better than his charges.

From the window of our railcars we saw the world go by — flat grassland, bustling factories, heaped snowdrifts taller than a man, the mile-wide Mississippi, frozen lakes, ramshackle slums, the expanse of the Atlantic Ocean, hillsides speckled with grazing sheep, and once, in Kansas, the heart-stopping beauty of a burning prairie at night. Our leader was always refining her act, of course, and as she became more famous, our audiences grew. Our skirts got shorter and our tickets more expensive. But the basic rhythm of the show itself was the same.

The curtain came up on our most elaborate set, a facsimile of a Hindoo palace, backed by tall pale columns with bright banners of chiffon strung between them, a riot of color surrounding a golden throne. Five veiled girls swathed in those same bright colors spun onto the stage, swaying to Hindoo rhythms, each bearing a snake with a yellow blaze down the center of its flat head, and we spun quickly enough that the snakes seemed to writhe and hiss,

241

though in fact they weren't real snakes at all. We had rehearsed the dance once with the real snakes, but Adelaide decided they looked much less impressive from the audience, so we went back to the fakes, with some relief. Once the snake dance was complete, we struck the poses of jacks, queens, and kings, and then we vanished in a flurry of playing cards, just as Adelaide strode out regally to seat herself on the golden throne.

The music swelled and then stopped. The hissing of the snakes faded away. And Adelaide began to perform the first of three sets of card tricks she claimed were taught to her by the Hindoo mystics themselves, in the dark alleyways of Calcutta. No matter where we were or how long we'd been at it, my breath always caught a little when she fanned out the thick flat cards in her long fingers. There was always such promise in that moment. I looked forward to it every night.

There were songs and sights and more and more illusions. The Hindoo set was traded for a more feminine, abstract one, a kind of ladies' dressing room, draped with pale lace, for a Night's Alteration. Playing the role of an overly curious maid, I was folded into the sheets of a great bed and vanished inside it, then the next season when we changed the illusion to keep it fresh, three of us were folded up inside the bed and vanished and were replaced by a dove, a dog, and a peacock. The season after that, new girls were the dove and the dog and the peacock, and I was the one who turned the bed and waved the wand and made all the disappearances and transformations happen, at least as far as the audience was concerned. When the final transformation was complete and the peacock spread its tail wide, the audience always broke into gleeful applause, and I raised my arms to drink it in. For however long it lasted, mere seconds or much longer, I let the sensation pour over me like cool water on a hot day, delicious and welcome.

Toward the end of the entertainment, all the sets were swept away until the stage was hung with only a dark scrim. A lone violin began to play in the darkness, a crooning, charming song. The evening's final dancer, and the most accomplished — Adelaide herself, danced a graceful pantomime. What was most arresting was the effect of the robe she wore, a dark dress patterned in swirling, pale sequins, lit with lamps of shifting colors, first a royal blue, then sea-green, then a delicate pink, and so on and on.

Every year, the robe was more ornate, the lamps more artistically arranged, the spectacle more riveting. Everything was the same and yet different, and that was how I liked it.

I'd found a true home, even if that home never stayed in one place very long. I had settled into the pattern of Adelaide's show, of my own expertise, of the rhythms of traveling, setting up, performing, breaking down, and traveling again. I slept far more soundly with the deep bass thrum of a moving train in my ears than I did without it. I took joy in the sameness of my conversations with Jeannie, and the way Belladonna stopped talking anytime I entered a room, and the little nod the prop master gave me each night when we put the last of the trick boxes away. We had our little rituals, and we held fast to them.

Until Hartford.

We were two nights at the Pope's Palace in Hartford, and on the second night, one of the girls fell ill on bad oysters. As a result, Adelaide involved me in the show in a new way: the second sight act, which was her grand finale.

"You understand, Vivi, it's just this one night. No matter how good you are, you won't be better than Miranda."

"Yes ma'am," I said. I'd seen Miranda in the act, and she was very good, so I had no reason to think I could surpass her. But I would be better than she was tonight, when she couldn't even rise to her feet without retching.

The night was a disaster from the beginning. Nothing was quite right. In the opening dance, Scarlett tripped and stumbled so fiercely she literally fell off the stage. Adelaide waited for her in the wings, noticed that her slippers were too loosely laced, and slapped her across the face with one of the offending slippers before she herself went out onstage to start her cards and coins. The audience didn't seem comfortable. This was sometimes the case, especially in the largest cities, where the crowds wanted to be impressed from the very first moment since they'd paid good money to come. Tonight, they were restless, and that made us restless, and Adelaide most of all.

When it was time for me to assist with the second sight act, I stepped forward carefully and chose the woman in the seat I'd been told to choose. Third from the front, fourth from the left. She was undistinguished, in a dress the color of sand with a hat and gloves the color of mud, but when I pointed to her, a light of excitement came into her eyes.

"Now concentrate on your thoughts," I told her. "Think hard. What is your question? Don't say it aloud. Summon it to your mind with a firm clear thought and keep it there. Then Madame will tell you your answer."

The woman screwed up her face in concentration, and I gestured elegantly up to Adelaide, who stood ramrod-straight in her blindfold.

Then Madame said, "Yes, your answer is yes," and the woman gasped in delight and clapped her hands together merrily, but the audience didn't ease.

"Will you tell us what your question was?" I asked, as I was told to.

"I asked her whether her magic was real!" squealed the woman. "And it is! It is!"

A man in the center of the theater rose and screamed, in a hoarse voice, "Charlatan!"

I froze. This had never happened before, not anywhere.

Adelaide's voice rang out strong from the stage. "What do you mean by this, sir?"

The man was impeccably dressed in a black suit and vest, as if he'd just left the haberdasher's, but everything else about him seemed worn-out. He wore no hat, and though the back of his hair was thick and lustrous, the top was thin and bare. He strode up the aisle, approaching her. "Mind reader, my foot. You just stand up there guessing. If it hadn't been right, you would've backpedaled, like women always do. Trying in vain to cover their lies like a dog covers his mess."

The audience was nearly silent, but I heard a woman or two gasp at his indelicacy.

"You didn't even know her question. She told us herself!"

Adelaide said, "Do you have a question of your own, sir?"

"You bet your life," he said in that worn-out voice, and I feared for her.

My heart suddenly galloping, I looked wildly up at Adelaide, who gestured me back to her. I brushed past the man and walked out of the audience up onto the stage. He didn't seem to take any notice of me. He was entirely focused on her.

"Take my blindfold off," she whispered to me.

I aimed my mouth at her shoulder, turning my face so the audience couldn't see, and said, "Should I do anything? Call the police?"

"Just go," she said. "Wings."

I did exactly as she said. I stole one more glance out at the man in the audience. Even from here, I could see how powerfully he glared at Adelaide. He was far enough away that she'd be able to see him coming, so I didn't think he'd attack her. But oh, how he looked like he wanted to.

"You can't read my mind without looking at me?" he said.

"I could," answered Adelaide, "but the blindfold is window dressing, a put-on for show. You, you don't want show. You want truth."

"Yes."

It was like the two of them were the only people in the world and the rest of us didn't matter. The entire audience was dead silent. I huddled in the wings next to the trembling, nervous Scarlett, who was waiting for her cue with the other Hindoo dancing girls, and watched. I was afraid. It felt like the bullet catch all over again. A burning threat, an inescapable danger. For a moment, I wondered if this was a new part of the act, something she'd added without telling any of us. But why would she? And if the man was an actor, he was extremely convincing. His body fairly vibrated with fury. It was hard to watch but impossible to look away.

Adelaide said, "So get on with it. You've brought me a question."

"Yes."

"The answer matters to you. It matters to you more than anything ever has."

"Yes, of course!" the man said, sounding impatient. "Why would I ask you otherwise? I thought you said you weren't going to give me the empty show!"

"I just want you to be sure. That you want a true answer, not just one that will make you happy."

"Yes!" he shouted.

"Spirits, hear my call!" she shouted back more loudly. "Answer this man's question, with absolute truth, for he insists on the absolute."

The man said, "Forget the mumbo jumbo! Tell me now!"

Adelaide walked forward to the very edge of the stage, stared down at the man, and said, "Very well. No."

"No?"

"The woman you love," said Adelaide. "She doesn't love you."

I could hear Scarlett take in her breath. This wasn't how things were supposed to go. I'd seen the second sight act over and over, and I knew the news was always, always good. If she couldn't find something nice to say, Adelaide would either shake her head and complain that the spirits wouldn't come clear tonight or she would make some vague pronouncement about a journey, one that shouldn't be undertaken without purpose. It had never happened like this.

The man's voice sounded strangled as he said, improbably, "Thank you."

Adelaide raised both arms, turned like a whirlwind, and said, "The spirits are with us tonight! Shall we see what else they have in store?" It was the cue for the Hindoo dancing girls, and they all swirled out of the wings to the sound of a high piping flute, spinning almost too fast to follow.

Adelaide herself exited the stage on our side, and I didn't see until then how deathly pale she was. But there was no time to talk. She turned her back on me and shrugged into the gown Jeannie held out for her, checking the hidden pockets for props, making sure everything was in place. Then she was dressed and out onstage again, weaving in and among the dancing girls.

Jeannie and I looked at each other, worried.

"Is it real?" I asked her.

She said, "I don't know. I honestly don't."

That night was a quiet one, so quiet that when the sound of a brandy glass breaking against the side of Madame's railcar came much later, it rang out almost like a gunshot. None of us slept well.

■ ■ ■ ■

Two days later at breakfast, I was tearing a roll in half and wishing for butter when the mostly recovered Miranda slid carefully onto the bench beside me. She set a newspaper on the table.

"Is this him?" she asked without preamble.

"Who?"

She pointed, and I picked up the paper. The front page headline screamed: NATIVE SON SLAYS FIANCÉE, SELF IN TRAGIC MURDER-SUICIDE. There were two pictures. The woman was unfamiliar. She had a heart-shaped face and was pretty in the way that all rich girls are pretty, smooth-skinned and unmemorable. The man, on the other hand, I recognized instantly. His receding hairline, his remaining brown hair woolly and uncombed.

It was the man who'd asked the question in Hartford and gotten his answer.

I opened my mouth, but before I could speak, the paper bowed in the middle and crumpled, torn from my hands. I looked up to see who'd done it. The person holding the remains of the crumpled paper was Adelaide.

"Bad luck to read bad news," she said.

"I'll take this."

I knew I should remain silent, but I was still in shock. I'd never known anyone who died. I didn't really know this man — I had only ever seen him the one time — but I felt responsible for him somehow. I wondered if Adelaide felt the same way. She'd told him the woman he loved didn't love him. She'd said it flat out. It seemed he'd taken action, in the most terrible way.

"What happened?" I asked her.

I didn't expect an answer, but she gave me one, of sorts.

"Too much truth is dangerous," said Adelaide. "For all of us."

CHAPTER EIGHTEEN

Janesville, 1905
Three o'clock in the morning
She looks distraught now. The tears on her face are different from her earlier tears. Her whole face seems to blur with sadness. He reaches out with his handkerchief to dab her tears without being asked. She doesn't thank him.

"Was it real?" he asks intently, standing over her, staring down.

"I thought about it a lot, for a while," she says. "That man, that answer. I don't know how she could have known what he was asking, but she did. On the other hand, none of the rest of her magic was real, so why would that have been?"

"None of the rest was real?"

She nods. "Nothing she did onstage, none of her illusions. Lady to Tiger, the Dancing Odalisque, Light and Heavy Chest, all of them were mechanical. Different secrets, but knowable ones. Mirrors, misdirection, sets, costumes. She taught me the tools to manipulate the audience's reality. It's amazing how you can make people think they're seeing something they're not. Especially when they want to believe. Then there's nothing easier."

He prods, "And then what happened?"

"After the second sight act?"

"Yes."

Her shoulders sink. "Nothing was the same. Adelaide just — she just — didn't care anymore. She didn't say why, but it was obvious. Two people had died because of her words. Because of what she'd said to him in that theater. Had she said something different, or nothing at all, he might not have killed himself and that poor young woman."

"She thought it was her fault? But she couldn't know for sure, could she?"

"She was sure enough," she says grimly. "It was like a light went out inside her. She did all the same illusions, with all the same results, but they didn't make people want to stand up and applaud. Audiences lost interest. Somehow there was no magic in her magic. And of course, she never did the second sight act again."

"But what happened? Did people stop

coming to see her? Did she quit? Did something else happen to her, once she stopped caring?"

The magician gathers herself and speaks more crisply, shaking off the rough, wet sound of her earlier tears. "What happened was nothing. She performed the shows that were already booked, but she didn't book any new ones. She wrote off the future. I asked about it once, and she told me to mind my own business, that if she wanted to drop off the edge of the world, she'd drop off on her own time and thank you very much, so I never asked again."

His exhaustion strikes him then, out of nowhere. The adrenaline and the story have been carrying him. But there's something about knowing that a successful woman like Adelaide Herrmann — the name sounds familiar, this part of the story must be true — could just crumple into nothingness. It reminds him that he, who is far less, has little to hope for.

He thinks about sneaking a look at his pocket watch but resists. He knows what he needs to know about what time it is. Evening is long gone and the night is headed toward morning. Time is running out.

He says, "She was like a mother to you."

"She was. Like a mother isn't the same as

a mother, is it?"

"No."

She eyes him, saying, "Tell me about your mother."

"She's dead," he says. "She died in childbirth. I never knew her at all."

"I'm so sorry, officer. I mean that. I can't think of anything sadder."

"Oh, I'm sure you can," he says gruffly and walks back to his desk while he collects himself. He makes another decision. He crouches down behind the desk, pretending to look for something, so she can't see. He unbuckles his holster and slides the whole thing, holster, gun, and all, into the bottom drawer. He uses the key from his belt to lock the desk. Hiding the gun leaves him defenseless, but he's not worried about that. He's far more worried about her using it against him. He can't think of a way she could possibly escape the wrist cuffs, but then again, he couldn't think of a way she could escape the ankle cuffs, and she's already done that. He has to calculate the risks, and based on the calculation, do the best he can.

At length, he turns back to her and says, "Adelaide's magic wasn't real then. But yours is."

"Not what I do onstage."

"Even the man you heal at the end of the Halved Man?"

"No. That's a trick. I told you already."

"Always?"

"Always. But you would believe me if I told you it was real, wouldn't you? You believe in magic."

"Does it matter?" he stalls.

She says, "It's interesting. I just wouldn't think it of you. A practical young lawman. I would've thought you more — skeptical."

He's surprised when an explanation comes easily to his lips. This, like the truth about feeling like Iris's second choice, he's never told anyone. "My mother believed in it. I was told so, anyway. Small magic. The idea that people can sometimes do little things, for themselves or each other, that make life easier. Soothe babies. Encourage crops. Calm disagreements. Each according to their particular gifts."

"Did you get Iris with small magic? Pry her away from her suitor? Put the other girl in his way?" she asks with a glint of mischief.

He knows her motives. He knows she wants to distract him, get him off the subject of her healing powers. He looks down to where her wrists are still linked tight to the chair and allows himself to feel superior for just a moment. Concentrating, he keeps a neutral expression on his face.

"She knew how I felt about her, even when she was together with Mose. I was patient. Then after Mose's family announced his engagement to Prudie, she became much more receptive. I saw my opportunity, and I took it."

"I think she's better off with you," she says, which surprises him, largely because it's certainly not true.

Had she chosen Mose and he her, Iris would be married to a county sheriff instead of the only lawman in a one-horse town, a lawman who might not even keep that position for long, given what's happened. Their family is still just the two of them, two years after the wedding, and she'd give anything for the baby that Prudie has. No, she's not better off at all. He recognizes the magician's empty flattery for what it is.

"Oh, ma'am. Don't be obvious," he says.

"Just so." She bobs her head, a quick nod of acknowledgment. It doesn't seem to bother her at all to be found out. "But right now, I'd like to ask you to do one kind thing for me. Would you?"

He braces himself but asks innocently, "What thing?"

"Take one pair of cuffs off my wrists?"

"Why would I do that?"

"Because you're kind. Because they're cutting me. Because there are still two left, so it doesn't make any difference. It's a favor. If you could do me just this one favor, I'd owe you, wouldn't I?"

"Do you ever expect to be in a position to do me a favor?" he asks. Then his heartbeat begins to speed up as he answers the question for himself before she even speaks.

"Never know," she replies.

"It would have to be a big favor, wouldn't it?"

"I imagine it would."

He knows it's unwise, but his mind is churning and churning. If she can do the favor he wants her to, it will change everything. Too soon to ask now, but not too soon to start laying a foundation. Doing her a kindness can't hurt his case. If they can be cordial with each other like this, it's a breakthrough.

Pulling the key on a long string from his belt, he unlocks the bottom cuff from her right wrist, then her left. Now only two steel circles are stacked on each wrist, with two chains stringing the distance between them.

"Thank you," she says softly.

He's relieved she didn't try at all to kick or bite him or dash her skull against his while he was so close to her. She knows the exact spot of his weakness, that bullet hiding in his back, waiting to kill him. Either she genuinely trusts him or she's playing a longer con. As much as she's told him, he still doesn't know which is more likely.

Right now, she looks helpless. Bound to a hard chair in a small room with a locked door. Trapped, pinned down. Fragile in her useless finery.

As if she can feel him trying to read her, she says, "You still think I'm some kind of monster, don't you? A dangerous creature? But I'm not. I'm just like you, trying to get by."

"You're not like me."

"You're a good person," she says with enough force that he almost believes she means it. "So maybe not. You gave me that whole apple to eat instead of keeping it for yourself, which was a kind thing to do. You took off the cuffs when I asked, and I appreciate that. My wrist feels much better, by the way. I could sit the rest of the night like this now. So let me do something for you."

"No."

"You don't even know what I mean to say!"

"Then say it."

She turns her fierce gaze on him, three-quarters blue, one-quarter brown, and says intently, "Ask me one question and I'll answer. Yes or no. Any question at all."

Without the slightest pause, he asks, "Did you kill your husband?"

"Absolutely not."

"How do I know you're not lying?"

There is a pause. The beads on her dress clack softly as she shifts position, tucking her legs demurely to one side, one ankle crossed over the other. She looks down at her ankles and the silver cuffs still attached to them and back up into his eyes once more.

Then she says, "I said one question, not two."

"All right," he says, resigned and exhausted. Maybe they haven't made much of a breakthrough after all. "Tell me what happened to Adelaide."

CHAPTER NINETEEN

1900
Woman on Fire
After a final show in New York, an empty road stretched out ahead of us. Not the right kind of road, to say the least. Emptiness, loneliness, poverty, and worse, no bookings. The business lived and died on bookings. Every single person in the company could tell you of a case where that was literally true. Everyone knew someone whose act fell apart when they couldn't get booked, ended up in the poorhouse, and then one way or another — starvation, illegal behavior, bad company — met an untimely demise.

I didn't want to become one of those people. But I didn't know how I would go forward, how I would forge a new life. I didn't want to give up the nightly ritual of applause, which had become like air to me. I needed to be onstage. Perhaps I could find another job dancing on Broadway, but I wouldn't be content in the fourth row of four anymore, and I was older now than the average chorus girl. I had turned seventeen, eighteen, nineteen, twenty, all without fanfare. If I couldn't perform, I might be driven back to service, but that was also a poor answer. My skills onstage were unusual, maybe even unique; I was far less remarkable in a parlor or a laundry room. Given all this, I sank into a sadness. I knew a happy ending wasn't the only kind of ending I might have.

We returned to New York for Adelaide's last show. The city had changed in the years I'd been gone. Where there used to be a reservoir on Forty-Second Street, now they were building a great, huge marble palace. I couldn't tell what it was going to be, but it was going to be grand. A new terminal for the Grand Central Railroad was also under construction, and there were so many electric lights that the city seemed to glow at night in every direction. There was more of everything. I found it just as overwhelming as I had when I rode into the city for the first time, yet the energy was undeniable, and I could understand why people gravitated toward this place.

Our last show, at the Casino on Broadway at West Thirty-Ninth, was a celebration. Adelaide seemed to regain all that she had lost, just for the night. It was beautiful. The crowd was our happiest crowd, and our peaks were our highest peaks. Our magic was flawless, our dances magnificent, our music enchanting. Adelaide was generous and beautiful and impressive. The audience clapped for us, appreciated us, loved us.

We closed the show with the Navajo Fire. It was not our most elaborate illusion, but it always pleased the crowd. There were five of us dancers in buckskin fringe with feathers on our heads, but we looked like a lot more, whirling in a circle with long scarves. We pantomimed capturing Adelaide and tying her to a tree then danced around her in celebration, whooping and stomping. But we, foolish tribesmen, hadn't reckoned on her magic. She got one arm free and raised it. All she needed to do was snap her fingers, and the dancing Indian nearest her vanished in a plume of fire, leaving nothing but smoke. We danced on, seeming not to notice, until she snapped her fingers again and another of us disappeared. By then it was too late: snap, snap, snap; gone, gone, gone. At the end, Adelaide stood alone. Usually, she clapped her hands and the rope holding her to the tree fell away, freeing her in a flash, and she strode out to the apron of the stage to do either the second sight act or one final card flourish to close the show. But this last night, instead, she snapped her fingers a sixth time, and she too became fire and then smoke, and she too disappeared.

The audience's thundering applause in the dark was the loudest, most welcome sound in the world.

Everyone dispersed afterward, almost immediately. No one even lingered to say good-bye. But I knew where Adelaide would be, in her railcar. It was parked in the Grand Central yard for the night. And when I knocked on the door, she answered and poured me a brandy just like hers, halfway up the glass.

"Where will you go?" I asked.

"I'm moving out to a farm on Long Island," she said. "No more road. No more travel. None of this."

I began to cry.

"Stop that," she said. "If you let this be the end for you, you're not the girl I think you are."

"I just want one night to be sad."

"A night's too much," she replied. "You have three minutes."

For three minutes, we sat in silence, sipping our brandy. The artwork on the wall was familiar enough now that I felt the painted ladies and gentlemen were my good friends. It seemed I would never see their faces again.

She flipped open her pocket watch, which had been Alexander's, and said, "Time's up. How do you feel?"

"Not sad anymore," I lied.

"Good."

I sipped my brandy again.

"Because I have something I want to tell you," said Adelaide.

"Yes?"

"Vivi, I'm proud of you."

"Thank you," I said, trying hard not to cry again and failing.

"Oh, toughen up. It's not the end of the world."

"It's the end of my world," I said.

"And you don't think it's the end of mine? I've been at this a lot longer than you. I've lost a lot more than you've lost."

"That's not what I meant."

"I understand, chérie," she said gently. "You're young. When you're older, you'll understand. Life is long. If you're lucky. You never know what it will bring."

I replied, "So you think there could be

other things as wonderful as working in your show?"

"For you? Absolutely."

"Such as?"

Raising her glass, she said, "Working in your own show."

"I don't think I'm ready," I said.

"You're ready."

"But I'm not like you," I said. "I'm not strong enough. I can't fake it. I can't build a world out of nothing."

"You don't have to. You've already got it."

"I've got a fat goose egg," I said, frustrated.

"Don't be stupid," she said. "Listen to what I'm saying. I'm giving it to you."

"What?"

"I'm not proposing you make something out of nothing. I'm proposing you take over what's already here. I'm handing the company over to you."

It was starting to sink in. I was overwhelmed. "Truly?"

"Close your mouth. You'll catch flies," she said. "Honestly. You're smart enough, Vivi. I assumed you'd thought of this."

"I didn't," I said, but I realized I should have. I'd been too busy mourning our demise without stopping to check first if we were dead. Adelaide leaving the business didn't mean the show couldn't go on. Not if someone else was willing to step up and be Adelaide.

And she wanted that person to be me.

"No guarantees," she said. "If things fall apart, things fall apart. I won't come to rescue you. If your employees desert and your animals escape and the audiences throw horse apples on the stage, that's your own problem, not mine."

"I understand."

She said, "I'm doing the best I can for you. You can have the sets, the illusions, the whole noodle. In return, I want a cut. Twenty percent."

"I'll give you ten," I answered quickly.

She roared with laughter, wiped her mouth, and said, "That's adorable. I'll take twenty."

"Thank you. I don't know what to say."

"Don't say anything. Just make good at the box office and keep me happily retired."

"I'll do my best."

"Oh," she said. "One other condition."

"What's that?"

"I hired you a manager," said Adelaide. "A sharp young man. You're great onstage, but you're ignorant of the business."

I couldn't disagree.

"He'll protect my investment, keep an eye

on you, book your circuits. Cut the checks and all that."

"Experienced?"

"Not as much as some. But he knows what he's doing."

And just like that, there was a knock on the door.

"How did you do that?" I asked.

"Magic." She smiled, going to open it.

I heard a low voice, a man's voice, in the darkness. His tone was light and teasing. Adelaide laughed and said, "Yes, perfect, right on time."

The low voice rumbled again, but I was seated too far from the door and couldn't hear his words. I sipped at the last of my brandy.

"Well, come on in then," she said. "Come and meet my protégée. Or should I say, meet her again."

He stepped up into the railcar, and my world tilted on its axis.

The first thing I noticed was his dark hair. It looked like it was wet. And though I would never have been able to describe him to a stranger, once I saw him again, I recognized everything. The familiar slant of his shoulders. Thick fingers and forearms that showed his ability to dig. The way he leaned forward a little, even at rest, as if something interesting were always right in front of him. The intensity.

And that smile. I knew that smile.

"It's good to see you, Ada."

"It is not good to see you, Clyde."

"You jackass," Madame said to him. "You said she liked you."

"She did," he said, a familiar softness in his voice. "Very much."

"Once upon a time," I said frostily. "Madame, this man doesn't keep his word. He can't be trusted."

"Addie," he said, "have I ever steered you wrong?"

She looked back and forth between our faces, reading us both. "You haven't," she told him.

"But he was — he once —" I searched for the right words. "He broke my heart."

"Did I?"

I said, "He told me he would be honest, and then he deceived me. On an important matter. How could I trust him to have my best interests in mind?"

Adelaide replied, "Well, that's very odd to hear, considering . . ."

"Considering what?"

Clyde said to me, "I told her who you were and where to find you. Back when you were in the chorus. It's why she hired you,

270

and why you're here."

I turned to Madame for confirmation, and she nodded. "He did. He suggested you, insisted I go to watch you dance, said you were perfect for the company. When your predecessor had to leave the business."

"The pregnant girl?" I asked, suspicious, eyeing Clyde.

"Yes."

He caught my look. "Good God, Ada, it wasn't me."

I shrugged.

Adelaide said, "Here's the trick to it, Vivi. The deal's already done. You take the company, I take my cut, he's your manager. It's a solid deal. If the two of you can't work together, fine. It would be a tragedy, of course."

"Because?"

She said, "I would be very sad that you'd decided to leave a business that suits you so very well."

I knew what she meant. I was still reeling from all this — Clyde Garber not only in my present, but also more involved than I'd known in my past and with a proposed role in my future — but I wasn't slow, despite the brandy. If the deal was done, it was done. And just because it wasn't what I expected didn't mean it wasn't good for me.

Rushing to say yes and rushing to say no were mistakes in equal measure. I needed to think it through.

At length, I said, "All right."

"You two will have a lot to talk about." She stood. "I'm going to go for a walk."

"A walk? Are you sure? In the dark?" I asked.

"Aren't you sweet," said Adelaide. "I am walking as far as the next tavern, because I am going to get good and drunk just once more in New York City before I leave it forever."

"Thank you," I told her as she left, and she did the most typical thing she possibly could have done: she pretended not to hear me at all.

Then Clyde and I were alone again, together, for the first time in years. He smiled at me the same, the shape of his body under his clothes was the same, the warm look in his eyes was the same. It was so familiar that it hurt.

"So," I said. "You again."

"You again," he echoed, grinning.

"I don't see why you think I should be happy about this."

"Because your life is coming up roses?"

"An interesting way to put it. So you're not a gardener anymore, I see."

"A lot has happened to both of us," he said. "Look. I understand why you were angry, why you ran away. It took me a while to figure out. I hurt you. I didn't mean to, but I did, and I'm sorry."

He sounded sincere. Of course, he'd sounded just as sincere, years before.

"But we were kids then," he said. "Weren't we? Just stupid kids."

"Speak for yourself."

"Okay. Two of us were kids and one of us was stupid. Me. You can let it go now. Water under the bridge. You have to find a way to trust me."

His insistence made me push back. It was a reflex. "No, I don't."

"Ada," he said. "Please. For once. Don't resist."

"The hell I won't. What's to stop me from firing you?"

"Addie says you have to work with me."

"Addie knows how good I am at what I do." My confidence was bolstered by the brandy, and I let myself be bold. "I'm not replaceable. But I bet you are. And I bet I can convince her of that."

He extended his hands, palms up. "Maybe you could. Or maybe not. Why take the risk? Wouldn't it be easier just to work with me? And let the past be past?"

"I don't know."

"This is a good opportunity, Ada. No, an amazing one. Addie thinks you're incredible, and I'm inclined to agree with her. If you don't do it this way, you'll have to build your own company from the ground up. Are you prepared for that?"

"Sure," I lied.

"But this would be better. So much better. And you'd be willing to let that go because of a teenage grudge?"

"You make it sound like it was nothing," I said hotly. "It was not nothing." His argument was solid and logical, but the history between us was beyond logic, and I wanted to be sure he wasn't taking me lightly.

"I know," he said, "I know. But think about what good sense it makes to do it this way. Forget our history. Pretend we're meeting new, and we're just colleagues. Professionals. Can we do that?"

Finally I had to admit it was the right choice, at least for the present. I lifted my chin. "I can, anyway. I don't know about you."

"That'll do for now, I suppose. Would you like to have some supper?"

"No," I said. "I'm not hungry."

"All right. You want to be businesslike?" he said, sounding resigned. "Then let's do some business. Come on."

We walked out into the night, and as we walked, he told me his story in an unending stream of patter. Mr. Olmsted, who had once promised him a job, wasn't in the city when we arrived, but he had provided an introduction to a Mr. Hastings, who was key in the design for a new library building, replacing the Croton Reservoir. Clyde worked for Hastings & Cutter as a general errand boy, delivering plans and managing supplies in support of every kind of construction from churches to theaters. He met the managers of the best theaters in New York, charming a few of them, and saw an opportunity. He announced his availability as a talent scout to agents who managed acts in the city, charging each one well under market rate but making ends meet by attaching himself to half a dozen. When the time was right, he chose one agent to assist full-time, who happened to be Adelaide's agent, for whom he scouted talent all up and down Broadway. That was when he'd spotted me in the chorus of *The Belle of New York,* and when Adelaide needed a new Odalisque, he suggested my name. In the years since, he'd become a full-time talent manager himself, booking acts onto vaude-ville circuits all throughout the East, having some solid success. And although Adelaide was too loyal to abandon the agent who'd been with her and Alexander since the beginning, her retirement opened up this new possibility, and for me, she wanted a younger and savvier man.

Listening to his familiar voice and walking next to him made me feel fifteen years old again, young and foolish. By many standards, I was still young, but I hadn't felt that way since the day the train took me away from New York the very first time and Adelaide told me to write down my address for the boy. I'd felt like a grown-up then, like someone with the world waiting on her. I'd felt old when I was young. Now it was all reversed. I was only angry because he'd fooled me, once upon a time. He was right that it would be easier to work with him than to force him out. In this case, perhaps the devil I knew was better than a devil I didn't. Now all I had to figure out was whether my professionalism was stronger than my pride.

Fifth Avenue was broad and long, and at this time of night, empty. It was cold enough that I could see not only my own breath in the night air but also his, and there was something intimate in that sight. I snuck a peek at him. The arched eyebrows and the

276

high cheekbones, they hadn't changed. He looked a little wider in the shoulders, and he wore thin-rimmed eyeglasses over those piercing blue eyes, but otherwise, he was the same. I knew he was examining me just as closely, though I pretended not to see. I turned my gaze back to Fifth Avenue.

The mansions were stunning. Broad-shouldered and pale and grand, each and every one. They loomed out of the darkness like sleeping giants, noble and silent. Most had the faint glow of lights deep within, veiled behind lace curtains and velvet drapes. Despite how large the windows were, you couldn't make out even the faintest shape of what was inside. You had to imagine. Their faces were blank and forbidding. I'd heard about them, of course, but I'd never walked into this part of the city.

As if he could hear my thoughts, he said, "You've never been here before?"

"No."

"Why not?"

"Never had a reason," I said.

"I love New York," he said. "No matter how long you're here, there's always something else to see."

"But there's a whole country to be seen too. Not just this one city."

"Then I suppose we're both best off doing what we do. I'll hold down the fort here, operating out of the Broadway office, and you'll take to the tracks."

That heartened me some. Adelaide insisted we work together, but we wouldn't really be together at all. Perhaps it wouldn't be so bad. Casually, I responded, "Oh yes. I'd almost forgotten why you're here."

"Never forget the bigger picture, Ada."

"Don't lecture me," I snapped back. "I don't see any gray hairs on your head."

"Sorry. Sorry. Anyway, here we are."

He gestured up at an imposing marble building, one that looked just as much like a mansion as the rest, but with no signs of life inside.

"The Lenox Library," he said.

The building was enormous and white, and I could feel the cold radiating off its surface. Two imposing wings jutted out toward the street while the central entrance sat demurely within a large courtyard, recessed and regal. Huge arched windows were arrayed on the first and second floors. On the first floor, each arch was large enough to drive a carriage through, but only the top half of each window was glassed, to keep out prying eyes. On the second floor, the windows were even grander, furnished with six separate panes of glass, curved gracefully on the top but solid and rectangular at the middle and on the bottom. The center of the building had a third floor, with smaller windows, paired and rectangular. From here, they resembled French doors, but at such a distance, it was impossible to know their true size. Both wings of the building were crowned with Greek-looking pediments, intricately carved, but with what I couldn't say, as they were so far overhead, nearly disappearing into the darkened sky.

I had to admit the entire effect was breathtaking. "It's beautiful."

He led me away from the street, around the side of the building — no small distance — toward a series of low windows. He counted under his breath, one two three four from the left, and crouched in front of a window that looked identical to the others.

"In case you ever need to know this," he said, "the best way to get through a lock isn't to pick it. It's to slip something in between the bolt and the frame so it never locks in the first place."

He reached down and swung the glass of the window open, as silky silent as you please, and gestured for me to proceed through the open window, which I did gladly and landed softly on a floor not too far down. He followed.

Once we were inside, he turned back to me from the dark and said, "Welcome to the whole world." I looked around, letting my eyes adjust to the dim light from the high windows.

Books.

Shelves of them, walls of them. Down to our feet and high above our heads. Books everywhere. The last time I'd seen shelves of books was back at the Biltmore, in the library where we first began our affair, but these shelves held twenty, thirty, fifty times more. It was stunning. I didn't realize how much I'd missed them. I wanted to run my fingers along the endless series of spines, rub my cheek against the cloth and leather covers, press my nose into the pages and inhale until I was drunk on the smell of old paper.

"All the books anyone could ever want," he said. "And this is only half of what's going to be in the public library. All these, and all the books from the Astor Library, that'll be the start of the collection. For anyone to read."

"It's amazing." I couldn't help whispering, staring up at the rows on rows of spines stretching out into the distance. I knew it wouldn't last — we weren't supposed to be here, and I doubted we'd stay long — but it still felt like a sort of homecoming.

"And tonight it's ours," he said.

"No watchmen?"

"The watchmen are at the front doors, the main entrance," said Clyde, gesturing to indicate I should follow him along a row, which I did. "They won't bother us."

"What won't they bother us doing?" I asked, suspicious.

"We're going to find you a name."

"Why?"

"No one goes to see the Amazing Ada. Or the Amazing — what did she call you?" he said.

"Vivi."

"Vivi? Awful. Won't do."

"You have a better idea?"

"I'm full of ideas," he said and then, jauntily, "Oh, don't look at me in that tone of voice. Come on."

We stopped in front of a shelf next to another window, this one larger and higher than the one where we'd come in. With only two of us here in the huge dark space, only a small puddle of light around us, it felt like the most private place in the world. It was warm. Clyde shed his overcoat, and I followed suit, letting the coat fall in a heap at the end of the shelf before we stepped further in.

"Duck, duck, duck, duck," he said, running his finger over a long row of books and then stopping at a series of matching brown spines, "goose."

I leaned in to read the gold lettering. "Shakespeare?"

"Only the best," he said. He reached for the leftmost book and opened it.

I brought my face close to the book — *The Merchant of Venice* — so I could make out the words in the dim light. He leaned closer, but not too close. He brushed his finger across the page, saying, "Portia?"

"It might suffice," I said.

"It won't." He took the book from my hands, tucked it back into its place, and handed me the next.

I flipped the pages into motion then stopped them with an outstretched finger. "Here. How about Cressida?"

"No, not enough poetry to it. Cress is like salad," said Clyde.

He lowered his hand on top of mine and removed it from between the pages, sending a long and trembling shiver up my arm like the bubbles in champagne.

I jerked my hand back. It was a powerful reminder, and I knew it was the moment to speak.

"Clyde," I said.

He turned to look at me, and I held his gaze. "Yes?"

Then I said, sharply so he couldn't mistake me, "Look. We need to work together. That's a fact. And I'll do it because it's necessary and for Adelaide's sake. But let me make this clear. If you touch me again, I'll kill you."

Nothing registered on his face. Not surprise or fear or amusement. Nothing at all.

After a pause, he said, "You won't."

"You doubt me?"

"No," he said calmly. "I don't doubt you in the least. What I mean is, I won't give you cause."

I had no idea whether to believe him. But I'd made myself clear, and at the moment, I could do no more.

We tried book after book. Juliet was too obvious, he said; Constance sent the wrong message, I countered. He suggested Lavinia, but I refused to be named after a girl with her hands cut off and her tongue cut out.

Just when it seemed we'd never reach agreement, he said, "Here! I found it."

"Okay. Tell me."

"Arden," he said.

"No," I said, "that's not right. There's no

character anywhere in Shakespeare named Arden."

"You're right. But you're wrong."

He brought the book closer to my face so I could see. The word was right there at the tip of his finger. Arden.

They say he is already in the forest of Arden, and a many merry men with him; and there they live like the old Robin Hood of England. They say many young gentlemen flock to him every day, and fleet the time carelessly, as they did in the golden world.

"The first time I read this," said Clyde, "it sounded like heaven to me."

" 'Fleet the time carelessly, as they did in the golden world,' " I said. "It does sound wonderful."

"And there's this," he said, closing the book and showing me the tiny raised letters along the bottom of the spine, which I'd missed in the dim light: The Arden Shakespeare.

"Arden. Do you think it's a sign?" I asked.

"I do."

It seemed right to me somehow. "All right then."

"All right. You have a company. You have a name. You have a manager. I think we're in business. Only one thing left to do. Shake on it."

"I suppose."

He lifted his hand then hesitated, looking down. "Though you said not to touch you."

"For a handshake, this once, I'll make an exception."

"Truce, Arden?" he said, and offered his hand.

"Truce," I echoed, and shook it.

Chapter Twenty

1900

Light and Heavy Chest

As the Amazing Arden, I booked a dozen shows before I'd even performed my first. Part of it was Clyde's hustle and his excellent connections. But part of my appeal was inherent. A female illusionist was a true curiosity. There were no others. Men were the magicians and women the assistants, and any woman on the stage was clearly being acted upon, not acting. Wives of famous magicians were often privileged to be more active assistants than the average, but they were still merely assisting. In this world, the next-best curiosity was Harry Kellar's wife Eva, whose role in his act also included playing the cornet. Adelaide Herrmann herself had been the only true female illusionist, the only woman whose company was in her own name. And she had withdrawn from the field.

Those first weeks, I thought about her every moment, every day, wishing I had had more time with her, more guidance. But I respected her decision. She had given her youth and her looks and her husband and half her life to magic. It would be churlish to ask her to give anything more. Anything I hadn't learned in more than three years on the road with her, I would have to figure out for myself.

In the handful of years we'd been performing as a company, the competition between stage magicians had become somewhat more fierce. It was obvious there was money in magic. Vaudeville audiences enjoyed singers and dancers, but every small-town Susie with a mouth and two legs thought she was the next Lottie Collins, and magicians were somewhat harder to come by. With fewer of us available, we could negotiate for more money, because the booking agents were gladder to have us. Neither was vaudeville the only option for a magician with a good name and reputation. Harry Kellar, whose star began burning brighter after Alexander's death, even alternated tours on the road with much longer engagements in a single city. While I loved traveling, there was something that sounded utterly luxurious about a seven-month run at the Egyptian

Hall in Philadelphia. If things went well with my act, I knew settling in was a strong possibility, but for now, I knew just as certainly I had to take to the rails again.

I couldn't quite pick up where Adelaide had left off, not exactly, but neither was I starting from scratch. When the members of the company came to get their final pay from the office, I was there to explain what I needed from them. On the surface, for them, it was good news. They didn't have to go looking for something new. They could stay on in the same role for the same pay, if they chose. They only had to hold on for two weeks until our debut, not far away at the Golden Garden in the Bronx. It would be easier to stay than to go.

Explaining the situation to them one by one was excruciating. Seeing the flicker in their eyes when they saw me sitting behind the desk. The distrustful way they reached out for the check Clyde handed them. And it was unpredictable, which ones would say yes and which no. Billy seemed confused and reluctant, but in the end, agreed to stay. Jack, on the other hand, didn't even stay to hear my speech. He grabbed the check and was gone.

"We'll find someone new," Clyde said. "Don't you worry."

"I'm not worried," I said, and I wasn't.

I knew part of the gift Adelaide had given me was the freedom to make the act my own. We put half of the illusions in storage, especially the bulkier ones with the more complicated sets, and I said a fond good-bye for now to the picture frame of the Dancing Odalisque. I decided to part with the animals, reluctantly, because their care and feeding complicated things, and I didn't want to be an animal act. We sold them at auction, which I didn't attend, trusting Clyde to handle it in all aspects. I spent that afternoon with the musicians, thanking them for their service and paying them a generous farewell.

I was careful about what I kept and how to deploy it. I revised Light and Heavy Chest, planning a new presentation where larger and larger men would fail to pick it up, then smaller and smaller women would succeed. The trick was not new, but the message was. No one else dared put women above men onstage in any way. It was an outrageous statement. I hoped it would be unusual enough to begin to build my reputation. The novelty of being a woman would get audiences in the theaters once, but I needed to handle them just right once they were there.

The night of my solo debut, I trembled in the wings as I watched the audience trickle in. Even after I should have taken my position to start, I lingered with my eyes on the empty seats, praying more theatergoers would appear at the last minute.

"Arden," Clyde said from behind me. His voice was firm but not without sympathy. "You're not here to watch them. They're here to watch you."

I always fed off the energy of the crowd. I said, "I need them."

"The only one you need is you. Curtain time. Go."

I'd chosen a haunting flute, three notes repeated, as my cue to begin. Clyde signaled to the musician. The curtain began to slide aside, and as the third note sounded, I stepped onto the floorboards for my first appearance as the Amazing Arden.

I began with cards and coins, a few small tricks to warm my hands up, and immediately I realized that had been a mistake. The crowd occupied about two-thirds of the small theater, and without a strong start out of the gate, their early applause was polite and scattered. I feared their lack of enthusiasm would sink me.

Even worse, as I gestured to cue the two assistants who would help me with Light and Heavy Chest, only one appeared. Otis was here — dragging the chest behind him, because what else could he do? — but Billy hadn't shown. My mind racing, I called out to the audience for a volunteer and assigned him to help Otis carry the chest out. As a result, there were several long, still moments as I struggled to get the audience member to do what a trained assistant would have done by instinct. Still, I'd chosen luckily. He followed orders well enough. And again I chose luckily when it came time to conclude the illusion. A cheerful little girl, no more than seven years old, happily bounded up to the stage and lifted the chest in her two little hands, exclaiming in the most charming soprano voice, "My word, that was easy!" It brought the house down.

A half hour into the show, I took my first breath in the wings while Jeannie stripped off one gown and quickly buttoned me into another. Then I caught sight of Billy, chatting easily with Otis, as if he hadn't caused any trouble at all.

"You," I said.

He turned, offering a sheepish smile.

I didn't return it. "You're fired."

The smile disappeared. He said, "I had trouble finding the place."

"Funny how no one else did. You're fired,"

I said. "Get out."

He scowled and started toward me. I thought for a moment he might even hit me, but I didn't let myself cower.

Clyde clapped a hand on his shoulder and stopped him still. "We're done here."

Deliberately, silently, I turned my back.

My heart was hammering as I readied myself to go back onstage, but I wasn't sorry. Boundaries had to be set. If I didn't establish my authority now, I would never get it back. The first time had to be the only time for any misbehavior, or we'd be sunk.

That unpleasantness out of the way, I found the audience more responsive as we presented our second half hour. They applauded in the right places and laughed as they should. When I asked for volunteers, a smattering of hands went up, both male and female, which I was heartened to see.

At the end, as we made our bows and curtsies, the audience cheered us. It hadn't been the success of Adelaide's farewell show — not even an echo of it — but neither was it a failure. It would do to start with, and to build on.

With the next twelve shows set up and the logistics of the train already arranged to get us from one to the next — the gift of Adelaide's railcars, including her sumptuous home on wheels, being one of her most valuable — I knew we were only at the beginning of everything. I was ready to look forward, and go forward, an optimist.

The first month, at Clyde's suggestion, I didn't emphasize my womanhood. I wore a man's evening suit of tailcoat and trousers, carefully tailored to my slightly curved shape, complete with a matched waistcoat, white bow tie, and black top hat. It was his belief that this would make me seem even more of a novelty, a woman with the spirit of a man and yet not one. The audiences liked it fine, but I liked it less and less each night. I didn't feel like myself. As we began the second month of shows, I appeared on-stage one night in one of Adelaide's old costumes altered to fit my smaller shape, a frothy confection of white organza that made me look like an elegant ghost, and after that, the tails hung unused on one of Jeannie's costume racks. Clyde said nothing. I felt like I'd won an important victory, even though we hadn't been in battle. It was harder to hide away props and charges in the sleeves of a gown than of a tailcoat, but I assumed the challenge as part and parcel of the female magician's lot and adapted quickly.

And as the second and third months went by, every part of the act become second nature. My gestures became more confident. My patter between illusions got smoother. I developed a better sense of what played best with a particular crowd and learned how to adjust my presentation on the fly. The longer we were on the road, too, the more confident and relaxed the other performers became, and we could all feel the difference, both onstage and off. We'd started out as survivors of Adelaide's company, but now we were our own company, and I was glad.

Once things were solid enough, we hired two more performers, a round-cheeked Pennsylvania farm girl named Doreen and a dusky-skinned young woman named Giulia who could pass for Hindoo, Italian, Spanish, or any other exotic nature called for. Giulia kept her name, but Doreen I renamed Contessa. She protested that she felt odd not using her real name, and I felt a bit of Adelaide's spirit in me as I informed her, "They are all real."

And instead of hiding my gender and trying to do a man's work onstage, I redesigned the whole act to celebrate womanhood. I dreamed the name Woman on Fire and devised an illusion to match it: a young woman dances alone on a stage in a soft white light then dances with a handsome young man as the light begins to glow red like embers, and as he spins her faster and faster, she seems to explode, leaving his arms empty, and the lights give way to darkness. It could be done in nearly any theater, since the lighting did most of the work, and a nimble girl could do the rest. The implication was a bit risqué, but not too shocking for the audience if the rest of the evening were properly reserved. To balance it, I invented the Magic Milliner, a version of the Dove Pan that produced a beautiful hat out of nothingness, which one woman a night from the audience was allowed to keep. Clyde found a place below Canal to buy them by the dozens. I dropped the card tricks entirely, feeling like they didn't make sense for the new act. Instead, I taught them to the newly christened Contessa so I could call on her to fill time between illusions in an emergency and gave her several of Adelaide's treasured decks.

I also invented a new coin trick, almost by accident. For some of the close-in magic, I liked to walk down into the audience, so close to them that my skirt would brush their arms. I was spinning a silver coin between my fingers, saying, "And this coin, I must tell you, it's simply an ordinary coin.

Would anyone like to take a closer look? Prove to us all it's nothing remarkable?" And as I always did, I scanned the audience to find someone to offer the coin to then noticed an unusual pair a few rows up.

The man was brightly dressed in a resplendent suit. His silk tie was a brilliant crimson, the silk square in his pocket perfectly chosen to coordinate, in a repeating pattern of crimson and cream. The woman next to him, clearly his wife, was drab by comparison, in a faded dress the color of bricks. She was craning her neck to get a closer look at the coin, her hand outstretched, offering to take the coin for examination. Her husband, not even glancing her way, pushed her hand back down to her lap, not gently, and reached his own hand out instead.

I felt sorry for the woman, clearly the peahen to a peacock, and I wanted to do something for her. The idea came to me immediately. "Ah, I seem short of coins tonight. Sir, might I have the coins from your pocket?"

Clearly proud to be singled out, the man didn't hesitate. He produced a leather wallet and poured a small river of coins into my waiting hands. I also asked for and received the square of silk from his pocket, wrapping the coins inside. I raised the bundle over my head, shaking it vehemently, repeating the words "Shake, shake, shake, shake." On the final shake, I thrust my hands upward, and the square of silk flew up into the air, empty, and fluttered slowly back down to earth.

There was a murmur, and people looked around.

"Madam," I said to the peahen, "if you'll look into your purse, you might find a pleasant surprise."

She opened the purse, and with a cry of delight, pulled out her own coin purse, now heavy with her husband's coins.

I announced to the crowd, "You see here I've taken the money from a husband's pocket and put it in his wife's. And this is what we call the Fair Shake."

The applause started immediately, but what truly gave me joy was seeing how the woman put the purse in her lap, coins still inside, and folded her hands over it with a satisfied smile.

The new act was a hit. I noticed right away, after only a few weeks, that the audiences were changing. Not only were we filling the house, but there were different people in the crowd. More women, of every stripe. Contessa remarked on it, and so did Otis.

The whole company realized that we were doing something no one else had done, and it was a source of joy to us as well as them.

It was not a bad life. It wasn't perfect, but it was good. And I was becoming more of a success every show, every night. I wasn't into the big time yet, but the whole company could feel that we were headed in that direction. Clyde had booked individual shows at first, but as my reputation began to spread, we were ready for our first three-month vaudeville circuit. We began in the South, a lovely place to spend the winter, and traveled through Georgia, Mississippi, Arkansas, and Louisiana, concluding with a performance in New Orleans at the St. Charles Theatre that took my breath away. The applause got louder, and every night as I heard excitement and surprise ripple through the crowd, I felt ever more powerful. The optimism I had forced myself to adopt in the beginning was now earned, and I couldn't imagine feeling any other way.

And the truce with Clyde held. We worked together exactly as Adelaide had intended; I was the performer, the creative one, and he had the head for business. He spent most of his time in New York while I was on the road, but I returned to the city once a month, and we went over the books and the act and our plans for the future. He occasionally bristled at my suggestions for new illusions — "Why fix what isn't broken?" he'd ask and expect an answer — but once he saw how the attendance numbers were not just holding but rising, there were few complaints.

The more time I spent with him, the more I came to respect him. He was sharp as a tack and good with numbers. Keeping track of who owed us money and who we owed money to would have driven me to distraction; he not only embraced it, but also displayed a gift for getting reluctant debtors to cough up what was past due. He put on his wire-rimmed eyeglasses and leaned over the columns of numbers as if nothing in the world was more important than those little red and black figures. When I heard him talking to theater managers, I was always impressed with how natural the conversation sounded, as if every man running every theater was his true friend. There were still elements of his character I wasn't sure about — his tales of what he'd done in New York City were endless and seemed like years' worth, not months — but he was a man of his word. Other than the handshake I'd agreed to in the library, he never even tried to touch me. If from time to time I looked down at his well-kept fingernails and remembered the feeling of them years before, gritty with dirt from the rose garden, hauling my bare legs up onto his lap, I brushed it away instantly and came back to the present. We were no longer the children we'd once been.

Chapter Twenty-One

1901

The Suffragette's Trunk

After six months, everything felt stable enough to build on. The company grew and so did the act. We began a northeastern circuit, playing midsize cities, some large theaters, some small. We played to a packed house at the Leonard Block in Taunton, which seated a few hundred, and at the much larger Mechanics Hall in Worcester, more than half of the seats went begging. Even when I knew there was no difference in size between the two audiences, I hated to see empty chairs. Without applause, I couldn't breathe. With it, I felt all-powerful. And as the tour proceeded, even the larger halls began to fill up.

Like Adelaide had done, I gave my favorite girls more responsibilities onstage, and while I was certainly the main attraction, we had a dozen wonderful players, and I wanted to show them all off. Doreen, as Contessa, had developed an impressive talent for fire dancing, so she had her own spotlight, in between the Magic Milliner and the Fair Shake. I brought the Dancing Odalisque out of storage and asked Giulia to invent her own new spin on it, and she came back with the suggestion we make the girl in the picture Botticelli's Venus and worked with Jeannie to design a costume that cloaked everything precious while seeming to reveal all. Clyde and I discussed its potential and agreed it would be a knockout. It was a hit with the husbands whose wives had dragged them to the show, for certain. The night we performed it in Springfield, rose after rose flew through the air and landed at our makeshift goddess's feet. A true performer, she did not bend to pick them up. But afterward, I saw the flush in her cheek and smiled that I'd played a part in making the girl so happy.

It was good that I was revising and enhancing the act, since we soon found that my success had inspired some imitators. Clyde brought me word that Arthur Burlingame, an established illusionist in the South, was performing an illusion he called the Enchanted Hat, quite similar to my own Magic Milliner. Other magicians had made key changes to their acts as well. While no one else was bold enough to give a woman billing equal to a man's, they added to the roles of their female assistants and made their dancers more prominent, to appeal to some of what we'd awoken in the audience's minds. I smiled to myself even as I muttered under my breath that we'd have to do more, do better, to stay ahead.

While my competitors aped the illusions I'd already done, I worked on newer and more elaborate illusions. One of my favorites was called the Suffragette's Trunk. It was a variation on a well-known trick called the Saratoga Trunk Mystery, where a man puts a woman into a large bag, locks her in a trunk, then sits atop the trunk. Assistants raise a cloth in front of him, and when they pull it away, the woman is sitting atop the trunk with the man inside, tied in the bag. The mechanisms were simple. There was a false seam in the bottom of the bag where the woman could slip out; there was a panel in the trunk that slid open for the players to make the switch. The main issue was making sure the players moved very, very quickly, as the longer the curtain was up, the less impressive the switch was to the audience. I made it far harder. In the Suffragette's Trunk, the man and woman took their positions in the bag and the trunk just the same as the Saratoga, but when the curtain was pulled away, the woman was not only sitting on top of the trunk, she was wearing the man's suit. The man, when freed from the bag, was wearing the woman's dress. Jeannie, always a genius, had made tearaway clothes for Otis and a new girl named Della, so all they had to do was pull off their first outfits to reveal the second ones underneath. Della was pert and pretty in a brown tweed three-piece suit, and Otis was perfectly lovely in a dress of emerald-green serge. In some cities, the audience laughed so hard they cried.

Also during this time, we added to the company a pair of twenty-year-old twins Clyde found for me in Ithaca who were absolutely ideal. They were like angels with their ringlets of blond hair, and they called themselves Michael and Gabriel. I would have turned them down — their pale curls reminded me of Ray's — but they were so clearly more talented and eye-catching than all the others, I set my personal feelings aside. It had been so long since Ray. He was in the past. I had only the future. I had a long solid set of bookings yet to come, and a brand new life as the Amazing Arden.

I did many things the way Adelaide had

done them, but in one area, I'd chosen to be very different. I wanted my company to feel like a family, and like the mother of any good family, I imposed rules. Every member of the company was required to eat dinner together and make conversation, telling their own stories and listening to others'. We had a very strict curfew and a ban on fraternization. The stiff punishments — a night's suspension from performance on the first violation, a week's suspension on the second, and dismissal from the company on the third — kept the boys and the girls out of each other's arms and beds. There were no repeats of young Jonah's fate. So as many young people as we added to the company, they treated each other more like brothers and sisters than anything else, which was certainly how I preferred it. My old bunkmates had all left the show when I'd taken over from Adelaide. I occasionally wondered what had become of them, but truth be told, not all that often.

Me, I had found my calling. I loved the crowd, of course. I loved magic. I loved being onstage and making things seem to happen that didn't really happen. I loved to be looked at and admired. I loved pretending to be a witch one minute and an artist the next, then a society lady, then a woman on fire. I even loved walking onto a stage in a room full of people I knew didn't like me and working hard to turn them and turn them until I'd won their favor, and at the end, they stood to applaud in a thundering crowd as loud as a train.

What I loved most about the magic I did as the Amazing Arden was that it wasn't real. I always wondered about Adelaide's second sight, and whether she had a true power by which she divined people's secrets. In my act, I left the audience's secrets alone. I wanted to dazzle them, impress them, fool them in a way that helped them escape their lives. I didn't need to know anything about them in order to do that. They could be a mystery to me the same way I was a mystery to them. My healing magic was a private secret, not something anyone needed to know or witness. I'd keep myself to myself, and all would be well.

And all was indeed well, until we played the Rialto in Poughkeepsie.

A man shouted "Charlatan!" from the audience. Not remarkable, that a man would shout, but his choice of words set me back on my heels. It was what the man in Hartford had called Adelaide, at the fateful second sight act, and I didn't care for it. But I soldiered on. The spirit of the show swept me up, and I was deep into the Magic Milliner, with a hat in my hands that I had seemingly produced from nothingness, when I heard the shout again, louder and nearer, "Charlatan!"

I wasn't on the stage. There was a little staircase we used for this illusion, so I could produce the hat and then walk down into the audience to hand it to an audience member to take home. I was halfway down the aisle, and what scared me about the shout was not its volume, but its direction; he was between me and the stage.

I held the hat above my head in both hands. Usually I would call out, "To whom shall I award this fetching chapeau?" but I couldn't focus, not with the man coming at me. He was moving slowly, but he was moving toward me, unmistakably.

A fierce cold shiver ran through my whole body, one I hadn't felt in years. I'd let down my guard. I'd been too comfortable too long. All my good luck was about to change.

Suddenly there was more light — the stagehands had turned the footlights on the audience; I'd missed my cue but they hadn't — and my vision shifted.

And for a moment, I saw Ray, hulking and dangerous and unstoppable.

It had been years, and I was no less

haunted. Suddenly my leg ached where he'd broken it, and I flexed the hand the horse had crushed when I fled from him.

But the man was not Ray. His hair was darker, and he was heavily mustachioed, fingering a lit cigarette.

"You, miss, are a charlatan," he said, not loudly this time, walking toward me. "A phony. A fake."

"Sir, I don't know why you'd accuse me of such a thing." I spoke with all the calm I could muster.

I lost that calm the moment he lunged at me with the cigarette up and out and forward, aiming to put it out in my eye.

I half fell sideways, desperate to get out of his path, partly succeeding. The burning cigarette landed on my shoulder instead of my face. The man's weight knocked me off balance. We both tumbled to the floor. The aisles were not wide, and I banged my head on the arm of a seat, and I could see feet scurrying out of the way. Shouts of surprise broke out immediately around us, but for the most part, the audience seemed to be holding its collective breath.

The fear gave me strength, and I wrestled him with my fingers twisted tight in the sleeves of his shirt. The cigarette had slipped under the fabric of my dress, and I could feel it searing my shoulder, smell it burning both flesh and silk. Without another weapon, he was simply trying to punch me in the face, and I kept twisting, dodging, barely avoiding his jabs.

The old litheness, the flexibility I'd built doing Cecchetti exercises for years and years, was still with me. Despite my far smaller size, he was tiring rapidly. I saw an opportunity and took it. I grabbed the hat from where it had fallen and held it over his face. Disoriented, he raised his hands to grab at it, and I reacted reflexively, striking him in the face with the top of my head. My skull rang with the impact. He fell back onto the carpet and lay still for a moment, stunned. I straddled his fallen body and raised my fists and pummeled him, aiming for the center of that hat over and over. I lost track of who or what I was fighting and became pure punishment, nothing but a set of fists.

Someone grabbed me from behind and lifted me off the fallen man, who did not move.

The tension in my body was so fierce it stung. I looked out over the crowd — they were all still seated, watching, waiting, except for whoever had lifted me off my assailant. Perhaps they thought it was part of the act, that one or both of us might transform or disappear. If so, they would be disappointed.

Whoever had grabbed me turned my body around to face him and kept hold of my wrists. He was middle-aged, old enough to be my father if I'd had one. I struggled but not mightily; this one wasn't trying to hurt me, only hold me still. Even in my desperate state, I could tell the difference.

The new man said, "You're the stage magician known as Arden?"

"You know I am." I spoke harshly. Only after that did I recognize that he was wearing a uniform. It was navy blue and heavy, with an insignia on the sleeve. He had a nightstick in his belt. I wished I would have noticed these things earlier.

"Would you come with me, please?"

"I will not!"

"You will," he said. "You're under arrest. I'm Officer James Gould of the Poughkeepsie Police Department, and you will come with me right now."

"Your badge?" was all I could manage. He produced it.

And that was how I found myself arrested for assaulting a man who had assaulted me first, and spent my first night in prison.

I never found out whether my attacker was

mad or drunk or simply mistaken. Officer Gould hustled me off the premises with dispatch. As the only female inmate of the local jail, I spent a chilly night in a silent cell, pretending to sleep, fully dressed in a gown and corset with a cache of flash powder still wedged uncomfortably up my sleeve, against my elbow. At least it wasn't a dove. I whispered a wish under my breath to heal the weeping burn on my shoulder, and within hours, it was a shadow. I was released the next morning, not much worse for wear. The next show, just up the river in Kingston, sold out. By the time we got to the Smith Opera House in Geneva for the show after that, there was a line out the door and down the block. And we began to book larger venues, at ever-better billing, with the added notoriety from my run-in with the law.

While I wished the assault had never happened — how could I enjoy being in fear for my life? — I was grateful to Officer Gould. The publicity from my arrest was better than a thousand posters. Some headlines boldly declared sides: the *Albany Argus* chose "INNOCENT FEMALE STAGE MAGICIAN VICTIM OF UNPROVOKED ASSAULT," which I appreciated, while somewhat less generous was the *Schenectady Gazette*'s

"ILLUSIONIST OR PUGILIST? WOMAN MA-GICIAN BEATS AUDIENCE MEMBER WHO DARES CHALLENGE AUTHENTICITY OF HER MAGIC." When the news spread wider, the *Philadelphia Public Ledger* decided on a more neutral "FEMALE ILLUSIONIST AT-TACKED MIDSHOW BY DOUBTING PA-TRON." I remembered what Adelaide had said: *As long as they say something and in large type.* The type got much larger after Poughkeepsie.

Clyde, who had been in New York at the time, was furious upon hearing the story. He made a special trip to tell me so. He berated me for confronting the man instead of turning tail and fleeing, and he turned so red that I wanted to laugh at him, but out of politeness, I kept my face grave. I fibbed about how serious it had been, leaving out a number of details, but even so, he insisted I had been in true and unacceptable danger. So he added two bodyguards to the com-pany entourage, just in case. My fame had grown, and I reveled in it, but somehow it felt like it was happening to someone else and not me. I barely recognized myself in the photographs and illustrations that ap-peared next to the newspaper stories. And despite the moment in Poughkeepsie where I was convinced that Ray had found me at last, there was barely a shred of Ada Bates in the Amazing Arden. Only the eye was the same, and its unique coloring was invisible in black ink. Everything I did celebrated the new person I had become.

I didn't mind the bodyguards; actually, they were nice boys. They fit in well enough, always watchful but rarely obtrusive. And when several months had passed without further threat — the newspapers continued to growl their same stories about the dangers of a woman taking a man's role onstage, but their tone grew more and more admiring — I offered the big-shouldered one a job as a prop hauler and the long-fingered one a position onstage, and they both accepted.

It was the night after I released the bodyguards that things changed with Clyde. It had been exactly a year since I'd become the Amazing Arden, and I was in New York for just one night, going over our accounts in the office. We'd planned to go to Keen's to celebrate the occasion with mutton chops and red berry bibble, but we got to talking and lost track of the clock. By the time he checked his watch, we decided to content ourselves with sandwiches and keep working.

Truth be told, we hadn't spent every

minute talking true business. I'd come to look forward to talking with him on my return visits, sometimes for hours. He confessed his greatest dream was to build a theater of his own, and we fell to talking about it when other business was done, dreaming it grander every time. We changed the name over and over — the Perennial? Garber's Grove? the Modern Taj? — but settled on the Carolina Rose. Each time we talked, we gave it ever more prestigious addresses, furnishing it with chairs and curtains and carpets, down to the last detail. I advocated for a streamlined, elegant scheme of black and white furnishings, but he wanted something more baroque, full of scrollwork and ornament. It was a subject of fun, but also something we shared with each other and no one else.

In a way, it was intimate, a word from which I once would have shrunk where Clyde was concerned. I found I minded that thought less and less. There was still a wall between us — the wall I had put there to guard against being hurt by him again — but it had sunk lower with every passing month, and after all this time, I could see over it. We could laugh together once more. But there was no hint of anything romantic, not until the night he chose to declare himself.

We'd finished the sandwiches, and I'd asked a question about our receipts for June, so he reached into the middle of a stack of papers, and the top of the stack toppled and fell. I leaned over to begin picking them up, but he shooed me back. So I sat in the desk chair and looked down at him while he gathered up the sheets of figures and neatly squared their edges again. When he was done, he handed the papers to me, and I put them back where they belonged, but he didn't get up. Instead, he removed his eyeglasses, folded them slowly, and placed them on the edge of the desk. Then he pinched the bridge of his nose as if it pained him and sat back on his heels.

"Clyde?" I prodded.

He didn't meet my eyes. "Arden, do you know what you want?"

"Sure," I said. "I want to be famous enough to make front-page headlines just for coming to town. I want to invent an illusion so original I'm forever known as its creator. And I want those marzipan candies they make in that little town outside Binghamton, the ones dipped in chocolate, in the box with the red ribbon."

I was partly joking, but I watched his reaction, and he was serious. He knelt at my feet and laid his hands on the ground, his fingertips almost but not quite grazing the toes of my shoes. Awkwardly I looked down, waiting.

"I want you to forgive me," he said. "That's what I want."

I knew what he meant instantly, of course. My answer took a bit longer to form. "It was a long time ago."

"But you were right," Clyde said. "I did you wrong. I never should have let you believe I was going to marry you. It was a trick, and badly done. And I'm sorry."

I looked at his bent head, and my heart ached. I'd pictured this before, down to the last detail. If I'd been truthful when he asked me what I wanted, I'd have included this: him, on his knees, begging my forgiveness.

"So that's what you want," I said. "More than that theater of yours? More than the stacks of money you keep in the safe? You want me to forgive you?"

"Yes."

There was something about the way he looked up at me that turned on a light. I'd been lying to myself. I hadn't been enjoying his company just for conversation. I had wanted something more, something I didn't want to let myself want, but if he was truly repentant? Maybe I could have it after all.

Boldly I said, "Is that all you want from me?"

He lifted one hand to hover over the hem of my dress, stared up into my face, and said, "No. It isn't. But that doesn't matter."

"Why not?"

"It only matters what you want from me. And you've said I can't even touch you. So I won't, until you give me permission."

"Done." I surprised even myself with how quickly, how eagerly, I said it. "Touch me, then."

He gaped a little bit, taken by surprise. Seeing his shock was almost more gratifying than watching him beg. "I don't know where to start."

"I do," I said and leaned down to him, cradling his face in both hands. I could feel the whiskers just under the skin of his cheek. After so long, it was almost too much, and I gave myself over instantly.

His lips on mine were warm and sweet. I parted my lips and felt his tongue slip in, shocking me a moment, and then the sensation took me well beyond warmth into a delicious, undeniable heat. I came down out of my chair, down to my knees, to meet him.

"Are you sure?" he said low in his throat,

urgently.

"More," I said in response and pulled him to me and pressed my hips against his hips as if I could pass my body into his like two magic rings struck together so hard they interlock. His lips were soft but insistent, and I could feel the scruff on his chin scratching me, making my face feel tender, then as he trailed fierce kisses down my neck, the scruff rubbed against the skin there, and my face and neck were aflame as surely as if I were standing in the Navajo Fire itself.

I pressed against him, feeling the delicious, unfamiliar heat of another person's body against mine, chest to chest, waist to waist, thighs to thighs. We knelt facing each other for what seemed like hours. His hands twisted into my hair, his fingers wrapped around my head as he held my face to his, as if to devour me, and I wanted nothing else in the world in that moment but to be devoured.

When kisses were no longer enough, we both knew it. I could feel his need against me, and I lay back so he could have what we both wanted. He pushed at my skirt, sliding it up over my knee, and he was so maddeningly slow about it that I grabbed two fistfuls of skirt myself and hauled the layers of fabric out of the way. He smiled at that, and I kissed the smile off his face, shocked by my own boldness, but so gripped with urgency I couldn't slow down.

I couldn't say which of us unlaced the front of my dress, our fingers were both tangling and lunging, but when the front hung open, I felt a rush of cold air and then a warmer rush as he lowered his mouth. A wave of heat ran down between my legs and up my spine to the back of my head where it exploded, and I gasped out loud.

I had waited a long time without knowing what I was waiting for, and for all the months and years I'd waited, it was worth every minute.

"How beautiful you are," he said, murmuring the words against my bare breast. The sensation was new and unfamiliar and wonderful, and the heat was everywhere at once. I couldn't feel his hands on me so I reached out for them and found one at the waist of his trousers pulling them aside, and when I brushed something I didn't expect to brush, I heard him groan. He sounded like an animal, but not in a frightening way. I wasn't afraid. I reached out for him and he groaned again, lowering his hips onto mine. His skin was so hot. His face came up to mine, and there was a question in his eyes, and I tipped my hips up to meet his, pressing and pressing, which was all the answer he needed.

"Beautiful," said Clyde, "beautiful, beautiful, beautiful," as he pushed aside the last scrap of fabric separating us and plunged inside, and there was pain and joy in my answering cry, until neither of us were making words, only sounds, though at the end when we lay down next to each other, he ran his hand over my face and cupped my cheek in his palm and said, "Beautiful, beautiful Arden."

CHAPTER TWENTY-TWO

Janesville, 1905
Half past three o'clock

"I'm sorry, Virgil, have I shocked you?"

"Officer Holt," he says, "or Holt. Or officer."

"Virgil is a lovely name though. Traditional. And have I shocked you? Made you uncomfortable?"

"No."

"I don't mean to. But your reaction, just now, it tells a different story."

"Story," he scoffs as sharply as he can, given that she's right. He was already uncomfortably warm, but the prickling of his skin now is more than just a rising sweat. The hot, bare room feels as small as a closet. His heart is pounding and that's not all. "You're the storyteller, not me."

"Stories are often true."

"Sometimes true," he says and keeps his distance, still trying to calm himself down.

She didn't need to tell that story that way, getting into those details. He should have cut her off. But he didn't want to, and he's sure she knows it. He might as well tell her everything, all his hopes and fears, since it doesn't take much effort for her to figure him out.

Then something interrupts.

At first it sounds like the wind, like a tree branch on a window, except that he knows there are no trees close by. Fast wind over flat land has thrown things against the building before — broken cart wheels, lost shirts, newspapers — but none have sounded quite like this.

The sound keeps coming, something between a whistle and a scratch. He knows he's not imagining it. Partly because it's persistent, but partly because of the magician, who has also turned her attention toward the door, cocking her ear to listen.

"Is that a cat?" she asks. "Do you have a police cat?"

"No."

Then the sound comes clearly, soft but unmistakable: a knock.

He doesn't move to answer it.

She says softly, almost in a whisper, "Will this be like the telephone? Will you ignore everything for my sake?"

"Nothing for your sake," he spits in irritation, striding in three long steps straight to the door, unlocking it, throwing it open.

No one is there. No one and nothing. No tree branches or carriage wheels or cats.

They both breathe in the soft summer night, a relief after hours of the tiny police station's stale air. The breeze, with its slight perfume of grass and earth, is a pleasure. He takes deep, sweet, hungry breaths. The sleeping town is framed squarely in the doorway: houses with darkened windows, perfectly straight and silent streets.

"Ah, lovely." She sighs, which snaps him out of his reverie, and he closes the door on her vision.

"What did you do that for? I was looking at your sweet little town."

"Well, don't. It's not yours."

"I didn't say it was. What do you think I could do to it anyway? Terrorize the citizenry? Lead them like the Pied Piper in a merry parade, out of town and into the river?"

The heavy, stale air of the station closes in on him as if the sweet outdoor breeze had never been. He tries to ignore her, but the words keep coming.

"Need I remind you," she says, "I am still chained to this chair. Terrified. Weak from lack of food and sleep. I would think you wouldn't be so afraid of me. Just for breathing your precious Iowa air."

He turns the key in the lock, and he doesn't hear the click he should hear, the sound of the bolt sliding into place. But she's chattering at him so loudly that it's hard to hear anything, still talking, still nattering on and on and on. His head is buzzing again. She keeps talking. The later it gets, the harder it is to hold on. It's her fault. If he hadn't found her, if she hadn't been so obvious with her sequins and her fairy eye . . .

"Be quiet!" he shouts at her.

She falls silent instantly.

He says, "Enough of this. Tell me about the murder. Now. I've been very kind to you, considering."

"Have you? You hauled me off, nearly knocked me unconscious —"

"And I've listened to your story. But I need the end of it. If you don't get to the end of it, the rest of it doesn't do me any good at all."

"And I'll get there."

"When?" He feels like the floor is lurching underneath him, and it's all he can do to plant his feet and stay steady.

"Soon."

He snaps sarcastically, "Before the end of time?"

"Lord," she says, "are you all right? You look like you're about to fall over."

He sits down, setting his weary body down in the chair across from her again, almost sighing with pleasure at getting off his feet. There's no point in arguing with her when she's right.

"I'm sorry," he says. "I'm just — tired."

"Me too," she says, almost in a whisper. "Me too."

"I suppose it's all taken a toll. The bullet, the bad news from the doctor. Worrying about it all."

"What was it like? Being shot?"

"It wasn't like anything in particular," he says. "It was just — it was a fact. I'd been shot. I was going to die. It was a certainty."

"But then you didn't."

"I was a fool to think there were ever certainties."

She smiles.

"It's nothing to be glad about," he says. "When I woke up under the doctor's care, when I realized I was alive, I was overjoyed. In that moment. But this life, it doesn't even feel like life anymore."

The smile disappears from her face.

He says, "I told you, I'll get driven out for

sure. I'll lose my position, my wife, the only things that give my life meaning. I might as well have died. It'd be faster."

"Hogwash," she says.

"Excuse me?"

"Life is always better than death. Always. No exceptions."

"You don't understand." He leans in toward her, speaking more loudly, intently, trying to drive his point home. "I could die right now, sitting across from you in this chair, having this conversation."

"Well, don't," she says. "If you do, I'll never get out of here."

"I'm serious."

"I'm sorry. I know what you're trying to say. You think your life is so compromised that there's no joy in it anymore."

"Exactly."

"Still. Even when life is full of pain, it's better than the alternative."

"Every minute of every day, I'm aware it could be my last," he says, still trying to make her understand. "The worst is, when it was happening, and I was lying there bleeding, I thought, all I want is to survive. And I did. But now I'm not sure it's better this way."

She says, "I don't want to sound rude, but officer, that doesn't make you special.

It's the story of modern life. You want something, and you get it . . . and it's not what you thought it would be."

"Sure," he says. "That's what happened to you, with Clyde?"

"With everything," she answers softly.

CHAPTER TWENTY-THREE

1901–1903
The Iroquois Fire

In the days and weeks following, Clyde and I fell quickly into a pattern, as if we'd always been together. It was difficult at first to focus on anything but each other. I did learn to take precautions, because the two of us was enough and neither of us wanted to make it three. I wasn't about to risk my career. I still remembered the example of the nameless girl who had preceded me as the Dancing Odalisque. In a way, I had her to thank for all of this, for her foolishness had made my entire career, and now my love, possible. If she'd had a Mr. Vanderbilt to counsel her, to encourage self-control, who knows where that would have left me?

When I was in New York, Clyde and I spent all day each day in the office on Broadway and returned at night to his rented rooms on Jane Street. Even then, even as we were rushing to discard our clothes, we would still talk business, reminding each other of appointments or obligations in between each kiss. Figures and illusions and ticket prices and billing were all the food for love. One night when Clyde knelt at my feet, introducing me to a new form of pleasure, I had a new understanding of Woman on Fire. Instead of a woman destroyed by fire, I would create an illusion of a woman bursting into flame but withstanding it, letting the flames caress and surround her. It was a delicious inspiration. We were each the person the other needed, at the right time, in the right place, at last.

"I wish you could come on the road with me," I said to him afterward as we lay in bed together, an idle wish in a quiet moment.

"You know I can't. It's a cutthroat business, Arden. We can't just do it halfway."

"I know." Of course my career was the important thing, and if the choice was between staying in New York and being no one, or traveling alone as Arden to perform in front of crowds night after night, my choice was never in doubt.

"Not that I wouldn't love that. To be with you. It's all I've wanted since the moment I saw you again."

He trailed his fingertips over my body, knees to shoulders, and cupped my face in his palm. I savored the lovely feeling that there was nothing more important in the world than how his fingers felt against my skin. Our world could be just the two of us, small and wonderful.

"I've been so in love with you," he murmured. "I couldn't believe you couldn't tell. I counted the days until you'd be back, and every time you were, I sat there every moment fighting the need to touch you. Like this."

He let his hand roam, and I gasped.

"But you said you'd kill me if I touched you. And so I didn't."

"You didn't," I said. "You kept your word."

"This is better," he said, lowering his face to mine for another kiss and stroking me until I could barely breathe.

When my mouth was free to speak again, some time later, I said, "I don't want to leave you."

"You're not leaving me," he said. "I'm yours, wherever I am. We'll keep you in a tighter orbit as soon as you're established. Medium time, the next step up. There's no reason to go west — the Orpheum circuit is already lousy with illusionists, and that does us no good. We need to build your profile in the East."

He went on, "I've got a real talent for this."

"If you do say so yourself."

He grinned, never one for false modesty. "It's a stepping stone for me to meet the people I need to help me build my theater in New York. Once you're known and your act commands the highest prices, we'll install you as the main attraction at the Carolina Rose. I'll be a real impresario, and you'll be a flat-out star. And we'll be together, here. We just need to be patient and smart about it. I believe we'll get what we want."

I looked at him. He was right. It was what we both wanted. That didn't make it easier, being apart.

"You're so beautiful when you're sad, with those eyes of yours. They break my heart," he said.

"Mine too," I said and curled my body into the curve of his, until I could feel his breath as if it were my own.

I was riding high, thrilled and amazed at my own luck, feeling more powerful than Houdini himself. I wasn't just a female illusionist; I was a woman in full, a woman with a man who couldn't get enough of her.

It made me even more confident and seductive onstage.

We debuted the new version of the Woman on Fire, which I reveled in. My costume was crafted of white layers of chiffon with red, orange, and yellow ones underneath, and as I spun, the brighter colors looked like flame. With carefully placed lamps and wisps of smoke, the illusion that I was on fire was complete. I loved it because I could be my true self onstage for once. For the purposes of the Woman on Fire, I didn't need to pretend myself fearful or foreign or shrouded in mystery. I only needed to be happy. And I was.

The crowds grew larger, my billing more pronounced. I found myself in a familiar cycle. In the earlier days with the Great Madame Herrmann's company, we'd played smaller theaters, and as she built her fame over the years, we'd visit larger venues in the same cities. And so it was with the Amazing Arden's company. We went from the Howard Athenaeum to the Hollis Street Theatre in Boston, no small leap, and from the Locust Point Theater to the Ford's Grand Opera House in Baltimore. As he had many times before, Clyde displayed his worth as my business manager and suggested it was time I begin to play on a percentage basis at certain theaters. My up-front salary would be smaller, but every ticket sold would yield a bit more silver for our coffers. Enjoying the gamble, I agreed. At three out of every four shows, it paid off, and it would be hard to say which of us was more pleased.

Clyde was both my inspiration and my reward. I delighted in the stage and the road, collecting anecdotes and tales to tell him, and when we were together in New York, I disappeared into bed with him for hours and then days, and when he insisted we go and eat something, I mumbled and dragged my feet until he swept me up in his arms to carry me out, blinking, into the light. We could have griddle cakes at a lunch counter or shrimp bisque and spring lamb at Delmonico's, and I'd hardly notice, so thrilled to be sitting across from him, looking at him, knowing he was close enough to touch.

And when I was with him, I learned the compromises of intimacy, the way the pillow you fall asleep on disappears in the night sometimes, the way the other person's smell becomes more familiar to you than your own, the way you learn the phrases they repeat and the foods they avoid and in which direction their hair grows. In the years before we found each other again, I couldn't imagine what it would be like to be loved and needed; now it had become such a part of my life I couldn't imagine what it would be like not to.

And so things continued in the same way, for a full year and then some, until Christmastime of 1903.

My little family of performers had grown together, and not a single one I'd hired had left the company. They also began to come to me for counsel and reassurance, which was something Adelaide's employees had never done, forbidding as she was. Sometimes they only wanted my advice. Sometimes they wanted to ask to be included in or excused from a particular illusion or to be granted a particular day off here or there. On occasion, they asked for more meaningful favors. The long-fingered former bodyguard, whose name was Hugo, asked for a loan to get his sister out of a bad situation, and I was happy to advance him the money, though it was a substantial sum. He paid it back promptly, reaffirming my trust.

We still had our curfews and our mandatory dinners. During these mealtime conversations, we were fond of going over and over our memories of every venue we knew, talking about which were the best theaters and which the worst, debating the pitfalls and benefits of each one. Late in 1903, Hugo told us of an ornate new theater built in Chicago, a beautiful, soaring place. Not only was there room for nearly two thousand audience members in the high, vaulted auditorium, but great thought had been given to the comfort of the acts as well. We'd never heard of a backstage area so luxurious. Five levels of dressing rooms had been built — surely, we exclaimed, that could only be a rumor — and an elevator constructed to shuttle performers from there to the stage level. Its opening had been much delayed, but all was now well at last. It was called the Iroquois Theater, and none of us could wait to play it.

Clyde booked a show for me there in early January, but I decided to go a few days in advance, at the end of December. Holidays were a quiet time for us. What audiences there were tended to congregate for family entertainments, especially the seasonal ones, Yule-themed ballets and musicals and the like. So we made a plan: I would go on ahead while Clyde settled the year's business. After this single show, I'd join a small circuit called the Castle for a month of shows in Missouri, and after that, we were very close to a deal with a northeastern circuit, the Monrovian. Once that paperwork was signed, Clyde could afford to spend a week without hustling for the next bit of business. When the deal was done, he'd follow me out to Chicago, stopping over for one night before turning north and heading into Canada, where he wanted to look at a plot of timber he might buy as an investment. He'd been eager to put some of his money into land, and as a man who knew growing things, he thought he might be able to turn a profit in lumber. When he described the virgin stand of pine to me, "trees so close together they rub shoulders," he sounded giddy as a schoolgirl. I teased him for it, but to be honest, I only wanted him happy. Sinking money into the Canadian forest would delay his plan to build the Carolina Rose in New York, but we were in no rush, and the longer I spent on the road building my name, the better off we'd be when he did.

Our Christmas presents to each other were simple. I gave him an expensive pair of leather gloves to keep his treasured hands warm, and he gave me a copy of the book that gave me my name: a lovely pocket-sized edition of *As You Like It,* which I looked forward to reading yet again. Life on the road had given me many things, but it had made it impractical to maintain a collection of books, a rare regret among so many joys.

The real present was time together, uninterrupted hours of pleasure, and we treated ourselves to the finest hotel we could find, heedless of the cost. I loved Clyde's Jane Street rooms for sentimental reasons, but for luxury and indulgence, two days at the Astoria were like living in another world. We tumbled between the soft, lovely sheets, and every minute was glorious. The bed was enormous, like a sailing ship in the middle of a carpeted ocean, white draperies billowing from the framework of the canopy like sails from a mast. Rich, savory food was brought to us, whenever we wanted it, under silver domes. The faucets yielded up water at every temperature from Arctic to scalding. We looked down from our high window at the soundless streetscape below, the dots of people scuttling about their everyday business, then let the curtains fall closed upon them again. We plopped our bodies into overstuffed chairs, extended them across cool velvet sofas, settled them into the steaming, lavender-scented embrace of the marble bathtub. What I loved most in these moments was that we were still ourselves. Even among abundant, outrageous luxuries, even isolated from the forces that had brought us together in the first place, we still reveled in each other. Clyde of the cramped, cold office and Clyde of a richly appointed suite at the Astoria were still the same man. The man I loved. The man who — I could never believe my luck in it — loved me.

After our Christmas together, I left for Chicago, arriving three days before year's end. The soft languor of my holiday was worn away by hours of train-borne rattling. Accustomed to my private railcar, I found even a good journey by public rail exhausting, and I could barely keep my eyes open until I finally arrived at the hotel Clyde had arranged for me. All I wanted to do was sleep, but there was an envelope on the bed with my name on it, so I had to read it before I collapsed. I was delighted at what I found inside — a ticket waiting there for the next day's show at the Iroquois, with a note reading *"Go see it for us. — C."*

Walking into the theater was like walking into a dream. The Biltmore had been a palace, but the Iroquois was dazzling on a different scale. The entryway was larger than it seemed like any building could be, its ceiling impossibly far overhead. I had dressed in a plain brown shirtwaist and a low-brimmed hat, eager to avoid attention, but now I felt underdressed. A spectacle like this deserved better. All gold and ivory, it was like a song-and-dance man's version of heaven. I drank in the details, trying to capture as much as I could in my memory so I could share every bit of it with Clyde later.

Heading through a winding hallway lined with dark red carpet, I trailed my fingers along the brocade wallpaper, a heavy gold-and-red pattern almost too bold to be elegant. It felt like velvet.

My seat was in the very first row. I smiled, thinking of Clyde, and took my seat. I imagined myself concluding a performance on the immense stage, drinking in the applause of a stunned and grateful crowd, and felt my limbs grow warm with the thought of such a triumph. But before long, I twisted around and looked behind me, risking a crick in my neck to take in the sight of the gorgeous theater filling up. Even though it wasn't my own show, the excitement of an audience filing in still thrilled me.

From my vantage point at the foot of the stage, the size of the room was simply astounding. Hugo had told us the theater could hold nearly two thousand people, but hearing the number was nothing on seeing it. An enormous orchestra section stretched out on the ground floor, with a dress circle and balcony stacked above, and as I watched, all three filled up completely. Women and children lined the rows. Not just in the seats but between them, up and down the aisles. People packed themselves in, sitting or standing, wherever there was room. My audiences were large, but never like this, and my theaters were rarely as grand. It was more than twice the size of the Walnut Street Theatre in Philadelphia, far more opulent than Ford's Opera House in Baltimore. Gorgeous draperies of heavy scarlet damask lined the walls and boxes, and even the aisles were lined with deep carpet. Clearly, no expense had been spared.

A chime played to indicate that it was almost time to raise the curtain. The bustle slowed and stopped, the only movement a set of ushers who locked the gates between the levels to keep patrons with cheaper tickets from sneaking into the more expensive sections. But even though everything was still, even when the lights went down, you could still hear the enormous audience breathing in the darkness. It was impossible to keep such a crowd completely silent.

The orchestra played its merry fanfare and the show began. Again, I was overwhelmed

340

and impressed. The bounty onstage was enormous, all colorful costumes and fast movement. The children in the audience roared with laughter at all the right moments. I'd never seen so many children in one place at one time — school must have been shut for the Christmas holiday, because these were children who should have been in school — and it was a strange sight to me. Then the sound of the calliope caught my attention, and I looked up at the pageantry on the stage, and I lost myself in the magic of the theater.

Midway through the second act, it started, with a soft roar. Quiet at first, but growing louder.

I couldn't see anything out of the ordinary, but the sound built and built until I couldn't ignore it. I looked around. What was going on? What wasn't right? At first, everything looked as it should have. An octet stood on the stage, four men and four women, singing a lovely ballad about moonlight, the stage lighting tinting their white garments softly blue.

I returned to the sound, trying to remember where I'd heard it before, imagining what it might possibly be. It wasn't the children laughing, and it wasn't the audience applauding, and it wasn't some kind of effect, like the metal sheets sometimes hidden behind the curtains and shaken to imitate the sound of thunder. It was softer than all that.

Then the smell reached me, about a minute into the roar. The smell of smoke. Right after that, I saw the bright light, and with the evidence of my eyes and ears and nose all together, I knew what was wrong.

The curtain was catching fire.

The flames were roaring upward, and the sound was the air they ate as they soared up faster than any human could go.

Panic spread in an instant.

As soon as ten patrons stood and fled, it was twenty and then a hundred; women in the gallery were running before they could have possibly realized what they were running from. But the truth was clear to everyone soon enough. The fire leapt from the curtain onto the hanging sets that were waiting above the stage, and dozens of yards of painted canvas were swallowed up with hungry tongues of flame. The crowd surged away from the stage, away from the fire, in a blind scrum. Quickly people realized that the aisles were clogged, and they began to surge over the seats as best they could, stepping on seats and backs of seats and in some cases other people, too panicked and desperate to know the difference. They surged for doors — or what seemed at first to be doors but were only glass-paned decorations meant for show, an ornament no one could have guessed would turn cruel.

I stood stock-still, terrified, not knowing which direction to run. The smoke had descended on me almost instantly, and my eyes burned with ash. I heard the sound of hundreds of feet. A boom sounded from somewhere distant — had a metal door been flung open? Had the windows burst? The smoke began to rise, lifting and rolling with the air currents, and the scene became clearer. I wished it hadn't.

The fire was spreading to the wooden trim on the boxes and the walls, and the audience was fleeing toward the sides of the theater where they'd come in. But the gates across the staircases were still locked, trapping the crowds in place. And there were too many of them. They were tripping over each other, searching for a way out in any direction, and in some places, people were horribly, horribly still because there was nowhere to go. Large bodies and small ones, tangled. To my left in the orchestra section, I could see people pressing against a closed door, pressing and pressing, but going nowhere. Smoke hung low over everything and everyone.

The screams were loud and alien, and it was raining fire.

Behind me, I heard a single voice, the only one shouting words: "Get out! Get out!"

I turned. The stage itself was right behind me, and unbelievably, it was not burning. One of the members of the octet who had been singing was still there, dressed in white, and she beckoned to me. Behind her, a stream of performers — shepherdesses, gypsies, knights, men and women costumed as animals of all kinds — was moving toward a single destination.

There was a way out.

I didn't want to die. The stage in front of me was too high, but I could see a half staircase at the side of it, and clambered up the stairs before leaping across the gap onto the stage. I hit the wood of the stage hard on my knees, one foot dangling back over the orchestra pit below, but I made it.

I scrambled to my feet. The smoke was thicker again, heavy and gritty and every-where, here where the fire had begun. I felt my lungs fill with it, my throat close. I coughed out what I could. I swatted the air around me as if that could clear a path, but I was still disoriented and could barely tell up from down, let alone downstage from

344

up. My eyes failed me, so I focused on my ears, which picked up the sound of footsteps, headed all in the same direction. That was the back of the stage. I scanned in that direction with all my senses, knowing there must be a way out. And then I might have been imagining it, it was so very faint, but I thought I could smell fresh air.

Foolishly, I turned one last moment to look out at the auditorium again, seeing at a glance scores of people, scores of bodies, those who would never escape. Too much stillness under the smoke.

I swayed and fell.

Someone carried me. In moments, I was aware. Desperate men ripped the hinges off the stage door. A horde of survivors huddled in a frozen alleyway. Performers scrambled up out of the coal chute, their spangles smeared with coal and ash. Then the moments were shorter, punctuated with darkness between. The horns of the fire companies arriving, steam from the horses' nostrils looking like smoke in the frigid air. Near the exits and at the bases of the unfinished fire escapes, dark clusters of bodies heaped like flies.

After that, when the darkness swum up at me again, I welcomed it.

■ ■ ■ ■

When next I woke, I lay on a cold stone floor. The smell of smoke and ash was less but unmistakably present. A basement? As dim as one — a room with few windows, small and placed high on the walls, giving very little light. Perhaps it was evening, or even night. Stacked wooden crates lined the walls, but they were too far away for me to read the lettering in such low light, so they might contain anything. It seemed like some kind of storeroom. I redirected my gaze nearer and felt reassured when I saw another woman's face sleeping peacefully close to mine, only to recoil in horror when I realized she wasn't sleeping but dead.

I tried to scramble up, but my body failed me, my lungs and throat still seared with smoke. I had been carried to this place and laid down next to a dead woman. And next to her was another dead woman, and another, a whole roomful of the dead, and I lifted my arms, as heavy as lead, and covered my face and prayed it was only a terrible dream.

When I let my hands fall again and dared to look, my awful company still surrounded me, so I turned my attention to my own body to try to shut out the horror of this place of death. The interior of my throat felt burned away. My eyes stung. A pervasive ache had settled in my veins. But on the whole, none of this mattered. I was alive, and safe, or so it seemed. Where to start? I wished soundlessly that my throat would heal itself. One step at a time.

The door opened and closed, and I discerned a shape in a white coat. A doctor. Familiar somehow. He drew nearer, smiling at me with a broad, open grin. The sight of a living, breathing person was almost as welcome as the scent of fresh air in the burning theater had been, and I thought, *Thank goodness, this isn't just a nightmare,* and I smiled at him until I heard him speak.

"Ada." He breathed out, and the longing and the triumph in that single word, it nearly destroyed me.

My joy fled and left me hollow. All the pain, and more, returned.

Even if I'd wanted to return the greeting, to call him by his name, I couldn't. I couldn't speak. My burned throat, healing but not healed, wouldn't yield up any sound.

My smoke-stung eyes, however, could see well enough who it was. The years had changed him, weathered him. His hair was cut shorter but still showed the wave of the ringlets he'd worn in his teenage years. The thickness of his limbs was still evident. He'd grown larger and stretched out somewhat. He was taller. And, I suspected, even stronger.

Ray had finally found me.

Chapter Twenty-Four

1903

Feathers without Birds

"I can't believe it's you," he said, falling on his knees next to me, reaching for my face but not touching it, just like all those years ago. "I knew it was, once I saw your posters, even though the name wasn't yours. Who else could it be? But I thought maybe somehow I was mistaken. I was afraid of that, deep down. But it isn't so. My God, Ada, I've missed you so much. You're my other half. The only one like me. I haven't felt complete without you."

I was glad in that moment for my wrecked voice, as I didn't know what to say. My mind reeled. Maybe I was dreaming. I prayed I was. But as long as I'd feared Ray, as many years as the memories of what he'd done to me had haunted my waking hours, he had never appeared in my dreams. This was all too real.

"You'd be proud of me," he went on. "I'm a doctor now. I told you I was a healer. I came here to Chicago since I knew you'd been here . . ."

The card to my mother, I realized. *I am well.* I'd sent it from here. Years ago. All unknowingly, I'd brought us both to this moment.

". . . but then you weren't, but I just trusted to fate and stayed. It's been years, you know, but this place was as good as any other. I worked and waited. Then finally I saw the posters for the Amazing Arden. And I knew it was you. You were coming back to me, and I'd be complete at last again. I bought a ticket for your show. I knew we were about to be reunited. But I didn't know it would be today. Today — today is unexpected."

I croaked out, "Today is horrible."

"Oh — well, yes," he said, seeming to sober and take in our surroundings, as if seeing them for the first time. "I'm sorry I had to put you in here with these people. I came to help, we all did, and there were so many we couldn't save, so there had to be a place for them. And someone brought you to me, they weren't sure if you were alive, and I saw my chance. It was like it was meant to be. I planned to be back before you woke up. I'm sorry I wasn't here for you. But now it's all right. Here we are."

I closed my eyes.

"Ada?"

I didn't, I couldn't, respond.

"Open your eyes," he said, "or I'll open them for you."

I complied.

He shed his doctor's coat. He rolled up one sleeve and showed me the scars on the inside of his arm, a solid mass of lines that followed the bone of the arm, right up the center. He unbuttoned his collar and other cuff and reached one hand up to the back of his neck to grab his shirt and then pulled it off in a long single stroke, and I was powerless to look away.

In the intervening years, he had made a project of his scars. Now they showed every bone. Not just the rib cage but the breastbone, the shoulders, everything. The pale, clustered shapes outlined his whole skeleton. He turned slowly so I could see the scarred curves of each knob in his backbone, the wide triangles of his shoulder blades. Either he was infinitely talented and patient with the razor or he'd had help. He shrugged back into his shirt again and then his spotless white coat, and no one looking at him now would know what a danger he was on the inside.

"You're not impressed?" He sounded petulant.

I only said again, "Get the hell away from me."

He shook his head. "I can't do that, Ada. I've been searching for you all this time. And now I've found you."

I made to sit up, and he put the palm of his hand in the center of my chest and pushed me back down.

"Now," he said, "let's catch up."

And in his other hand was the old straight razor with its worn bone handle and its sharp square blade.

I couldn't fight anymore.

Lying on the floor of that room, the life force drained from me. The world shrank and almost disappeared, and all I could feel was an enormous ache wrapped around my skull and the cold bare floor under my broken body. I'd fallen too low and could see no way out. It was all I could do not to stretch out and surrender to sleep, like a girl in a fairy tale who would either awaken transformed, or not at all.

He leaned over me with the razor, pushing my dress and underskirt up almost to my waist, and began to cut into the flesh of my thigh. I didn't move. It must have disappointed him, my lack of reaction, because he lifted the razor and brought it toward my face instead.

"You're hurt. Let me fix you," he said in that old long-ago voice, and that was what gave me the strength to move. Just one more time.

I moved fast.

I closed both of my hands over his fist with the razor in it and immediately shoved as hard as I could, bending his arm back toward his body. Surprise was on my side. The upturned razor blade slashed across the front of his neck, and blood immediately began to fountain out.

His eyes were stunned, unbelieving. He dropped the razor, and his hands went to his throat, clutching at the wound. The blood still seeped out between his fingers, running over his white coat and shirt, running everywhere.

I threw my body sideways. With what little presence of mind I still had, I grabbed the discarded razor so he couldn't use it on me. I pushed it against the stone floor to fold it and tucked it into my bodice. There was so much blood.

And then I looked at Ray. His eyes were wild, panicked. I knew who he was, and I knew he'd caused me so much pain and anguish. He'd driven me from my home when I was little more than a child. He was damaged and he was dangerous. But he was also a human being, frightened for his life, and I felt no joy at what I — I! — had done.

Desperate to take it back, to do whatever I could, I pressed my hands over his hands, the slick blood coursing, and said out loud, "I wish you well again."

Nothing happened.

The blood kept coming, red and warm. The calm that had come over him when I spoke quickly disappeared, and his eyes were even wilder. He opened his mouth to speak but of course he couldn't. And I, horrified, knew that if I couldn't heal him, there was only one thing I could do. Escape.

I left him there. I dashed up the stairs. There were two doors at the top. I opened the colder one. This took me outside, and I slammed the door behind me, exiting into an alleyway between the theater and the restaurant next door. Standing next to the restaurant's window, I could see the entire room was full of survivors from the fire, standing or crouching or laid out on tables, and white-coated doctors were moving from person to person, giving directions, pointing, shouting. It seemed clear they were separating patients into those who could be helped and those who couldn't. I'd been in the restaurant's storeroom. The warmer door would have taken me inside. Someone might use it at any moment to take more of the dead down into that awful room. I couldn't be nearby when they found Ray, untouched by smoke or ash, dying or already dead.

I plunged my hands into a snowbank to wipe away as much of the blood as I could. I looked around to see if anyone was watching me, but the scene was so frenetic that no one had time or inclination to take any notice of someone who wasn't visibly injured. The fact that I was on my feet and moving meant I could safely be ignored, and so I was.

I forced myself to walk, heading up the alleyway toward the street, and stared for a moment at the firefighters, still battling the blaze. From here, I could feel the dreadful radiant heat of the fire on my face. The firefighters were curiously silent. Then I realized I couldn't hear anything at all, as if the sound of the world had been wiped away. I wished everything else were as easily gone. With no warning, I vomited on the stone of the alleyway.

I felt my life would now be divided in half: everything that came before this, and every-

thing that came after. I didn't want everything after to begin.

After an infinite amount of time, when I
could hear again, I toddled like a child to
the street. Someone in a dark blue uniform
with a high collar asked me where I lived. I
whispered the name of my hotel.

When next I thought about it, I was there.
I lay sprawled across the bed on my back,
still wearing the soot-smudged dress, surrounded by smears of ash on the white
coverlet. I closed my eyes, and when later I
opened them, I saw I was no longer alone:
Clyde had arrived.

He leaned in and cradled my face and
whispered, "Oh, thank the good Lord.
Beloved, come join the world."

"No," I said. "I can't." It felt too soon.

"You have to."

"No."

"Are you hurt?" he asked and pointed
toward the front of my dress. I looked down
at a great dark streak of blood all the way
across my bodice, and all of a sudden, I
stank of death. Was it Ray's blood? My own?
Another victim's? Was it the blood of a living person, or a dead one? I leapt out of the
bed and attempted to tear the dress off my
body, my shivering fingers fumbling with

the buttons.

He said, "Let me help you," and reached out for the buttons, and I slapped his hands away, even though I was shaking too hard to manage them. One at a time, struggling every moment, I tore at them, breaking the button or tearing the fabric more often than not. When I finally got the dress off, I threw it on the floor and stepped away from it. I backed away and backed away until my body bumped into the wall and there was nowhere else to go. I huddled against the wall, half naked, shivering in my undergarments and not just from cold. Clyde wrapped his arms around me, and I sagged against him, crying.

"Here," he said. "Here."

I sobbed in his arms. It already would have been the worst day of my life, the horror of that disaster, all those dead mothers and children, and then Ray had found me. And I had done what I had done. I could still feel the folded straight razor inside my corset, cold against my skin. It was too much. All of it.

"Here, get back in bed," he said, and he helped me lie down and pull the covers up over myself. He sat on the edge of the mattress, looking down into my face and brushing my tangled, stinking hair away.

"I'm sorry," he said. "This is so awful. I'm so sorry. What can I do?"

The answer sprang to mind immediately. "Cancel the next month of shows. Take me off the road."

It was plain my answer had shocked him. He had probably been thinking I wanted tea. But I'd almost died because he'd sent me there, all unknowing. I could feel a faint burning still in my throat and lungs, and only because of my gift did I have a voice at all. If I hadn't been there, the fire would have been only a headline, not a memory. It would have been someone else's tragedy. Now everything was different. My life was horror, and I was a murderess. I couldn't tell him what I'd done; I never could. We were well beyond tea.

Quickly, he was all business. "We can't cancel. You know how much that costs?"

"No," I said honestly.

"I suppose that's why you have me," he said. "The answer is too much. It's not even the money. No one will trust us again if we cancel so many shows on such short notice. Word spreads like wildfire when you go back on a booking. We have to protect your reputation."

"Less, then. What about three weeks?"

I could see him calculating. "No."

"Two weeks, then? I can't. I'll panic." Even just thinking of the hardwood boards of a stage, I could smell the smoke. My knees ached, and I felt the hard landing from my leap over the orchestra pit all over again. Then I saw Ray's face looming above me, and blood, a fountain of blood. I backed farther into the bed, clutched the pillow across my chest like a shield.

"No."

"You can't force me," I said a little hysterically. "Let someone else do it."

"No one can take your place. You're the one people come to see."

"Dress someone else up like me. Tell them it's me. How will they know?"

He said, "They'll know, Arden. Maybe we should wait and talk about this later, when you've had some more time."

"No, now," I said firmly. "I won't change my mind."

He thought about it. Nervous, still trembling, I watched him think.

"Ten days," said Clyde at last. "We can cancel the next show, the one in Moberly. It's a small venue and they don't talk to anyone. And of course the show here is canceled."

"They won't shift it?"

"The mayor closed all the theaters in

Chicago. For six weeks. I don't think you realize how bad it was."

"I know how bad it was!" I yelled, angry at myself and him and the world. "I was there! I watched people die! I could have died, because you sent me there! Don't tell me I don't know!"

"Do you know how many people are dead?" he yelled back. "Six hundred! The world didn't stop for them, and it's not going to stop for you."

On any other day, I would have found it a stunning number. Today, it didn't even make a dent.

But I could hear the anger in his voice, and if both of us flew off the handle, things would come to a bad end. I couldn't take that on top of everything else. I was sad and furious, but I knew what I needed to do next, and shouting wasn't going to accomplish it. I could only tell him the truth.

"I don't know if I can do this anymore. I need to go back to New York," I said. "To rest. To think."

He sighed and said, "Okay. I'll change my plans. Canada can wait."

"No."

"But you can't be alone."

"I have to." With effort, I set the pillow aside. I reached for his hands and held them. His fingers were cool and dry. "I would love to go to Canada with you, but I can't. And I can't stay here. I can't be on the road right now. I need to be alone with my thoughts. New York is the best place for that. I need to go, and I need to do it today."

"Tomorrow?" he said, ever the negotiator.

I relented in the one small way I could. "Tomorrow."

He brushed his lips against my forehead with such a gentle, feathery touch that it made my whole poor body dissolve.

We slept in each other's arms without making love, the first time we'd ever done so, and in the morning, I left.

I took a passenger train instead of the private railcar. Somehow I thought it might help. I didn't want to feel pampered. I wanted to feel anonymous. I missed Clyde terribly — hiding in his arms might let me forget things, at least for a few blissful moments — but it was best that I was alone. I was melancholy and not fit company. If Clyde had been there, I just would have pretended things were fine, and things weren't fine. So I let myself be melancholy and settled into a dark frame of mind.

Regret for what I'd done quickly bloomed into fantasies of what I might do, what I could do. I could just disappear, I realized. I could get off this train anywhere, and no one would have to know. I could make a new life somewhere else, anywhere else, where no one knew me as a magician or a dancer or any of the other things I'd been. I could start over. It was a beautiful fantasy, and indeed I almost followed that whim. I found myself standing, even, to make for the door. Had I had even a little money with me, perhaps I would have done it.

Then my fantasy turned even darker. I wouldn't even have to wait until the train stopped moving in order to step off. Taking a life meant it would be fair if I lost mine as well, in some fashion. Dying would mean no more torment, no uncertainty, no regret. But quickly I let go of the idea. People would think some weakness or hidden fault had gotten the better of me — *Drink? Gambling? A secret love affair?* they would speculate — and I didn't want that to be my legacy. And it would destroy Clyde. I had to get back to him, to be with him, even if I wasn't ready just yet.

As I stared out the window at the country-side, I felt as if the train was bearing me back in time. Back before I'd cut Ray's throat, before I'd had my heart broken and my lungs burned by the Iroquois Fire, before I released Clyde from his promise and he laid his hands on me and we fell headlong in love. I'd taken great joy headlining my own act as the Amazing Arden, no question. But in a way, the happiest time of my life had been before that. It had been when I was a member of Adelaide's company, learning the ropes and forging my way ahead into the unfamiliar world of stage magic, making it my own. And then I knew where I needed to go and who I needed to see.

She was more mother to me than my own mother had been. Neither of them had instructed me tenderly or shared their feelings with me, but Adelaide and I were more of a piece: canny and distrustful on one hand, but on the other, whores for the crowd. She had trusted me, encouraged me. She had handed something meaningful down. If I was going to leave the stage and its attendant world behind — which it had just occurred to me I might — I'd be wise to talk to someone who knew exactly what that was like.

Adelaide's farm looked like it had been copied from the pages of a picture book. There was a wooden mailbox at the end of the gravel-lined drive and rows of tall trees that flanked the lane. The farmhouse was faded but clean, the worn lines of its white clapboard sides still straight and true. The one detail that stood out as odd, which I only noticed as I mounted the steps to the porch, was the tiger sprawled out in the sunbeams that fanned out from the slats in the porch railing.

The weather had turned shockingly warm for the season, and Adelaide was sitting in the porch swing with an open book on her lap, her bare feet almost but not quite brushing the tiger's back. There was more gray to her hair; the same was true of the fur around the tiger's muzzle. "Same tiger?" I asked.

"The very same."

"Is he safe?"

"For now, she is. She's just had her supper."

I noticed then there was a thin chain running from the tiger's collar to the thickest post of the porch railing, and I breathed a little easier. "You bought her at auction?"

"I did."

"I'm sorry I didn't ask you before selling the animals."

"That's why I gave you the company, no strings attached," she said. "I expected you would do with it what you wanted. I didn't want you to ask me anything. I wanted you to make your own decisions."

"I seem to remember there were two strings attached," I said.

"Eighty percent of a great deal is far better than one hundred percent of nothing. You're doing quite well for yourself, it seems."

She was bold, but she wasn't wrong. I said, "I suppose it was the other string who told you that."

"And that one's worked out in your favor as well, hasn't it?"

"Yes, he's done a great job with the business."

With a sly smile, she said, "I'm not talking about the business. Not the money kind of business, anyway." I realized he must have told her what had happened between us. Well, we hadn't hidden it from anyone in the company, so why hide it from Adelaide? I wanted to ask if she was happy for me, but it didn't seem right. If she wanted me to know how she felt, she'd tell me.

"You look wonderful," I said.

"You've become a better liar," she replied.

The tiger sighed in her sleep, a deep rumbling noise, and stretched one paw farther out before settling back into stillness. I watched the soft, pale fur of her

underbelly rise and fall, almost impercepti-
bly, with her breath. It was hypnotic.

"So what's the occasion?" said Adelaide at
last.

"I almost died in a fire," I said. I left out
the part where I'd cut a man's throat; in
case someone figured out the connection
and came to accuse me of the crime, I
didn't want to ever have spoken aloud of it.
The less she knew about that, the better.

"But you didn't," she said. "That's life."

"But I don't know what the point is
anymore. Playing tricks on people. It's a
frivolous thing. Night after night, the same
games, fake flowers, fake pictures, a fake
world. That whole crowd came to the Iroquois to escape their ordinary lives for a
couple of hours, and it killed them. I don't
know if I can ever look out over an audience again without remembering that."

Adelaide said, "Are you going to give up?"

"I don't know."

"Hmm."

"What?"

"Never thought of you as a girl who gives
up, that's all. The strong ones don't quit."

Without thinking, I said accusingly, "You
did."

"That's different, Vivi. And I suspect you
know it. I lived an entire lifetime onstage,

and it was glorious. I wouldn't trade those years away for anything. But then it wasn't my time anymore. It's still your time. Why would you toss that away?"

"It's hard."

"We deal with the hard parts because we have to. What's the alternative? Not living?"

I thought back to the horrific scene in the burning theater, and to Ray looming over me among the shrouded dead, and how I'd felt lying there helpless on the ground. "Maybe."

"Good Lord, girl. Stop feeling sorry for yourself. It's embarrassing."

"I almost died," I said again.

She seemed unmoved. "Life's a bullet catch."

"You're pitiless, aren't you?"

"And I suspect that's why you're here. You don't want someone who'll coddle you and tell you you're right. You wanted a level head, and here I am. You almost died? You've got fear and amazement in you. Use them."

I looked down at the sleeping tiger and smiled. "Is it all right if I stay the night, then?"

"If you promise to drop this malarkey about how the world owes you a bucket of fine red roses."

"Consider it dropped."

She rose gingerly from the swing and folded her book closed with an audible thump. "Then let's have a steak and talk about the time you got arrested in Poughkeepsie. I've been dying to hear your side of the story."

The weight on my heart lifted. I followed her into the house, saying, "It started with a man at the back, in the middle of the act, shouting, 'Charlatan' . . ."

CHAPTER TWENTY-FIVE

Janesville, 1905
Four o'clock in the morning
"You don't just heal your body. You heal your mind," says Holt.

She stares at him, wordless for once.

"I mean, you clearly have some way, some magic, beyond what normal people have. To keep you going."

The magician cocks her head. The half-brown eye blazes.

He goes on, the words drawn out by her silence. "A disaster like that fire, it stretches the mind beyond imagination. People aren't the same afterward. They just give up."

"I almost did," she admits.

"But you kept going. You're still going. Despite Ray, despite everything. And it's like you draw your strength from disaster. You only get more determined the more of these horrors you endure." Her story is so real to him now; he imagines he can almost smell the smoke and blood. The room around him is unchanged, but it feels darker somehow, as her story takes more and more sinister turns.

"I don't know that it works like that," she says. "And anyway, you're wrong. My mind doesn't heal like my body. I remember everything. Being able to go on, the kind of determination you seem to admire so much, it comes at a price."

"Your soul?"

She laughs, but bitterly. "That's just newspaper talk. The Devil and whatnot. I'm just a woman, a human woman."

"Despite your magic."

"Yes. That doesn't mean I'm any more or less human than anyone else."

"Doesn't it?"

She rattles her hands in the cuffs. "You tell me."

"Well, you cut a man's throat," he says, hoping to jar her. "Whatever he'd done to you, however horrible he was, he was human too. What did that feel like?"

Nothing changes in her posture or her manner. She only says, matter-of-factly, "I wished to God I could have taken it back. I tried to heal him. I tried my best. But the wish didn't work."

He can think of a dozen reasons her healing power might have failed her in that moment, but he doesn't want to focus on that right away. He has another question for her first. "Why did you tell me that story? You must know it makes me more suspicious of you. To know you've killed before."

She is slow in responding. When she does speak, her voice is still matter-of-fact. "I'm telling you the whole truth. The whole story. So why wouldn't I tell you that part?"

"Because you're trying to convince me to let you go?" He doubts she truly needs to be reminded. It's life or death for both of them now; that kind of thing doesn't slip a person's mind.

"As I said. It's the truth. I need you to believe me. I think the best way to do that is to tell you the whole story, warts and all."

"Tell me this, then." A dark question has been nagging at him, and as many questions as there are to ask her, he can't help putting this one next. "Why did Ray do what he did to you? What makes a man like that?"

She shakes her head. "It's impossible to know. I think the fever he survived as a child, the one that killed his sisters, left him touched in the head. Not that it made him stupid, but it changed him. Burned away some part of his brain. And made him think he was better than human. He thought he had some godlike healing power, and he thought I did too, and that gave him rights to me somehow. I don't know. I don't want to talk about Ray anymore. Do we have to talk about him?"

"No," says Holt. "We can talk about the murder instead."

She's staring up with those otherworldly eyes. He wants to ask her to close them. He wants her to look away. But if he told her that, she'd know she's getting to him. And he feels so close to knowing the answer now.

She's dangerous. She slashed a man's throat open, let his life drain away. And she and this Clyde were in love, but they'd also fought each other. Disagreed. He sees clearly how she could be guilty. Almost every piece of the puzzle is in place.

He taps the folded razor on his wrist again. And realizes what he's holding, all of a sudden. Almost involuntarily, he drops the razor, which clatters loudly on the floor.

"That's it, isn't it? His," he says.

"Yes."

"That's awful."

She swallows hard and says, "Yes, it is."

"Why do you keep it?"

"I didn't mean to," she says. "I took it with me so I wouldn't leave it there with him. It was just a reflex. And then — well, I'll tell you that part in a bit."

"Tell me now."

"First, can you do something for me?"

"What?"

Looking up at him with the fairy eye, she says, "Take off another pair of handcuffs."

"Why?"

The words pour out of her in a flood, unchecked. "Because I'm asking you to, Virgil. Because none of this matters, does it? The how and the why? I'll end up dead whether I did it or not. We both know that. And I am so, so scared of dying. And my only hope is that you'll show me mercy, but the longer we talk, the more I think maybe it's already too late. Maybe at first the easier thing to do was to let me go, but the longer I'm in this chair, maybe the easier thing to do is to keep me. Maybe you've already made up your mind. And I'm not asking you to release me right this minute. I'm not asking for your answer. I'm just asking you . . . could you just make me a little more comfortable?"

He makes her wait while he pretends to consider it, although he already knows exactly what he'll say and why. He bends down and picks up the fallen razor, which feels like it's burning his fingers, now that he knows its history.

Then he walks around the desk, to the far side so it's between them, and crouches behind it. He tucks the razor into the right drawer, the one he can get to fastest if he needs it because it doesn't lock, but low enough that he knows she can't see which one he's using. He nears her again and stands facing her. He touches the key at his belt, as if absentmindedly, but really the furthest thing from it.

He watches her watching him, that unsettling gaze so flat and level, and stares hard and straight back at her until, at last, she blinks.

"Not until you do me a favor," he says.

"What favor could I do for you?"

"I think you know," he says.

She opens her mouth to speak, appears to think better of it, and closes it again.

He feels a surge of power so strong that it makes him light-headed. There are two pairs of cuffs left, chaining her firmly to that chair. Unbreakable, inescapable steel. Two is enough, he tells himself. She has no way out unless he lets her out. She has to know that. So once he makes it explicit — the favor only she has the power to deliver for the release only he can grant — she'll jump at it. She has to.

She stares down, down at her stockinged feet in their dangling shackles and the scattered sequins shed from her dress in the struggle. The loose tendrils of her hair fall to obscure her face. He can imagine what she's thinking, but he doesn't want to imagine. He wants to hear it straight from her mouth.

He reaches out and pats her knee. It feels like the right thing to do, somehow.

"I said I don't want to talk about him," she says. "But I can't avoid it."

"Ray?"

"Ray," she says, barely whispering the name.

He's confused. "But you told me the whole story already, didn't you? He attacked you, and you killed him for it. What else is there to say?"

She gasps. "How can you be so glib about it?"

"I didn't mean —"

"No!" she shouts, and fresh tears spring to her eyes. "You don't realize. You don't have any idea! I was a child when it started. A child! And him following me, tracking me, watching me, every single day! Do you have any idea what it's like, to live on the knife's edge like that? Knowing yesterday you stopped it, but tomorrow you might not? There's only one thing worse."

"Giving in?"

"Yes."

"So — you gave in?"

She slumps in the chair, her eyes shadowed. Her hair and her clothes and her posture all give her the air of perfect defeat. "I can't do this anymore. With you. These questions. I can't."

He doesn't speak right away. He waits and watches her face, trying his best to read it. There is something about her now that seems emptied out, and he chooses to believe her. She seems to be well and truly overcome.

At length, he says, "Then what shall we do instead?"

She says, "First I want you to wipe my face before the tears dry on it."

Reaching out with the handkerchief, he dries the nearer cheek with a light and tender hand and asks gently, "And then?"

"And then I want to tell you the rest of the story. When things took a turn. When it all started going bad, and I couldn't stop it."

"Good," he says, drying the other cheek. "Good. That's what I want to hear."

CHAPTER TWENTY-SIX

1904

The Halved Man

Clyde and I were reunited in New York upon his return, and once I was in his strong, sheltering arms, I never wanted to leave them.

"But are you all right?"

I nodded fiercely, yes.

"You'll be ready for your show in two days, won't you?" he asked, and if I was a little disappointed that talk had turned so quickly to business, it helped me calm my own heart.

I drew back and collected myself. "Yes, I'll be ready," I said.

He pulled me toward him again and said, "I missed you. I can't even tell you how much I missed you," and I tried to let myself relax against him. He pulled at my skirt playfully, but mindful of the wound on my thigh, I murmured something about waiting a little longer, and he didn't insist. I hadn't tried to heal it yet. I was afraid somehow I wouldn't be able to, that whatever magic had once been in me was gone. Seeing Adelaide had bolstered my spirits and reminded me I was capable of soldiering on, but it hadn't made everything fine and safe and right. Neither of us had the right kind of magic to pull off that trick. No one did.

I couldn't rest, not really, but travel and emotion and fatigue meant that at least I slept.

The next day, I woke up curled against the warmth of Clyde's body, which had always been wonderful to me. So long known, so long familiar. But in the first breath when I woke up, I inhaled his masculine, musky smell, and for a moment, I didn't recognize him, and I sat bolt upright, heart pounding.

As soon as I recognized my surroundings, the bedroom of the Jane Street apartment, my world settled into place again. I lowered myself back down, and Clyde shifted in his sleep to put his arm back over me. I lay still, but my mind was still spinning. That fear was far too fresh in me, too close to the surface. I needed to find some way to drive it down again.

I had been afraid of Ray more than half

my life, but the fear had gone dormant with distance. Now it was fully awakened again. Terrified and threatened, my head spinning, I had lashed out with all my strength and loosed a waterfall of blood from a fellow human being's body. He was the only thing in the breathing world I feared, and he had turned me into a killer. I could feel those surging moments of desperation again, wishing over and over to heal the gaping wound and stop the coursing blood, going mad at my failure. Even the thought of him dead at last, a cold body among all the other cold bodies, didn't kill the fear.

Was it him I was afraid of, or myself?

The fear was up against me, inside me, under my skin. Adelaide had said to use it. How could I do that? How could I push it away, or transform it into something else?

I lay on my back, staring up at the blank white ceiling, thinking of that awful day. How entirely helpless I'd felt, right up until I lashed out, and how regret had washed over me afterward. How the terror was like a djinni escaped from his lamp, never to be crammed back in. How everything had spiraled out of control, and how fervently I wished that everything could come out differently.

And that was the seed of the illusion. How

I didn't need to fear either Ray or myself if I could take back that day. If I could end the confrontation my own way, on my own terms. How I could bring death, yes, but afterward, if I chose to, bring life.

By the time Clyde woke up and turned his sleepy gaze on me, I had the idea fully formed. The illusion. Powerful and magical and unique.

"Good morning," I said.

"Good morning."

"I have an idea."

"So do I," he said, nearly purring, and ran his finger up my arm in that tickling way he knew I loved.

"Not now."

"When?"

I couldn't hold back a smile. "Soon."

He rolled over, stretched, kissed me gently on the lips, and settled himself back against the pillows. "So what's your idea?"

"A new illusion. One of the boys. Who's the best?"

"At what is the question." He eyed me, half suspicious.

"Not anything in particular. He doesn't need to be a dancer or an acrobat. Well, an acrobat might be good. But not necessary. It's a passive role, really."

"Go on." Idly, he rubbed my shoulder.

"He just needs to have presence, mainly. Oh. And act scared."

"Scared about what?"

"About what I'm going to do to him."

"And what are you going to do to him, love?"

"Cut him in half," I said.

"What?" Clyde's hand dropped from my shoulder.

"Well, someone cuts a girl in half, doesn't he?"

"A lot of someones do. Kellar, certainly. Atwood. Burlingame."

"And a dozen more. So I'll cut someone in half. Why shouldn't I?"

He looked at me blankly. He didn't have an answer.

I kept going. "But not a girl. The girls can't defend themselves. Cut a man in half, and see how he likes it."

"Arden, are you all right?"

I bristled at the question. I'd expected him to embrace the idea, but he was clearly made uncomfortable by it, and I wasn't sure why. He was usually head over heels for sensation. I said, "Of course I am."

"You almost died."

"Yes, I remember that," I said with a touch of frost. "But I'm fine now."

"I don't like this," said Clyde. "It's not you."

"It's me. Truly."

"No. I know you."

He sounded more than confident. He sounded territorial. It rubbed me wrong. Accusingly, I said, "Do you?"

"Arden, please, don't be like this. I love you, and everything I want is your happiness."

"That's not even my name," I said.

"Arden. Ada. Miss Bates. Whatever you'd like. It's you and you're mine."

"Yours? I can't talk to you about this anymore. I need to go."

"No, no, don't run, not from me, please," he said and grabbed my arms, the worst thing he could do, and I ripped my body out of his grasp and stood.

He started to rise from the bed, and I held my hand up, blocking him.

"Don't. Don't." I stepped into the dress I'd worn the night before, a forest green gown too fancy for the circumstance but the closest thing to hand.

"Don't go," said Clyde. "You can't very well wander the streets alone."

"Oh, can't I?"

"I mean — Ada, please — at least let me go."

"No, I'm leaving. I don't care what you do. Please yourself," I muttered, closing the top button of my dress on the way to the door, which I left hanging open behind me.

I threw myself into revising the act. The excitement of the Halved Man was bubbling inside me. I stayed after Clyde with all my might — wheedling and cajoling, then insisting and demanding — until he agreed to find someone to make the new trick for me. The mechanics of it were relatively simple. The construction itself didn't require a master, as an intricate cabinet illusion would. There were no hidden hooks or mounts. This only called for a competent carpenter with a bit of imagination, absolute discretion, and two weeks' time.

Hundreds of illusionists were cutting women in half, and despite the differences between men and women, they came apart just the same way under a blade. Or, rather, gave the impression of coming apart — of course no one was really getting severed. Men's bodies could be reflected by mirrors or hidden under the false bottom of a trunk, just like women's. There were as many different ways to stage the illusion as there were illusionists, but I chose one of the simplest, knowing the shock of seeing a man in a woman's place at the end of the blade would be shock enough.

The cabinet design I chose was a coffin-shaped box in which the body would appear parallel to the ground, on four narrow poles that raised the box to the level of my waist. The poles were wheeled so the cabinet could be freely moved about the stage. But the cabinet was actually two cabinets, the separation in the middle cleverly concealed with thin panels of veneer. The saw that seemed to sever the cabinet only slipped into the existing gap, cutting nothing at all. One of the twins would lie down in the top half of the cabinet, jackknifing his legs up and to the side, and Hugo would lie down in the bottom half, curled tightly and carefully so only his legs protruded through the cabinet's holes. When the cabinet halves were pressed together, it looked like one man's body, but it never was. Any viewer would assume Michael's or Gabriel's angelic curls connected to Hugo's polished black boots, but they were entirely separate. The audience was off the track from the beginning.

Even after I healed the cut Ray had made on my thigh, when Clyde and I made love, I always insisted on darkness. Whenever his hand roamed too close, I shifted and stirred to keep his fingers from touching me there. I knew my wish had worked and the cut had healed completely, leaving no sign, as my cuts always did. But I could still feel it there, burning against the tender skin, and I couldn't stand the thought of my love's fingers resting on that unholy spot.

I was so careful in this respect I became careless elsewhere, and Clyde found among my things Ray's straight razor, which he took for a gift I'd brought him. He loved the smooth unadorned bone of the handle and exclaimed over its perfection. He kept it on the sink and used it every single day he was with me. It made me sick to my stomach to see it in his hand, but there was no question of setting the record straight. I couldn't even begin to explain. So I let him think it was something lovely when in fact it was something awful. For his sake. And every time I saw it, I tried to force myself to forget what that blade meant, what its sharp edge had done, but I always remembered. Always.

The night before the new act was to debut, there was a long, heavy thunderstorm. Clyde was next to me, and I was idly stroking his hair while we lay on the floor of the railcar together. The bed was far more comfortable, but sometimes we were too eager for it, and this had been one of those times. We'd drawn the shades against the lightning. I could hear the steady patter of rain on the roof, and it made the world inside seem small and dark and private. I reveled in the feeling.

Clyde said, "I need to talk to you."

"So talk."

"Please. It's serious."

I set my shoulders and turned toward him. I was ready for another fight. But he didn't look angry, not exactly, and I tried not to rush to judgment.

"I love you so much, you know that?"

Soberly, I nodded. "I know that."

"And I think you love me."

"Yes," I said, and my voice cracked, because for a moment, I realized he was a little unsure. That maybe I would say I didn't love him. But I did love him, as much as I loved myself, probably more.

"I've been thinking," he said. "If we love each other so much. Maybe we should do something about it."

"What?"

"I want to be with you. I've been waiting for the perfect time, to have everything settled, and now I realize maybe that's no way to live. Maybe we should jump at the chances that we have. You're my Juliet, my Rosalind, my everything. My Arden. I want to be with you."

"But you are with me."

"Not in the way I want."

I wasn't sure what he was getting at, so I asked. "Do you want me to come off the road?"

"Not yet, no."

I was growing more confused, not less. "Then I don't understand. If you don't want anything to change, what do you want?"

"I want you to marry me."

The minute felt like an hour as I searched his face. He looked sincere. There was no trace of guile, no angle. And yet. I couldn't help but think of the last time he'd proposed marriage to me, years and years ago, under circumstances that knocked me flat. He hadn't meant it then, and he hadn't looked any less sincere. He'd always been a good actor. The only difference was that now, unlike then, I knew it.

I had the same feeling I had the first time he'd proposed: an overwhelming instinct to say yes, throw myself into his arms, mold my body to his. But this time, I didn't give in.

As soon as I got my breath back, I asked,

"I see. How would that change anything?"

He looked down. "It wouldn't, really, I guess."

"Then why do you want to?"

"Arden," he said, a pleading note in his voice that I'd rarely, if ever, heard. "This is absolutely not very romantic. I had pictured it very differently."

I reached my hand out, cradling his beloved cheek in my palm. "You know I love you. Completely. And desperately."

"And I love you."

I said, "So you don't need some certificate to tell you that. It wouldn't make a bit of difference. We belong to each other already. Don't we?"

He said, "It makes a difference to me. It's what I want, Arden. Please."

"Okay."

"Okay?" There was hope in his voice.

I said, "I mean, okay, I'll think about it."

He was silent for a minute. The next question he asked seemed unrelated. "Are you going to do that trick?"

I didn't tell him it was an illusion, not a trick, and I didn't ask which one he meant. I told him bluntly, "Yes."

"I wish you wouldn't."

"My mind is made up."

"And marriage? Is your mind made up on

that too?"

I tried to be gentle. "No, darling. Please. That I need to think about."

"Of course you do," he said, his voice rough. "You never do anything the way a normal girl would do it. Of course you have to do this your own way too. You'll probably want to buy your own ring."

"I don't," I said. "I don't even know if I want a ring."

"You know. You just won't tell me."

"That's not true. Please. I truly need time to think. You took me by surprise."

He still looked suspicious, but in the end, he said, "All right, then. A few days enough?"

"Yes," I answered and hoped it would be.

We tried it first in Baltimore. It was somewhere we could put up posters, create mystery, pay people to whisper. We spread a rumor someone had been killed in a rehearsal. We spread a rumor it was as dangerous as the Bullet Catch, as fatal as Parisi's Chainsaw Folly. We spread every rumor we could to guarantee a packed house for opening night, and we got exactly what we wished for.

I'd never felt more powerful. I'd designed and performed dozens of illusions, but they were all some form of pageantry, turning the most prosaic items into flowers and ribbons and flames, embracing the lush impossible. I was the undisputed queen of creating opulence from nothingness. Nothing like this: savage and beautiful, with all the artifice of stagecraft stripped away. Nothing else had put me alone on a stage with the object of my actions, just the two of us, in which I could have complete victory. In a way, it was like Adelaide's performance of Lady to Tiger, but instead of the physical form of a tiger, I took on the spirit of one. Instead of a delicate grace, I had a strong grace, a grace to be feared.

Frankly, I liked being feared for a change.

I had begun as a dancer, and a dancer's allure was as a creature too light for the earth. My new allure was as a creature too dangerous for it. Jeannie outdid herself with a striking black gown, beaded and spangled all over, to suit me up like a modern witch, both graceful and grim. Unfortunately the gown turned out to be her swan song as my wardrobe mistress, as she was called home to Abilene to care for her mother, who'd taken ill. An unwelcome surprise, but I couldn't begrudge her. I would miss her terribly, but the excitement of the Halved Man swept me along, carried me forward.

The old act had incorporated many things — fire and beauty and mystery and magic — but this was the first time we reached out into the seats to take our audience by the throats. This was the first time we made them afraid. And as strange as that was, as unexpected as it was, they found that they liked the feeling.

I raised up the long bright knife and plunged it into the center of the coffin. The man cried out. Then I laid down the knife and picked up the saw, which I heaved back and forth with obvious effort, leaning my whole body into it to emphasize how heavy it was, how hard to move. The man howled as I sawed.

The audience howled along with him.

With a flourish, I spun half the man away, leaving the other half in place. Some nights, I left the head and shoulders behind, some nights, the legs and feet. The audience seemed to embrace both possibilities. No matter which half went where, they cried out in unison, disbelieving. They sucked in all their breath and let it all out like a single breathing person all together. The shock and the terror and the shared impossibility made a single fantastical creature of them. I made a creature of them.

I spun the second half of the man off the

stage after the first, clouds of smoke filled the stage, and I pointed with a terrible, straight finger toward the center of the front row. There a young man with a head of bright blond curls stood and opened his white shirtfront to expose a line of fresh red blood across the center of his waist. I clapped twice, hard, two sharp noises like gunshots. He wiped away the blood from his skin with the palm of his hand. He wiped again with his other hand until the blood on his stomach was gone, the flesh clean and unbroken underneath, turning so all could see. He was identical in every way to the man I'd cut in half, but whole again.

Of course, earlier in the act, they'd already seen that the twins were part of the company. They knew there were two of them, identical blond things with cherubic faces and teenagers' lanky frames. They saw one and started looking for the other. They felt smart, thinking they were too smart to be fooled.

When the twin sprang up, as an unexpectedly whole person, the audience was suspicious. "Impostor!" they called. "It's the other one!"

And in the next moment, his brother sprang up at the back of the theater. Everyone looked back and forth between the two twins. The second one pulled aside his shirt to show a waist as unmarred as his brother's. They both turned to one side and then the other, giving the audience a good look, from the cheap seats on down. Someone had been torn apart and made whole again, but it was impossible to tell who. They were both flawless.

Then the audience shouted "Brava!" and "Amazing!"

The twins took their perfectly synchronized bows, moving as one. Then I took mine.

And the theater erupted in applause, long rippling waves of it, until the echoes threatened to deafen us all.

The headline in the *Sun* read "WOMAN MAGICIAN'S SPECTACLE DIVIDES MAN, DUMBFOUNDS AUDIENCE. WHO IS THIS AMAZING ARDEN?" There were other headlines, less flattering ones, but the *Sun*'s I clipped from its page and tucked away for safekeeping. I wasn't given to keeping mementos, but this felt like a worthy occasion.

It was an immense success, the Halved Man. It was like and yet unlike what everyone else was doing. It created a stir. There had already been press about my unfeminine business, but it multiplied a hundred-fold. Some said I was possessed by the devil. Some said I should be stopped before I hurt someone. A preacher in Conestoga gave a sermon about the killing of a man by a woman being the sign that Armageddon was upon us, and he called for my destruction, so we had to have a police guard for a couple of weeks, but all that meant was more attention.

The twins were ecstatic. Not content to simply take turns, they drew straws every evening to determine which of them would be the one in the box, and the excitement of this ritual brought the whole company together to lay bets and play favorites every night. They were all involved. Contessa, née Doreen, snuck down into the audience and watched, even though she had to be onstage for the next illusion. She couldn't help herself. When the knife took its first plunge into the coffin, there was always a bloodcurdling cheer of joy, and I knew it was hers, because it happened in every town.

The audience cheered and booed and whooped and cried, and when it was all over, they threw more flowers than they'd ever thrown before. It was amazing how their enthusiasm changed everything. The show seemed brighter, smarter, faster. All of us in it seemed more beautiful, more clever, more alive. The new energy affected every member of the company. I could see the difference clearly.

In short, everyone was happy but Clyde.

CHAPTER TWENTY-SEVEN

1904–1905

The Ring in Danger

He gave me a ring, of course. Maybe he thought that's what I really wanted. It wasn't. I wasn't holding out for a bauble, some kind of material proof of his commitment. It shocked me that he thought that might be what I required. Then it shocked me again that I assumed I knew his reasons. It's amazing how well you can know someone, how much you can love them, and still not really know what it is they're thinking.

The ring was lovely and simple. A gold band with a gemstone channel-set into it, very thoughtful, since it wouldn't catch on my clothes while I was performing. It was a light blue stone, but when I looked at it carefully, it seemed to me to have a kernel of brown inside it, almost like my half-brown eye. If he'd searched to find something unique that reflected my own uniqueness, it was a touching and wonderful gesture. But I didn't ask him about it. I couldn't. If I asked about the ring, he would take it as an invitation to talk about the proposal, about whether or not I might accept. I wasn't done thinking yet. I was afraid to talk at all to him until I knew what it was I was going to say.

I didn't know what to do with the ring, so I stuck it to my chest with a bit of spirit gum to keep it close to my heart. When I put on my first dress for the evening's performance, in a spangled blue gown I knew flickered gorgeously in the gas spotlights, I dressed right over it. Between the spirit gum and the tight fabric of the undergarment, I thought it would be safe.

My emotions were affecting me more than I wanted to admit. It was too much at once. My brush with death at the Iroquois. The horror of Ray immediately afterward. Regrets and uncertainties I couldn't silence. Worst of all, the volatile situation with Clyde, who I needed as my rock. Everything was coming unmoored.

I could almost hold myself together. I knew every moment and every action so well, I only needed to let my body find the memory to carry me forward. We got through Light and Heavy Chest, Woman on

Fire, the Magic Milliner, one bit of business after the next. But three-quarters of the way through the act, at a crucial moment of stage patter where I stood alone on the stage, things began to fall apart. I found myself reaching for a coin that, for the first time, wasn't there.

Had anyone else been on the stage, I could have motioned to them for help. We had a set of prearranged signals for exactly this type of situation. But I was alone, with no one there to assist and a mind as blank as an unpainted canvas.

My choices were to invent a way out or to walk off. I invented a way out. It was all I had been thinking of for days, this ring, and while I didn't usually do any ring illusions, I remembered the name of one I'd seen in Adelaide's old notes. It was all I had to help me. I used it.

I reached into the front of my dress, freed the ring, and held it high to catch the light.

"The Ring in Danger!" I cried.

First I made it vanish inside a dainty flowered handkerchief, a simple palming with a misdirect, and it reappeared in the spot over my heart again. I strung it on a flowing crimson scarf, then cut the scarf in tiny pieces and brought it whole from my pocket, with the ring still threaded over the fabric. I used the spare charge up my sleeve from Woman on Fire to make it appear to melt in a burst of flame then pretended to find it intact in the most unlikely place, in the sock of a man in the fifteenth row, nowhere near the aisle.

The illusion was a success, but I felt no pride, only a flat and hazy relief.

After the act, I went to Clyde. I took off my sparkling gown and stockings and corset and underdress and hung them neatly so they didn't wrinkle. I removed every layer, down to the bare skin. I still felt the wound on my thigh, but I knew what I felt was invisible — while I hadn't healed, my body had. I scratched away the patch of spirit gum on my chest and left an angry red streak in its place. I tugged the ring off the finger where I'd kept it after the illusion and held it in the palm of my hand. I lay down next to him on the bed, raised myself up on my elbow, and gazed into his face.

He looked at me and said, "You have an answer for me, don't you?"

"Yes."

"It's not going to be the answer I want, is it?"

"I don't think so."

"Go ahead and say it."

"Beloved, I'm not going to marry you

now," I said.

He lay back with his eyes closed, his head against the pillow, and said, "I was afraid you'd say that."

"I love you more than anything else in the world."

"I know." He reached out and stroked the side of my face. The feeling of his fingers against my cheek shook my resolve. He was offering me a kind of certainty. The chance to know that no matter where we were or what we did, that I had a person who loved me that much, who always wanted to reach out for me. Proof, or as close to it as one could ever have, that we believed this love would last. Linking just the two of us, for-ever.

But I couldn't. It was a trap. He might not mean it as one, but that's what it would be. I had no second sight, no magical power to see what life would bring, but all the same, I could clearly see our future. We were too strong-willed to be locked together in marriage, a permanent institution. If we tried to hold each other too close, it could destroy us. On some level, we would never trust each other. I was no longer trust-worthy, and neither could I believe it of him. Even with the best of intentions, one of us would do the other wrong. It was only a matter of time and chance which one of us it would be. And if we married, my property would be his. My money would build his theater, whether or not I wanted it to. I hated to think that entered into his decision to propose, but I couldn't be certain it didn't.

And I couldn't say any of that out loud.

Tentatively, I told him, "The timing just isn't right. Maybe we can talk about it after this tour's over. It's only a few more months."

His jaw tightened, tensed. "Fine. I suppose. I just wish we didn't have to do everything your way."

"We don't have to."

"Yes, we do," he said. "I have suggestions, I make recommendations, but we always end up squarely where you want to be."

"And is it so bad?"

"No, darling. I'm happy," he said, and he sounded like he meant it, or was trying to. "But I think sometimes we could be happy if I got my way too. It would just be different."

"I'm not ready for different."

"All right."

"Can't we just keep things the way they are? For now?"

"Including your new trick, I suppose."

I said, "Yes. I'm not going to back down on that, I think you know."

"I was afraid you'd say that too."

"And it's not a trick."

"Let's go to sleep."

The fame of the Halved Man grew. Some audience members were still shocked by the boldness of it, but more and more of them bought tickets because of, not in spite of, the illusion. We got more coverage in the papers, higher billing on the posters, more attention in every regard. Even the people who hated it couldn't stop talking about it. They might even have been talking the loudest. And for every minister or temperance crusader who complained that the Halved Man was a travesty and a sacrilege, there were two or three more citizens who wanted a front-row seat for the hubbub.

To stoke the flames, I decided to make the illusion even more shocking. I did so with the help of our prop assistant who had staged dozens of battles at a Shakespearean theater in Philadelphia and knew all there was to know about fake blood. Eagerly we worked out the best position and the best moment. At the next performance, the blade of the saw pierced a thin membrane, and bright red blood seemed to pour from the severed body, completing the illusion that a man was dying right onstage in front of the audience's wide, hungry eyes.

And as dark and disturbing as the Halved Man seemed to the world, it made me happy. It made me regain my joy in performing. The fear that had crept back into my life was banished. I could enjoy the applause again, revel in the audience's amazement. When I bowed low and heaved the blade of the saw through the cabinet, I was fully the Amazing Arden, without even a trace of the Ada I had been. Afterward, once I had shown them I had full dominion over life and death, I raised my arms and drank in their admiration. I'll admit I enjoyed the power. I think anyone would. Suddenly I was an overnight success, half a dozen years in the making.

I even got a card from Adelaide. She didn't sign it. She didn't need to. She only wrote, *"Well done. — A."* and I knew I had finally brought myself up to her standard. She was, at last, truly proud of me. That gave me a warm thrill of satisfaction I sorely needed while the other person I most cherished was deserting me inch by inch. Seething. Pulling away.

In New Haven, Clyde and I finally had the

fight we'd been spoiling to have for weeks. He'd signed me up for a very close-in circuit, New York and Connecticut and New Jersey only, never more than a three-hour train from New York City. The show was starting to command high prices, the kind of numbers that had seemed out of reach when we conceived our plan, what seemed like a lifetime ago. He wanted to make the particular people who ran this circuit happy, for business reasons. It was a favor to them. It was also easier on me. I didn't ask him which reason weighed heavier.

Clyde was preoccupied with business in New York, and he didn't say exactly what, but I was fairly certain I knew. He was talking with investors who might help him build the Carolina Rose. If he built the theater, it would be time to bring me back to New York as we'd agreed. If I became his head-liner under exclusive contract, the act would still be mine in name but his behind the scenes. He had swallowed his pride for the time being, because I was so inflexible about the Halved Man, but I knew he wasn't truly at peace. He went along because he had to. There was a distance about him, a tension in his muscles. We made love as usual, and his motions were the usual motions, but he didn't look into my eyes, and I knew exactly what that meant. He hadn't forgiven me.

What made it even more evident was the mark he made in my book. While paging through my copy of *As You Like It,* I found that he'd turned down the corner on a single page and underlined a short passage with a few sharp strokes of the pen. I expected it to be the line about fleeting the time carelessly, but it was another mention of Arden:

Ay, now am I in Arden; the more fool I; when I was at home, I was in a better place: but travelers must be content.

In New Haven after the act, I climbed into the railcar, traded my silk gown for a cotton shift, and poured myself a finger of brandy. My body ached. It didn't look it, but the Halved Man was an intensely challenging physical illusion. It wasn't just about the speed and the gestures, which so many of my illusions were. Raising and lowering the knife with precision required very careful control, and the saw itself was remarkably heavy. I was starting to think maybe I should reengineer the opening, so instead of pushing the box into place myself, I'd have one of the assistants push it, but I was reluctant to cede even that much control.

My complete power over the box was one of the things that made the illusion so remarkable. I had designed it without spectacle on purpose. There was nothing else to look at but me, the box, the man inside, and the weapons I would use to cut him apart.

There was a noise at the door, and I started, but then recognized the sound of the key turning in the lock, and since only one person had that key, I raised my brandy to welcome him with a smile.

"I wasn't sure you were coming tonight," I said.

"I wasn't sure either," Clyde said. "But here I am."

I raised my lips for a kiss, but he didn't respond, and I knew he had something to say.

"Tell me," I said.

Without preliminaries, he said, "I want you to stop doing the Halved Man."

I laughed.

"Don't laugh!" he said, wounded, angry. "I'm serious."

"I know you are! I'm sorry. But it'd be ridiculous to give it up now. This is what we've worked for all this time. Enough success to give us our dreams."

"I don't like the trick," said Clyde.

"Don't call it a trick."

"It's a trick," he said, sitting down on the bed, resting his head in his hands. "More than anything else you do, it tricks people. It makes them think something other than what they want to. Your illusions, the rest of them, they make people believe in a better world. This trick makes them believe in a worse one."

"I'm not changing the world. The world is what it is."

"I think it upsets people."

"They love it!"

"*You* love it. Maybe too much."

"What are you saying?"

"It scares me," said Clyde. "To be honest? I'm a man, and to see you cutting a man in half, it makes me worried that you might want to do that to me."

Fortified by the brandy, I decided I needed to answer him. There was something that had been tickling the back of my brain, another reason the illusion appealed to me, and it was another part of the truth. I couldn't just tell him the Halved Man was meaningless. I couldn't tell him what Ray had done to me or what I'd done to him. But I could tell Clyde the alternate meaning, the one that was his anyway.

"Now don't be scared by this," I said, "but

407

in a way, I do."

"How do you suppose I could not be scared by that?" he shouted, springing up.

I sprang up too, holding my hands up, barely noticing when the empty brandy snifter fell on its side. "No, no, no. I don't want to harm you, not at all. If anything ever happened to you — it would wreck me. I love you more than my own self. Believe me."

"Then what did you mean?"

"If I could — not cut you apart, no, but if I could, I'd divide you. I'd have part of you with me every day on the road, lying down with me, loving me. And I'd have part of you back in New York keeping the books and building both our careers. You understand? I'm sure you wouldn't mind dividing me too. Making me two separate people. Your business partner, and the woman you love."

He leaned in then, placing his forehead on my shoulder, and I wrapped my arms around him, tight. I could feel his heartbeat, his breathing, the heat of his skin. He was my love, my whole love. He was not divided.

I asked tentatively, "Do you understand?"

"I understand."

I said, "You're my world, my golden world. I need you. If I can only get half of you sometimes, that's what I'll take."

"You're right," he said, cradling my cheek. "It's not fair. I want to be with you too, all the time. My whole self."

"We can't have the impossible."

He said, "Someone will have to compromise."

I tried to think of what else I could do, but I didn't know how to fix it. Finally Clyde was the one who spoke.

"Then I'll come with you," he said. "We'll find someone else to settle the apples."

I hadn't expected him to say it, and at first, all I could think of were reasons why not. "But you're the best. I don't know who else I could trust."

"I'll still be responsible. You'll still be in my hands." He smiled at the double meaning. "But I know a young man who needs an opportunity, and he can answer the telephone calls and balance the accounts. We're established enough I don't need to go knocking on doors anymore. Our door is the one getting knocked on."

I had to ask one more question. "And what about your theater?"

"It can wait a little longer," he said. "I don't want to be divided anymore. I want to be with you."

"Thank God," I said and held him forever.

■ ■ ■ ■

He booked me on the Beauregard circuit, a guaranteed three months of shows, one last act as my business manager to settle our future, undivided. At night, our safe little self-contained world, our movable home, rode the rails through the dark from Kalamazoo to Grand Rapids, Gary to Richmond, Charlotte to Charleston. We played to sold-out crowds. Local dignitaries, mayors and governors, attended in seats of honor. On the second night in Washington, DC, there was a rumor that a well-disguised President Roosevelt entered Ford's Theater and watched the show from the back of the orchestra level, and whether or not it was true, it brought us all great joy.

If I thought that the weeks of my life where I stopped traveling and spent my days with Clyde were wonderful, it was even more wonderful to have him with me all the time. He was there with me when the sun first began to peek through the curtains in the morning. He was there when we arrived at each dark, empty theater and transformed it into a thrilling place of magic, a carnival of color and light. He shared in that tense moment in every performance after the first flourish — *ta-da!* — when you hold your breath for what seems like an eternity, waiting for someone, anyone, in the audience to begin applauding, praying this won't be the time when the entire crowd just stares at you in hollow, awful silence. Most importantly, he was there with me, to wrap his arms around me, when I donned my nightgown and crawled under the covers to sleep. The bed in the railcar was small, and there was always some part of us that hung off. One arm or another, sometimes my feet, sometimes his head. But we managed. We were in love.

It was that simple. At least, I hoped it was.

CHAPTER TWENTY-EIGHT

Janesville, 1905
Half past four o'clock

"You said you wouldn't marry him then."

"Yes, that's what I said."

"But you married him later?"

"That would be reasonable. But you know not all of this story is reasonable."

"To say the least," he says wryly. It all seems so plausible, and she tells it so smoothly. Reasonable, no. Believable, yes. But is it true? Now it seems he will never be sure. But his decision isn't about that anymore. Whether he believes her innocent is less important than what she can do for him now. It's the simplest of all trades: a life for a life. If she saves him from the bullet, she will save him from everything. He'll keep what he has, what he treasures. That's all he wants.

He says, "And now I want to ask you for that favor."

She doesn't look at him. Her eyes are downcast, modest. She says, "Virgil. You don't have to ask."

"Yes. I do. Very much."

"That's not what I mean. I know exactly what you want."

"All right then, tell me." The situation is so absurd but so vital that it starts to make him light-headed. This can't be happening, yet it will change the course of his life. He lets himself be a little sarcastic. "Give me your second sight act, Madame."

"Not like that," she says. "You've all but said it. The bullet."

"Yes," he admits. He can feel his pulse quicken at the mere thought. "The bullet."

"You want me to heal you. To put my hand on the small of your back, make a wish, and draw that bullet out. Science has failed you, so you need magic."

"Yes. I need magic." It's a relief to admit it, to say it so nakedly. In front of anyone else, he'd be embarrassed. In this way, as in so many others, she is an exception.

"Because science has its limits."

"Yes."

There is no emotion in her voice, he realizes, and it worries him. It's as if she's reading someone else's words from someone else's script. There was passion in every

413

word when she was telling her story, but now she tells the facts: bald, cold. "Magic has limits too."

"Don't be coy," he says. They're so close now. He's so close. She can't hold out on him; she can't. "I said it's a favor, and it is, but I'm not asking you just to do it out of the goodness of your heart. I'm asking it as a trade."

"I understand perfectly. If I heal you, you'll set me free."

"Yes."

She sounds almost disappointed. "So I'm telling you all this for nothing. My story makes no difference to you."

"It's a fascinating story. Truly." He wants to put his hand on her arm but doesn't dare. He can only hope his words will be enough. "But how could I care about your life more than my own? That's what I'm asking you to give me. My life."

The moment she waits before answering him is days, months, years long. It stretches on far longer than he thinks he can bear.

Then she finally raises her blue-and-brown eyes, meets his gaze, and says in an almost whisper, "Would that I could."

"But you can! It's easy! Heal me. Draw the bullet out and you're free." He raises his hand, snaps his fingers. The sound in the small, bare room is as loud as a gunshot. "Nothing could be simpler."

She speaks slowly. The quiet night around them has never been quieter. It seems hard for her to choose her words.

"Virgil, when I — struck out at Ray, cut his throat — after the fire. You remember, I told you exactly what happened. I tried to heal him. It didn't work."

"You were in a rush," he says without the slightest pause. He's already thought of every reason. "You didn't take the time to do it properly. And you hated him anyway. Why would it work on him? You didn't really want him to get better."

She shakes her head and leans slightly forward in the chair, intent. "I'd never been sure about the limits of my gift. After that time with Ray, I suspected I'd found them."

"That was just —"

"Hush," she says, not unkindly. "So I tried it out. People are always getting injured on the road — not through any acts of mine. It's just dangerous to be moving all that equipment, especially in a rush. Since they were my family, my company, it wasn't odd for me to insist on taking a look at their injuries. So I'd put my hands on them and whisper a little something under my breath. They thought it was a prayer. It was a wish."

She takes a moment, squares her shoulders.

He has to prompt her. "And . . . ?" Even then, he trails off. He both does and doesn't want to hear the answer, to know where the story goes. If it were good news, she wouldn't be so slow to tell it.

"I've tried to heal broken fingers, bruised ribs, bloody toenails, every injury large and small and in-between. It never worked."

"But you said — bruises, cuts, broken bones —"

"*My* bruises. *My* cuts. *My* bones."

The air goes out of his lungs.

She swallows, as if she doesn't want to say what comes next, but she goes on anyway. "I can't do it, Virgil. I can't help you. My own body, I can do anything. Someone else's body, I'm powerless."

He feels like he's fallen from a great height. This must be how she felt, being thrown from the hayloft and crashing to the floor of the barn all those years ago. Like there isn't anything to breathe, and nothing to breathe it with.

"I'm sorry," she says, but she doesn't sound sorry, not at all, and her indifference is what finally leads him to reach out and put his hands on her.

He puts both hands on her shoulders and

shoves her backward, and the chair tips over with a crash. The sound echoes off the wall.

The crash of the chair is the only sound. She says nothing. Doesn't cry, doesn't scream, doesn't move.

She lies still.

For a moment, he's afraid he's killed her. Any normal person would have screamed. She just lies there on her back, the chair underneath, her eyes open and staring up. The only other woman he's ever seen lying on her back is Iris, and the sight disturbs him so much he reaches down and rolls the magician over on her side and the chair with her.

She still makes no noise, and he watches her for a moment, watches the side of her neck, until he's sure he can see the pulse beating there under the skin. She's alive. The noise he heard, the cracking noise, wasn't her skull. Thank God.

"I'm sorry," he says.

In a very small voice, she says, "I understand."

When he bends down next to her, behind her, he sees what's happened. The middle bar of the chair has snapped off. That was the noise, the sound of wood snapping. Both pairs of handcuffs were laced through it, and now they aren't. She is barely restrained at all. He grabs the chain of the handcuffs in his fist before she notices that her wrists can move farther than they have in hours.

"I'll right you," he says, as if she weren't completely free of the chair, as if nothing at all has changed.

He takes her silence as assent. He bends down and picks them up together, her body and the chair, to right them again. He can feel her heartbeat against his shoulder. He smells the sweat of her neck, an earthy, salty smell, not the same as his wife's, and that tickling scent of citrus from earlier. His body holds hers in place, and his breath stirs her hair. She remains silent.

When he settles her feet and the chair's feet both squarely back down on the floor, he releases everything but the handcuff chain, which he grips so hard his knuckles are white. Luckily, she can't see his knuckles.

"It looks like this one has been cutting into your wrist," he says. "I'll fix that."

He unlocks the right wrist, laces the chain through one of the remaining bars, and re-locks it in place. He hustles to do the same with the other set of cuffs, unlocking it from the right wrist, lacing the chain behind the bar, then locking it to the wrist again. Now she's set, back in two pairs of handcuffs holding her tight to the chair, fully secure.

Her silence and lack of resistance since the fall begin to worry him. It's getting later, and he's getting more vulnerable. He's sure she must sense that. Maybe she hit her head harder than he thought.

"Are you all right?" he asks. He comes around to the front of the chair so he can look into her eyes when she answers. He's seen a man kicked in the head by a horse so hard his eyes never did both look in the same direction again.

She locks her eyes on his. They are the same. Three-quarters blue, one-quarter brown, a strong fierce gaze, boring into him like she can see into his brain. He doesn't know what she sees there.

"There's really only one question. Do you believe me?" she asks.

He's tempted to make her spell it out, but he knows what she means. The murder. She's been telling him all night she's innocent. All night, he's been resisting that fact. "I want to."

"But you're not sure."

"No."

"Lies are harder than the truth," she says. "They have a way of falling apart. So tell me. Have I contradicted myself yet? Slipped

419

up? Have you caught me in a lie?"

"Not yet."

She raises her chin. "You remain hopeful. I can tell."

"Well," he says, deciding to tell the truth. "Your story is awful. You were abused and attacked, terribly. And it all ends in murder. So yes. I hope it's not true."

She seems to smile a little at that, in the midst of her sadness. "I wish it weren't. But this is life, and when bad things come to us, there isn't much choice. You survive them or you don't."

"And you hope to survive this one."

"Dear God, yes," she says intently, "I do. I do."

He doesn't know what to say to that. When he doesn't reassure her, she seems disappointed. But it would be hypocritical, given his role. Hours ago, she asked if he would be her executioner. He denied it, but she was right. If he turns her in, he might as well use his own two hands to fashion the noose. Don a black hood and be done with it.

He wants to know the truth. He needs to know.

He circles around behind her. She doesn't even lift her head to look. The night has been long. And whatever happens, one way or another, it's almost over.

He inspects her hands and says, "You're not wearing the ring."

"No."

"There was no ring, was there? Just one of your many inventions. You haven't been able to prove a single lick of your story all night, and this is no different."

She says, "In the valise. The muff. Put your hands in it."

He feels both foolish and excited as he does what she says. He retrieves the muff, which appears to be rabbit fur on the outside and silk on the inside, and positions it on the desk. Of course, he's never placed his hands in something like this before and is surprised to find it isn't just a hollow tube but has a shaped lining that draws tight around each hand. The fingertips of his left hand strike something round and cool.

Gingerly he draws out the object. A ring. Exactly as she described it. A beautiful blue stone with a brown flaw. Eerily like her eye.

The feeling that floods him is overwhelming. If her story is true, if the man she loved was neither her husband nor her victim, that gives him something to hope for. He doesn't want her story to just be the old sad tale of a man and woman whose love turned to poison. He wants something better, something more.

"Arden," he says. "Please. If you'll finish the story, we can settle this, and I can go home to my wife, who you're so curious about."

"To Iris."

"Yes, to Iris." That's all he wants. To go home to Iris, as soon as this is over. To be done with this and return to his life, however much of it is left to him. He needs to be home. As soon as the sun comes up. He's been away too long. He's spent too much time chasing an impossible dream of erasing what's happened to him, when what he needs to do is accept it and move forward.

"Well, I'm truly sorry to keep you from her. But I have my limits. I won't admit what I didn't do."

"But now you're getting into the right part of the story. How you got a husband. Tell me how you came to hate him. And then, how you planned and decided on murder. Was he unfaithful? Were you in a rage? How did it happen?" He doesn't add *now that I know it matters.* Most of the night, he's been planning, hoping, thinking he knew how this would all end: healing, and release. Now everything has changed. Now he needs to be a police officer again. Not the Virgil Holt who's terrified of death coming upon him without warning; instead, a man of the law following the rules, searching for the truth.

"The answer is the same," she says. "I didn't kill him."

"Then tell me that, if it's true, but tell me the whole of it," he says, softening his voice. "Maybe you didn't swing the ax, but you were there. Maybe you only saw it. Were you there when he was murdered? Did you watch your husband die?"

"Clyde was with me every night until he wasn't," she said. "And that's when it happened."

"The murder?"

"No," she says. "Worse."

CHAPTER TWENTY-NINE

1905
Resurrections

Three weeks before the end of the circuit, it was time for Clyde to go back to New York for a few days to work with the new kid he'd hired for the practical work and get everything settled up right. I had three nights in a row booked in Savannah, challenging but hardly outlandish. I had gotten so used to having Clyde around. I missed him too much now that he was gone again. I wasn't sleeping well — I was restless, constantly waking up over and over to find only minutes gone by — but a couple of fingers of brandy helped with that.

On the third night in Savannah, I was looking forward to my brandy. I was exhausted from the demanding routine and from the lack of good sleep, and I wrapped my linen robe tightly around my tired body and poured myself a good heavy glass, and all was well until I heard knuckles rap against the door, which I hadn't yet locked for the night.

"Yes?"

I expected Doreen, who had stepped into a certain role as my proxy most nights, accepting bouquets of flowers and sending away unwelcome visitors, but it was not her voice that answered. No voice answered. Instead the handle turned, and someone stepped up into the car and swiftly closed the door behind him, and quickly it was already too late.

The lamplight glinted off his pale hair. He looked almost angelic, with the light hitting him like this, at this angle. But he was earthbound enough, a sandy-haired man in a suit slightly rumpled from travel, with a grin that would have looked cheerful and welcome on any other face. He paused with his back pressed against the door and waited. Perhaps he was waiting for me to panic, to scream. Instead I only stared.

It couldn't be him. It couldn't. It wasn't.

It was.

"Ada," he said in a new voice, one with a hoarse scratch to it, where there had been none before.

The shock of seeing Ray alive and well

and here froze my blood, and I was helpless.

"So," I said, but no other words would come. I remained at the table and sipped at the brandy to wet my dry mouth, still somehow hoping that this wasn't happening to me.

"So," he echoed me. "Offer your cousin a drink?"

"No," I said and didn't dispute him on semantics. I took another sip instead.

It was impossible. He couldn't be here. It could be a look-alike, or a brother, or a bad dream. I had seen enough illusions to know things weren't always as they seemed. But it was perfectly him, his hair longer than it had been in Chicago, the face just a little more worn. And I saw the mark on his throat, a sharp straight line. I knew I was awake by the spiraling dread in my belly, too insistent for the dream world.

I had killed him, hadn't I? There had been so much blood. I remembered how it gushed, how my hands were slick with it, how neither pressure nor magic would keep it from flowing. How I wished so hard to save him but was certain I'd failed. Yet here he was. Not a facsimile, not a look-alike, not a dream. Ray, in the flesh.

There was only one possible explanation.

I hadn't killed him after all. The wound had been deep and terrible, but no matter how close he'd come to death, he hadn't crossed over. His heart hadn't stopped. His body hadn't gone cold. Of all the bodies that covered the floor of the storeroom next to the Iroquois, left for dead, one had risen.

In some small way, that should have made me glad, I supposed, not to be the murderer I'd thought myself for more than a year. But I couldn't rejoice at seeing him walking and talking, not in the least. If I hadn't taken his life, it seemed certain he would take mine. It couldn't end any other way. The railcar was a prison now, just another box from which there was no escape. I had never wished more that I could be Houdini.

I desperately needed to think of something to say. If I could keep him talking, maybe he wouldn't touch me. If he touched me, I would fall apart.

He stared at me, seemingly waiting for more words. I didn't have any. I didn't have anything. I had my brandy, which I drank, and that was all. I remained in the chair as if welded to it.

While I drank, Ray finally stepped away from the door, though we both knew he was still close enough to lunge back in an instant. He reached over to the sink where

427

the straight razor sat — Clyde had forgotten it there, and I hadn't wanted to touch it — and placed it on the table between us. I knew how strong he was. He didn't need the razor at all. Alone in the private train car where no one could hear me scream, all it would take was his bare hands.

"You don't scare me," I said, which was a bald lie. He terrified me. He always had.

"You don't think I'll hurt you? I've done it before."

"You have."

"And you're not scared?"

"If you hurt me, it hurts, and then it goes away," I said, chin up, fierce. "I'll survive it."

"You're not the only one I could hurt. There's that boy."

"He's not a boy." A wave of cold crashed over me. I hadn't immediately thought of the threat to Clyde, but of course, my tormentor had.

"Whatever he is." Ray sneered, stepping closer. "Your manager. Your lover. The slender one with the dark hair and the fine eyeglasses. The one who rubs his thumb along the bottom of your spine when he thinks no one is watching. The one who lives in New York, in rented rooms on the second floor of a house facing Jane Street. You care about him. And if you don't do what I say, I will kill him."

How long had he been following us, stalking us, watching, learning? I thought I was scared before, but when he threatened Clyde, all the fear before was just like a shadow of a hint of fear. This fear hurt more than being thrown twenty feet down from a hayloft. More than the guilt of surviving a fire in which many better people had perished. More than any broken bone. It hurt the most because I didn't know when it would end. It might never.

If he knew where Clyde lived, all bets were off. Because I had no doubt at all that he would follow through. I felt the panic set my bones alight then, worrying that perhaps he'd already hurt Clyde and this was all just for show, but I made myself think like him. Of course his ultimate goal wasn't to hurt my lover; it was to hurt me. He would give me a choice, because the consequences would be so much worse for me afterward if I knew I'd had the power to choose. Every way he'd hurt me before would be like a bee sting compared to how I'd feel if Clyde were killed, knowing I was the one responsible.

I forced myself to stand and look Ray in the eye. Then I asked, because I couldn't ask anything else: "What do you want?"

"Everything."

Cold and growing colder, I said, "Be specific."

"You let me do what I want. No objections, no conditions. I want to break you and heal you."

"For what purpose?"

"Because I want to," he said. "I've wanted to since the beginning. You've always looked down on me, and I want you to know you can't do that, not ever again."

"You're insane," I replied.

"I don't see how that changes anything," he said, almost cheerfully.

With that, he stood close to me and reached his hand around my back, stroking the base of my spine lightly, running his thumb along the thin skin over the bone, just as he had seen Clyde do. It was a threat and a promise, and it paralyzed me, because I knew exactly what he meant by it. He wouldn't just break my bones. He would break me, period. That was his intent.

I hoped for a knock on the door. I hoped for a burst of inspiration. I hoped for the strength to bluff my way through and refuse him, catching him off guard so I could turn the tables. I hoped for anything and everything. Nothing came. Nothing at all.

I did the only thing I could do, then.

I gave in.

After a restless, sleepless, awful night, I sent Clyde a cable telling him we were through. I wrote and rewrote it a dozen times, searching for the right words, searching for a way to send a secret message that Ray couldn't see through. He was watching me, of course. He watched silently the whole time, standing behind me without a word. He only moved when I crumpled up each failed attempt in order to discard it, reached across me to grab the ruined sheet of paper, and deposited it in the wastebasket.

On the thirteenth attempt, I finally settled on the right lies, simply told. No secret codes, no hidden cry for help, just a plain, clear message bringing everything to an end. I told Clyde I didn't love him anymore. I told him I'd grown to hate him over the past months, unable to trust or forgive him for the wrongs he'd done me, and that his appalling suggestion of marriage was the straw that broke the camel's back. I accused him of seducing me for money, doing what a poor boy with a handsome face and few other talents does best. I tried to be as horrible as possible, harsh and petty, hoping he would believe me capable of such cruelty.

Fortunately or unfortunately, I was sure he could. I'd been distant lately, ever since we'd started sparring over the Halved Man, and perhaps he thought there was more to it; this explanation could easily make sense to him, even though it wasn't anything close to the truth. I told him our business and personal relationships were now at an end. An intermediary would contact him to manage the separation of finances in due time, ensuring that he didn't profit from our association any more than he should, by the letter of our signed contract.

I also told Clyde not to contact me, that I never wished to hear from him again. I threatened lawsuits and worse if he even tried. This was a specific instruction Ray had given from over my shoulder, but I quickly realized it didn't matter. He had watched me write the telegram and watched me send it. I realized he would be with me every sleeping and waking moment. Even if I did receive a reply, he would be there to intercept it. My life was no longer my own, just like that.

Deep in my girlish heart, I wished Clyde would come rescue me. The rest of me knew better. If he came, a rescue wouldn't be the outcome. Not when Ray was ready to kill him on sight if I didn't obey. All I'd be doing was delivering my beloved more swiftly into the grave. A living Clyde was preferable to a dead one, no matter whether I'd ever see him again. This way at least I could daydream of him, imagine him free, his happiness in trade for my sacrifice. This way one of us would survive. And perhaps, I told myself darkly, he would be better off.

Then I made changes. Some were suggested by Ray, in a tone that indicated they were not really suggestions, and some I did for my own sanity. I gave the twins their walking papers, then Tabitha, then Doreen. All knew me too well to think I'd throw Clyde over. They had to go. The twins stormed out, their angelic faces dark with anger. Tabitha sobbed. Doreen begged me for a reason, and while I tried to muster a frosty, imperious voice to dismiss her, the best I could manage was a simple "Because it's time." Ray stepped in and hustled her to the door, patting her back soothingly, and shot me a dark look. He wanted me to be a better actress, I supposed. It was all I could do to act like a human being.

Then there was a blur of work. Shifting the less experienced assistants into new roles meant more training and more trouble, and I had to overhaul the program completely. I gave up the Halved Man for several nights, which caused grumbling in the crowd. I had come up with a new version of the illusion that didn't require twins, but I needed a new assistant to pull it off. We held hasty auditions in Bloomington. I chose a promising deaf boy who I knew would be both grateful for the work and undisturbed by the noise of the crowd or the rumors.

I missed Clyde like I would have missed a limb.

Everyone in the company knew he and I had been together this past year. It wasn't known by the general public because we'd kept mum when asked by the newspapers, but among our little family, we'd made no secret of it. Now I wished we would have, but it was too late. They would think me a fickle whore. I couldn't change that. I'd prided myself on building this strange family, on sowing the seeds of warmth and trust, but now a switch had been flipped, and they weren't family anymore. I couldn't let them matter. I couldn't let concern for their welfare distract me from my own. There was something far more important to be done.

I had surrendered on the outside, but on the inside, I knew there were two things I could do: I could escape and outpace Ray to New York, hoping that Clyde would still be there, or I could figure out how to kill him.

Killing him should have been easy. I'd stabbed him before in desperate anger, and now I was twice as desperate and infinitely angrier. Could I do it with the straight razor again, do it right this time, in an unguarded moment? Stab him in the gut if I needed to, when he bent over my body to hurt me in whatever way he pleased? Or better yet, wait until he was asleep. He had to sleep sometime. Didn't he?

But Ray was smart. Always had been. He was with me all the time, at every moment, when we were awake. He installed a new lock on the railcar door, and when he slept, he locked it from the inside, with the key hidden on his person, in a place he knew I'd never reach willingly. Everything sharp disappeared from the railcar. I searched in vain for the straight razor, a knife, a knitting needle, anything. He laughed, watching me hunt over every inch. He'd even stripped the car of mirrors so I couldn't break one for a sharp edge to use against either of us.

With the mirrors gone, he did my makeup himself before each show, wielding brushes and powders with what I had to admit was a doctor's skill. Every night, we went through the ritual. First was the flesh-toned cream, which he spread across my nose and cheekbones and blended with fluttering fingertips up to my hairline and down over my chin. The brush of matching powder danced lightly over my entire face, followed by a lighter variation of the same dance, softer, smaller bristles applying peach-colored powder to the apples of my cheeks. Gently, he held each eyelid closed with a thumb while he drew a kohl pencil along the very edge of my lashes, one eye and then the other. Last, and possibly worst, was the feeling of another, sharper pencil outlining the tender nerve endings of my poor lips, and then a wet brush of waxy lipstick filling in the outline. I was vulnerable at every moment, and I never knew if the precise, methodical application of these paints and powders would be interrupted with sudden pain, which could come from any direction. He might jam the brush down my throat, or curl his hand around a paint pot and slam it into my gut, or slowly work the point of a hat pin under my fingernail. Some nights there would be pain every minute; some nights, none at all. It seemed impossible that after such torture, I always looked beautiful. I had never applied my own makeup with such care. Ray was a brute with the hands of a surgeon, and I would have admired him if he hadn't been as dark as the devil himself.

I knew what the future held, at least for a few weeks. The tour schedule was already in place; Clyde had set us up through the end of July. The tail end of the circuit was set. Indiana, then Illinois, then Iowa. Three states to live through, I told myself. Only three states. By then, I'd figure out my exit, one way or the other.

At first, I had plans. I'd slip out through the stage door, the moment before the show was to begin, and run for my life. I'd call for the doctor and wheedle him for laudanum, with which I could drug Ray's coffee. I'd buy a gun from someone in the company, secret it in my blouse, shoot him dead in the railcar. But quickly, too quickly, the pain took over. I hadn't realized exactly how, and how much, it would hurt.

The physical pain was bad enough, but the other pain, deep inside, was worse. I hurt because I'd lost. I had fought so hard to get away from that girl I'd been, the one who'd let herself be brutalized, who had accepted for a long time that she wasn't worthy of being saved, and now I realized I'd never stopped being that girl. All those years, all that money, all the gleeful crowds, and I was still exactly as weak as ever. She had finally caught up with me.

Within a week, I had dark circles under my eyes. After two, I moved more slowly, my legs and arms turning to lead. At my best I was exhausted, and I was rarely at my best. In a town called Flora, I almost missed the show altogether, because he'd knelt on my forearm and slowly, slowly bent my right pinkie back until it cracked. The pain of the broken finger was excruciating, but just as bad was the pain of knowing he could do that, or anything else, to me that he wanted. I'd given him permission. To save Clyde, I'd signed on for that deal.

And as bad as each act was, the anticipation of the next one made it worse. Because I knew he would only escalate. Cuts and bruises were the opening act. Bones came next. Small bones first, and then larger. And after that, along with that, I knew one night he would violate me in a way that didn't show at all on the outside, a way that I would never be able to heal. He could have done it the very first night or any night after, but he knew that I expected it, and he held back, waiting. He tortured me with the things he hadn't yet done as much as with the things he had.

He climbed on top of me, over and over, always looking for something new to bend or crush or break. If I wasn't looking at him, he'd lock his fingers around my forehead and twist my head around until I did. I thought I could probably recover from a broken neck, and some nights it was bad enough I thought it might be better if I didn't, but he seemed to know just how far to press or pinch or wrench to have the effect he wanted. He'd made a lifetime study of bodies, and before long, he knew more about mine than I would have thought possible.

Perhaps the rumormongers were more right than they knew about me. In the end, I did just what they'd accused me of. I sold my soul to the devil.

No one knew what a nightmare my life had become; I doubt they even suspected. The ones who might have read the signs and guessed my misery were gone. Of those left, none were inclined to rock the boat. It was easy, too easy, to see it with their eyes. To them, Ray was charming and jovial, a pleasant man to have among the company. If we spent rather a lot of time alone together in the railcar, well, that was easily explained away as the thrall a new romance — a honeymoon, perhaps — could bring. He had only kind words for anyone in the company. By all outward appearances, he was no one's enemy.

The days and nights became a blur. I was no closer to figuring out how to get away. My body was weakening from the abuse. My mind was clouded by exhaustion and fear. I was healing myself over and over, muttering a wish for every wound, letting him believe that he was the one with the healing power, the reason my cuts and bruises could disappear in a matter of hours. Yet I had to keep up an illusion greater than any that had come before: the illusion that nothing was wrong.

In Terre Haute, the reporter asked me all sorts of prying questions about my life, and I smoothly answered him back with the usual vague claptrap. No, I wouldn't say where I'd come from, before I'd come up through the ranks with Adelaide Herrmann, as everyone knew. No, I wouldn't reveal the source of my powers, nor comment on the rumor that the brown part of my eye was a sign from the devil that he had taken one quarter of my soul as a promise of payment of the rest. No, I wouldn't discuss the inspiration for the Halved Man.

The reporter, persistent, began to follow me back to the railcar, and I was so distracted I didn't notice him until I was almost to the stairs.

The door swung open and Ray leaned out, clad only in a long, purple silk robe, cooing, "Welcome home, my dearest darling. Did you bring any more brandy? We're fresh out."

Before I could say anything, the reporter called out behind me, "Oh, is this your husband?"

"You caught us out," said Ray. "That's exactly who I am."

The reporter was behind me and couldn't see my face. I stared up at Ray with hatred. I didn't say anything. I didn't need to. Rightful or not, there he was. He'd already taken his place.

CHAPTER THIRTY

Janesville, 1905
Five o'clock in the morning
"It was Ray," says Virgil Holt, realizing. "Your husband."

"He wasn't my husband," she mutters.

"I realize that. But people thought he was. That's what matters. It wasn't Clyde. You didn't marry Clyde."

"No, I didn't."

He doesn't think he's imagining the sadness in her voice.

He says, "But the reporter from Terre Haute put it in the paper that you were married and your husband was with you on the road. And the rest of the company thought it was true. So when the body was found, they said it was your husband's body. That's what they told the reporters. He was your victim."

She protests weakly, "He wasn't . . . I didn't," and rattles the two remaining pairs

442

of cuffs.

He believes her now. Fully and completely. He's had doubts all night, but the story has gone to his core. She would never make up something so outlandish to sell him on her innocence. If that were her goal, a simpler story would have done. The fabrication is too elaborate to truly be fabricated.

But now he needs to decide what to do with the truth she's told him, which is the harder part. And there's still one gap to fill.

"But who killed Ray? Who beat him, and broke him, and sank that ax into his gut? Who made him into the Halved Man and left him there?"

She glares up at him, her gaze burning brighter than ever, but he doesn't stop. They're at it now.

"It's your specialty, Arden. Your illusion. Your idea."

"You can't hang a woman for her ideas," she says, a note of hysteria in her voice. He knows she doesn't believe that. She thinks they'll hang her no matter whether she's a murderess. She's almost certainly right. "In any case, I wasn't there."

"If you weren't there, where were you?"

"I don't know."

He pushes. "How is that possible? You remember everything."

"Not everything."

"Everything else. This whole night, you've proved it. You remember what happened when you were twelve and fifteen and twenty years old. You can recall conversations word for word with people you haven't seen in a decade. You remember what you want to remember. It's all in there, every bit." He reaches out and lays a finger in the center of her forehead, a firm quick tap. "So only last night, not twelve hours ago, you expect me to believe you can't remember where you were?"

"I don't know what time he was killed. How could I know?" He hears the edge of desperation in her voice, the trembling uncertainty.

"But how could it have been anyone else? No one else there even knew who he was. They thought he was a good man, you said it yourself. Only you hated him. So you killed him."

"No."

Generously, with a broad gesture of his arm, he says, "I don't know if I'd even blame you for it. The world is probably a better place. You already thought you killed him once. Wouldn't it be easier the second time? Like running a sword through a ghost."

"Look at me, officer. Please."

He avoids her gaze. He stares instead at her discarded boots next to the door, laces trailing, one fallen on its side. Beautiful things now smeared with grime that will never come out.

"I didn't kill him. I can only tell you that so many times until you have to decide if you believe me. And it's time, Virgil. Make up your mind once and for all. You have to decide whether you're going to let me go. Just you. No one will make that decision for you. Like Mr. Vanderbilt said. You have agency. Use it."

"I remember you telling me he said so."

"And now I'm saying it. To you, Virgil." She leans forward as far as she can, her shoulders straining, her chin thrust out. "You want to set me free? Do it. You want to turn me in? You can do that too. You're the only one with the choice. And that bullet in your back doesn't mean you've got any less choice than you ever did. Live free of fear if you want to. We all carry something inside us that could kill us; yours just has a name. You want to change your life? Change it. You have no less of a right to be happy than the rest of us."

He's reeling from what she says. It's too much. He snaps at her instead, with sarcasm. "You're the perfect example of happiness?"

"Not at the moment." She smiles ruefully and shrugs a little, as best she can. "But whatever happens, I've been happy. I've been loved. I've amazed crowds and drunk in their applause. Not because of luck or favor or magic. Because of will. My will. I've been willing to do whatever it takes. That's the closest thing I have to a secret. And now it's yours."

It's a lot to think about, and he can't quite digest it. But there's a spark there. Maybe she's right about him. Maybe it is up to him, how much he lets the bullet, and the fear, take over his life. Maybe. Not a curse, but a choice. His agency and no one else's.

She says, "You're right about one part of it. I hated him. With my whole self."

"But your will failed you there, did it?"

"Not exactly. I was ready to kill him," she says. "I was absolutely ready. I swore to myself, before the show, that I would find a way."

"And then?"

"And then, in Waterloo," she says, pointing across the room, "I found what was in that valise."

CHAPTER THIRTY-ONE

1905
The Slave Girl's Dream

In Waterloo, I did something foolish. It was a silly impulse, and I knew it would make no difference, but I had left logic behind. The railcar that had once been a lovely refuge was now a prison. Sometimes he locked himself in there with me and sometimes I was alone, but either way, I was thoroughly a prisoner, and I grew to hate the ornate ceiling and the framed art and the rich bedclothes and the empty spaces on the brocade walls where the mirrors used to hang. I hated him and I hated myself. There was only one time each day when I was free in both my body and mind. It was the golden time, the beautiful time, as the late afternoon shaded into evening, when he had to let me out to go onstage.

Onstage, he couldn't stop me. He'd never interfere with the show. He escorted me all the way there with his hand on my elbow, his steps in perfect concert with mine. During the performance he would stand in the wings, watching, and follow my every move. The moment I was offstage I was in his grip again, literally. But for a precious hour on each stage in each theater in front of each audience, I was still myself, still in control.

Ever since the Iroquois, I'd made a point of finding out what each theater's precautions were in case of fire. In Waterloo, there were buckets of water in front of the footlights, which was a standard precaution, but there was also an ax hanging on the back wall of the stage, which was not. Nearly every theater had fire axes on the premises to break doors and windows during a fire, to let either people or smoke escape. They were just usually offstage. This one was not, and the moment I saw it, I knew what I would do.

The evening unfolded in the usual pattern, at first. Majestic, I strode onstage in an exquisite gown to a surge of welcoming applause. I entranced the audience with coins that multiplied and disappeared. By turns the stage was a riot of colorful scarves, then a still and silent temple, then a blaze of light and motion. I did not even venture a glance into the wings, but looked out instead over a sea of rapt spectators, their eyes shining. I announced the fire dancers, the Dancing Odalisque, all the other illusions. I performed. We performed.

But this night, not everything was exactly the same as it had been. Just the sight of that nearby fire ax had reawakened me to myself, and I was thinking more clearly than I had in weeks, seeing the act with new eyes. What I saw and felt onstage pleased me. The new assistants were settling into their roles, and although they weren't yet as expert as their predecessors had been, they were growing in confidence and strength. As an act, we were finding our shared rhythm. And as we crescendoed to the Halved Man, I became more and more eager, every muscle a taut wire.

I wheeled the box out onstage, the deaf boy's head seemingly connected to another boy's feet. I made the usual gestures. But instead of reaching for the saw on the table stage left, I turned my back on the audience and walked to the back of the stage, lifting the ax from its tether. I strode downstage again, taking a brief moment to lock eyes with Ray in the wings as I did so — he looked murderous at the improvisation, which pleased and energized me — and then I stood over the box, and instead of gently sawing back and forth through the precut center, I raised the sharp ax blade over my head as high as it could go and willed all my strength into the downstroke.

I swung it down furiously, splintering the wood. It was satisfying. I did it again, and it was more satisfying yet. I considered crouching for a moment to whisper to the boys in the box that no harm would come to them, but there wasn't time for it. In any case the deaf boy wouldn't have heard. And I was barely aware of anyone but myself in the moment. I was transported, transformed. I was merely an extension of the ax. We were one, a single instrument of punishment and destruction. We were revenge. I pictured Ray's face as I smashed and smashed. Every blow was an answer to some wrong he had done me. Every upswing of the ax was an opportunity to bring it down again, hard and swift.

Then I heard the blast of a horn, possibly repeated, certainly loud enough to jar me. It was my cue. That brought me back into my body, onstage, and I realized where and who I was. The middle of the box was nearly split into kindling. But no one knew this wasn't what was expected. I had to give them the rest of what they'd paid for.

So I finished up as usual, in a near daze

— smoke and mirrors, deaf boy through a trapdoor, a sudden reappearance to amaze them all — and I took my bow. The audience thundered its applause. I raised my arms to thank them. They had no idea what they'd done for me. Without Clyde, I could barely go on, and without them, I wouldn't want to. I wasn't a mere prisoner — not at that moment, not anymore.

The curtain slid closed with a heavy and final-sounding *whoosh.* I stood alone on the bare stage, panting. My shoulders were already beginning to cry out from the effort, but there was a smile on my face, frozen there, my cheeks aching. I still gripped the ax.

I didn't stop smiling when Ray grabbed the ax out of my hands, nor when he marched me to the railcar, hissing at me to go faster, faster, at every step. I didn't stop smiling when he shoved me through the open door of the railcar and slammed it behind us with a mighty thump. I didn't stop smiling as he screamed at me, pushed me to the carpet on my back, and held the wooden handle of the ax against my windpipe with two hands, nor when he pressed down so hard no air could get through, bruising my neck deeply. I must have stopped smiling when I lost consciousness, though it tickled me to wonder if maybe I hadn't, which would have driven him to absolute distraction. When I came to, Ray was gone, and the ax with him. I was alone.

I reached for the brandy as I usually did but stopped myself. It would only deaden the pain for the moment. Drinking would leave the ache on the inside untouched and add a dizzying physical ache to wrap me like a shroud in the morning. And tonight was different. Tonight, I remembered the most important lesson of my life: I had agency.

Tonight I could surely find some better use for these minutes without Ray, however long they lasted, than to drink them away.

I pulled my suitcase out from under the bed. I was torn. Could I try to run away just one more time? Would he be gone long enough for me to get away, free and clear? Seeing and wielding the ax had made a difference. It reminded me that I might be a prisoner but I didn't have to be a victim. Earlier in the night I had told myself with certainty that I would finally kill him, without knowing how I would do so but utterly sure that one of us would be dead before the next day's sun came up. If I searched every inch of the railcar again, might I find something that would make the difference? Should I flee, or stay and fight?

Inside the suitcase was a smaller valise, which I recognized as the one my mother had bought me, all those years ago, in hopes of sending me off to ballet school. My life had certainly turned out differently than she'd intended. That little bag had seen me through many years, lean ones and fat ones, but right now it only reminded me of my failings. I kicked it, hard, so it flew a few feet across the railcar and struck the bed, and when it bounced and popped open, something fell out of the lining.

The straight razor that had been both Ray's and Clyde's.

Ray had hidden it well, but not well enough. I'd found it. And the moment it was in my hand, I knew what I was ready to do.

I positioned myself next to the door, razor at the ready, to kill him.

My body tense with anger and fear, I waited by that door for what felt like hours.

Darkness fell and I didn't light the lamp. My eyes had adjusted to the dark by then, and when he came in, there might be a chance that his hadn't. It would add to the element of surprise. I needed every advantage I could get. My hand still smarted from the broken finger, but I didn't trust my left

453

hand to bear the weapon any better. I would simply wait, in the dark, until he came, and then I would lunge, and it would all be done at last.

Only he never came.

CHAPTER THIRTY-TWO

Janesville, 1905
Quarter past five o'clock in the morning

Holt asks quietly, "He never came?"

"Never."

"So that's where you were, during the murder. In the locked railcar."

She says nothing.

"Waiting there to kill him," he goes on. "Not knowing someone else already had."

"Yes," she says, staring down at her feet, looking exhausted. Her hair seems more gold than before, which makes him realize there is a little light peeking through the high, barred window. The false dawn is here, and sunrise can't be far away. They've lost the night. What comes next?

"And then you ran," he said.

"I ran."

"But how could you?"

She looks at him blankly then, as if she doesn't understand what he means, but he knows she must.

He asks, more insistently, "How did you get out? If the railcar was locked? Did one of the girls come and rescue you? Did you realize he left the ax after all? Did you use the straight razor somehow? What was it?"

She shakes her head.

And then, insight comes in a flash. One part of the story doesn't add up. About what she's told him she's done, and who she's told him she is.

"You didn't escape from a locked railcar, did you? That's something only an escape artist would do. And you've told me that's not what you are. See? I was listening."

She mumbles down at her feet, and it's so soft he has to ask her, "Say that again?"

Instead of answering she shakes her head again, side to side, so fiercely another thick tendril of red-gold hair falls across her cheek, obscuring half her face.

His triumph begins to fade. He expected her to sass back with a ready answer, like she has before. But clearly, there's something more here. "Please. I didn't hear you. It's important."

"Is it?" she whispers.

"Yes. You're telling me your story. This is how it ends. This is the only thing I don't know."

"And it matters?"

"Arden. You said you'd tell me everything, so tell me everything." He reaches down and pushes the hair out of her face, tucking it behind her ear, so he can see her better. "How did you get out?"

She seems to come to a decision, meeting his gaze with tears shining in her eyes, and says, only a little louder, "The door wasn't locked."

He doesn't bother to hide his shock. They're well past that. He even reels backward a step, his single footfall audible in the quiet. "What? You said it was. You said he locked it."

"I did say that."

"And?"

Still meeting his eyes, her gaze burning, she says, "I lied."

"Arden . . ."

"But understand! It's the only lie I've told you all night." Her words come in a rush. "Everything else was true. The barn, my mother, Biltmore, the Iroquois, Adelaide's tiger, my healing power, every last bit of it. All true. I swear."

He has to ask. He has to. "Then why didn't you run?"

"I did."

"You said —"

"I mean, last night. Remember? I was running when you caught me."

"But why not earlier? Before he could hurt you?"

"I was so goddamn afraid," she says, the tears coming hard, running down her cheeks and neck into her high, open collar. They run over the pale, perfect skin where the bruise used to be and pool in the hollow in her throat. "My fear was all he needed to keep me there. I was too afraid to run. I didn't want to admit that to you — you understand, how shameful it was, how weak I'd been."

She pauses for a breath, and he wants to reassure her that he understands, but she forges ahead before he can.

"He'd threatened Clyde, and that was enough. One threat and I was his puppet. I let him damage me and try to heal that damage with his delusions of magic. I talk a good game about risk, but when it all came down to it, I chose something awful and safe. He's a brute and a horror, and I was a fool to let him intimidate me into giving up everything that I cherished, but I did."

"But you did finally run." He wants to comfort her, soothe her. "You were brave enough, last night."

"For all the good it's done me," she says,

sniffling. "I'm a prisoner again now, aren't I?"

He looks down at her, not sure what to say. The crying has reddened the whites of her eyes, making the blue irises even bluer, strikingly so. He reaches out silently to wipe away her tears, as he did much earlier in the night, while he thinks. Morning will be here shortly. He has to make his decision. He promised to hear her story, and he's heard it. There's nothing more to wait on.

"You're not his prisoner," he tells her. "That's the difference."

She takes a rasping, hiccuping breath.

He tucks the damp handkerchief back in his pocket and says, "Ray won't ever hurt you again. Whatever else happens, there's that. He's dead."

"God, I hope so."

"Hope?"

The telephone rings so loudly, piercing the silence, that they both jump.

He crosses the room and reaches for the telephone, mostly to quiet it, without thinking about who's on the other end. His thoughts are still a storm of uncertainty, his body reacting by reflex. He puts the earpiece to his ear without taking his eyes off the magician.

But when he hears Iris's voice, soft and

hesitant, his world cracks open wide.

"Virgil?" is all she says at first.

"I'm here," he says. "It's me, yes, I'm here. Is everything all right?"

Iris says, "I was afraid you wouldn't be there. You weren't there before."

"I should be home with you." He sits down in the chair behind the desk, hard, as it hits him. All this time, she's been waiting, wondering. He owes her more than that. The magician's story reminds him how fragile this all is, but also how important.

"You should. I was worried."

"I'm so sorry," he says.

He can tell she's crying but trying to hide it, and that touches him more deeply than he can say. He's been holding her at arm's length and it was all wrong. He can spend all his time with Iris in fear that she'll leave him, or he can spend that time telling her how important she is to him, how much he needs her. Now he knows which he'd rather do.

He says, "Oh, darling, I love you. You must know how much."

Her voice is soft, and he has to lean in to hear it. He leans hungrily, pressing his ear against the warm black horn-shaped metal.

"What did you find out?" she's asking. "Tell me. Tell me the doctor can help you.

460

Tell me everything will be all right."

He can't find the words to answer her. There's no guarantee of a future, but how could he say that? He needs to live the life he can live.

Her voice comes down the line again, passionate. "Tell me you'll be here for me."

"I will. I will." He says it and believes it.

Arden watches him closely. Watches to make sure that his attention is fully elsewhere. She'll be fast, but it will take a few long moments. Misdirection. She didn't create the opportunity, but she'd be a fool if she didn't take advantage.

It would be better if it were only one pair of cuffs, but she can do it with two. It will just hurt more.

Half turned away from the magician with his head down, straining to listen to his wife's words, Virgil Holt doesn't hear the cracking, wrenching sounds.

All he hears is Iris, so happy to talk to him, relief plainly evident in her voice. "Thank the good Lord. I want you home," Iris says. "I miss you."

"I miss you too," he says. "So much."

"Will you please come home to me?"

He says, "In the morning."

461

"Isn't it morning yet?"

"Almost. Once the sun comes up. I promise. There's one more thing I have to do first, and when I get home, I'll tell you all about it."

Iris says, "That sounds ideal."

Then he catches a blur of motion off to the side. Sequins and flesh. He sees the blur move and shift, rising up. She's getting up out of the chair. It's almost like he's imagining it. He's so tired now.

He turns to look at her, and he isn't imagining it at all. It's real. She is real, and free.

Both pairs of cuffs swing free from her left wrist. Her right hand looks awful, scraped and bloody, from being shoved against the metal. The thumb hangs off to the side of her hand almost like it isn't connected at all. And he realizes suddenly, it isn't. The bone, there's something wrong with it. The skin is all that's holding her thumb on.

In training, they told him that there were only two ways the average person could get out of cuffs. One was to pick the lock, which was harder than it seemed. The other was to break the thumb to make the hand small enough to fit through the cuff, which no one was foolish enough to do.

But she's done it, and she's not foolish.

She just knows her limits, which aren't the same as other people's.

"You broke your hand," he says.

"Whatever it takes," she says and bolts for the door.

Dropping the telephone and leaping out of the chair, he goes after her. The chair clatters madly, falling to the floor. He grabs for her and catches hold of a fistful of her skirt.

He thinks the locked door will stop her, but even as he has the thought, she has already flung the door open and is lunging out. It should have been locked, but it wasn't; belatedly he remembers the knock at the door, the click that didn't come, too late to regret that now. He holds tight. The fabric of the skirt rips with a shriek and comes off in his hand, scattering beads, so he topples over backward onto the floor of the station, landing on her discarded boots, and it takes him a moment to scramble to his feet before he can follow her outside.

It only takes a moment to spot her. She's easy to see, her long white limbs pale against the darkness, all alone on the empty road. He gathers his strength and gives chase.

She is running fast but barefoot, and he is sure the roughness of the road will slow her down before long. The loose cuffs bounce with every step, striking her bare skin; it must hurt almost as much as her broken thumb. She's thirty paces ahead of him and he can hear her panting. She'll never be able to keep up this speed. He's a good runner, and it should be an easy matter to catch her, but with every step he remembers the bullet, unsure whether it's drifting away from his spine or toward it, and a strip of sunlight is just beginning to peek over the horizon, and it's just the two of them sprinting down the gravel road through the last minutes of the night.

He doesn't count on the third.

A young man with dark hair leans forward out of the darkness, and before Virgil Holt can think anything other than *Yes, just how she described him,* a fist comes forward and strikes him between the eyes and he goes down like a felled cow at a Chicago slaughterhouse.

Virgil lies in the roadway on his back.

"Sorry," says the man's voice, but it is already faint. The man is running away in the same direction as the escaped prisoner. The two sets of footsteps grow quieter and quieter, until Virgil can't hear them anymore.

Maybe it's better this way, he thinks. Would he have let her go? He thinks he would, that his belief in her innocence would have overcome his need for the security her capture would win him, but he still isn't sure. He wonders if he would have really put the key into the lock when it came down to it. If after it all, he could let her get up and walk away.

But the magician was right. Everyone has will. It's time for him to start using his. He has a wife at home who loves him and wants him with her, and nothing else matters in the same way. He should be with Iris as long as he can, whether that's a day or a year or a decade. If a slip of a girl can live through more abuses than he can count, through misfortune and abandonment and fire, he can endure this one little knot of metal slumbering under his skin. And he is so exhausted by everything, by the uncertainty of the bullet and the long night and the long story and the girl who has fought so hard against her enemies, including him, that it takes him a long time to rise.

Woozy at first, he pulls himself up to sit and then to stand. He'll take it one slow step at a time. He looks in the direction he heard the suspects running, east toward the sun, already out of sight. Once he feels strong enough, he puts one foot forward,

then the other, and walks west instead,
toward Iris, toward home.

CHAPTER THIRTY-THREE

Janesville, 1905
Half past five o'clock in the morning
Arden looks back over her shoulder as she runs, even though there's nothing to see now, and it makes her sad. In different circumstances, she might have liked Officer Virgil Holt, and he might have liked her. All she can do now is wish him well and keep running.

Alongside her, Clyde runs, matching his stride to hers. She wants to stop and swoon and melt into his arms, let the rest of the world go hang, but there isn't time for it, not now. If they're caught, she doesn't want it to be like this, with so many questions unanswered on both sides. If they can get away free, there will be hours and days and years yet for kissing. If. She glances back again, hoping for an empty road.

"Don't look back," he says. "It slows you down."

"I know."

They run on the hard-packed road, past squat dark houses one after another, houses full of good people still asleep. Her hand hurts, her feet hurt, her lungs hurt, everything hurts. But the pain doesn't stop her from relishing the feeling of running. She is going forward with a freed mind and a freed body, and Clyde is beside her, and there is so much they are leaving behind.

"He'll be all right, won't he?" she asks, her breath coming harder but not so hard that she can't form words.

"Yes, of course. I barely touched him."

"He thought I killed Ray," she says.

"I know."

"But I didn't."

"I know."

"Because it was you," she says, even though she doesn't want to say it out loud, but if she doesn't say it now, she'll always be thinking it, for the rest of her life. The rest of their life together, if they're going to have one.

"Ah," he says, slowing then stopping. He stares down into her face. She looks away, looks behind him. Have they run far enough, for now? They're at the edge of this small town. It seems like a lovely place to live. A haven. But because of the choices they've made, it's a place to be escaped. Behind her are sleepy, closed-up houses. Behind him are trees and the open road.

"You shouldn't have done it," she says.

Instead of responding, he looks behind them and says, "Was it just one officer?"

"Yes."

"There's no one else chasing us?"

"No."

"Just to be safe," he says and nods toward a stand of trees off to the side of the road. She shuffles into the shelter of their covering branches, Clyde following closely. The sun is nudging up over the horizon now, but its light is blocked and scattered by the leaves, so they stand in a pocket of shadow.

He says, "I wasn't sure. That's why I didn't come in. I didn't know how many there were, whether we were outmatched, and I couldn't take the chance you might get hurt."

He kneels down at her feet silently, and something small and silver flashes in his hand, and she feels the first of the cuffs on her ankles give way. Instead of throwing the cuff away, he tucks it into a small bag at his waist and then starts on the next.

Now that they are safe, at least for now, she feels a dizzying relief everywhere in her body. The worst she feared hasn't come true, and the best thing she could hope for — Clyde, here, alive — is right in front of her. She begins to cry, and when she can reach up to her face freely with both hands to wipe away the tears, the joy makes her cry even harder.

"I wasn't sure it was you, at the door," she tells him. "He kept talking about a dead man, but he couldn't tell me what the dead man looked like. I thought it was probably Ray. I prayed it was. I was terrified he might have meant you."

"It wasn't me," he says, head down. He picks the lock on the second ankle cuff, it pops open with a soft clang, and he tucks it away. "At the door, knocking, that was me. I would have figured something out, you know. I would have gotten in to rescue you."

"No need," she says. "Rescued myself."

"It's not a joke."

"I wasn't joking. Now I want to know what happened."

He doesn't look up, still crouched at her feet, turning the silver stub over and over in his fingers. "I heard there was a man with you on the road. Doreen came back to New York, after you sent her packing. I thought I was stupid for not seeing it, that the reason you didn't want to marry me was that there was someone else. We were apart so often, it made sense that you'd seek comfort in another man."

"Never."

"That's what I thought. But I wasn't sure. That seed of doubt got in, and —"

"I know." She breathes out. "I know."

"So I needed to see for myself. Who you'd chosen over me."

"But I hadn't. I was trying to protect you," she says, her voice trembling. "He said he was going to kill you if I didn't . . ."

Clyde stands up, leaning in, his eyes shining with tears. He lays his palms flat against her shoulders. She can feel the warmth of his hands. That soft welcome feeling, after the torture of the past few weeks, makes her light-headed with happiness. His touch is so gloriously ordinary that it almost undoes her completely. She puts her hand against his rough cheek and leans forward to kiss him, a soft, swift kiss, as simple and honest as their very first, under the mistletoe.

"I couldn't stand it if anything happened to you."

"Nothing did. At least nothing fatal."

He lifts his shirt. She squints to see in the half dark, but once she sees it, it's clear. His stomach is wrapped with something white, with a slash of dark brown cutting all the way across it. The dark stain is soaked into

471

the bandage, a few inches above his waist. Drying, darkening blood. Only hours ago, it would have been red.

"Knife?" she asks him.

"Ax."

She shudders. She knows the very ax he means; she'd held it in her own two hands. "Tell me what happened."

"I watched the show in Waterloo — you were magnificent, Arden, you amazed me all over again — and I watched to see who was there afterward." Clyde tucks his shirt into his waistband in a swift, smooth motion, in no obvious discomfort, so the wound must not be as bad as she first feared. "Everyone left, and I was afraid I'd missed my chance, but he came back in and hung that ax on the wall. So I confronted him. I asked how long he'd been your lover, and he laughed. He knew exactly who I was, and he wanted to taunt me. He boasted. He told me what he thought he was, what he thought he could do."

"Oh, God," she says, feeling faint.

He reaches out for her left wrist, raising the cuffed hand to his mouth, and kisses it, once, twice, three times.

"Why didn't you tell me?" he asks.

"I was sure he'd kill you."

"Not just that," he says. "Before. It must

have been awful for you to keep that secret."

"Talking about it wouldn't have made it less awful."

He inserts the metal pin into both cuffs in turn and slips them from her wrist. She should feel lighter, now that she's free. She doesn't.

Clyde says, "It was him or me."

"I know," she says.

"We fought. I got in a few good blows; he was bigger, I was faster. Then he grabbed the ax, chasing me across the stage, swinging the whole time. I took a risk and let him swipe me with it, so he'd think I couldn't move faster. It's shallower than it looks." He gestures down at his wound. "Because what I noticed and he didn't was the open trap door. I stepped around, and he stepped through."

She pictures Ray falling, falling, landing hard.

"I couldn't tell if he was moving or not, so I took the long way down instead of jumping through the trap door. By the time I got there — he was gone."

She thinks she knows what he means, but she still asks, "Gone?"

"He landed on the ax. Curled around it like he was holding it close. All the sets and props were under the stage, right there, and

I thought maybe if I hid the . . . evidence, that I could find you before anyone found him, that everything might still be all right. But I heard footsteps. I had to run. I just got out of there, went north as far and fast as I could until I had my wits about me again and stopped at a restaurant on the road. Then I realized they were going to suspect you. I was about to double back. To turn myself in. So you'd be safe."

"Oh, Clyde."

"Then I saw him" — he gestures back in the direction of the fallen officer — "riding off with you. I couldn't keep up, but I kept on following, and finally I saw the horse in front of the station, and I knew that's where you were. So I waited."

She looks up at him, his face so familiar and loved, and knows they've both done things neither will ever want to talk about. She doesn't want to think about his any more than she wants him to think about hers. That's not the person she is. That's not the person she wants to be.

She says, "I want to start over."

"Yes, yes," he says, stroking her cheek. "We can fleet the time carelessly."

"As they do in the golden world?"

"But you won't be Arden anymore."

She shakes her head. "Right now, I don't

want to be."

"Do you think you'll be happy? Without an audience?"

"Maybe I'll start again. Maybe I'll get a new name, a new act."

"In Canada," he says, catching on. "Or California. London, even. Somewhere far away."

"Yes. In the meantime, you're my audience," she says.

He whispers softly as he lifts her hand to kiss it, his lips brushing her skin with each word, "And I will applaud, and applaud, and applaud."

She closes her eyes and savors the tickling warmth of his mouth. Then he lifts the injured hand, squeezing it lightly as he does so, and she can't help but wince.

"Arden!"

"Shh," she says. "It's okay. We need to go."

"Go?"

"It's morning."

He squints through the leaves, now dappled with half sun. "Almost." But first he takes the injured hand in his own gently, turning it over, looking at it closely.

"This is how you got out?"

"Yes."

"It must hurt."

"Just for now. It'll be as good as new

tomorrow."

"So soon?"

"Like magic," she says.

She puts her good hand in his, and they walk away from the town, together, toward the brightening horizon.

READING GROUP GUIDE

1. The action of *The Magician's Lie* alternates between a single night in 1905, with Arden imprisoned by Officer Holt, and the story of her life that Arden tells him, which ranges over a number of years. Did you find one storyline more intriguing than the other? Were you eager to get back to one or the other?

2. As the novel opens, Virgil Holt has just received the bad news that the doctor won't operate on the bullet lodged near his spine. How does this affect his actions? Do you think he would have behaved differently if he were uninjured?

3. "The law is perfect. The men in charge of executing it are not." Officer Holt decides early on that if Arden is innocent, it's his responsibility to free her instead of turning her in, since the courts can't be trusted

to determine guilt or innocence. Do you believe this? Do you think he should have turned her in either way?

4. After Ray breaks Arden's leg, preventing her from dancing for Madama Bonfanti and having the chance to enter ballet school, she says, "There were so many what-ifs." What do you think would have happened if he hadn't done this?

5. Arden's unique gifts set her apart from the other characters in the book, but she also has a lot in common with them. Who in the book is the most like Arden? Her mother? Ray? Clyde? Adelaide? Who is she least like?

6. When Arden confesses that Ray has hurt her, her mother tells her, "You must be mistaken . . . we all depend on that boy's father, for our lives, for everything . . . I think you know Ray won't be the one he'll punish. We will all suffer instead." Do you feel Arden's mother bears some responsibility for what happened to Arden at Ray's hands? Should she have spoken up, even though it could have endangered their family's well-being?

7. Fleeing Tennessee for Biltmore is a huge, pivotal moment in Arden's life. Do you think it was the right choice? Should she have stayed with her family and tried to find another way to fight Ray?

8. In a key scene, the master of Biltmore tells Arden, "We all have agency," and she later repeats it to Holt. What does this quote mean to you? Do you think it applies to your own life, and if so, how?

9. Arden is surprised that Holt easily believes in magic. Did this surprise you as well? Did you believe from the beginning that the disappearance of the bruise on Arden's throat was magical, or did you suspect some sort of trick?

10. Ray pursues Arden for years, eventually finding her first in Chicago and then again in Savannah. "My God, Ada, I've missed you so much. You're my other half. The only one like me. I haven't felt complete without you." Why do you think he was so obsessed with her?

11. During their romance at Biltmore, Clyde is a slightly shadowy figure, and Arden learns that he's not entirely trust-

worthy during their trip up the coast. Is Arden right to distrust him when they meet again years later? How hard is it to reevaluate your relationship with someone you've known for a long time?

12. Arden is suspicious of rich people at several points in the book and feels she can only fit in at Biltmore as a servant. Yet she was raised in wealth by her grandparents. Why do you feel she identifies so strongly with the life she led starting at age twelve instead of her life before that?

13. Adelaide Herrmann maintains emotional distance from everyone who works for her, except for Arden. Why does Adelaide choose Arden as her protégée?

14. Adelaide Herrmann was a huge success as a female magician. Does she seem satisfied with that life, up until the ill-fated Second Sight act? Does she seem satisfied after her retirement, when Arden visits her many years later?

15. Virgil is convinced that he was his wife's second choice after her childhood love Mose married another girl. Do you think this prevents him from being honest with

her about his hopes and fears?

16. Arden's near-death experience at the Iroquois Theatre, including her unhappy reunion with Ray, frightens her deeply. Yet she doesn't share the full extent of her feelings, or the truth of what happened, with Clyde. Why do you think she keeps this from him? Does it contribute to their problems later in the story?

17. Arden's illusions, such as the Fair Shake, comment on gender relations in a time when that would have been very controversial. How would the same illusions be received today? Do you think a woman cutting a man in half onstage would still be shocking to some audiences?

18. When Clyde asks her to marry him, Arden refuses, telling herself, "It was a trap . . . We were too strong-willed to be locked together in marriage, a permanent institution. If we tried to hold each other too close, it could destroy us." Did you believe this reasoning? What other reasons would she have to accept or refuse his offer of marriage?

19. "I let him damage me and try to heal

that damage with his delusions of magic. I talk a good game about risk, but when it all came down to it, I chose something awful and safe." When Ray threatens Clyde, Arden gives up and allows him to hurt her and essentially keep her captive. Did you feel she had other options? If so, what should she have done instead?

20. Arden claims that "in different circumstances, she might have liked Officer Virgil Holt, and he might have liked her." Do you think this is true? What about their interactions makes it seem more or less likely?

21. Arden isn't guilty of the murder of Ray, but she did cut his throat in Chicago, and she tells Holt she was "ready to kill him" before Clyde did so. In your mind, does this compromise her claims of innocence?

22. As the book ends, Holt has resolved to begin living his life anew, without letting his fear of death get in the way. Do you feel he has been profoundly changed by his experience with Arden? Or do you think these resolutions will fade in the harsh light of day?

23. Where do you think Arden and Clyde's story might go from the ending onward?

24. Whether or not Arden is telling Officer Holt the truth is a key question throughout the book. When did you most believe her? Were there times where you were sure she was lying?

A CONVERSATION
WITH THE AUTHOR

What inspired you to write _The Magician's Lie_?

In the beginning, it was a very simple idea: I realized that I had read and seen countless references to male magicians cutting a woman in half but had never heard of a woman cutting a man in half. I decided to research it and found that stage magic is one of those fields that has really historically been dominated by men all along, with a few interesting exceptions. One of those exceptions was Adelaide Herrmann. I decided that her performance of the Bullet Catch in New York City in 1897 (a real event) would be the perfect inspiration for my protagonist to enter the world of magic. And the Amazing Arden was born.

Was that the reason you decided to set _The Magician's Lie_ at the turn of the

century?

Yes and no. Integrating Adelaide into the story intrigued me, but the main driving force was the place in culture I wanted Arden to occupy. In the present day, we're intrigued by professional stage magicians, but they don't occupy a central place in popular entertainment. Most people could probably name a couple of magicians: Criss Angel, David Blaine, David Copperfield, maybe Doug Henning (am I dating myself?). I wanted Arden to have true fame and true infamy because of the Halved Man. And for her to be a real pioneer in the field, I decided that right at the turn of the century was the best possible time.

So Adelaide Herrmann is real. What about the other characters? Fictional, inspired by real people, or somewhere in between?

George Vanderbilt, of course, was a real person, though I've played a little fast and loose with what we know of the early days of Biltmore. "Somewhere in between" fiction and fact would describe how I've integrated history throughout the book. The guests I mention attending that first Christmas party at the Biltmore — like the future President McKinley — are on record as visiting Biltmore, but not necessarily on that date. The prima ballerina assoluta Madama Bonfanti was real, though there is no evidence she visited Biltmore or even traveled seeking students for her school.

Some of the magicians Clyde and Arden discuss are real players of the time, and some aren't. Same with the theaters in which she performs. The Iroquois Theatre fire, tragically, was very real, resulting in more than six hundred deaths due to the exact conditions described in Arden's retelling — doors that opened in instead of out, locked gates between the levels of the theater, really terrible contributing factors that made the disaster so much worse. That was hard both to read about and to write about.

My intent throughout the book was to integrate history in a way that enriches and expands the story I wanted to tell, without feeling hidebound by exactly what happened to whom and when. After all, Arden has a magical power of healing her own wounds. This is a novel and not a historical document, clearly.

Speaking of that, where did Arden's healing power come from?

Actually, there were drafts of the story

both with and without the magical element. But I was fascinated by the idea of a magician who really does have magical powers, and even more, by the idea of a man of the law who is practical and realistic, but also has no problem believing that supernatural things can happen. I wanted Arden's power to have limits. She's not a superhero. So her healing power only goes so far.

You said there were different drafts of the story. Was the ending always the same?

That was one of the few parts that stayed the same the whole time! The beginning changed, the characters changed, the magic changed, nearly everything changed. But I always knew what I was working toward: the reveal to the audience and Holt alike that Ray was the dead "husband" we saw at the beginning of the book, followed closely by Arden's successful escape. I just love that kind of pit-of-the-stomach realization as a reader, so as a writer, I wanted to deliver on that for my readers. Arden was never guilty of the crime in any draft that I wrote. I did want the reader to have lots of doubts about her along the way, but I always wanted her to get her happy ending, or as close to it as possible.

How long did it take you to write this book?

Sometimes it feels like forever! I think from the first moment I wondered "What if a female magician cut a man in half onstage?" to turning in the final draft to my editor was about five years. Part of that was the research. I'd been writing fiction for years, but never historical, and it really changed my writing process. I kept getting distracted — if there was a scene where I wanted a character to put on a hat, I wanted to know what kind of hat it would have been, so I'd stop writing and go to the Internet. And you know what happens with the Internet. Two hours later, you know everything about hats of the 1890s, but you haven't written a single word. Eventually I found a way to put in placeholders and come back later with details, but that took a while. There were also a couple of major revisions, and I'd set myself a pretty serious task by interweaving what happens in the "present" story (the 1905 police station scenes) and the story that Arden is telling in the "past" (from 1890 onward). Every change rippled through the whole book. I'm really thrilled with the result, but there were some tough days in there. Writing is rewriting.

Arden is very clearly the central character of _The Magician's Lie_. Is she the character you feel most closely connected to?

Well, yes and no. Arden keeps most people at arm's length throughout the story, and I felt like she was doing that to me a little too. I knew she was telling the truth to Holt, but I also knew she didn't entirely trust him. And even though she loves Clyde desperately, she's still suspicious of his motives. That's not really me. In a way, I identified more with Adelaide. She's brusque and sharp and imperfect, but you know where you stand with her. I admired her courage and intelligence just as much as I admired Arden's. Most of my early readers picked Adelaide out as their favorite character. I'm actually thinking about giving her her own book next.

What do you love most about writing?

I love creating something out of nothing. It starts with just the spark of an idea, some small inspiration, and grows into this entire world of the novel. A full cast of characters who feel real, all the words they speak, all the actions they take. It's all just words on the page. And then to have a real effect on readers? That's the most amazing thing. It's the closest thing to magic I think we really have in life, other than love. Writers are illusionists who work in words. I love being that kind of magician.

ABOUT THE AUTHOR

Raised in the Midwest, **Greer Macallister** is a poet, short story writer, playwright, and novelist whose work has appeared in publications such as *The North American Review, The Missouri Review,* and *The Messenger.* Her plays have been performed at American University, where she earned her MFA in creative writing. She lives with her family in Brooklyn.